Uhura Was at Her Post When Suddenly Her Console Began to Flicker and Beep . . .

". . . *Enterprise,* come in *Enterprise* . . . Gamma 7 calling *Enterprise,* come in please. . . ."

The signal was faint, full of gaps and heavy with static, and the voice was not Sulu's.

"*Enterprise* here," Uhura said crisply. "You're very faint, Gamma 7. I can barely read you. . . ."

"This frequency too risky. Can't hold channel long. We have a priority data feed. . . ."

The relays fed in a whole string of numbers and Uhura's pulse began to race. These were the trade route coordinates Sulu had promised just before they lost contact! It meant he was alive and still free to move about. Or had been, at least long enough to broadcast his findings. . . . If Sulu can't get out on his own steam, she thought, they'll never be able to retrieve him. . . .

Look for STAR TREK Fiction from Pocket Books

DWELLERS IN THE CRUCIBLE

MARGARET WANDER BONANNO

A STAR TREK® NOVEL

POCKET BOOKS

New York   London   Toronto   Sydney   Tokyo

An *Original* Publication of POCKET BOOKS

POCKET BOOKS, a division of Simon & Schuster Inc.
1230 Avenue of the Americas, New York, NY 10020

This book is published by Pocket Books, a division of
Simon & Schuster Inc., under exclusive license from
Paramount Pictures Corporation.

ISBN: 0-671-66088-8

First Pocket Books printing September 1985

16 15 14 13 12 11 10 9 8 7

POCKET and colophon are trademarks of
Simon & Schuster Inc.

Printed in the U.S.A.

For Diane, t'hy'la:

> "If my slight muse do please these curious days,
> The pain be mine, but thine shall be the praise."

Author's Note

The Klingon and Rihannsu (Romulan) material herein owes its accuracy and dimension to the eminent xenosociological research of two authorities in the field. To John M. *(The Final Reflection)* Ford, and to Diane *(My Enemy, My Ally)* Duane for their contributions to our knowledge of the Empires, the author is most grateful.

DWELLERS IN THE CRUCIBLE

Prologue

THE DECISION WAS reached in the Inner Holy of the Summer
Palace of the Praesidium.

Only the Praetor's throne and six of the divans were
occupied; the empty couches fanned out and above the
Seven in the subdued light, mute witnesses to an event no
one could have heard in any case. The Praetor's chamberlain, having seen to the installation of the Praetor's sedan
chair, had activated the auditory baffles with the touch of a
panel before removing his presence from the Holy. None but
the Seven in the room, no matter the sophistication or range
of their listening devices, would hear what was spoken there
that day.

Of the Seven—a Mystical Number, XenoResearch had
recently reported, in Vulcan and Terran cultures as well as
their own Rihannsu (only Klingons subscribed to six as a
more potent talisman—something to do with their obsession
with the Games; allies or no, they were a reprehensibly
superstitious lot)—only the Praetor was Unseen, seated
behind the artfully wrought mirror screen so that he could
observe without being observed.

Some said his almost constant recent use of Unseen meant
that he was seriously ill—perhaps as a result of the latest

1

attempt on his life—or even that he had died of that attempt and had been replaced by his nephew Dr'ell, heir apparent. The latter rumor had been scotched by Dr'ell's appearance as one of the Six now present—as newly appointed Security Chief, to be precise. As Unseen, the Praetor was still the Praetor. His voice, as always, projected his personality beyond the parameters of his invisibility.

"If it fails," he pronounced in that slightly mincing tone that proclaimed his clan status and planet of origin, "it must be absolutely deniable."

"It won't fail!" Admiral-Superlative Meru'th snapped impatiently, not bothering with the honorific as only she could and get away with. She was old enough to be the Praetor's grandmother, had in fact suckled his father when her girlhood friend, his grandmother, had had the radiation sickness in the Earth Wars a hundred-year before, and that was her immunity. "As a masterwork of espionage and military prowess it is flawless, Excellency. My question is, is it necessary?"

"Exploiting the Federation's weaknesses is always necessary, Little Mother," the Praetor said with a fondness in his voice. "And the final decision is mine."

"*t'Lr m'th!*" Meru'th barked back; her background was Navy and her language had always been salty. Defense Minister Lefv tittered behind his hand, disguising it as a cough. "If it were, the Senate wouldn't insist the rest of us be here!"

In the end, Meru'th was persuaded of the necessity of the action she had helped orchestrate in the Empire's continuing cold war with the Federation, and the Praetor was assured by both her report and that of Security Chief Dr'ell that each phase of the mission was completely sealed from each subsequent one in case something went wrong. The Seven voted, and the vote was, not surprisingly, unanimous.

"Whom have you selected to undertake this glorious mission?"

The Praetor's voice percolated with satisfaction; his use of the old watchword was doubly indicative of how pleased he was. Every plot that pleased him was a "glorious mission," no matter how sordid its details or how many died in its implementation. The Praetor, whose long-nailed hands

2

(some few had died for calling them "effeminate") had never been soiled, did not concern himself with how others might soil theirs in serving him.

His question was addressed to Meru'th and his nephew simultaneously; the old battle-ax and the young rapier studied each other's reflection in the mirror screen before Dr'ell answered:

"Delar, Centurion late of *Gauntlet,* Excellency. His credentials are impeccable, his languages without accent, and he is dark enough to pass for Vulcan."

"Good," the Praetor said, and dismissed the Holy with a languid gesture.

Somewhere along the outer arm of a spiral nebula the Klingons had designated Haktuth, a battlecruiser commander named Krazz gripped the arms of his command chair and bared his back teeth in what he hoped his superior on the commpic would read as an obedient smile. Inwardly, Krazz wished Tolz Kenran's testicles in a vise—all three of them. He would personally turn the screws. Someday . . .

Tolz had finished pontificating. Krazz snapped alert; it was his turn to speak.

"Respect, my Lord Tolz, I am not a babysitter." Tolz outranked him by only a hair, but Krazz had to be careful. "I've logged my complaint. But I will obey."

"Affirm. You will obey," Tolz rasped. He did not add "bumpkin" or "hayseed" as he would have in their cadet days, though he was thinking it, Krazz knew. "You have coordinates for rendezvous with the Rihannsu?"

Ri-hann-su, Krazz thought. Pretentious smooth-browed freaks. Call them Roms the way the Feds did and puree them all for gel pastries! Although, he thought, the green-filled ones always give me the trots. Ri-hann-su!

"Affirm, my Lord. Anything else?"

"Suggest you learn to change nappies."

Tolz signed off, laughing at his own joke. Krazz gripped the armrests until they squeaked.

A multispecial merchanter hung just beyond the orbital approach limit of an arid red-orange world, awaiting permission to dock.

"Permission granted," came the inflectionless voice from Space Central. "And from all of Vulcan, welcome."

In the transporter room where the first shore leave party had gathered, three crewmen whom the humanoids aboard took to be Vulcans exchanged lightning glances.

Implementation of Phase One successful! Delar, Centurion late of *Gauntlet,* thought. Unlike a Vulcan, he had begun to sweat.

One

THEY WERE ENGAGED in the herb gathering ritual when it happened.

Cleante made a face which T'Shael had come to recognize as chagrin, clasping her hands at her temples in frustration.

"You have made an error?" T'Shael inquired, careful not to say "another error" because humans were so sensitive about such matters. However, it was a fact that Cleante had been making errors all morning.

"I'm sorry!" Cleante sighed, sitting back on her heels in the midst of the herb garden, letting her hands fall into her lap. "I keep forgetting the order."

With a Vulcan's patience, T'Shael abandoned her place at the drying screens and knelt beside the human.

"K'rhtha, mah'ta, sh'rr, kh'aa," she recited, plucking three leaves of each with a single motion as she said their names. "Lhm'ta, hla'meth, tri'hla."

Cleante nodded, absorbing it as T'Shael made the benediction.

"I'll keep trying," she said softly.

The ritual gathering of the proper herbs for the Masters' tea was many millenia old, perhaps as old as the origins of the Vulcan Masters themselves. It was not strictly logical, in that the herbs need not be picked by hand nor in any particular order since they were later sorted into different mixtures for the various teas, but the ritual also served as a premeditative exercise. Repeated often enough to become second nature, it enabled even a human to aspire to certain contemplative levels. It was this that Cleante, under T'Shael's tutelage, was attempting, with as yet little success.

"Your task would be easier were they Terran herbs," T'Shael offered by way of consolation. "You are contending here with three levels of meaning—the ritual itself, unfamiliar names, and equally unfamiliar flora. Perhaps if you were to employ Terran names, however inaccurate—"

" 'Parsley, sage, rosemary and thyme'," Cleante murmured softly, perhaps a little sadly.

"Your pardon?" T'Shael asked.

"An ancient Earth ballad," said Cleante, who dearly loved to sing. She began to pick the herbs again, whispering their names under her breath as she did so. She was far clumsier at the task than T'Shael, who had been doing it all her life; still she persevered.

T'Shael waited until she had completed a round of seven, spreading the leaves in their individual compartments on the drying screen. The Vulcan nodded her approval.

"And lastly the benediction, to thank the plants for serving us," she reminded gently.

Cleante nodded.

"I'd forgotten that too," she said, making the gesture.

This was what she loved about Vulcan culture, this sense that everything had a purpose, and that even a plant ought to be thanked for its generosity.

"Perhaps you will sing your ballad for me," T'Shael suggested as they labored side by side now. "I would be honored to hear it."

"Maybe another time." Cleante wiped small beads of perspiration from her upper lip. A native of Earth's Middle East, she was more adapted to the Vulcan climate than most humans, yet today it seemed to affect her more than usual. "I'm not much in the mood for singing."

T'Shael analyzed this. She had studied xenopsychology in preparation for her role as instructor in the settlement at T'lingShar, and her specialty was humans. She recognized this particular human mood as the one called "depression."

"It is my observation that something disquiets you," she said cautiously. "If you are in need of an auditor . . ."

Cleante shook her head.

"I'll be all right. But thank you for your concern, my friend."

The word gave T'Shael pause, and she did not respond to it.

"No doubt you find the herb ritual foolish," she said instead, rising with her race's gracefulness, waiting until Cleante had completed another round of seven and made the thanking gesture before she finished her thought. "For the outworlder such stylized behavior—"

"No," Cleante responded, and she too rose from the task, becoming animated where she had been languid all morning. " 'The Vulcan knows there is a time for everything'," she said, quoting one of the few things she could remember from the Kahr-y-Tan, the Way of the Vulcan. "And I am eager to learn."

They made an attractive picture, these two young females among the fragrant, breeze-blown herbs—their voices melodic, their soft clothing teased by the arid wind. Born under different stars, reared in totally different cultures, they were come to dwell in this place at this time for differing reasons but for a single purpose. They were but two among the many gatherings of races from throughout the Federation known as the Warrantors of the Peace.

It might have been difficult at first glance to tell which of the two was the Terran, if Cleante did not smile as often as she did. She was fine-boned as many Vulcan females were, athletic and darkly beautiful, and with her heavy black hair hanging in a single plait down her back and covering her rounded ears she might easily be taken for a Vulcan. The word Byzantine had been used by her first lover to describe her eyes. T'Shael, a linguist by profession, might have found the term "Nilotic" more applicable. Nilotic applied to she who was born on the banks of the Nile, as Cleante had been. Nilotic also applied to she who was dark and lithe and exotic, as Cleante was. The word suited T'Shael's dual requirement for logic and aesthetics.

T'Shael, being the Vulcan, naturally did not smile. She was the elder of the two, and if the Vulcan as a race was

7

considered beautiful, she was no exemplar. Her features were austere, her straight dark hair cropped at her shoulders and unadorned, her manner retiring. Even among her characteristically silent kind she was known for the quality of her silences.

As was expected of her, T'Shael was a virgin, betrothed from childhood to one chosen by her family, one whom she had not seen since her seventh year, one who would someday soon summon her to *koon-ut-kal-if-fee* and the madness of *pon farr*. Even as it was considered improper to speak of such matters, T'Shael did not so much as permit her conscious mind to dwell upon them. The traditional small ruby that glittered in her left earlobe was sufficient to designate her as an unwed female, and no Vulcan would presume to inquire further.

T'Shael was unable to articulate why it was that she preferred the company of this Terran female to all others in the settlement at T'lingShar. Like all Vulcans, she had been instructed from birth in the equality of all sentient life forms and in the equal value of each individual within a given species. Why, then, did she permit herself this exclusivity? Logic suggested that one might be curious about a denizen of Earth, a planet T'Shael had never visited. One could attribute one's attraction to Cleante merely to a desire for cultural exchange. Yet why, when Cleante called her friend, was she visited with such a mixture of exaltation and shame?

No matter. T'Shael would live out her life within the confines of T'lingShar, and Cleante must remain here for as long as her maternal parent was High Commissioner of the United Earth Council, which could be for a great many years. There would be time enough to examine such conflicting responses to a single concept. T'Shael's immediate concern was with whatever secret trouble had beset Cleante in recent weeks, and her own wish to alleviate some portion of that trouble. Was this not the function of a friend?

T'Shael would blame herself ever afterward for being so preoccupied with her thoughts that her delicate ears did not discern the approach of the hovercraft until it was almost upon them.

T'lingShar was a densely populated urban area, and airborne craft of all descriptions came and went constantly, though they were forbidden to fly so low near a dwelling. This should have put T'Shael on her guard.

But was it logical for one who had never known violence to anticipate attack?

The hovercraft lacked markings, which puzzled T'Shael. It was too large for a personal vehicle, and all official craft bore plainly visible identicodes. What did it mean? By its erratic flight pattern the 'craft was disabled or else its occupants lost; it was only proper to offer assistance. T'Shael hesitantly moved toward the clear space at the end of the plaza where the 'craft was about to set down.

"It's only a 'craft," Cleante said uneasily, alarmed by the transfixed expression on the Vulcan's face. "T'Shael, what's wrong?"

"Unknown." T'Shael shook her head slightly. Humans possessed an instinctive, atavistic fear of the unknown; she could hear it in Cleante's voice, feel it emanating from her. Should she heed this, or her own race's dictate, bred out of a thousand years of peace, that the unknown was merely that which merited investigation? "Perhaps nothing. Perhaps we may be of service."

The hovercraft's engines stopped and the pneumatic doors hissed open. Three males emerged, catlike and swift, one behind the other. They wore desert suits with no markings to indicate profession or status. They were more overtly muscular than the average Vulcan and could have been taken for professional athletes. The traditional *Klarshameth* troupe was touring T'lingShar. T'Shael reasoned that perhaps they had been exploring the city and had lost their way. She moved forward without hesitation now. No Vulcan would harm another. Cleante, still uneasy, hung back near the colonnade that led to the living quarters.

"Live long and prosper," T'Shael said to the apparent leader, raising her hand in the *ta'al* as was proper to the native in welcoming the stranger. "If you are in need of assistance, perhaps we may serve you. I am called T'Shael."

The leader turned to the two who flanked him, one of whom held a small portascreen upon which he studied certain images. The one with the portascreen nodded, and the leader did something no Vulcan would do. He smiled.

9

Rather, he leered—an ugly, feral baring of teeth that gave T'Shael pause.

"Our task is made the easier," the leader said to his cohorts. "Here are two of them already!"

His words were Vulcan, but his inflection—T'Shael, trained linguist, whirled toward Cleante, abandoning all propriety in the face of what translated as Romulan, as danger, and shouted: "Run!"

Knowing it futile but instantly calculating odds against the maze of small streets in the Old City where Cleante might conceal herself, T'Shael dared to buy time. She saw Cleante hesitate for a fraction of a second before bolting like a gazelle. T'Shael stood to face the aggressors.

"I will serve your purpose," she said evenly.

"No one has consulted you!" the leader sneered with his Rihannsu cynicism, sharpening his sibilants and biting off the ends of his words. He and his second moved toward her, while the third made to pursue Cleante. T'Shael threw herself in his path.

It was no contest. All Vulcan children are trained in the protective arts, and T'Shael was no less skilled than another. But they were three and she was one, and her purpose was not her own protection but Cleante's. She dodged, she whirled, she took blows which she knew would gratify Rihannsu aggression, but at last a powerful hand grasped her by the hair and yanked her head back, and a nerve pinch out of their common ancestry and harder than necessary brought her down.

She was at least spared the look of terror on Cleante's face when they cornered her in a *cul-de-sac* in the Old City and closed in on her.

"I'm bored," Jim Kirk announced to all and sundry lounging around the null-grav pool during their offshift. "God, but I'm bored!"

Uhura propped herself up on one elbow under the ultraviolet and looked over her sunshade at McCoy. McCoy returned the look. Uh oh. Whenever the Big Guy was bored, the rest of them invariably got caught in the crossfire.

"You're just annoyed because Ensign Chen beat the pants off you at five-card stud," was McCoy's opinion.

He meant it literally. The game had nearly degenerated into old-fashioned strip poker until the Admiral remembered the dignity of his office. Or realized how badly he was losing, depending on which version one believed.

"She didn't beat me; I let her win," Kirk said, all innocence, tugging at the ends of the towel draped around his neck after his recent swim. "Don't want to intimidate new crewmembers the first time out. Besides, she cheats. There's no such thing as a Ho Chi Minh straight."

Uhura lay back and readjusted her sunshade; no way was she getting involved in this one. McCoy just grunted.

"I don't know . . . is it me, or is Command shoveling us a lot of dull assignments lately?" Kirk mused, not really expecting an answer. "Mapping expeditions, training cruises, milk runs. Are they trying to tell us something?"

Uhura rolled over to give her back equal time under the rays and began to hum a little tune. McCoy stopped scanning the freckles on his arms for latent melanoma and took the bait.

"You know what annoys me about some people?" he addressed the high vaulted ceiling of the Rec Dec. "I'll tell you what annoys me about some people. Stick them up to various parts of their anatomy in Red Alerts and they complain about how overworked and under-appreciated they are, how all they ever wanted was a beach to walk on—you know the speech. Give them a little slack time to sit around the pool at the country club with friends and what do they do? Gripe about how *under*worked, under-appreciated and bored they are!"

Kirk sat on the edge of a lounge chair, stretching his back muscles against the towel's resistance, getting the kinks out.

"I'm not asking for a Red Alert, Bones. Just something more challenging than nursing a pack of green cadets through Standard Evasive."

He stared out the main viewpoint wistfully; no matter where the man's body was, his spirit was always somewhere Out There. A supernova had been roaring its life away in the lower lefthand corner some fourteen parsecs distant for over a week now; spectral dampers had reduced it to a pale blue flicker. Tame stuff, supernovae, after a while. If you've seen one—

11

"There are hotspots all over the map out there," Jim Kirk said plaintively, waving his hand at the starfield. "Disasters waiting to happen. At this very moment any one of a hundred worlds could be in need of our unique brand of troubleshooting. So why do they ship us off to the boondocks?"

McCoy rendered a fair version of "It Was Paranoia" to the tune of "Fascination" in his cracked baritone. Uhura smiled quietly. Be careful what you wish for, Jim, honey, she thought, the ultra-v making her sleepy. A dose of McCoy's sarcasm brought her awake.

"Now here comes somebody who's never bored. Bor*ing*, maybe—"

Uhura flipped the sunshade up to see Spock crossing the Rec Dec in their direction.

"Oh, Leonard, don't be so mean!" she said, always ready to defend her favorite Vulcan.

With Spock was Lieutenant Saavik, brightest of the new crop of cadets and his unofficial protege. The two of them were engrossed in the sort of uniquely Vulcan dialogue that closed in around itself, shutting out everyone and everything but its participants. (M'Benga used to regale the others in Sickbay with the story of his first assist on a cryocardial bypass and how the Vulcan on the table had carried on an animated conversation about wildflowers with the attending surgeon while the surgeon held her frozen heart in one hand and sutured with the other, neither surgeon nor patient nor heart missing a beat.) As Spock and Saavik came closer, Uhura realized what they were doing.

"They're playing *cha*'!" she said excitedly, sitting up, flicking off the ultra-v and stretching like a cat, all attention.

"They're playing *who?*" All McCoy could tell was that they were engaged in a rapid-fire verbal fencing match in Vulcan interlayered with another language so alien all he knew for sure was that it *wasn't* Vulcan.

"*Cha',*" Uhura explained as if to a child. "The Game of the Word. *You* know."

"Oh," McCoy said.

He knew *of* the Game, of course. Humans called it the Vulcan National Pastime, subtitled "What They Do for the Seven Years In-Between." But the rules for the Basal Game alone would fill an old-style Brooklyn telephone directory if Vulcans didn't carry them around in their heads. McCoy had never been able to follow even the infant school level of play, and the cutthroat intensity with which *these* two were going at it . . .

Kirk was listening too, but with that bemused I'm-not-going-to-admit-I'm-out-of-my-depth expression he had. Uhura was the only one who seemed able to follow entirely, and when Spock concluded the match with a gesture of acquiescence giving it to Saavik, Uhura applauded loudly. Several other crewmembers looked up to see what the excitement was about.

Spock raised an eyebrow, as if only now realizing there were others in the room. Saavik looked mildly embarrassed at all the attention.

"Brilliantly played!" Uhura said. "May I have the next match?"

Spock gestured toward Saavik as if to say, "She's all yours." Uhura threw a robe over her tank suit and she and Saavik went off to find a computer con to set up the rules for whatever variants on the Basal Game they selected between them. While Uhura was quite good for a non-Vulcan, she still didn't trust her memory against any Vulcan's innate eideticism.

"That was Klin trade patois you were using as an alternate, wasn't it?" Kirk asked as Spock joined them by the pool, incongruously impeccable in his uniform compared to their varying degrees of dishabille. Spock was also the only person Kirk knew who could sit ramrod straight in a lounge chair.

"Correct. Lieutenant Saavik was instructing me in its nuances."

"I thought so." Kirk was pleased with his erudition, even if Spock took it for granted. "I didn't recognize the Variant, though."

"*cha' Damyath*," Spock replied. "The *Sim're'At cha'* or Masters' Game, where the object is to sacrifice points rather than to accrue them. Sometimes imprecisely called the Loser's Game. Not a Variant you would find congenial, Admiral."

Kirk decided to ignore that.

"Where've you been all morning?"

"Casting this month's ballots," Spock reported. "At this distance I will barely meet the deadline."

Voting from deep space was a sometimes sticky procedure, complicated by time-warp distortions, differing residency laws from planet to planet, and the difficulty of sending secret ballots on hyperchannel. Uhura's least favorite day of the year had to be the Federation-wide General Election; Communications was always in a tangle what with everyone trying to call home at the same time. The Vulcan system was at once simpler and more complex.

"What is this—Vulcan Election Day or something?" McCoy wanted to know. "Somehow I just can't envision Vulcans stumping the campaign trail."

"Possibly that is because we do not, Doctor."

Spock launched into a detailed explication of the Vulcan legislative system, in which balloting was exclusively on issues, never on candidates, where every Vulcan was eligible to vote on every issue, and where "politicking" and the concept of electing public officials on the basis of popularity were unheard of. McCoy's eyes began to glaze over.

"And what else is new on the most peaceful world this side of Halka?" Kirk cut in when McCoy seemed in danger of toppling out of his chair.

"All is well," Spock reported. "Ambassador Sarek sends his regards. And my mother says 'Hello.' "

Kirk smiled at the distinction in greetings so typical of their senders. He sought out the Eridani system in the viewport; it wasn't visible from where they were, of course, but he knew approximately where it ought to be.

"Vulcan," he mused, his restlessness less obvious now. "Probably the only place in the galaxy where I know we aren't needed."

"Amen to that," McCoy said.

Before McCoy had changed out of his swim trunks, taken an antidote for the sunburn he could feel prickling across his back under the uniform and ambled down to Sickbay, an All Points Communique had flashed from Vulcan Space Central, leaping across hyperspace in the direction of the Federation

Council Emergency Session and the headquarters of Starfleet Command. Over the next several stardates it would radiate out to starbase after starbase down the line, and thence to every ship in the Fleet. *Enterprise,* owing to her particular locale and a mess of intervening ion storms, would be among the last to know that six of the Warrantors of the Peace had been abducted by force or forces unknown.

Blackness. Impossible even for Vulcan eyes to penetrate. Blackness and a throb of engines and a subliminal odor of some kind.

T'Shael analyzed. It was not actually an odor, but a sensory impression somewhere between olfaction and tactility, in a range usually more disturbing to humans but affecting Vulcans nevertheless. Now she knew.

Deltan pheromones. Negative ones. Anxiety, fear, terror—stay away! T'Shael stirred and sat upright on the cold metal deck.

There was an unpleasant taste in her mouth, a dryness at the back of her throat. She had been drugged, then. Her acute hearing distinguished the heavy breathing of several others in like condition. How many had been captured, and for what purpose? T'Shael groped along the floor until she made contact. Whoever it was let out a whimper of fear; the pheromones increased sharply.

"Who?" it cried in Deltan.

"T'Shael," she replied in the same tongue. "Resh, it is you?"

"Yes," he sighed in some relief, and the negative pheromones he'd been exuding since he'd awoken began to recede. "Where are we?"

"In a 'craft of some sort. But as to where . . . who else is here?"

"Krn and Jali slumber beside me. Others—two more, I think. I know not who."

"Indeed," T'Shael acknowledged, listening for each one's breathing past the insistent thrum of engines. "What do you remember, Resh?"

She knew how Deltans craved contact, communication, for their very survival. She shied from Resh's touch, but

15

would let him speak his fill while she tried to analyze the situation.

His story was not unlike hers and Cleante's—a surprise attack by Vulcan-clad Romulans with prior knowledge of their victims. He and his two cousins had been touring the points of interest in the Old City, Resh explained. They had stopped to rest and take refreshment in one of the many parks and naturally, as Deltans will, had fallen to gentle sex play among the shrubbery where none could see them. They knew they shouldn't, Resh explained, its being Vulcan and thus, but it was hard to resist Jali when she was in a whimsical mood and thus . . .

Resh'da Maprida'hn, Jali'lar Kandowali, Krnsandor L'am, T'Shael thought with relish, strangely gratified with the beauty of their names. One could almost transform them into a meditative chant, she thought with a small part of her brain that was not engrossed in the problem at hand. Deltans had beautiful names and essentially sublime souls. As to their sexual practices . . .

Infinite Diversity in Infinite Combinations, T'Shael reminded herself dutifully, and returned to her analysis.

They were, to judge from the power of the engines vibrating the deck beneath them, in the hold of some interplanetary vessel. "They" were herself, the three Deltans, and two others. Six in all.

T'Shael did not presume to touch unnecessarily, but followed the sounds of breathing to a hard, wiry form curled defensively against a bulkhead. Rapid breathing and the presence of antennae—an Andorian, male, and not to be awakened abruptly lest he strike out. Andorian aggressiveness was less predictable even than human, Andorian strength almost equal to a Vulcan's.

One other, T'Shael thought, continuing her groping progress across the throbbing deck. She touched. Oh, by the All and why? she thought with what in a human might have been despair. Why must you be here?

Cleante.

The drug had affected some more profoundly than others. The Andorian stirred and hissed in his sleep; he was coming around. T'Shael sought the pulse in Cleante's wrist. There it was—human slow, but strong.

Why must you be here? T'Shael wondered again. Why are any of us here except through my error?

"What becomes of us now?" Resh lamented. His cousins were awakening; he would have to be brave for them, hide his fear—no easy task for those as psionically interdependent as Deltans.

"Whatever our captors deem necessary."

T'Shael had meant it as a statement of the inevitable. It sent Resh into a fresh bout of whimpering.

"They know who and what we are!" he cried, wringing his hands in the darkness, resisting the urge to clutch at T'Shael because he knew it would be improper. He tried to keep rein on his pheromones, but without much success. "They will destroy us and the Federation with us!"

"I submit that the fate of the Federation hardly hinges upon ours," T'Shael said drily.

Must it depend upon her alone to counterbalance the emotions of all of these? She crouched between Cleante and the Andorian, waiting. Jali and Krn clung to Resh now, pheromones intermixing, imploring explanations, seeking comfort. Resh soothed them absently, stroking them in a way even a human would call lascivious. T'Shael could not see his actions in the darkness, but heard the purring responses they evoked. She had observed Deltans doing this to each other in the most public of places and instinctively averted her eyes.

"They know who we are!" Resh mourned. "They had identicards for each of us; I saw them. They know that we are Warrantors!"

"If they did not know before, surely you have succeeded in enlightening them," T'Shael said with a touch of impatience.

The planet Vulcan, in the year of T'Shael's birth, had begun its second millennium of peace. Surak, Father of all the Vulcan now holds true, brought about the final unification of a brilliant and violent race after untold millennia of barbarism; his codification of the teachings of the Masters was the salvation of the Vulcan as a species, though it cost them their emotions and Surak his life. What is less widely known is that for all his seeming innovation, Surak never disturbed anything which was already viable. Whatever innate moral principles feudal Vulcan possessed were preserved and cherished despite the carnage. Among these was the concept of the Warrantors of the Peace.

In Vulcan prehistory, it was the custom for the firstborn of a tribal leader to dwell among a rival tribe once a truce had been declared. If the least of that tribe's members died in a renewal of hostilities, the rival chieftan's offspring was forfeit. The practice kept the peace, sometimes.

By the time of the city-states which characterized Vulcan's Middle history the tradition had been refined and expanded. It was not only an offspring or consort who might be exchanged for a member of the other faction, but also *t'hy'la*, the soul-sibling of the leader, who went to dwell in the principality of the others. In the event of war, this one was the first to die—a death calculatedly brutal and, where possible, enacted before the eyes of those who cherished him.

Surak had weighed the inherent violence of this practice against the greater good, and decided it must be retained. In his wisdom, he refined the concept further. At his behest, the Warrantors came to have the formulae for global war implanted in their hearts.

The term "first strike capability" appears in the language of every world's nuclear age, along with appropriate rhetoric assuring that no civilized nation would ever consider employing it. The Vulcan was no exception.

By Surak's time, scientific evolution had far outstripped moral maturity. Vast intelligence provided the Vulcan with nuclear power and the potential for interplanetary travel a full millennium before Earth, yet placed these capabilities in the hands of savage feudal lords and petty dictators. If the Vulcan as a species had not yet succeeded in destroying itself, this period provided ample opportunity.

Surak drew upon the gifts of the High Masters, especially those skilled in the sciences and the healing arts, and developed a procedure whereby an indestructible capsule containing the encoded formula for nuclear first strike could be surgically implanted in the heart of a Warrantor. In order to start a war, a leader must first, and with his own hand, cut out the heart of his child, his consort or his closest friend. With this as the finalization of Surak's Reforms, the first millennium of peace ensued.

Similar concepts evolved independently on other worlds, including Earth. On Earth, the idea was first put forth by pacifists in the late twentieth century (Old Calendar), but was slapped down by the majority as "barbaric." Only within the past five years, despite the Vulcan delegation's repeated introduction of a referendum on Federation-wide Warrantorship at every Council meeting from the First Federation Congress in 2124 forward, was the concept adopted by the Federation as a whole. Surak's original settlement at T'lingShar, long a cosmopolitan gathering place for artists and travelers from many worlds, was expanded to include permanent residences for outworlders.

A vast complex of buildings in the Old City—part commune, part university campus, part cultural and arts center—the settlement was literally a city within a city, exhibiting the traditional aesthetic tranquility that was Vulcan. T'lingShar lacked for nothing. Outworlder and Vulcan alike intermingled freely in an atmosphere of social and cultural exchange. New Warrantors could emulate the Vulcan way of life or adapt it to their own or, as some of the less evolved like the Elaasians preferred, remain within small enclaves of their own kind. No security measures other than the usual planetary screening were deemed necessary on a world that had not been conquered as far back as collective memory, and Warrantors were free to come and go as they pleased, required only to register at the settlement once in the Vulcan solar year. Each Warrantor remained on Vulcan for the duration of the term of office of those who had sent them there.

Cleante alFaisal had come to T'lingShar on her mother's accession as High Commissioner of the United Earth Council two years before. When her mother's term of office expired in an additional two years, the peace capsule within her heart would be deactivated and she would be free to return to Earth. She had been the only possible choice as Warrantor for the formidable Jasmine alFaisal. They had no other acknowledged relatives, and Cleante's mother did not allow herself the luxury of friends.

Cleante spent her days on Vulcan dabbling in a variety of academic studies and pursuing her particular passion, which was archeology.

As a child she had clambered ecstatically among the excavations in the City of the Dead in Old Cairo, delighting in the antiquity of her people and the mysterious past they whispered to her. On Vulcan she could study the relics of a people even more ancient, more mysterious than her own. Vulcan reminded Cleante of her native Egypt in so many things, and everything else was an adventure. T'lingShar was one of the best things that could have happened to her.

Her imminent departure for Vulcan had also given her an excellent opportunity to extricate herself from a messy love affair on Earth Colony Seven, only the most recent of several. Her love affairs always seemed to be messy, at least toward the end. Cleante enjoyed being with men, but they became easily infatuated with her and she had never mastered the art of easing herself out of their lives gracefully. What better way to discourage a lover than by telling him she'd be spending the next four years on Vulcan? Cleante was only too pleased with the way things had worked out.

A woman whom men find exceptionally attractive often has difficulty retaining close friendships with other women. There is always a tinge of jealousy, an unvoiced competitiveness. With a Vulcan female such considerations did not exist. Cleante had been drawn to T'Shael from the beginning, and told herself it was only a Vulcan's innate reserve and T'Shael's particular shyness that prevented a return of her overtures of friendship. At least it had seemed that way until recently.

Cleante did not know what turmoil thrived in T'Shael's heart. But it saddened her to think that in two years she would leave T'lingShar, while T'Shael would remain for life.

T'Shael was one of the few who had become a Warrantor at her own request. She was parentless in a society where family ties were strong, and in a world where every individual was of equal worth, a leader would no more sacrifice the life of a stranger than of one of his own. Volunteers could take the place of those whose presence was required elsewhere, or simply choose the life of a Warrantor as their personal commitment to intergalactic peace. This had been T'Shael's choice.

As the most politically stable Federation member and the origin of the concept of Warrantorship, Vulcan was the logical place where the Warrantors of the Peace should make their home. Surely none would molest them there.

But none had anticipated an attack which in a single pristine morning netted a human, a Vulcan, three Deltans and Theras of Andor, transporting them against their will to an unknown destination and for an unknown purpose.

"Shall we submit or shall we fight?" Theras hissed, his Andorian-soft voice shaking with rage.

He had, as T'Shael had expected he would, sprung up from a deep slumber ready to attack, groping for his deadly-sharp *flabjellah,* the ubiquitous Andorian dagger, which had of course been taken from him upon his capture. Not content to accept his situation, he frantically sought some escape, stumbling over the others in the darkness and banging his antennaed head against the low bulkheads.

"We must *do* something!" he hissed now, not a little fear edging his anger.

"Indeed," T'Shael observed. "You must restrain yourself, or be restrained."

She heard his sharp intake of breath, sensed his coiling in on himself, preparing to spring. T'Shael readied herself.

"Would you fight me, Vulcan?"

"I would fight no one. But if you would fight, as I surmise you would, it might be more logical to fight your own fears than to turn your aggressions upon a fellow captive."

The Andorian subsided. He was a stranger to most of them, though Jali had taken a course in socioeconomics with him once. Like all his race, he was terrified of any form of enclosure. Andorians were bred to the outdoor life, and certain primitive instincts raged in them still, despite recent centuries of advancement under Federation. If Theras's claustrophobia proved contagious . . .

No fear for the Deltans, who were happiest in a clump.

T'Shael listened to Cleante's breathing in the dark and found it calm. The human was fully awake now, apprised of the facts and strangely silent.

"T'Shael!" she had half-shrieked, coming awake abruptly in the darkness.

"Here," T'Shael had said and, after a moment: "Are you harmed?"

Cleante seemed to examine herself, listen to her body in the darkness.

"No. Are you?"

"No." T'Shael would have been unable to put words to her experience had Cleante's answer been otherwise.

They sat together in the darkness, listening to the insistence of massive engines taking them no one knew where, none but their captors knowing why. Jali cuddled up to Theras in an attempt to ease his fears. Even an Andorian could find solace in the Deltan touch.

"If only we could see!" piped a small voice. Krn had been quiet for as long as he was able. Small Krn, child of eleven Deltan years, well-versed in the love arts but inexperienced in all else, wrung the hearts of his auditors. "I would not fear if we had light!"

He said the last word loudly, hopefully. Lights on many Federation vessels were voice-activated. Not so Rihannsu craft, apparently. It was the first thing T'Shael had attempted when she woke. Now she realized why it had not worked.

She spoke one of the few words she knew in yet another language, a language none of the others had heard before. Like most of the words in the abbreviated Battle Language of this particular species it had a harsh, grating, guttural sound to it. Spoken in T'Shael's soft voice it was especially incongruous.

Yet the lights turned on. The others blinked in stunned silence, studying each other for a moment before murmuring their relief. Only T'Shael retreated into a thoughtful silence.

"How did you do it?" Cleante asked wonderingly, though she was already convinced that the Vulcan could do anything. "What was it you said?"

"It is the word for light," T'Shael replied softly. "In the Battle Language of the Klin."

The silence this time was electrifying. The group surveyed their surroundings more closely—a barren cargo hold, sealed from the outside and provided with minimal life support—a holding pen for the exotic fauna of several worlds. But for what purpose?

They could surmise any number of reasons why they had been taken—none of them pleasant to contemplate—but by whom? Their captors had been Romulans, but acting on their own or at the behest of their uneasy allies the Klingons? Rihannsu honor was legend, but the Klin—

"The Rihannsu have utilized Klin vessels since their alliance," T'Shael, whose mother had been in Starfleet, observed. "Yet, were this manned by Rihannsu, one would have expected them to recalibrate the voice control."

Whatever frantic speculation this might have evoked halted with the abrupt sliding open of the cargo bay doors.

The same trio that had captured Cleante and T'Shael—garbed now and not surprisingly in Romulan military uniforms—stood framed in the cavernous opening, the leader bracketed as before by his two muscular cohorts. The light seemed to surprise him.

"Clever!" he remarked in heavily-accented Standard. His eyes scanned them—Theras coiled and vigilant in a far corner, his clawed fingernails scoring the metal of the bulkhead in his tension, small Krn cowering between Jali and Resh, Cleante drawing calm from T'Shael and neither moving—and locked on T'Shael. "And which of you has managed this?"

Before T'Shael could speak, he leered at them as he had on Vulcan.

"It makes no difference. We shall soon restore your darkness."

His two lieutenants drew their disruptors as he casually produced a hypospray from a pocket of his uniform tunic. Singling them out, he began with the Andorian, who presented the greatest threat.

As first Resh and then Jali abandoned him in heavily-drugged sleep, Krn let out a wail and flung himself at T'Shael. She swept him up in her arms by reflex—he was feather-light and rife with pheromones—fighting her reluctance to touch in response to his need. His psionic impulses exploded dangerously into her consciousness until Cleante realized what was happening and pried his desperate fingers from around T'Shael's neck, wrapping the little Deltan around her own body instead.

"How touching!" the Romulan leered as he pressed the hypo against T'Shael's unresisting arm.

T'Shael thought her gratitude to Cleante in the engulfing darkness.

Two

"It is of the utmost importance to remember one thing only," Master Stimm had said in the very beginning to his student T'Shael. "Question this not for its simplicity, but consider: It is not that the Vulcan has not emotions. It is that the Vulcan has powerful emotions that are kept ever in check. Emotion must be ruled lest it rule. She who sees this not would do well to remove herself to a solitary place to reconsider."

T'Shael spent much of her life in a solitary place.

Outworlders came as Warrantors to T'lingShar, took advantage of the many things the settlement had to offer and, for the most part, contributed something of their own gifts. They would stay their year or two or four or ten—as long as those they represented held office—then return to their home worlds.

T'Shael stayed.

"It must be lonely for you," Jali said the first time they met, fluttering her very long eyelashes—they and her feathery soft eyebrows being her only hair—and drawing closer then T'Shael would have wished. "To acquaint yourself with so many persons for so short a time and then to have them depart—to have no friends . . ."

She had wanted to say lovers—the word was the same in Deltan, with only a slight variation in inflection to distinguish, and T'Shael noted the distinction—but she knew that was impossible for a Vulcan. Jali fluttered her eyelashes again and drew closer still, exuding a special level of warmth that few could resist.

"I am of service," T'Shael had responded tersely, retreating into herself; she was too well-mannered to physically withdraw from Jali's allure. "And 'friend' is a word too easily spoken by some."

"How long have you been here?" Jali asked, knowing such a direct question was a breach of Vulcan etiquette.

"Since my sixteenth year," T'Shael replied remotely. "Is that pertinent to your calculations?"

Jali had then given up, and gathered the diskettes for her math course, before going off to seek more receptive companions. The humans in the settlement—and they were the major concentration of outworlders—were more appreciative of her talents.

She could not have known what levels of meaning were held in check by the Vulcan mask; Deltan behavior is so overt that it sometimes overlooks the nuances of others'. Jali had felt only pity for the soul imprisoned in the angular, seemingly sexless body swathed in its somber clothing—no throbbing Deltan colors or giddy florals for this one, ever.

Jali did not know that a Vulcan of T'Shael's circumstances might find this question of friendship disquieting despite her disclaimers. Constant exposure to outworlders could prove expanding to the mind or dangerous to the Vulcan soul, depending upon one's perspective.

"If this one may speak, Master—" T'Shael ventured; it had taken her weeks of silent listening to find the boldness.

"It is permitted," Master Stimm replied, masking a secret satisfaction at her presumption. He was an old one, and even a Master could fall prey to an excess of words. Further, it was a sign of growth that his student could open out of herself even this much. If T'Shael had a fault, it was an excess of reticence.

"Given the premise that knowledge is a good—" she began softly.

"Does thee consider this so?" the Master asked.

He was wont to task her with continual re-examination of the self-evident, but T'Shael had never given any indication of impatience. It was this docility that her mentor found most disturbing.

"This one's simple gifts indicate to her that it is among the greatest of goods," T'Shael answered simply.

Master Stimm let her words fall into a careful silence, allowing her to weigh them even as he did. Simultaneously, he studied the figure kneeling on the bare floor at his feet—her slender back straight, her quite beautiful hands folded gracefully in her lap, her less then beautiful face downcast and showing no trace of what roiled in her mind. Her soft dark hair was unadorned, contrary to the custom among females of her age; she wore no jewelry or ornament of any kind, but seemed content with her plainness. She was one for whom self-denial was a natural state, one who could attain the status of Master with alacrity, if only she desired it. From her present train of thought, it was apparent that she desired something other.

T'Shael thirsted for something she could not name.

Master Stimm repressed the sigh that rose from his soul. This one's father, the reknowned musician Salet, had studied with him many years before, and had entrusted his offspring to the Master's care. There had been no possibility of persuading Salet to achieve Master; his soul, his being, had been music, his fate chronic illness and early death. But the musician's daughter possessed gifts which were less clearly defined. If her spirit could be guided in the proper direction. . . .

Stimm considered. He was contending with the allure of the outworlders, toward whom T'Shael with her aptitude for languages and a Vulcan's innate curiosity was inexorably drawn. Her pliability concerned the Master. Yet was his concern completely objective, or was it colored by the Master's having no offspring?

"Indeed," Master Stimm said at last in response to T'Shael's statement. "But it is to question whether thee speaks of knowledge or merely of information."

T'Shael took his meaning—that the mere gathering of data on other species, the mere absorption of their languages and

27

forming of acquaintances, was insignificant. This is not my purpose! she wanted to cry, but such an outburst was beyond her.

"If this one may presume to an analogy," she said. "If it is the Master's purpose to attain levels of meaning ever loftier and more complex, rising upward in the soul from one reach to the next, then it is this one's purpose, through the linguist's gift which has been given to me, to seek levels of meaning that expand outward toward a spiritual horizon in ever-enlarging circles."

"Thee waxes poetic," Stimm observed, though not as an accusation. "And one wonders if in expanding outward thee also considers the other purpose of the Master, which is not only a reaching upward, but a reaching inward, not only to the more complex, but also to the most simple."

T'Shael had no ready answer to this. As to her presumption to poetry—

"I ask forgiveness," she said, self-effacing.

Stimm repressed another sigh and softened his posture slightly.

"Consider this," he said. "That which is good leads to tranquility of soul. I submit that thy soul is far from tranquil."

T'Shael lowered her eyes and said nothing.

Perhaps one must pass through degrees of turmoil in order to arrive at tranquility, she thought.

T'Shael had begun as a student at the settlement; her place now was that of instructor. She taught advanced linguistics and the intricacies of Ancient Vulcan to the youth of T'ling-Shar proper, and basic Modern Vulcan to any and all in the settlement. All but the most primitive members of the Federation spoke Standard in addition to their native tongues, but Vulcan was the language of scientists and mathematicians and, to some degree, of musicians and philosophers. As T'Shael meticulously unfolded the mysteries of her language to her students, she absorbed each of their languages in turn, with as much enthusiasm as a Vulcan could permit herself.

To know a language intimately is to understand the soul of those who speak it. Salet her father had taught her that. He had meant it of music, the ultimate, universal language, but the concept applied in greater degree to words. T'Shael's mind mastered words as her being struggled with the concepts behind them. The more she learned of all these many species, the more she desired to learn. It was a hunger.

But the Vulcan knows there is a time for everything. In addition to her studies, her teaching, her meditations under Master Stimm, T'Shael somehow found time for two other things—music, and paleoarcheology.

She whose father had been perhaps the greatest musician of his time played the *ka'athyra* with but a pedestrian gift. Nevertheless, a transcendent look came over her austere face when she played. If a Vulcan could not admit to joy, then this would perhaps serve.

Her interest in the ancient artifacts of her people stemmed in part from the ever-presence of the tumbled ruins beyond the Old City of T'lingShar. T'Shael knew them intimately. She who had no friends could find companionship in the shattered columns and broken monuments, the somberfaced friezes and heroic statuary of another time.

It was among the ruins that she first encountered Cleante.

No one else was mad enough to go scaling the ruins in the heat of the Vulcan noon, Cleante decided, not even bothering to ask any of her classmates to accompany her. She would go exploring on her own.

She had been at the settlement for several weeks and had yet to find time to visit the ruins. After her morning classes on a half-day schedule, she slipped out of the city in the briefest of walking shorts, the most minimal of halters, and a staunch pair of hiking boots. Her backpack held a ration of water and some dried fruit, a magnifier, a minitricorder, and some soft brushes to gentle the sand away from any inscriptions or fine work she might want to study.

Winded from the long hike, Cleante rested in the shadow of the first of the mammoth colonnades marching in silent witness almost to the horizon, letting the breezes cool the sweat from her body. There were no birds here, she realized, no desert creatures. The silence, accentuated by the arid wind, was awesome.

Vulcan ruins were an endless source of puzzlement to the young human. In her part of the world great pains had been taken to restore the relics of the past; she herself had been one of the student volunteers responsible for the discovery of the long-lost tomb of the mad pharaoh Akhenaton, whose body had been stolen by his enemies four thousand years before. For all its drive toward modernism, Terra had at last come to recognize the need to preserve its past.

Yet the Vulcan, for all their preoccupation with what they called "the time of the beginning," let these archeological treasures stand untouched, prey to the ravages of wind and sand and the killing sun. In the heart of the Old City many ancient buildings had been rebuilt into the structures of newer edifices, but here on the outskirts all was ruin, and silence.

Cleante knew enough of Vulcan history to date much of the architecture to several millennia before the Cataclysm, but later additions indicated that they were in use up until that time. There were no "lost civilizations" on Vulcan; new cities were always integrated into older ones. Yet the ruins remained, wounded and profoundly disturbing.

Why would a species so concerned with aesthetics, with order and harmony, permit such a wasteland of broken columns, crumbled facades and tumbled statues to exist untouched for so long? Cleante knew that as a newcomer, an outworlder on probation as it were, she risked a breach of Vulcan propriety in asking too many questions. Yet she asked her professors, as indirectly as she could, about the ruins. The answer she was given only raised further unanswerable questions.

"The ruins serve their purpose," she was told, and knew enough not to inquire further.

Rested now, she meandered among the columns that remained, broken, wounded-looking things, stroking their carved sides lovingly with her fingertips as if to derive some knowledge from them in that way.

"Why?" she asked, not knowing that she spoke aloud. "What is your purpose? Why have they left you here like this?"

The ruins gave no answer.

"I wish you'd stop sulking," Jasmine alFaisal said to her daughter the night before she left for Vulcan. "It's very unattractive. And since you've gone to all the trouble of decking yourself out like a Maypole—"

"I'm not sulking, Mother," Cleante replied, too languid from her day in the City of the Dead (one last look at her childhood's growing place, macabre playground, which she would not see again for four years) to really argue. "I'm brooding. There's a difference. And I'm no gaudier than you."

Jasmine alFaisal, newly-elected High Commissioner of the United Earth Council, looked at herself in the floor-to-ceiling mirrors in Cleante's suite in the manse in Sadat City and had to admit that her daughter was right. She removed a few strands of native beryl stones from her neck and dropped them carelessly on the dressing table. She tugged at the waist of her formal ensemble in mild despair. If her physician's latest combination of injections couldn't keep her weight down better than this . . .

It's middle age, Jasmine thought with resignation. She was sixty-five, exactly midway into a human lifespan according to current longevity studies. Her jet-black hair had yet to be touched with gray, but there were lines around her eyes and mouth, a certain sagging about the jaw, that did not please her. Was that why her daughter's lithe beauty served as a constant irritant?

Of course not! Jasmine thought, annoyed with herself. Cleante is as much entitled to her years of beauty, with all the joys and sufferings such beauty brings, as I was to mine. What she is not entitled to do is to threaten my status in the Federation with her whimsies, her inability to settle on a career, and her blatant recklessness with the male of the species.

Isn't that last item the real issue here? Jasmine asked herself. Aren't you jealous of the way Cleante so casually attracts men, while you must work around your age, their awe of a High Commissioner and the fact that you're five kilos over your ideal weight? Isn't it the specific incident on Earth Colony Seven, that damned Rico Heyerdahl, that really galls you?

Well, four years on Vulcan will cure my proud beauty of all her bad habits, Jasmine decided, smiling a little cruelly. And with a little luck and my usual perseverance I may be reelected and she'll have to stay for eight. If only we can get through tonight's diplomatic reception without scratching each other's eyes out.

"I don't understand you," Jasmine sighed. "You're either dressed to the nines or covered with dirt from the excavations. Either way you're like a child. You play at everything, Cle, whether it's study or archeology or sex. When will you grow up?"

"When I'm thirty, Mother," Cleante laughed. Her laugh was artificial and clattered falsely against her own ears. "I do solemnly promise I'll become instantly mature as soon as I complete the next decade. I'll stop playing the perpetual student; I'll settle on a career. I may even get married."

She said this last with no small amount of irony. Her mother had married four times, finally abandoning the formalities and selecting lovers at random. Cleante's father had been a man she'd never met.

"Mother . . ."

Cleante felt a sudden tenderness toward this hard, glittering woman whom everyone else on this planet held in such enormous reverence. She would not see her mother for four years, possibly twice that. She was going to become a different person on Vulcan, Cleante promised herself. She was leaving on the interplanetary ferry early tomorrow, long before Jasmine awakened from her beauty sleep. There was so little time to assure her mother that she need no longer add her wayward daughter to her list of planetary burdens.

I'm sorry about Rico, Mother! she wanted to cry. I'll admit I went after him at first because I knew you wanted him, but it got complicated later, out of my control. Mother, I didn't mean to.

"Mother, when you were my age you knew what you wanted," she said instead. "It's taken you forty years to get it. Scratching, struggling, denying yourself everything except that goal, but here you are. Don't fault me if I haven't found anything I want that badly."

Except love, Cleante did not add. Hasn't it ever occurred to you that I seek solace in the arms of strangers because those who are supposed to love me don't? I have no father, but that hurts less than having a mother who resents me. You can't disguise it, Mother. I know I've always been the setback in your career, the little baggage that held you back all those extra years, the one mistake you've ever made or will admit to making. Shipping me off to Vulcan will make it so much easier for both of us. No more keeping up appearances.

"I promise not to nag you," Jasmine alFaisal said, resting her hands on her daughter's shoulders and contemplating them both in the mirror, though the comparison made her uneasy. "After all, this is our last night together. And I'll have no unhappy faces at my first official reception. Only the Vulcan delegation will be forgiven for seriousness. I want you to be happy. Just think of the notables gathered in that room tonight—Shras of Andor and Sarek of Vulcan and—"

"Wonderful," Cleante said with little enthusiasm. She did want to meet the mighty Sarek and his Lady Amanda, but she didn't care a fig about the rest of them.

Our last night together, Cleante thought bitterly. With a supporting cast of half the Federation!

"What is your purpose?" Cleante asked the great and silent columns at T'lingShar, so far from her beloved Egypt and yet so near in spirit. "Why have they left you here like this?"

"To remind ourselves of that which we once were," said a soft and somber voice.

Cleante turned sharply. She had thought she was alone, had not seen the slight figure more shadow than the shadows, had not heard her Vulcan-quiet approach even in this awesome stillness. T'Shael seemed at one with her environment, seemed to detach herself from it reluctantly to stand in the sunlight so that the human might see her better. Cleante smiled spontaneously, strangely moved.

"I don't understand," she said.

"Such as this serves to exacerbate the Vulcan's need for order," T'Shael said, making an elegant gesture with one long hand to encompass everything that surrounded them. She was about to speak more words in a moment than she usually spoke, beyond the limits of the classroom, in an entire day. "We would prefer to correct, to restore, to return this to a place of beauty as it once was. We come here instead to acknowledge that these ruins must always remain, as penalty for the violence of our past. The death of a city is preferable to the death of a living being. The Vulcan must never revert to what was, and this reminds us."

"*Memento mori,*" Cleante murmured wonderingly, not certain if the idea pleased or repulsed her. She looked long into the solemn dark eyes that appraised her. "A hairshirt."

"Your pardon?" T'Shael recognized the Latin; it was common enough. But this other expression was new to her.

Cleante shook her head.

"Nothing. I was thinking out loud. I didn't mean to disturb you. Were you meditating?"

She realized as she said it that such a question was a breach of Vulcan etiquette, and covered her mouth with one hand, a nervous habit she had whenever she was acutely embarrassed.

Was it that gesture that caused T'Shael to open out of herself in the presence of a stranger, to speak where she might ordinarily have kept her silence? Had she known, she who spoke of levels of meaning expanding outward toward a spiritual horizon, the ramifications of this moment, would she have dared?

"I'm sorry," Cleante said, blundering along. Humility was hardly her strong suit, but there was something here that humbled her. Was it the sense of place, the soaring columns emphasizing her smallness as their antiquity emphasized her youth? Was it the imbuing sense of history, the voices of the ancient ones such as had whispered to her in the City of the Dead, here speaking a language she did not know, but speaking nevertheless? Was it the disapproval she was certain she saw in those solemn eyes? Disapproval of what? Of the clothing she wore, or rather didn't wear (the Vulcan was swathed from throat to ankles, but surely humans were allowed to compensate for the heat), or her intrusive human questions which were a violation of the Vulcanness in the very air? "I didn't mean to be rude—"

"No matter," T'Shael replied, and though that was all that propriety required of her, she said more. "That you have come here indicates a curiosity about our old places. That you ask forgiveness indicates respect for our ways. You have not disturbed me. Meditation was not my purpose here this day."

"I see," Cleante said, and did not know what to say next. Again she caressed the stone, cool on the shadowed side, torrid in the sunlight. Every square centimeter was covered with carvings as far up as she could crane her neck to see. Cleante could only assume that with their race's integrity the ancient artisans had continued their designs to the very top. She puzzled over them. Hieroglyphs, runes, complex equations and merely decorative fine work wove about each other and intertwined their way about the columns, soaring upward. If she studied the Vulcan tongues for the rest of her life she could never begin to understand. "In my part of Earth there are ruins similar to these. Just as old, but not nearly as complex."

"The City of the Dead. Cairo, Old Egypt, Pan-Semite Union, Terra. Though you make your home in Sadat City of the same national division," T'Shael reported. "You are called Cleante alFaisal."

Would she ever be able to keep from laughing in the face of the Vulcan passion for accuracy and detail? Cleante tried masterfully, and was almost successful. Her sobriety returned when she realized her desire to remain relatively anonymous among all the other VIP offspring at T'lingShar was being threatened. She wished to be known for herself alone, not for being the daughter of a famous mother. Yet the Vulcan had made no mention of the celebrated High Commissioner.

"How did you know who I am?"

"I instruct at the settlement. New students are known to me. I am called T'Shael."

"T'Shael," Cleante repeated carefully, trying it out on her tongue. "It's soft, yet strong. As I suspect its owner is—oh, wait a minute!" she cried, sensing T'Shael's drawing into herself though the Vulcan's demeanor did not alter. Cleante's humility was shortlived. She was a diplomat's daughter, and could be persuasive or imperious as she chose. "You don't have to retreat into one of your Vulcan distances. I know all about those, and I'm not going to ask any personal questions like some blundering outworlder.

Look, I'm new here. I'll be here for four years, and I'm not going to spend that time hiding in some little human enclave. I want to learn about your world. Will you teach me, T'Shael?"

I am by definition a teacher, T'Shael thought, though the directness of the request disquieted her. It has been given to me to serve.

"If you wish it," she replied carefully.

"But do *you* wish it?" Cleante demanded incisively. "I don't want you to do it only out of a sense of duty."

"I am here to serve" was T'Shael's answer.

Cleante thought about that for a moment. It was not the answer she had wanted.

"I guess that's the most enthusiasm I can expect from a Vulcan," she said. T'Shael's eyes were hooded, unreadable. "And I promise to dress more appropriately, and conduct myself properly, in the future."

If T'Shael had an opinion, she kept it to herself. On this tenuous ground a friendship was about to take form.

"Come," T'Shael said shortly, moving away and indicating that Cleante was to follow her if indeed it was her desire to learn. "To learn about a world, one does well to start with its beginnings."

Cleante swallowed, squared her shoulders beneath her backpack as if setting out for a long journey, and followed.

In the evening of the day which had proved to be like no other she had ever experienced, T'Shael had activated the small teaching-aid computer in her solitary flat in the settlement.

"Computer," she had said softly, and it hummed its readiness. "Terran Standard, Dialect Subdivision Anglish. Definition and etymology of the term 'hairshirt.' "

The computer's response had been food for thought.

"It is a matter of acceptance of responsibility," T'Shael tried to explain. "A species which employs the term 'hairshirt' surely understands this."

"If you look at the history of Earth you'd think they'd forgotten," Cleante said wryly.

"Perhaps. But the Vulcan does not."

36

Moving among the friezes in a public building, T'Shael was translating the pictographs, pausing from time to time as the fading of the symbolic colors made her question her accuracy.

Cleante kept her tricorder running, unable to tear her eyes away from the epic snaking its way about the octagonal walls or the intense figure who explicated it, voice almost hoarse from so many words, eyes acquiring a kind of mystical light as she receded further into her race's past; those eyes, like burning coals concealing whatever she held inside. Oh, T'Shael! Cleante thought. How deep you are! Is it only duty that keeps you instructing a butterfly like me?

"Please go on," she urged her Vulcan companion, coming out of a sort of trance of her own. T'Shael tilted her head, not understanding. "Responsibility."

"Indeed." T'Shael nodded, framing her words. "It is to say that every action has its—one might call it 'ripple effect'—meaning that there is no action which is without significance. One's slightest gesture creates incalculable actions and reactions, possesses ramifications which cannot be foreseen, therefore—"

"If you tried to live by that you'd be paralyzed," Cleante argued. "Carrying the weight of the universe on your shoulders. You'd never be able to move."

Indeed, T'Shael thought but did not speak.

"You looked it up," Cleante said into her silence. "Hairshirt."

"Of course," was T'Shael's answer.

"The ruins at Gol are vaster," T'Shael had said on another occasion. Statuary was their field of concentration this day. Headless, faceless, limbless grotesques lying on their sides and flayed endlessly by swirling sand. Cleante had told T'Shael as much as she could remember of the poem about Ozymandias, and T'Shael made a mental note to discuss it with her computer. "And the statuary more refined. The best of the sculptors dwelt at Gol. The best of everything dwelt at Gol, which is why it is the place of the *Sim're'*, the High Masters, now."

"Were they gods?" Cleante asked absently, crouching to

touch one disembodied face lying like a gigantic Halloween mask at her feet. She knew they couldn't be; their features were too exactly drawn. They were Vulcans, true Vulcans. They could almost speak.

"Never," T'Shael said. "That is a curious difference between the Vulcan and most other intelligences. Perhaps it was our telepathic gift, but we never mistook natural phenomena for small pieces of divinity. We knew the All. We had no little gods, not even in the prewritten time, except of course the Others, and though we knew they were superior to us, yet we also knew they were not omnipotent.

"Our error was in attempting to deify those we knew to be mortal. An excess of honor perverts itself. Thus the Cataclysm. Thus these statues, erected to Vulcans who would be gods. And thus their destruction."

"It is called a bloodstone," T'Shael said on yet another day. She had brought her human companion to a vast courtyard on the very edge of the ruins which Cleante had somehow not discovered on her own. "There are many such extant in the old ruins. This is actually smaller than most, yet it has its distinction. It was here that Surak, Father of All We Became, came to meet his death."

She referred to an unadorned rectangular stone of some porous rock, perhaps two meters wide and three long, strangely scarred in places. It was an attractive jade green, unlike any type of stone Cleante had heretofore encountered on this world. As she did with each new discovery, she reached to touch it, finding to her surprise that it was damp beneath her fingers. A thrill of horror shot through her and she snatched her hand away, comprehending.

"Executions!" she gasped, expecting to find the blood of Vulcans clinging to her fingers. "Like the Aztecs on my world. T'Shael, how many?"

"Hundreds of thousands here alone," T'Shael said, and her voice took on a mourning note. "Ritual sacrifice not even redeemable by religious impulses, for we had no gods that demanded it. Poets and warriors, newborns snatched from the breast, all to gratify the base blood-lust of our own!"

She swayed slightly on her feet, lost in a kind of trance that frightened the human. Cleante reached out impulsively to touch her, knowing from past experience that she risked rebuke.

"T'Shael! It was your ancestors, thousands of years ago. Not you!"

"It is in all of us," T'Shael mourned. "Kept in check, but ever remaining. This place, this stone drenched with the blood of our own, with the blood of Surak, must remind us."

She seemed to shake off her trance, turning toward the human.

"You found the stone damp to your touch. Do you wonder why? Such blood was spilled here that it can never evaporate. The heat of the sun draws it to the surface that we may touch and be reminded, that pilgrims may come and add some portion of their own blood to that of the ancestors. This is, as you might say, our hairshirt."

"Are you a pilgrim, T'Shael?" Cleante asked carefully.

"That is not for you to know," T'Shael said abruptly, and Cleante laughed, nervously, irreverently.

"The trouble with not being able to lie, my Vulcan instructor, is that you fall prey to well-placed questions."

She grew sober. She could seize T'Shael's hand and, assuming the Vulcan would permit it, search for the mark of her personal blood-letting, but even she was not that rude. Nor did she need the physical evidence of a moral stance she could not comprehend.

"But why?" she asked plaintively.

"If you must ask the question then you cannot understand my answer. It behooves you to remember that you are human. Perhaps I have revealed too much to one who understands too little. That is my error. But you would do well to keep your place."

Cleante was silenced. It was clear that the lesson was over for today, perhaps for all time. Without another word T'Shael moved off in the direction of the settlement, not bothering to see if her merely human companion cared to follow. Cleante did, but she could not keep pace with the long and effortless Vulcan stride and soon lagged behind, the backpack digging into her shoulder blades, the sun even in the late afternoon making its presence felt.

I should hate you! Cleante thought, glaring doggedly at T'Shael's indifferent back, receding from her in the shimmering heat. You're morbid and cold and Vulcan arrogant; you instruct me out of duty and not out of care. I should hate you!

Then why do I keep coming back here with you, trying to understand you as much as I try to understand your world? What *is* it about you?

She was so furious she did not notice the change in the atmosphere until a sudden hot wind nearly knocked her off her feet. She glanced up at the still-unfamiliar sky and found that it was not its characteristic dull red color. It was suddenly filled with rapidly-massing storm clouds, leaden and lowering, and the temperature was plummeting. The wind turned cold, and it was hard to stand against it.

My first rainstorm on Vulcan, Cleante thought, shivering with excitement as she did with any new experience. She wondered if there would be lightning.

An ear-splitting crash answered her question and she grew alarmed, searching for shelter, thinking of tornadoes. She was midway between the settlement and the ruins; there wasn't so much as an outcropping to hide her. The parched desert plants about her flattened themselves against the desert floor; there was no shelter, none. Blowing sand stung at her. Cleante panicked.

Allah akbar! she prayed, instinctively reverting to her childhood's religion, though she didn't expect it to save her. She started to run toward the settlement, knowing it was too far, her arms flung across her face to protect her eyes from the sand.

She felt herself shoved face down into the sand as someone intervened between her and the elements.

T'Shael had come back for her.

There was rain now—cold, hard, needlelike rain, and hailstones several centimeters across. Cleante could see them pounding the sand around her, churning it into an oozing mire that threatened to smother her. She felt nothing. T'Shael sheltered her, taking the storm's fury upon herself. Cleante began to struggle.

"Get off me!" she shrieked into the wind, sand filling her mouth and nose. Gasping for breath, she twisted to look up at the face of the Vulcan whose spare body arched tensile-strong over hers. She could feel the hailstones pounding T'Shael's back through her own spine. "I'm all right! Don't—"

"Silence!" was all the Vulcan said, her eyes clamped shut, head bowed against the onslaught so that her lank hair whipped in Cleante's face. Her stronger hands pinned Cleante's at the wrists and held her down. Great branches of lightning slammed the ground on either side and Cleante understood T'Shael's wisdom. If she had continued to run through this . . .

Cleante stopped resisting until the storm did. She did not have to struggle to free herself now; T'Shael rolled away from her almost immediately.

"Just what the bloody hell did you think you were doing?" Cleante demanded, springing to her feet, trying futilely to clean great clumps of wet sand from her face and hair and sodden clothing.

"You are inexperienced in the vicissitudes of our climate. I must confess that I, too, was caught offguard. It is early in the season for such storms," T'Shael responded indirectly. She managed to look dignified though she was in worse shape than her companion. The sun returned blindingly, mocking their dishevelment. "It was my considered opinion that your safety superceded our mutual aversion to physical contact."

"I have no such aversion!" Cleante shouted at her, stamping her feet in her rage. "It's you and your damned Vulcan propriety. You who don't want to be touched. But you'll take the brunt of the storm for me, endanger your own life for a mere human whom you don't even especially like!"

"What has that to do with it?"

Cleante lost her anger in the face of such dispassion.

"T'Shael—I'm sorry. Oh, why do I always find myself apologizing to you? Are you hurt?"

"No," T'Shael replied, though not entirely honestly. Her back was a mass of assaulted nerve endings, but a light trance would ease the throbbing. "Is it of importance to you?"

41

Cleante looked at her in amazement.

"How can you ask me that? Of course it is! As obnoxious as you are, I'm concerned about you. It was obviously important to you to save me from the storm."

"There was no logical reason not to."

"And that's all it means to you?" the human demanded, wanting it to mean more, wanting her concern, her caring, to be reciprocal.

"Should it mean anything other?"

"I give up!" Cleante threw up her hands dramatically, disguising her pain. T'Shael's intention was never cruelty, but her words hurt all the same. "If I try to thank you I suppose you'll explain how it would have been illogical for both of us to suffer the effects of the storm. But why my well-being is more important than yours I don't under-stand."

"It is not," T'Shael said flatly. "You are the guest on my world, and the comfort of the guest must precede all else."

" 'Must,' " Cleante echoed. "How I envy you the sim-plicity of your life!"

She plopped down indifferently in the muck and began taking things out of her backpack, inventorying them for storm damage. The 'pack was filled with sand; she'd ex-pected that. The dried fruit she never got around to when she got lost in T'Shael's lectures was in the bottom, well-sealed and quite undamaged. The tricorder had not fared as well; it had been on top of the 'pack and the sand had penetrated the casing. The tape was ruined. An afternoon's labor, T'Shael's labor; Cleante had merely listened—destroyed. Nerves shat-tered from the whole experience, Cleante began to curse, tears of frustration in her eyes.

T'Shael listened, understanding only some of the invec-tive (sexual functions and the words for them were of no more significance to her than references to unnamed persons of dubious parentage, and what a human would call blas-phemy had no bearing upon the Vulcan concept of the All) but certainly recognizing the mood that evoked it.

"You speak of the simplicity of my life," she said, at-tempting to calm, to divert Cleante's attention. She took the

42

dysfunctional tricorder out of her hands and removed the tape, unreeling it centimeter by centimeter, blowing the sand away and allowing the tape to dry in the now cooling breeze. "Please explain."

"When everything is so black and white, how easy it must be to choose!" Cleante said bitterly, still shaky. She wiped the tears from her Byzantine eyes with the heel of her hand.

Cleante faced her biggest fear about the whole experience. Was it possible that T'Shael had been able to read her mind, had received some involuntary telepathic impulses as they clung to each other in the churning rain and sand? There were corners of Cleante's mind even she did not want to examine too closely. The thought of that morally incisive mind reaching into hers . . .

"How little you understand!" T'Shael said at last, and Cleante was not at all sure what she meant. The Vulcan handed her the tricorder, which was in perfect working order. She got to her feet and surveyed the landscape. "We must wait until the excess water has run off. There is a danger of quagmires."

Cleante laughed wildly. "Quagmires!" she repeated as T'Shael only looked at her. "A perfect emblem for our relationship, instructor mine." Her face hardened. "I wanted a friend. Instead I was blessed with a standup, prerecorded lecture on Vulcan archeology. Lucky me, audience of one for the invaluable wisdom of the reknowned T'Shael of Vulcan!"

T'Shael absorbed the insult as if it had not been uttered. "Your words were that you desired an instructor," she pointed out reasonably. "Had I known your requirement was friendship I should not have presumed to fulfill it."

"Why?" Cleante demanded. "Because I'm so mean to you? Or because I'm only human?"

T'Shael considered. Were she victim of her usual reticence she would have withdrawn from this conversation long ago. But there was need here, a need to which she could not help but respond. The comfort of the guest precedes all else.

"My words were not 'only' human," she began carefully. "You are human. That is fact. And even as I, as a Vulcan, do

43

not presume to understand the human heart, so I ask that you do not presume too readily to having knowledge of the Vulcan heart."

Cleante nodded, accepted it, humbled again.

"I only want to learn, T'Shael."

There was a child's plaintiveness here. T'Shael looked thoughtfully into the Byzantine eyes and was startled by what she found there. It was a hunger. A reflection of her own hunger—the insatiable hunger to know. How could she not respond?

T'Shael started to speak and could not. If Master Stimm was correct, if that which was good led to tranquility of soul . . .

She looked down and away from the Byzantine eyes to hide the hunger in her own.

They returned to the Old City to find citizen and outworlder alike out in force, removing the ravages of the unexpected storm. Vulcan cities were deflector screened against the worst weather, but a severe storm could sometimes slip through before the screens could snap on. With typical Vulcan efficiency, everyone who was able participated in the cleanup.

Some swept away the sand and debris filling the pedestrian streets with long, silent brooms. Others followed in their wake to scrub down the usually immaculate cobblestones, replace uprooted plants in the public gardens, and repair whatever the fierce wind had damaged.

T'Shael relieved an ancient female of her broom.

"In your place and in your honor, Venerable One," she said, and the old one nodded her acknowledgment, tottering off slowly. T'Shael looked hard at Cleante, daughter of the High Commissioner who, except for the digs, never got her soft hands dirty.

"If you would learn," the Vulcan said, a suggestion of challenge in her soft voice for the first time in their relationship.

Biting her tongue—humility was never her strong suit— Cleante sought out another elder, who was scrubbing the cobblestones on his hands and knees.

"In your place and in your honor, Venerable One," she said in slow and careful Vulcan, kneeling beside him to await his acknowledgment.

She did not dare look up to see the approval in T'Shael's eyes.

Three

"IF I KNOW Jim Kirk," Commodore Mendez said, "he's going to be the first one to jump on this thing."

"Then it's your job to rein him in, Jose," Admiral Nogura said. "This is no time for seat-of-the-pants heroics. You tell him that from me."

The years had not dealt badly with Jose Iglesias de Mendez. The stern, heavy-jowled face might have acquired a few more creases, his hairline might have receded a bit further, but the ice-blue eyes were as clear as ever, as was the steel-trap mind.

His long stint as commandant of Starbase XI and the surrounding sector hadn't diminished his reputation as a hardass, but he was still above all an eminently just man, and that reputation was legend as well. His repeated refusal of promotion or another starship command only emphasized his awareness of his own abilities and his place in the scheme of things. He *liked* being a paper-pusher. If he sometimes envied the reckless charisma of a Jim Kirk, the rainy-day twinge of a few old phaser scars earned in close scrapes quickly dispelled the feeling. Galloping around the cosmos was a game for the young, or the slightly mad. Jose Mendez was neither.

Nor was the individual on Code One Priority hyperchannel direct from Command HQ in San Francisco. No one knew how old Nogura was; his first act as Commander Starfleet had been to delete all references to his age from every memory bank from Earth to Memory Alpha. And nothing in his demeanor—public, private, or after a couple of bottles of rice wine—had ever indicated that Nogura was anything but deliberately, calculatedly, frighteningly sane.

"He's at least going to want a piece of it, Heihachiro," Mendez said. "What am I supposed to tell him?"

"A piece of *what?*" Nogura demanded, his opaque eyes becoming more inscrutable than ever. "Special Section has been swarming all over Vulcan for three days. Know what they came up with? An exosphere-converted hovercraft with its identicode infrarayed out, derelict in the asteroid belt. Vulcan authorities confirm it was 'borrowed' from the Space Central orbital station. Nothing's ever locked up on Vulcan; anyone with a grain of larceny could walk off with the entire planet. But that's it. A stray 'craft with a few hundred extra kilometers on the odometer.

"And I'll tell you something else—" Nogura went on.

He sounded out of breath, as if the sheer audacity of this thing was getting to him. Mendez watched, listened, fascinated. He remembered Nogura under fire, as captain of the old class-J *Horizon* when he, Mendez, was a wet-eared ensign. The Ice Man, they'd called him.

And a few years back, when V'ger had come home looking for its daddy and it seemed Earth and Heihachiro Nogura had bought it for good this time, and Jim Kirk's cavalry had come over the hill as usual—Nogura hadn't rattled then, either.

But right now he sounded as if he was close to rattling. Was it just the incredibility of this kidnapping, or was the old boy really past it?

"I'll tell you something else," Nogura was saying. "That 'craft was clean. No fingerprints, paw prints, scratch marks around the starter. No stray hairs or feathers or loose change in the upholstery. No nail parings, cuff buttons, candy wrappers—nothing. Not only do we not know how or why, we haven't a clue as to who. Just what's Jim Kirk going to want a piece *of?*"

"Maybe an espionage mission," Mendez suggested. "Maybe the answers to the how and why and who."

"If Special Section can't come up with anything, how in the Void is Kirk supposed to? Wait a minute. *Wait a minute.*" Nogura's entire face had gone inscrutable; he'd always considered Special Section a bunch of omni-thumbed dunsel-dusters anyway. "Jose, you may just have something there. Let Kirk tell me how under-utilized he is. I've heard the griping. We'll teach him when he's better off. When *Enterprise* hails in, this is what I want you to do . . ."

It was a desolate place.

They were hustled out of the cargo hold of the Klingon ship, legs rubbery from drugs and hunger and none knew how many days of unnatural sleep, and into a shuttlecraft of Rihannsu design. Whatever their destination, they had arrived.

"If only I had my chronometer!" Resh sighed as the shuttle lurched out of its bay and into velvet space. He seemed much calmer now, whether resigned to his fate or merely determined to keep his younger cousins cheerful. He was probably the eldest of the group at nearly forty (no one knew Theras's age), with that ageless maturity Deltans acquire for public decorousness and shed like a second skin for sex play. "They must have taken all our valuables when they captured us. I've only now noticed."

"Not all your valuables, cousin!" Krn piped up, poking his elder suggestively and falling into giggles. He had decided somehow that this was an adventure, and was determined to enjoy it.

"Perhaps some control!" Resh said with a touch of sternness. He was preoccupied with what Jali might be discovering at the rear viewport.

"What good is when if we don't know where?" Theras demanded, hissing and coiling in on himself.

There was a mad look in his aquamarine eyes as he measured the two guards against his own potential for snatching a disruptor. He kept glaring at T'Shael, hissing under his breath, trying to draw her into joining him in an attack; even at two against three and weaponless they might succeed with surprise and the Romulans' inability to get off a

48

clean shot in such close quarters. It was the closeness of the quarters that was telling on Theras; he could not take much more of this. T'Shael seemed to be in trance. At least she would not look in his direction.

"What have you come up with, Jali?"

Cleante crouched beside her at the rear port; the guards did not seem to mind if they chatted and explored their surroundings as long as they made no sudden moves. Deltans were gifted stargazers, the best navigators after Medusans, it was said, and if anyone could determine where they were it would be Jali. Cleante had always liked Jali; they had sometimes compared notes on the male of the species, a favorite topic of both. Jali made it a point never to approach a female as patently hetero as Cleante.

Now the Deltan shrugged and turned away from the viewport, swinging her legs over the sides of her seat carelessly.

"There is nothing here I recognize. We are far beyond any star system with which I am familiar."

The prisoners had no time to be depressed by this news. The shuttlecraft nosed into a sudden downspiral, and the arcing limb of a planetoid hove into the main viewscreen.

It was an unpromising dun-colored sphere, clouded by large atmospheric disturbances. Even as they drew closer and land masses distinguished themselves from water, there was nothing here anyone could recognize either.

Instinctively the Deltans huddled together, and Cleante returned to her seat. Captives and captors alike grasped handrails and braced against the shuttle's downslant. Theras took the opportunity to draw into T'Shael's personal space, his clawed hand gripping her arm, his fevered breath in her ear.

"We can take them!" he hissed, depending upon the softness of his voice and the acuity of her hearing. "Let the others create a distraction. You and I can take the three, seize a disruptor, then the shuttle—"

"And then?" T'Shael asked reasonably, staring straight ahead. His touch offended her. Impressions of bloodlust and madness intruded into her consciousness. Block them! she commanded herself. "We are inexperienced. None of us can navigate in a known star system, much less here."

49

"Lock into orbit!" Theras hissed frantically, spittle flying. "I am a historian. Military tactics are known to me. We can evade capture, send out distress flares."

"To be seen by whom? Rihannsu, Klin? Worse, no one? Locked into orbit around an unknown world with limited fuel, weakened by drugs and without provisions—madness! And what of our captors?"

"Leave them to me!" the Andorian hissed, confirming all the impressions T'Shael had tried to block, tightening his blue talon on her arm.

"Worse than madness!"

T'Shael wrenched free of his death-grip with sufficient force to alert the guards. She returned to her trance, if trance it was, though not without making note for future discussion with her computer of every Andorian curse now being rained upon her head.

The shuttle touched down on the night side, making it impossible for the captives to discern topography, to determine if this place was island or desert, jungle or tundra. One thing was certain. Except for the place where the shuttle-craft had come to rest there was no artificial light source as far as any horizon. If the planet had inhabitants, they did not dwell here.

It was silent! Cleante noted as the guard led them out of the shuttle one by one. She was always aware of sound or the lack of it. No birds, no night creatures, no far-off rumble that might evidence a city, a heliport, hovercraft, anything. Except for the wind, utter silence.

It was cold, T'Shael noted, even her usual stoicism unable to control a sudden tremor.

The shuttle stood in the center of a compound, a cluster of lowslung, apparently recently constructed buildings around a grassless quadrangle, completely fenced in. It was a desolate place.

He would not be kept here! Theras decided madly, the shreds of his sanity giving way to claustrophobia. With an animal shriek he rushed the nearer of the guards.

Had he bothered to ask her opinion, T'Shael might have told him the odds against his success. As it was, Theras of Andor never asked anyone anything again.

"It was an accident, Commander! He tripped the mechanism as we struggled. On my father's life I swear it!" the guard pleaded in a dialect which only T'Shael could follow. He surrendered the offending disruptor, pointing it toward himself should his commander wish an easy solution. The charred and broken body of the Andorian lay crumpled at his feet.

Cleante remembered screaming. The Deltans had turned inward to block the ugliness of the scene. T'Shael, unmoving and seemingly unmoved, thought a mourning chant. Such death was a waste. Worse than madness.

"—only another indication that we should never have been party to this in the first place!" the commander raged, the weapon upraised as if he would strike his subordinate across the jaw with it. The blow never fell; it would undo nothing. The Rihannsu had abandoned Standard now; the exchange became so staccato even T'Shael had trouble following it.

"Oh, my God!" Cleante cried, rocking herself, her face hidden in her hands. "Allah, is that going to happen to all of us? Did they bring us here to die?"

If she expected reasssurance from T'Shael she got none.

"Silence!" the Vulcan said harshly, straining to listen. Resh took Cleante into his arms, drawing her into his circle of cousins. T'Shael stood alone.

The Rihannsu commander whirled on his surviving captives, galvanizing himself.

"Inside, all of you!" he barked in painful Standard, waving the disruptor toward one of the buildings. His captives offered no resistance.

The building was a single room, a kind of barracks. The significance of its furnishing would become apparent in time. Three double-tiered bunks lined the unfinished concrete walls. Their design was not identifiably Rom or Klin and the bedding was Starfleet standard-issue, very possibly appropriated from some Starbase warehouse or ship's cargo hold. It was clear that the captors intended to leave no incriminating evidence in their wake.

Sleeping accommodations for six, the captives noted silently. As if whoever had masterminded this knew exactly who their hostages were to be.

There were a few windows high up in the thick walls and

sealed from the outside; atmosphere-control vents were too small to afford escape. A shower stall and primitive toilet facilities were housed in an alcove which made no pretense of affording privacy. The single entry was a clearsteel partition and opened only from without. This place was for captives who were to be kept under careful observation. But by whom, and for what purpose?

The second guard brought a large sack from the shuttle-craft and dumped it unceremoniously on the bare floor.

"Provisions," the commander reported, still in Standard. He seemed to have regained his composure with the language. "You are provided with food and you will be kept here. The rest is out of my hands."

That thought seemed to shatter his reserve. He reverted to his own tongue, and to a kind of dictatorial screaming.

"I charge you all!" he shouted in Rihan, and all but T'Shael looked at him blankly. He focused on her, jabbing his finger in her direction. "I charge you! You who cannot lie. You were witness. Tell them how it went, that it was no fault of mine. I am but a cog in the machine. I obey. You will tell whoever follows. I charge you!"

"I accept your charge," T'Shael replied, and it seemed to satisfy him.

He ordered the guards out and sealed the clearsteel entry from the outside.

The captives watched as the Romulans loaded Theras's body into the shuttlecraft and departed.

Uhura was so completely absorbed in the transmission from Starbase XI that she didn't notice Spock hovering behind her at the comm con. Until a moment ago, she'd had the bridge virtually to herself. She listened intently, disturbed by the content of the message, but smiling her radiant smile across light years of space to the old friend sending it.

It was hard to explain to the layman how it was possible to become so close to people one seldom met in person, and could reach only by voice and over vastnesses of space. It was perhaps that very remoteness, that lack of physical contact that made it imperative to share gossip and confidences and deeply personal things. Uhura could count among her closest friends beings whom she might never have met face to face, who lived and·worked beyond even commpic range, but whose every nuance of mood and voice was known to her.

Spock watched the frown vying with the smile for possession of the beautiful dark face and nodded thoughtfully. The human face in all its variations never ceased to fascinate him.

"Affirmative, Mai-Ling. I have the entire message now," Uhura acknowledged, her smile spilling over into her voice. "I'll have it decoded and ready for the Admiral's 1400 briefing. There's been no followup since the abduction?"

Abduction? If Spock's initial purpose in lingering near Uhura's console had been an aesthetic contemplation of the human face, it had suddenly acquired added dimension. His sharp ears grew sharper.

The response from Commander Hong on Starbase XI was apparently negative, for Uhura's face succumbed to the frown.

"Isn't that awful?" she clucked. "Those poor people! Oh, I know, intergalactic ramifications and all that, but I guess my primary concern is the people involved. Affirmative, Mai-Ling. Give my love to Tam. *Enterprise* out."

She took the transceiver out of her ear, half-turned in her chair, and nearly jumped out of her skin at Spock's proximity.

"My God, you gave me a start!" she gasped, her hand over her heart but her eyes dancing at him. "I swear you're getting quieter all the time!"

"It was not my intention to eavesdrop," he said in that whimsical tone he'd evolved over the years. He was about, Uhura knew, to make one of his oblique, self-deprecating Vulcan jokes. "Unnecessary, of course, since apocrypha among the cadets indicates I can hear through the very bulkheads. Commander Hong is well?"

"Yes, she is," Uhura twinkled. "She reports that her hydroponic garden is flourishing, thanks to your advice."

"It is the growing season on her world," Spock observed. "If her garden is any reflection of Ling Hong's personality, one may logically assume that it is flourishing."

"Oh—and she sends you her love," Uhura added, almost as an afterthought.

"Indeed?" Spock said, playing at the old formality.

"Yes, 'indeed,' " Uhura mimicked him fondly. "Did you think we were the only ones who loved you, Mr. Spock?"

Spock said nothing, and only someone who knew him as well as Uhura could discern in that seemingly unmoved face the slightest tinge of shy appreciation. But his next words gave no indication of his private thoughts.

"Ling Hong's transmission would seem to have been of a disturbing nature. Was it Security coded, or might one inquire?"

"If they let me in on it, you can bet it wasn't coded, honey," Uhura quipped, then stopped herself. If she wasn't careful her teasing would earn her some of Spock's wit, which, however infrequently used, could be murderous. "You'll get it at the briefing, just like everyone else. You'll just have to contain yourself for seven minutes."

"Seven-point-three-five minutes. You made mention of an 'abduction'—"

"Mr. Spock!" Uhura gasped, mock-horrified. "If I didn't know you better, I'd swear you were guilty of an old-fashioned case of human nosiness."

"To express an interest in matters of command, Ms. Uhura—"

"—is in this case to be nosey, Mr. Spock. You'll have to wait for the briefing. No scoops, no special privileges." She smiled seductively. "Unless you'd like to try reading my mind."

Their eyes locked for an instant and Spock might have smiled.

"A mass of conflicting impulses," he said solemnly.

It was an old joke. Uhura slapped at his hand playfully, beaming at him.

The Klingons arrived with the morning suns.

This world where the Warrantors had been abandoned by the Rihannsu, whatever its designation, was part of a binary system—two red dwarf stars wheeled sluggishly about each other in a trojan orbit, providing almost as much heat and light as a yellow Sol-magnitude star, though the light had a dull reddish tinge that rendered the sky a muddy brown, and the twin stars cast double shadows, disorienting to the uninitiated. But the dual system explained the Earth-equivalent gravity on such a smallish planetoid, as Jali explained to the others.

"Limbic curvature at the horizon indicates it is considerably smaller than any of our home worlds," she said with a fluttering of eyelashes.

"It would appear, at least for our purposes, to be uninhabited," T'Shael added.

"Must you keep bringing that up?" Cleante asked irritably.

None of them had slept through the long night, but the toll of uncertainty and fatigue was greatest on the human. Now her ears caught a sound that banished everything but terror.

T'Shael had been aware of the approaching vessel for some moments, but saw no logic in reminding her companions of their helplessness. Whatever came to them now, they owed her a few extra moments of uneasy peace.

"Klingons!"

This came from Krn, son of a senior Deltan ambassador, who with his parents and many siblings had spent much of his short life in transit between one embassy and another galaxy-wide. His father had encouraged him in the hobby of collecting models of every vessel he encountered in his travels, and Krn's dorm room at T'lingShar had been a small museum of such pieces, suspended from ceilings, mounted on walls, cluttering shelves and table tops. Before the vessel came clearly into view in the murky dawn light, Krn knew what it was.

"It is a Kzantor-style longrange, model 75ZX4 with modified forward nacelles. Four passenger," he reported proudly. He bounced down from the upper bunk where he'd been peering out one of the windows. "Meaning that they cannot intend to be moving us, in a 'craft so small. They mean to keep us here."

"They could always separate us," Cleante said without thinking. Klingons! Allah, what did it mean? She clutched at the hair at her temples the way she did when she was upset or, in this case, abjectly terrified. "Take us away individually, to different places."

She did not realize the effect her words would have on the Deltans. Nothing so terrified one of this species as the fear of

55

losing physical proximity to the others. The trio had spent the dark hours impossibly intertwined in a single bunk, not sleeping but comforting each other.

Krn wailed and Jali whimpered; Resh wrung his hands and crushed them to him, glaring at Cleante. She had never seen a Deltan angry before. Outside, the Klin vessel touched down in a maelstrom of ugly yellow dust. Whoever was inside would emerge at any moment, marching toward them. Cleante gasped for air, suddenly understanding poor dead Theras's claustrophobia, wanting to shriek at the Deltans to be still, to pull themselves together.

T'Shael touched her shoulder, lightly but with the strength of unshakable calm.

"Control," she said. "We have not time for such indulgence." She turned her gaze toward the threesome, focusing on Resh. "You must calm them. The Klin thrives on the weaknesses of others. You must prepare for this."

Resh nodded, drew himself up, and placed two fingers on each of his cousins' smooth and unlined foreheads. He began to hum a kind of mantra, to which first Jali and finally Krn added their voices, and together they surrounded themselves with psionic harmony. Cleante watched in wonder and in envy. The linkage lasted only a moment, but the change was remarkable. The Deltans seemed ready for anything. What she wouldn't give for some portion of their tranquility! Cleante thought.

"I'm frightened!" She whispered, looking to T'Shael, pleading. The worst she could earn was reproach. She heard the harsh crunch of boots on the gravel of the compound. Any moment now.

Extraordinarily, T'Shael drew close, closer than she had ever come, taking the human's face between her long, cool hands. Eyes like burning coals, hooded eyes in less-than-beautiful face drew the human's soul out into her own.

"Control," she repeated. "Whatever their purpose, they will look for fear. As I have endeavored to teach you—"

"Be strong for me!" Cleante pleaded, covering the beautiful hands with her own. "I'll try!"

"I am here," was all the Vulcan said, and it was enough.

The door burst open.

*　　*　　*

56

"Why does Command send us these things?" Admiral Kirk asked of no one in particular, pacing the confines of the briefing room irritably. His coffee had gone cold somewhere during Uhura's report. He put the cup down, spilling a little; it was the least of his annoyances. "These damn FYI bulletins—'All Fleet personnel to be informed but no action to be taken.' If Jose thinks I'm going to just sit here—"

He caught Spock's look and subsided. The others—Uhura, McCoy, Sulu, even Lieutenant Saavik, who was there to observe—sat silently around the table waiting for him to finish.

"Okay," he acknowledged. "I really didn't call you all here just to listen to me gripe, as some people have put it. Ladies, gentlemen—I need facts, and I need recommendations."

"One wonders at the merit of our recommendations, Admiral," Spock said rhetorically and out of turn. The others looked at him. "Unless of course they concur with what you have already formulated in your mind."

"Just what the hell is that supposed to mean?" Jim Kirk snapped.

"It means, if I may be so bold, Admiral, that you engaged your Knight on White Charger mode the moment you were informed of the abduction of the Warrantors."

Uhura giggled; Sulu struggled with a smile. McCoy developed a sudden fit of coughing. Saavik, puzzled by the reference, made a mental note to check with Linguistics following the briefing. Kirk glowered. Spock returned the look mildly.

"It's infuriating, that's all," Kirk said crossly, refusing to be teased out of his mood. "Innocents. Stolen out of the very heart of the Federation. Kidnapped from Vulcan, of all places, where you'd think they'd be safe. Students, some of them mere children, if Command's information is accurate."

"Only one is a child, Admiral," Spock interjected. He had accessed identities on all six Warrantors while Uhura gave her report, and was presently puzzling over the face of T'Shael on his computer's small screen. She was known to him, he was certain, but in what context? He would have time to cross-correlate later. "Krnsandor L'am is of eleven Deltan years. The others are of adult age."

Nitpicker! McCoy thought, controlling himself for once. That's not the issue here! Jim's right. If the Warrantors aren't safe on Vulcan, nobody's safe anywhere!

"Innocent people!" Kirk was fuming. "Children or not. Non-politicals. Peaceful, useful citizens donating a part of their lives to keep the rest of us from each other's throats. We still don't know who did it or why. All of the Federation's resources can't come up with an answer. We could comb the entire galaxy without knowing what we're looking for."

"Which is perhaps why we have been instructed to take no action," Spock suggested. He waited a moment. "I have a theory."

"Well, that's refreshing!" Kirk sat down at last. He clasped his hands behind his head and leaned back in his chair. "Shoot!"

Spock might have grimaced. He had never cared for that particular expression.

"Based upon the limited data supplied us by Command, I would surmise that the actual abduction was conducted by Romulan infiltrators."

Kirk shot forward in his chair, leaning across the table.

"That would explain how they could move about the cities unnoticed. But how did they get onworld to begin with?"

"For that I believe one must hold the mixed blessing of our common ancestry accountable."

Uhura shifted in her chair.

"I don't understand, Mr. Spock."

Spock folded his hands on the briefing table in a manner which indicated his auditors were due for a long explanation.

"No more than three or four armed Romulans would be needed to take six unarmed hostages. Such a small force would not require an entire Klin or Romulan vessel, which at any rate would be challenged and held by planetary defense screens. They could, however, assume the identities of Vulcans and infiltrate the crews of multi-special merchant vessels. A long-range scan of such a ship's crew complement would not distinguish between a Rihannsu body reading and that of a Vulcan."

Uhura nodded.

"Sounds plausible," Kirk said thoughtfully. "But wouldn't it be—logical—to anticipate something like this? Don't tell me it's never happened before?"

"The Vulcan and the Rihannsu share an ancient code of honor, Admiral—" Spock began.

"Meaning, it was humans who invented the polygraph test," McCoy chimed in. He'd been quiet for entirely too long. "Or to put it another way, them that don't lie don't expect to be lied to. Am I right, Spock?"

"Overly simplistic, Doctor, but essentially correct," Spock said drily. He knew where McCoy was leading him and decided to get it over with. "And this may have constituted a flaw in our logic."

"Pity the first admitted flaw in Vulcan logic had to be uncovered at the expense of six of the Warrantors of the Peace!" McCoy said.

"Gentlemen!" Kirk said automatically. He had a faraway look in his eyes. "Romulan infiltrators," he said softly. "Romulan infiltrators. Plausible, Spock, but why? The settlement of Warrantors has been functional for nearly five years. Why make a move on it now?"

Spock considered.

"Impossible to be certain, Admiral. However, the Rihannsu alliance with the Klingons has brought with it certain pressures which may be difficult to reconcile with their own moral code. And they may consider the Vulcan alliance with humans a betrayal of our common ancestry, hence a justification for their action."

"But humans and Vulcans have been allies for centuries, Mr. Spock," Uhura said. "Why would the Rihannsu wait so long to retaliate?"

"There have been other forms of reprisal, Ms. Uhura."

Spock's eyes rested on Saavik, who had been utterly, stonily silent throughout the briefing. The others assumed it was because she was a cadet and afraid to speak out of turn, or perhaps because she was a Vulcan and conditioned not to speak in the presence of her elders unless spoken to.

Or perhaps this dispassionate discussion of Romulans struck too close to the bone.

Spock continued, "And the Rihannsu have a long memory."

59

It was Kirk who broke the electrified silence which ensued.

"Romulans, then," he said. "Probably in cahoots with Klingons. But who's working for whom? And what would either empire hope to gain by kidnapping a handful of Warrantors?"

"Simple terrorism," Spock suggested. "Though why there have as yet been no ransom demands is unknown. Or, the abductors may think to gain access to our formulae for planetary destruction, not realizing that any attempt to tamper with the peace capsules will result in immediate self-destruct."

Uhura gasped. Most Starfleet personnel had a vague idea of how the peace capsules worked, but few understood all of their ramifications.

"You mean if someone tried to remove one of the capsules it would kill the Warrantor?" she asked incredulously. "How awful!"

Spock's delicate fingers flew over his console as he accessed as much medium-classified data as was available on the peace capsules. A complex chart appeared on the small screen, which he turned in Uhura's direction. Saavik, her curiosity overcoming whatever else she was thinking, leaned closer as well. Only Sulu seemed lost in some private funk.

"Each capsule contains the key sequential formula to inaugurate a global-scale attack," Spock began in his best lecturer's voice. Even Kirk and McCoy, who knew most of this already, found themselves listening intently. "It is surgically implanted in the left ventricle or, in the case, for example, of the multi-chambered Sulamid heart, the lower fifth ventricle, of the Warrantor's heart. Once the capsule is in place, the only way one Federation member can implement an aggression against another is for that world's leader to personally take the life of his Warrantor, thereby matching the code only he possesses with the code contained in the capsule. The capsule is encoded to deactivate once the Warrantor's term has expired, when it may safely be removed. Any attempt to remove or deactivate the capsule before that time results in self-destruct. The Warrantor's heart is literally destroyed, exploded from within. The system is tamper-proof. Without exception."

"Then those six people are walking time bombs," McCoy said after a sober silence.

No one else said anything. Spock's viewscreen returned to the holos of the six missing Warrantors, whose faces seemed to accuse.

"There may be yet another reason for the abduction," Spock said after a long thoughtful moment, still contemplating the holo of T'Shael on the screen.

Kirk held out his hands in a kind of plea. His anger had dissipated; the seriousness of the situation was weighing on him.

"We're listening," he said.

"The perpetrators may believe that, with four of our worlds bereft of Warrantors we would have no 'safety valve,' so to speak, and would fall to quarreling among ourselves. Both Empires know of the controversies which divide our worlds; it would be naive to believe otherwise. If the Warrantors were held incommunicado indefinitely, their worlds might begin to accuse others within the Federation, since the idea of Romulan infiltrators does on the surface seem outrageous. At least the abductors might reason that our diversity of cultures would lead us to destroy each other from within."

"Well, we certainly give them reason to hope," McCoy growled. "The kind of thing we tolerate in the interests of diversity must seem ridiculous to absolute dictatorships like the Empires. This nonsense between Elaas and Troyius that's been going on for decades. The renewal of hostilities between Vendikar and Eminiar VII. Tellarites gnashing their teeth at their immediate neighbors, Orions mixing it up with everybody. It isn't too far-fetched."

And Vulcans and humans sniping at each other out of pure cussedness, he thought but did not add. Next thing he knew he'd be agreeing with Spock entirely.

Kirk cleared his throat.

"So much for the facts," he said. "And the theories. Now—recommendations. Hikaru? You haven't said a word."

Sulu blinked, shook off some private reverie.

"I was just thinking. Command wants us informed, but inactive. They know us better than to think we're going to sit

61

still. I think they want us to keep an eye out. An ear to the ground, so to speak. As kind of an unofficial espionage network, on the assumption that the official network's also out fishing."

Kirk sipped his tepid coffee.

"I assume they've got Special Section working on it," he said, deadpan. He shared Heihachiro Nogura's assessment of the civilian Intelligence branch.

"Due respect, sir," Sulu said. "I've worked with Special Section—"

None of the others seemed surprised. Sulu had enough energy for three ordinary humans; they knew he often disappeared during their little training cruises when he wasn't needed at the helm, turning up weeks later somewhere between exhaustion and exhilaration alluding to "one helluva shore leave." Now they knew for sure.

"I've worked with Special Section," he said. "They're going to need some hand-holding."

"What did you have in mind?" Kirk asked. The thought had also occurred to him.

"We could put in a request for a more active role," Sulu said, mapping his plans out on the tabletop as he spoke. "Maybe a little cruise along one of the Neutral Zones. See if we can pick up any border violators, ask them some questions. Find out what's going on in either Empire that might have precipitated this."

Kirk was nodding. He and Sulu had been working together for so long their tactical minds had begun to merge.

"And you don't think Command's going to refuse us?"

"Of course they will, sir. They're not going to divert a red flag like *Enterprise* for that kind of assignment. Too conspicuous." Sulu grinned his best grin; the *samurai* blood was up. "But at least we can say we tried. That's when I brush up my Rihan, kiss you all good-bye and go undercover again."

"Now hold on a minute, bucko," McCoy objected. "Since when did this become a democracy? If you think you're going to go swashbuckling off saving the galaxy single-handed while we diddle around in the shallows. . . . Either we're in this together or—"

"All for one and one for all, huh, Doc?"

"Well, why not?" Uhura chimed in.

Jim Kirk said nothing, watching the wildfire spread. Sometimes that was the wisest thing for a commander to do. When he thought McCoy for one had gone on long enough he interrupted.

"Thought you liked the country club atmosphere, Bones."

"Well, I do. But when I think of those innocent kids out there . . . like you said, this is the kind of thing to get anybody riled. Are we going to leave this to the diplomats and the Special Section spooks or are we going to get involved?"

Uhura agreed. Saavik deferred to Spock, who merely nodded. As the word spread throughout the ship, several other department heads called in with their support. Scotty reported that he and his crew were ready for anything.

It was unanimous. *Enterprise* wanted in. Kirk put in a call to Starbase XI.

"I'm putting *Enterprise* on Standby alert, Jim," Jose Mendez told him. It wasn't what Kirk wanted to hear. "You'll be in the vanguard if there's any action to be taken. That's all I can do at this end."

Kirk leaned into the screen for emphasis.

"You can't leave me with that, Jose. I've got a ship full of people raring for action, individually or as a crew—"

"I'm not listening to you, Jim."

"Spock says it could be Romulans—"

"Spock's probably right!" Mendez blazed. He, too, was leaning closer to the screen, his cold blue eyes narrowed dangerously. "But it's not going to do you any good *at this time*. Do you read me, Jim?"

"Dammit, Jose, don't do this to me! Or to my people. We need this, and you need us. You may be Commandant of this sector, but I technically by God outrank you and I'll go over your head if I have to."

"Be my guest!"

Kirk stopped his next retort on the tip of his tongue, swallowed it, nearly choked on it. What was Mendez telegraphing? Was he daring him to go to Nogura? Regulation 46A. . . .

Jim Kirk took a deep breath.

"Message received, Jose. I'd thank you, if you weren't such a hardassed son-of-a—"

"My mother used to tell me the same thing. Warp speed, Jim. Mendez out."

Jose Iglesias de Mendez cleared the screen, counted to ten in all his languages, logged in his personal Priority One code, pressed the Scramble switch and waited for retinascan clearance. He paused only long enough to calculate what time it would be in Old San Francisco, Sol III right now.

Four a.m. Oh, well, they say the Ice Man never sleeps. Sorry to do this to you, Heihachiro, but you said to let you know.

He accessed Nogura's Personal Code, the one even his wife didn't know.

"Mendez," was all he said. "Kirk's coming in."

Four

THE DOOR BURST open.

There were four this time: two guards who immediately flanked either side of the doorway, weapons drawn, a leader of some high military rank, and his second.

Four pairs of piercing eyes raked the assembled prisoners. Heavy bifurcated eyebrows, vestigial vertebrae arching over gnarled skulls to the juncture of those eyebrows, prognathous jaws and a tendency to breathe through their mouths lent these hard faces menace no matter what the mood behind them. If a Klingon could smile, if a Klingon could soften into mercy, none of the prisoners knew it.

"Well! And what do we have here?" the leader inquired rhetorically. His Standard was good and almost unaccented, though one suspected it was limited. There was a swagger to his voice as well as to his walk. He was small for a Klingon, which meant only one thing. This one had learned to survive by his wits.

"I am Krazz," he announced, his eyes roaming over all of them in turn. *"Lord* Krazz, to you. I am to be your caretaker. For however long it takes.

"You wonder why you've been brought here," he went on when they did not respond, thumbs tucked into his weapon belt, booted feet planted firmly in the yellow dust swirling in from the quadrangle. "The Roms, being devious, told you nothing. As a Klingon I will tell you something, though it may not be what you want to know. I will tell you that you, and we, if I understand your Federation's way of doing things, will probably be here for a very long time. If you are cooperative, you will not be harmed.

"You will find no luxuries here. If my officers and I must subsist without servitors, you cannot expect to live better than we. You will be provided with whatever is necessary for your survival. You will tell your Federation that the Klingon Empire treated you well, if and when you are returned to it. That is not my concern. My orders are only to see to it that you are fed, sheltered and held in place. And I always obey orders."

None of the prisoners made a sound. They were a bedraggled lot—their clothes slept in for an unknown number of days, their efforts to wash frustrated by a mere trickle of cold water and a lack of soap or towels. Fingers could not replace combs, and human and Vulcan were equally disheveled, their hair tangled about their ears so that to the inexperienced eye they looked more alike than ever.

Nevertheless, all possessed a certain dignity. They stood motionless and separate. Even the Deltans, strengthened at least temporarily by their psionic link, were determined to show no fear. This seemed to disappoint the Klingon commander; he swaggered a little closer, studying them under his eyebrows.

"Talkative lot, aren't they?" he said over his shoulder to his second, who did not reply. He was taller than the commander, and seemed less menacing. There was a listening quality to him. "And three females! Quite a catch!"

Krazz drew even closer, and little Krn twitched nervously, but the Klingon did not deign to notice him. His eyes were for the females.

"Outside," he said softly, and that much more menacing. There was an ancient taboo against sexual assault within the confines of a dwelling. "The females only. The males remain."

"My Lord," his second began. His voice was deep, his manner properly self-effacing. "I respectfully remind you that these are political prisoners, not servitors—"

Krazz rounded on him sharply.

"You have an objection? There will be enough for the rest of you when I am through."

The two guards moved for the first time, exchanging glances in appreciation of their lord's subtle wit. His second hastened to explain himself.

"I only meant that our orders were to preserve the prisoners," he said in rapid, guttural Klingonaase. T'Shael, who knew only a few phrases, caught only the word "preserve." Nevertheless, the voices told her the content of their conversation. "In view of the mishap with the antennaed one, our superiors—"

"—have no say in how we choose to relieve our boredom in this godforsaken backwater!" Krazz cut him off harshly. He turned to the prisoners again, calculatedly reverting to Standard. "We will do nothing that can be proven later. There will be no—permanent—damage. Now, the females, outside!"

Cleante found herself watching the scene as if from outside. Was this what the Vulcan meant by Mastery of the Unavoidable, or was she numb beyond fear?

It is only my body, she told herself. They cannot touch my soul. Allah knows, most times even I cannot find my soul. I have had an insensitive lover or two in my time; if they're not too brutal I can survive it. Look at Jali—

She stole a glance at the Deltan, who walked with a kind of spring to her step, as if to say it was *only* sex they wanted. Was it possible for a Deltan to be sanguine even at the prospect of rape?

Rape. Just letting the word penetrate one's conscious mind . . .

T'Shael! Cleante thought, almost choking. Her insides churned; she thought she might be sick. T'Shael was a virgin; she couldn't, they mustn't!

The Vulcan's face was calmest of all. The burning eyes were hooded, the long hands relaxed at her sides. Her entire being breathed Control.

I'll try! Cleante thought, though her knees felt like water. I don't care what they do to me, but they mustn't touch you.

"I can't pronounce it," Cleante had said, chagrined.

67

"A difficult word for a difficult concept," T'Shael acknowledged. "It translates in Standard as 'Mastery of the Unavoidable.' "

" 'Mastery of the Unavoidable,' " Cleante repeated, puzzling over it. Her face seemed to brighten from within. "I think I understand."

"You frequently understand more than you are willing to acknowledge," T'Shael said with a suggestion of warmth.

Whether she meant this as a compliment or not, Cleante accepted it as such. She would need it to steel her for whatever T'Shael had in mind.

They had gone into the center of the city with a group from the settlement, students and instructors of many races, to browse among the shops and make a few small purchases, later to attend a performance by a visiting poet. Cleante found herself amazed as always by the quiet order of Vulcan crowds.

No one hurried, no one would presume to push or jostle another. Children walked with the solemnity of their elders, neither running nor frolicking in the marketplace, and of course making no extraneous noise. Vehicles passed in whispers along the traffic streets and the overhead telpher networks, and the cries of birds could be distinguished in the most densely populated areas. Soft conversation, accented by the plash of fountains and the clack of ubiquitous windchimes, was the only extant sound.

Cleante had to suppress a perverse desire to rend the soft, dry air with a very human shout, quell the urge to start a useless argument like a Tellarite. She would not embarrass her Vulcan companions, but there was something almost too perfect, too orderly here that her human spontaneity longed to disrupt.

T'Shael had something else in mind, some other particularly Vulcan thing, some object lesson in the concept of Mastery of the Unavoidable for her unschooled human companion.

"Put simply," T'Shael said, "it is to suppress overt reaction to that which one cannot prevent or remedy. Performed often enough, the exercise becomes internalized. One controls not only one's reactions, but the thoughts which might evoke those reactions. An example: If one observes from a

68

mountaintop as a hovercraft crashes into the center of a city, killing many, one is well aware that one had not the means to prevent such an occurrence. What is gained, therefore, by averting one's eyes against the sight, or giving way to rage or horror? If one is alone, one simply yields to her own weakness in so doing, but if one is accompanied, what right has she to add to her companion's discomfort by making a display of her own?"

"Maybe just letting off a little steam," Cleante suggested. "Avoiding an ulcer. I don't agree with you."

"That is of course your privilege."

"But what if you're not on the mountaintop, but right in the thick of the accident?"

"Then one is obligated to offer service if one is qualified, or to get out of the way if one is not. Still, one is not entitled to an overt display of emotion, which can only disturb others and impede rescue."

"But what if you can't suppress your emotions just like that? What if it's so horrible—"

Cleante's voice had risen above the whisper with which they'd begun this debate. The Vulcans around them in the streets did not so much look at her as *not* look at her, as if to imply that where humans were concerned one made allowances. Cleante found her temper growing short.

"What if your best friend were in the hovercraft, or in the crowd below?"

"That adds another level of meaning, which requires that Mastery be even more complete," T'Shael replied, masking an uneasiness. "Perhaps it would be better if you did not accompany me."

Cleante's eyes flashed; she recognized a challenge when she heard one.

"Try and stop me!"

"I do not offer this lightly," T'Shael cautioned her. "The privacy and the feelings of others are at stake here."

Cleante had never heard the word "feelings" from her instructor's lips. If she had not been intrigued before . . .

"I'm coming with you!" she said stubbornly. "It took your species thousands of years to develop this Mastery of the Unavoidable technique. Let's see what one mere human can accomplish in a single afternoon."

"If you wish it," T'Shael said, putting the onus directly on Cleante's shoulders, and went to speak to the leader of the group from the settlement.

"You would take her to the Enclave of the Faceless Ones?" he asked in Vulcan and with no little intensity when she told him. He gave her a penetrating look. It was known how much time this one spent in the company of the Terran. "She who has studied with a Master should not presume to the place of a Master."

"That was never my intent, Sekal," T'Shael said levelly. "We will return in time to honor the poet. The rest is my affair."

Surprised at her own uncharacteristic boldness, T'Shael took her market basket filled with purchases and departed. Cleante hurried to keep up with her.

Human followed Vulcan out of the marketplace and into a residential district. Cleante noticed almost immediately that the pedestrian streets in this quarter were absolutely deserted. After several blocks, T'Shael turned into a courtyard and stopped at a certain garden gate, ornately carved in the Vulcan fashion, but without the characteristic speaking-port through which the visitor announced her presence. In its place was a kind of touch-sensitive plate to which T'Shael put her hand in the Vulcan *ta'al*. Within seconds the gate swung open.

"There is a simpler phrase for the concept," T'Shael said softly as they walked the winding path to the dwelling. "It is *Kaiidth!*, meaning 'What is, is.' When one accepts what cannot be changed, one begins to think like a Vulcan."

Cleante nodded without speaking. This would be another of T'Shael's object lessons in how impossible it was for a human, or at least for this human, to think like a Vulcan. What horror lay waiting in the house beyond to challenge her humanness? Cleante wondered. She tried to keep up with her Vulcan companion, tried to lock her facial muscles into an expression as devoid of expression as T'Shael's, but her palms were sweating and she would have given anything to be back in the marketplace with the others. She would never create a scene again, she promised, if only—

The door of the dwelling opened to reveal one of the beings known as the Faceless Ones. Cleante gasped.

"Some years ago a comet passed too close to their world," T'Shael explained imperturbably. They had almost reached the portico of the dwelling where the being waited for them, yet she did not slacken her pace. "Most died. Those who survived are as this one, bereft of sight and speech and hearing, all vestiges of facial features burned away."

"Can't anything be done for them?" Cleante managed to choke out.

"Except for sight, much of the damage might be surgically repaired, but their religious taboo forbids it," T'Shael answered. She did not have to look at Cleante to know what effect this was having upon her. She persisted. "They have taken refuge on Vulcan, where none is repulsed by their appearance. Of this family, several were known to my maternal parent, who was among those instrumental in their rescue."

She approached the being on the portico almost reverently, and he reached up to touch her face in recognition. He took T'Shael's hand. Cleante imagined her being brought here as a child in the company of her mother, and growing up with the images of these faceless faces always before her. T'Shael signed something into the palm of his hand, and brought it to Cleante's face by way of introduction.

Cleante did not know how much of her revulsion was evident in her features and tried to draw away. She was aware of T'Shael's eyes burning into her. This, then, was the challenge. She drew upon whatever human equivalent of Mastery of the Unavoidable she possessed, and held her ground.

The Faceless One explored her features with a butterfly's touch, then gestured that he was pleased to form this new acquaintance. He led his visitors inside.

Cleante would never know how she survived that afternoon, how she sat calmly while T'Shael communicated in the fingers-to-palm language with any number of these hideously deformed beings as they came and went, pleased with the visit and with the few simple gifts T'Shael had brought in her basket. What she longed to do for the duration of the visit was to rush outdoors and empty her human insides into the immaculate Vulcan gutter.

She had asked for this, had accepted the challenge, but she had not known such beings existed. Their eyeless sockets stared hollowly at her, their sealed-over mouths and ears were mere air-holes where there might have been noses. Most heart-wrenching were the children, born later on this new homeworld of Vulcan and unmarked. The articulate, extraordinarily beautiful children with luminous gray-green eyes and masses of curls were living memorials to what their parents had once been.

Fighting nausea, Cleante searched herself, feeling a change. What if something similar had happened to her? She who had taken her beauty for granted all her life, what if a comet had burned across her sky . . .

She thought of the history of Earth and especially of her region, of centuries of eyeless, leprous beggars roving the streets of Tunis and Old Cairo, their faces covered with flies. Cast out, living dead. Humans had no Mastery of the Unavoidable. Only hardness of heart.

Point taken, my Vulcan instructor! Cleante thought across the room to her, though T'Shael might have been too preoccupied to notice. Have I come up to your expectations, atoned for the sins—no, excuse me, the *responsibilities*—of my ancestors? Have I passed your test?

She managed to wait until she got back to the settlement and the privacy of her own flat to vomit. Feeling raw of nerve and more than a little defiant, she informed T'Shael she was not in the mood for poetry tonight, thank you. Instead she looked up a former male friend from the Deneva colony, indulging in a little no-strings lovemaking. It almost took the sting out of the day.

Lord Krazz motioned his guards to stand the three females in a row in the dusty compound. His as yet unnamed second hovered behind him. He and his commander had focused on Jali, who fluttered her eyelashes but kept her pheromones carefully in check.

"Kalor!" Krazz barked, squinting at Jali in the murky light. He continued to speak in Standard. "What is this kind called again?"

"Deltan, my Lord," his lieutenant replied, masking his disdain at his superior's ignorance.

Unlike most officers, Krazz had little experience with other species. He was not from one of the old houses, had not been reared with the luxury of servitors on Klin Zhai or any of the other cosmopolitan inworlds, but had clawed his way up from an undistinguished agri-clan, teaching himself the Games and winning his commissions by craft. He had never lost his provincialism, and his enemies claimed he still had triticale seeds in his mane and that downwind the smell of dung still clung to him.

So while the more sophisticated scions of the old houses could distinguish a Withiki from a Cherwtl without so much as checking the color differential of the underwings, Krazz still got his humanoids scrambled.

"Deltan," he repeated now. "Are they as good as it is said?"

"Among the best, my Lord," Kalor reported. "Perhaps better than Orions, though I have no expertise with that category."

It was possible that Jali exuded a minute suggestion of her pheromones then.

"Hah!" Krazz triumphed. "Well, I've got you there. Remind me to tell you—"

He broke off, squinting at Jali as if he hadn't really seen her the first time. He took a step toward her, then changed his mind.

"Too easy!" he grunted. "I prefer a female with fight." He squinted at the remaining two to see if they would react. They did not. He moved toward them. "And these are—?"

"Human and Vulcan, my Lord," Kalor said. His eye caught Cleante's and held it for a long moment. This one was beautiful, he thought.

"They look very much alike, don't they? Except that one is ugly."

Kalor was about to respectfully point out the differences, but Krazz was not finished.

"I've heard it said that Vulcans do it only once in seven years. Can that be possible?"

"It is common knowledge, my Lord."

"But that's ridiculous!" Krazz exploded, his shoulders shaking with a kind of evil mirth. He enjoyed himself for a long moment, then leered at his lieutenant slyly. "Have you ever had a Vulcan, Kalor?"

Cleante's eyes darted toward T'Shael, who was unmoved. *I'm trying, as you have taught me! The human's thoughts pleaded across the few feet that separated them. But I will not let them touch you!*

Should she offer herself in T'Shael's place, or would that only increase Krazz's perverse interest in her friend? Her throat constricted; she could not speak. The Klingons continued their dialogue in Standard, a subtle form of torture.

"Have you ever had a Vulcan, Kalor?"

"Once, my lord. There was a disabled Federation border vessel, when I was an ensign on *Flyer's Pride.* It yielded some interesting prisoners."

Krazz pictured the scenario, savoring it. While his highborn second had been cruising the borders on Targa's flagship, *he* had been executing colonists on Ailig IV under the heading of "political expediency." *That* had yielded some interesting prisoners as well. Incredible what a female would bargain for a death without pain.

Krazz studied T'Shael. Once every seven years? Would that add to or detract from the effect?

"This Vulcan," he said, his eyes on T'Shael. "You had her and then you killed her?"

"Pride was a small vessel, my Lord. We had no room for prisoners. And for what little pleasure she afforded us, we might as well have killed her first."

"Unresponsive, hm?"

"If it is possible to be more so and still breathe, my Lord, I do not know. Even under agonizer she merely retreated deeper. Dull."

"You wouldn't recommend a Vulcan, then." Krazz leered at Cleante. "Humans aren't bad, though?"

"Fragile and easily exhausted," Kalor reported, getting into the spirit of Krazz's little farce. He was well aware of Cleante's silent pleading by now and had decided to use it against her. "But they'll do if nothing better is available."

Krazz stood between the two females, leering.

"Which is the human?" he barked suddenly, though by now even he could tell.

T'Shael cautioned Cleante with her eyes, a single look

74

over the Klingon's head. Do not speak! Let him work for the information he requires. Control! Cleante wrenched inside but kept still.

I will not let them touch you! her eyes blazed.

Krazz did not ask his question twice. The compound was strewn with loose rock, some of it jagged and quite sharp. He selected a fragment with the toe of his boot, hefting it in his hand, and drew close enough to T'Shael so that his rancid carnivore's breath was on her face. With a lightning movement he slashed the rock across her cheek.

"Well!" he said, pleased with the color of the blood that flowed. Tears had sprung to T'Shael's eyes, but she had not flinched. "That's one way to tell the difference!"

Cleante shrieked and lunged for him, only to have her shoulders nearly dislocated as the nearer of the guards yanked her arms back and held her. It hurt enough to bring tears to her eyes, but not nearly as much as the look on T'Shael's face.

Control! it seethed. Do not shame us both with such behavior!

Krazz rounded on Cleante, dropping the rock. His experiment had had the desired result.

"I like a female with fight," he leered, and he was upon her.

His hands were rough, brutal, violating, intending pain, delighting in her struggle. Cleante went rigid, refusing to give him what he craved, but her eyes sought T'Shael's desperately. Strangely, the Vulcan averted her gaze, abandoning her, or so it seemed.

There was no saying how far the Klingon would have gone had Jali not intervened.

No one had been paying any attention to the Deltan, and she had casually activated her most enticing level of pheromones, letting them waft about the compound, weave their irresistible spell. First Kalor, then the guards and finally Krazz became aware of her.

In predatory slo-mo they drew around her, circled her, abandoned the human, who clutched her torn clothing about her, sought refuge against the wall of their prison, one fist pressed against her lips to quiet her sobbing. Equally unnoticed, T'Shael moved to stand beside her. Her need overcoming anger and outrage, Cleante threw herself into the Vulcan's arms and T'Shael held her, sheltered her, though not without misgivings.

How vulnerable these humans are! she thought, awed at the intensity of emotions flooding toward her. Emotion must be ruled lest it rule.

The four Klingons had formed a close orbit about Jali—panting, feral. Something about Jali indicated that she was in absolute control, that she would take one or all of them, in whatever combination, and casually exhaust them all. If Krazz had not come to his senses she might very well have succeeded.

"Away!" he roared, first to lock into command mode and break the Deltan's spell. He backed away from her as if she poisoned the very air he breathed, waving his blaster at the others to break their fixation. When they had recovered themselves he leveled the blaster at Jali.

"You will not do that again!" he snarled at her. "Again, and orders or no I'll kill the little one inside. Don't underestimate me!"

Jali neutralized her pheromones—but casually, as if to imply that the Klingon had better not underestimate *her*.

"Physical damage would appear to be minimal," T'Shael observed dispassionately. "One assumes it is the severity of psychic trauma which causes your continued reaction."

Cleante swept her matted hair up off her forehead and wiped her tear-swollen eyes with the heels of her hands.

"Leave me alone, T'Shael. Please, please just leave me alone!"

She had curled up in a ball on her bunk, withdrawing from everybody, as soon as the Klingons had unceremoniously marched the three of them back to their cage. That had been hours ago. It was dark outside now; nights on this planetoid seemed twice as long as the days. In a far corner of their cell, as if to avoid disturbing anyone, the Deltans whispered among themselves, going over Jali's exploits—which Resh and Krn had been able to observe from a window—again and again. From time to time one of the guards would pass the transparent door, peer in, and move on.

"Describe it to us again, cousin!" Krn crowed, beside himself. "The looks on their faces—tell us!"

Resh hushed him, but the whispering continued. T'Shael would have reproached them, but to what purpose? Let them sustain their own morale—it was better to have them giggling than whimpering—while she tended to the human. Or tried to.

Tried to tend to her friend, T'Shael thought, thinking it in Standard, not daring to think the Vulcan word *t'hy'la* with all of its levels of meaning. Such was not for her. But friend, then, for she and the human had crossed that threshhold before this crisis, and it was Cleante who insisted upon the usage.

Or had, until today. T'Shael wondered what right she had to call herself anyone's friend. Would a friend have engaged her Mastery in the compound this morning?

T'Shael had examined her behavior repeatedly since. Everything she had done had been absolutely logical, yet she was not convinced that it had been right. She had never encountered such a discrepancy before, and it perplexed her deeply.

If it had not been for Jali, what might the Klingons have done? And how would she, T'Shael, have accepted the responsibility for doing nothing?

She sat beside the human now, lightly, on the very edge of the bunk, wanting to touch but not daring, keeping a barren vigil.

If I could make you understand, she thought to Cleante. When Krazz put his hands on you I averted my gaze to spare you further shame. Such would any Vulcan have done for another. I could not know that a human would have desired eye contact for comfort, for strength. I have failed you. Forgive me, my . . . friend.

But because she could not speak the words, and because the human, curled into herself, withdrawn, could not read her thoughts, it was as if they had not been thought. Human and Vulcan, separated by a matter of centimeters, were in fact divided by a vast gulf of misunderstanding. T'Shael's burning eyes looked up to find Jali's.

"Cold!" the Deltan clucked, plopping herself uninvited

onto the bunk, all but pushing the Vulcan aside. "Cold is worse than useless! If you are not being of help at least move aside for one who can!"

T'Shael gathered her desolation about her like a cloak and withdrew.

She did not observe how the Deltan activated a certain level of asexual, comforting pheromones, lightly stroking the human everywhere that Krazz had pawed her as if to eradicate all memory of his violation. If T'Shael was at all aware of what transpired between Deltan and human it only added to her desolation.

Worse than useless.

"Speak to me of love."

The request came not quite out of nowhere, but it startled Cleante nevertheless. For a time after the storm in the desert her role and T'Shael's seemed to have been reversed; it was now she who instructed the Vulcan in the ways of humans.

They no longer visited the ruins after that day. T'Shael no longer stopped at Cleante's flat in silent invitation on their off-days, and Cleante did not presume to go alone. She affected a Vulcan's sense of place, at least in this. And if T'Shael went to the ruins alone, melancholy pilgrim, Cleante did not inquire.

But they continued their student/instructor mode, now strangely inverted—sometimes in the parks that were everywhere in the city, or in the many study rooms and art galleries throughout the settlement, but most often in T'Shael's austere flat.

"Speak to me of Earth," T'Shael would say, hearing her own boldness, wondering at it. Was it the human's influence that made her thus? Would Master Stimm approve? "Speak to me of the ways of humans. Of your museums and cities and cherished places. Of your oceans and the blueness of your sky and this thing you call snow. Of your arts and languages and customs. Of your theatre and opera, these artificial displays of the emotions of fictional beings; these most especially I do not understand. Speak to me of the ways in which your world differs from mine."

Her words, spoken hesitantly and over many months, were certainly less than demands, yet more than requests.

Did their place between the two polarities render them neutral? Was that which could be refused, offensive by definition? Grappling with her many levels of meaning, swimming against the ripple effect that at every waking moment threatened to engulf her, T'Shael dared to slake her thirsting curiosity, dared to hunger, dared to know.

And thus as she sat cross-legged and dark-clad in the windowseat of her simple rooms overlooking a pristine and moonless Vulcan night, studiously restringing and tuning her *ka'athyra*, at ease in the presence of the human, who if nothing else had mastered the art of one Vulcan's silence, she summoned enough daring to say:

"Speak to me of love."

And Cleante's Byzantine eyes widened in astonishment.

"That's an odd request from you."

"Is it?" The Vulcan selected an H-string for her instrument from among several in an ornate box, pulled it taut to test its tensile purity, and expertly looped it about the intricate insides of the resonancer, stretching it across the soundboard with strong fingers. Her eyes did not rise from her task, and it was possible that her somber voice grew even softer, an indication of her interior struggle. "I have asked you of human emotions before."

"But why this one, now?" Cleante countered, perhaps thinking of the boy from Deneva and feeling a little guilty. The Vulcan couldn't know about that, could she? And what if she did?

"If you prefer not to answer—" T'Shael began, but Cleante cut her off.

"That's not good enough, T'Shael."

The human had learned to use the Vulcan's self-imposed restraints, her introversion, against her of late. She was not sure why she did this, was certain it was cruel, but found it sometimes revealed hidden and intriguing aspects of her cryptic companion's character.

"Why do you spend so much time with her?" her human friends asked Cleante. "Don't you get bored?"

"Not at all," Cleante would say, tossing her hair off her shoulders to hide her embarrassment. "She's really very interesting."

79

The others grouped in various languid postures about the fountain in the atrium of the Arts Hall expressed their skepticism. Most of them were from the Martian Colonies, possessed of all of the parochialism that implied. Some of them had never seen a Vulcan before coming to T'lingShar.

"Their voices always put me to sleep," one of the boys said.

Boys? Cleante wondered, looking at him with a Vulcan's eyes. A few weeks ago she would have called him a man, but he seemed suddenly to have shrunk in her estimation. How immature they are! she thought, wondering if her new perspective was any more accurate than the previous one.

"They all talk in monotones," he continued while the others nodded. "Their faces never move. And that one! She's worse than most."

Before Cleante could say anything someone else chimed in.

"You know, I tried to be friendly," she said, trailing one hand in the fountain. A kind of late afternoon sleepiness affected them all. Their belongings lay scattered about the atrium as they themselves lounged amid a profusion of outworld plants, listening to loud empty music on their transceivers and wasting time. "Okay, so I don't know much about their way of life, and maybe I put my foot in it a few times, but from the very beginning I always felt as if she was looking down on me. Passing judgment. That superior look they have all the time. I hate that!"

"You don't understand!" Cleante said loudly to be heard over the dull repetitive music which until recently had been a constant in her life but which now irritated her almost unbearably. She no longer felt any kinship with these people. How shallow they are! she thought. "T'Shael has studied with a Master. That makes her more introspective. But she doesn't pass judgment. That's not the Vulcan way. The philosophy of IDIC says—"

Her friend from Deneva reached for her wrist and pulled her down beside him. He'd become something of a nuisance since their single night together, but she acquiesced to his horseplay. Until he began playing with her hair.

"What're you doing?" she demanded, squirming out of his grasp.

"Watching the points grow on your ears," he teased.

Cleante jabbed him with her elbow so hard he yelped.

"Stop it!" she snapped. "It's an insult to both of us. I can never be what T'Shael is, never. And it's insulting to even think she'd want to be like me."

The boy from Deneva pulled her closer, wrapping his arms around her and whispering in her rounded ear.

"It's a good thing I know you like men," he insinuated, no longer quite teasing. "Otherwise I'd wonder what went on between you and that green-blooded ice maiden."

Cleante resisted the urge to scratch his eyes out. Why fuel his viciousness? She suffered his embrace, deliberately dissociating herself from this group of—of children.

What's happening to me? she wondered, growing so remote that even the Denevan sensed it and released her. Is this what it means to think like a Vulcan? Is this what I want? She saw one of the boys pulling the leaves off a nearby plant and went into a rage.

"Stop that!" she shrieked, jumping to her feet. "You're hurting that plant. It's not necessary!"

He jerked his hand away as if it had been burned.

"Excuse *me!*" he said in mock chagrin, then adopted what he thought was a suitable imitation of the Vulcan manner. "I ask forgiveness, honored one!"

Cleante stalked away to the sounds of convulsive laughter.

"You're all a bunch of idiots!" she shouted.

Well, that took care of that. If she hadn't been sure about dissociating herself from humans before . . .

"That's not good enough, T'Shael," she said now with her particularly human challenge. "If you're going to ask me about love, you'll have to tell me why."

She compared the scene at the fountain with the present one—two quiet beings, supposedly so very different that no amount of social exchange could ever alter what each one was, speaking of important matters in a manner which brought profound peace of mind to at least one of them, at least some of the time. With all their differences, with the sheer difficulty of maintaining their relationship in the face of multiplicities of misunderstanding, Cleante was more at ease with this one than with any human she knew.

"That's not good enough, T'Shael," she said, risking their tenuous tranquility despite her having severed all other friendship ties. This relationship was important enough to her to take such risks.

The Vulcan had secured the H-string to the frets at the neck of the *ka'athyra* and was about to select a K-string and repeat the procedure when her eminently skilled hands strangely faltered. She looked at the human for the first time.

"This thing you call love—" she began, struggling with her phrasing, her hands uncharacteristically idle yet devoid of tension. Did the human have any idea how long she had contemplated this topic before broaching it? Did anyone save Master Stimm know how long this one wrestled with a concept before she could put words to it? "I have studied it in the literatures of many races, including my own, yet it is a matter of which I in truth understand nothing—"

"I didn't know Vulcan literature dealt with love," Cleante interrupted, genuinely surprised. She leaned forward from her place on T'Shael's sleeping couch, the only other seating place in the room. "I thought it was considered the most dangerous of emotions—"

"The concept of love is written large in Ancient Vulcan literature, yet it is dimensioned by levels of meaning too complex. . . ."

T'Shael stopped herself. How to explain to the human the dimensions of *t'hy'la* when she did not comprehend them herself? As to Vulcan mating and all of its ramifications—if such could be considered in the context of love—she was forbidden to speak of such things. She put the *ka'athyra* aside and seemed to gather herself, speaking with great difficulty.

"Terra's poetry is eloquent on the topic of love. You, as a human, have experienced this emotion on a number of levels. I would learn from you."

Cleante sank back against the cushions on the couch. She shook her head and forced herself not to laugh her high-strung humorless laugh.

"I don't know anything about love," she said. "Sex, yes, but that's not what you mean. I can tell you what it's like to live without love—" She thought of her mother, and the thoughts were bitter. She, too, gathered herself. "But tell you about love? I can tell you nothing, T'Shael!"

An error, my human friend, T'Shael thought in the night of an unnamed planetoid, her desolation wrapped about her like a cloak. You were incorrect. You have accomplished what I asked you that long ago night. You have instructed me in love, and in its shadow side, which is loneliness. She who cannot love cannot know this emptiness.

I have failed you. Forgive me, my friend.

The bottle was half empty by the time Krazz invited Kalor to his quarters, and the commander made no secret of this. One stayed with fruit nectars in the Fleet, but a Klingon who couldn't hold his liquor planetside was no Klingon. Between them, commander and lieutenant would finish this bottle and the greater part of another before the murky red suns crept above the horizon.

"If I'd wanted to tend sheep I'd have stayed in the agricaste like my father!" Krazz growled. The encounter with Jali had shaken him more than he cared to admit. "I do not relish this pastoral assignment. It's an insult!"

"The strength of the Klingon is the strength of the whole," Kalor recited stiffly. He disliked it when Krazz was in one of these moods. Someday, his disaffection with his superiors would force Kalor to kill him, but this was not to be the day. "He who is strong is he who obeys."

"Stop spouting doctrine and have a drink!" Krazz roared; his words were already slurring at the edges. "If you are strong enough to obey, then obey me. Sit and drink with me. That's an order."

Kalor sat, straddling the chair, and Krazz poured them each three drinks in succession before he spoke again.

"Ah!" he declared with satisfaction, tossing the vitriolic liquor against the back of his throat and slamming the glass on the table top. "That takes the edge off an ill-omened day." He thought for a moment, his beady eyes glittering. "It was close, the moment with the hairless one. I'd heard they had that much power, but I didn't believe . . ." His eyes grew crafty. He knew how close he sometimes came to slipping, and how Kalor made note of it. "Obviously that was why I had to see for myself."

"Obviously," Kalor said slowly, nursing his third drink, "my Lord."

Krazz's eyes grew craftier still.

"As I recall, Kalor, you were the first to succumb to the alien's . . . influence. It might behoove you to remember that if you're thinking of reporting me, I, too, have a report in the works."

"If asked, I would respectfully point out that my Lord was—otherwise engaged—with one of our valued prisoners when the Deltan created her diversion," Kalor said evenly, downing his drink at last. He also slammed his glass on the table and met his superior's stare.

Krazz poured himself another drink; he did not pour one for his lieutenant. He grasped the edge of the table and leaned toward Kalor ominously.

"You'd like to see me blunder, wouldn't you, Kalor? Your aristocratic sensibilities are offended by having to serve under a bumpkin like me, and you'd welcome the chance to remove me. But before you make the attempt, take a moment to consider your opponent."

Kalor could not meet that knifelike stare forever. It suggested too many things to him—old secrets, perhaps not buried deeply enough. He broke his gaze and fumbled for the liquor bottle, pouring himself another drink without asking.

"I may be a hayseed, Kalor, but I keep up on internal politics," Krazz continued smoothly, his voice a serpent's. "Even old news. I have read your dossier thoroughly. And your father's."

Kalor's teeth gnashed involuntarily. The shame of Mertak *epetai* Haaral's treason had haunted his youth, excluded him from the Academy, and cost him access to all normal career routes despite his officiation at the old man's execution. (He still bore the claw marks on his throat and always wore his collars high, but the roar of his father's outrage remained in his ears, more profoundly scarring. They had grappled for the stunner with which he'd hoped to take the old dragon down without pain before dispatching him. Zoren, his boyhood friend, had caught Mertak in the spine with his blaster to end it, and Kalor had had to kill Zoren to erase the dishonor.) Only his mother's powerful connections—she was Gelfa; that and the long-standing estrangement from her spouse had been all that saved her life—had given him a solitary chance, as an enlistee on a merchanter, possibly the deepest humiliation for a scion of Haaral.

Kalor had won his commission in the Navy dearly. He would do nothing to jeopardize it now.

"My father paid for his mistake, my Lord," he said carefully. "And I have spent my life restoring the honor of my House."

"That's why I'm advising you now," Krazz said, affable, almost paternal, leaning back in his chair and tossing down another drink, then pouring another for his lieutenant. He had Kalor right where he wanted him. "Your father's activities will hang over your life like a cloud. These things sometimes take several generations to be forgotten. You yourself will always be suspect, no matter how you comport yourself. You must learn to look life straight in the eye and stare it down; get rid of that horrible sideways analytical squint you've acquired. At times you border on intellectualism, Kalor. It's a dangerous trait for a Klingon."

So saying, Krazz swaggered outside to relieve himself of the side effects of that much alcohol. He was blowing on his fingers when he returned.

"Incredible how cold it gets when those infernal suns go down," he remarked. "Two suns—what a novelty! And not another living thing on this entire rock but ourselves and the Federation's sheep."

"Lord Tolz and the Rihannsu chose our place of concealment well," Kalor said dutifully.

He wished he could excuse himself from the rest of the night's drinking. He knew not what other battles he would have to fight to stay alive and in his lord's good graces.

Krazz merely grunted at the mention of Romulans.

"*Ri-hann-su,*" he sneered. "I hope Tolz knows what he's doing." He glowered at Kalor to discourage any further spouting of doctrine. "I don't like Roms. They're too . . . subtle. Too serious. They deny the Game, yet they play it to win. And they'd rather intrigue than fight. It's not normal."

Kalor said nothing.

"This theory of theirs about corrupting the Federation

from within. What nonsense!" Krazz had begun to pace, working himself into a frenzy. "It's a test, you realize, Kalor. This 'privileged assignment.' Some mumble about 'future glories' which exist only in Tolz Kenran's fevered brain. Perhaps they've thrown us together on this rock in the hope we'll kill each other." Kalor was made of stone. "Rid of the upstart and the traitor's son in one swoop. Or perhaps the test is whether we will accept our sheepherding meekly or take the initiative and find some way of turning this against the Roms, which is the current favored tack, or was when we left port.

"If it backfires, of course, the Admiralty never heard of us. A variation on the Double Blind Game with us as dupes—clever, but obvious. Yet I sit here trying to read Lord Tolz's mind from a distance of a billion kellicams—which way, I wonder, does he expect us to jump, and does it profit us more to meet his expectations or to jump the other way? I am convinced this is in fact Triple Blind, the object of which is to slowly drive me mad!"

Something clicked in Kalor's brain just then, but he waited for Krazz to say his fill.

"And not so much as a chance to entertain ourselves with the females!" Krazz was ranting, pounding the walls in his rage as he paced; he was literally foaming at the mouth. He rounded on Kalor as if this morning's incident had been his fault. "What happened with the hairless one is not to be repeated. There will be no hands-on with any of the prisoners, not even the males. Gods know what tricks *they* have up their sleeves—or under their trousers. No further contact, is that clear?"

"Quite clear, my Lord," Kalor said, watching Krazz wipe the saliva off his chin. When he thought his commander might be calm enough, he played his move. "But there may be other ways to amuse ourselves."

Krazz's eyes narrowed.

"What did you have in mind, Lieutenant?"

"Perhaps a variation on the Game that even Lord Tolz has not anticipated," Kalor said, weighing his words. "But your opinion first, my Lord. Your opinion as a soldier, widely experienced in such matters."

Krazz was not immune to flattery, if it was well executed. He grinned.

"Speak!"

"How do you think the Federation will respond to the Rihannsu ransom demands?"

" 'Respond?' " Krazz snorted. "How do they usually respond? They will make highblown speeches about refusing to negotiate with terrorists, and we will have to kill the prisoners to make an example of them. There is of course an outside chance that they will attempt a rescue—a suicide mission, naturally. Humanoids seem almost as keen on those as the Roms. Oh, how I would relish that!"

"Then, in your expert opinion, my Lord, the prisoners are already as good as dead?"

Krazz shrugged.

"My orders are to keep them alive indefinitely. Until I figure out Tolz's plan I will do so. However, I have no desire to spend the rest of my life on this rock. If, after a judicious amount of time our sheep were to meet with an accident, or pine away as these inferior species tend to do. . . ."

The liquor was wearing off, and Krazz realized he was saying too much. His eyes grew crafty again. Kalor seized his opportunity.

"If our 'sheep' were to meet with such an unfortunate fate, my Lord, would the fault fall on us or on the Rihannsu?"

Krazz's face lighted up with glee.

"The Feds don't even know we're involved. And a dead witness is no witness!"

Kalor nodded, satisfied, and bided his time.

Hikaru Sulu took the cup of steaming *matcha* from Admiral Nogura, bowed slightly, and offered it to Jim Kirk. Kirk accepted the delicate porcelain object, trying not to wince as the hot tea burned his fingers through its eggshell thinness, and bowed in return, shifting his weight uncomfortably on the *tatami*. He sometimes thought Nogura insisted on the tea ceremony whenever he was in town just to make his Occidental posterior squirm.

"Not you, Jim," Nogura said, and Kirk knew better than

to argue this time. "Not Spock and not McCoy. The Romulans have a sheet on each of you as long as your respective arms. However, I can use that. As I can use Hikaru here and some other key personnel. And perhaps the *Enterprise,* but not as you might think."

"Heihachiro, I can usually follow your machinations, but—"

"Your sealed orders are being fed direct into ship's computer even as we speak. Just deploy your people as per instructions and leave the rest to those who have the whole picture."

Kirk sipped his tea deliberately before he trusted himself to speak.

"And what are the rest of us supposed to do in the meantime?"

"Why, just what you came back to Earth to do," the Ice Man said expansively, watching Kirk squirm. "Pick up a new consignment of cadets and take them out on maneuvers."

Five

"PURE GENIUS!" SULU was explaining to Saavik, surveying his new self in the full-length mirror in Sickbay one more time.

Whether he was talking about the mission Nogura and Special Section were about to send him on, or McCoy's surgical prowess, or his own reincarnation as a Rihannsu functionary, Saavik couldn't tell. She'd been assigned to help him polish his accent before he made the crossover into the Empire; for the moment she was his captive audience.

"Look at it as a tactical exercise, Saavik. Brilliant! You take a ship that's notorious in both Empires, load it to the rafters with cadets, send it on maneuvers just outside the Rom Neutral Zone, all innocence. The Roms immediately assume it's a cover for a spy mission, so they monitor it real close. At the same time, though, they're figuring we wouldn't be so obvious, so they suspect it's a decoy, and they deploy all available manpower looking for the real spy ship. You with me so far?"

Saavik just nodded curtly. Of course she was "with him;" she'd worked out far more complex permutations than this as exercises for Tactics I when she was a plebe. If *she* were a Rihannsu commander . . .

The thought was an uncomfortable one and she dismissed

it, concentrating instead on the personage Sulu now presented after a morning under McCoy's knife. He had the
facial structure and basic coloring of a Rihannsu colonial to
begin with, and with his newly pointed ears and upswept
eyebrows he could conceivably pass. As long as he didn't do
anything foolish like cut his finger on a paring knife and start
bleeding red. However, his demeanor—

"So, okay," he went on, warming to his topic, admiring
himself in his Record Clerk's uniform from every possible
angle. "Meanwhile, you do a chatter blitz on the subspace
channels, the gossip wavelength. The Roms have broken
Codes 3 and 4 by now, but we're not supposed to know that,
and they seem to get a charge out of listening in on the who's
sleeping with whom stuff. So we gradually feed them some
juicy bits. Like the 'fact' that yours truly is purported to
have gone civilian, last seen as a consultant for an aerody-
namics firm on Colony 5; I've already set up a series of time-
delayed commpics to an uncle in Hokkaido to make it look
authentic. Like the 'fact' that Montgomery Scott has been
remanded to medical rest leave after a three-day binge and
busting up a pub on Argelius; I just hope Scotty doesn't hurt
anybody when they stage *that* brawl. Those two 'facts' will
leave Scotty and me to do our thing. Then you throw in the
'fact' that Kirk and *Enterprise* have fallen under some sort
of political cloud and been relegated to the boonies indefinitely. You follow?"

"But, sir—those are outright falsehoods—" Saavik objected, struggling with the true word, not wanting to give
offense, "—*lies!*"

Sulu grinned at her reflection in the mirror.

"You're learning, kid. You're learning!"

Kids, Sulu thought, watching the disillusionment on that
face, a face that, gods, was enough to make him wish he *was*
Rihannsu. In a way you hated to steal their innocence, but if
you didn't break them in gradually, as a friend, before
someone came along and snatched it from them . . .

"Okay," he continued—reflective moods never lasted
long with him. "While the Roms are running the gossip
through their linguanalyzers and falling all over themselves
shadowing *Enterprise* along the border, Special Section slips
me over the border and we're in business." He grinned at

himself in the mirror, adjusting his collar and admiring his ears. "By the way, how do I look?"

You look, Saavik wanted to say, like a human surgically altered to pass for a Rihannsu colonial employed in Records Section, and if you don't stop strutting about drawing attention to yourself and adopt the proper self-effacing manner suitable to your rank and station all of Dr. McCoy's handiwork will go for nothing because you'll be stopped at the border and gutted like a sea-hare.

She stopped herself, remembering something Spock had said to her when he first undertook her instruction.

"Beware of letting facts obscure your perspective," he had said.

She had thought he was being ironic, if not paradoxical. She had not understood him then and didn't now. Or did she?

She looked at Sulu again, forgetting everything she knew about him, removing from his present appearance all preconceptions, the patina of familiarity, her certain knowledge of him as human and Starfleet officer. (He was the first full human who had ever touched her, guiding her hands the first time she took the helm without the autopilot, steadying her, all businesslike and cool; but the sensation, his unguarded human thoughts made accessible to her through physical contact, had been most peculiar.)

She must forget this complex, sometimes disturbing individual, and concentrate not on what he had been, but on what he had become.

("Tolerance," Spock had also said, over and over until she had wanted to scream at him for all her Vulcan discipline. "You who were born between worlds, who will coexist with those of all worlds, must above all master tolerance. Tolerance is logical.")

She saw that Sulu had turned away from the mirror at last, was looking at her expectantly, awaiting her approval.

"You look—adequate," she answered bluntly, watching his face fall. "What name have you chosen?" she asked quickly, to assuage his tender human feelings.

"Lel," Sulu answered. "Lel em'n Tri'ilril." His accent was flawless, Saavik noted. "We've researched. The Tri'ilril matronymic belongs to several clans, so it's obscure enough

91

to be difficult to trace. It could buy me some time in a pinch, *Ie?*"

"*Ie,*" Saavik agreed. "*Yll hrarizhmeliil ssri'ith?*"

"*Shsaa'ed vresish thlaymv,*" Sulu assured her, growing serious, assuming a character with the transition in language, the character of a humble Records Clerk, subaltern, blender-into-the-middle-distance, the perfect role for his task. He bared his left shoulder to show her the "dueling scar," one of McCoy's extra touches.

Saavik nodded her satisfaction, both with the authentic look of the scar and the flawlessness of Sulu's accent. The sudden change in character should not have surprised her; she had forgotten how transmutable these humans could be. "Natural actors," Spock would have said.

"*Yr mewsatheth kri'iw,*" she said, and Sulu's grin was eradicated forever, as if it had never existed, as he answered: "*Sedith mer'vri.*"

Together they moved down the deserted corridors of *Enterprise.* The new consignment of cadets would not begin to arrive until after Sulu had beamed down to a Special Section secured holding area. Once altered, he must be seen by as few as possible. They spoke exclusively in Low Rihan, the everyday language of the Romulan and probably the only language a colonial would be permitted to speak in public. It was the language Sulu would think, breathe, eat and sleep in until he slipped across the Zone to give his newly pointed ears a workout.

The Warrantors' days devolved down into a kind of routine.

After the incident with Jali, the Klingons kept an almost comically careful distance between themselves and their prisoners. At least Krn found it amusing, snorting and giggling behind his fingers until a look from Resh silenced him. The two guards, ever-present in alternating shifts, their hard faces peering through the transparency—as if despite it and their weapons and the electrified fence some escape were possible (and escape to where, with neither food nor shelter on an uninhabited planetoid?)—did not speak to the captives at all. As for Krazz, whatever he had to say was issued in the form of an order from where he stood in the doorway with legs astride and thumbs hooked into his belt.

"You will surrender your soft, decadent pre-synthesized clothing," he announced as the guards tossed each captive a coarse gray uniform several sizes too large for any of them. "It will be destroyed. Also your footwear. We are the only living things on this miserable rock, so there is no place our sensors cannot find you. But the thought of the sharp native stones under your soft civilian feet should discourage any contemplation of escape."

It was T'Shael who dared to speak to him about the food and the lack of sanitation.

"Your rations consist of animal flesh," she said, holding the bundled uniform against her thin chest, retaining her dignity. The Rihannsu had left them packets of dried field rations, mostly a variety of highly spiced dried meat and coarse biscuit. The others had complained but managed to choke down the execrable stuff; T'Shael had subsisted on water since her capture. "As a Vulcan, I cannot eat this."

"Well, the ugly one has a tongue!" Krazz exulted. "And it doesn't care for the Rom's fine soldiers' rations. Suppose I say I don't care if you starve?"

"That is of course your privilege," T'Shael acknowledged. "But since your mission specifies that you are to *preserve* the lives of your captives—"

She deliberately spoke the word in Klingonaase, and Krazz gave her an evil look.

"There is a danger in knowing too much," he cautioned her. He was accustomed to craven submission, and found her impassiveness unnerving. He countered it with sarcasm. "And what would milady's refined palate prefer?"

"I will eat neither animal flesh nor the products of living creatures," T'Shael said evenly. "Since you have no synthesizers—"

"This is not a health resort!" Krazz roared, incredulous. "Next you will demand servitors to cut your meat for you— except that you won't eat meat, is that it? I will see what sort of silage I can find for you, my Federation sheep, between now and the next supply ship, but I make no promises. Small wonder your blood is green!"

He translated this for the guards' benefit and together they enjoyed the joke.

Supply ships, T'Shael noted, exchanging glances with the others. Such information might prove useful. The Vulcan dared one thing more.

"There is the matter of hygiene—" she began.

"More complaints!" the Klingon commander despaired, making a few salacious comments for the guards' entertainment. They laughed until the tears came. *Kahless,* but their lord was clever! When Krazz decided the merriment had lasted long enough he grew surly. "I didn't have a hot bath until I was an adult. If cold water was good enough for me, it is good enough for you."

"We will require soap and towels," T'Shael said, equally indifferent to mirth or anger. "And the wherewithal to keep our place of confinement clean. And a change of bedding. If dirt is the natural order for the Klingon, it is not for us."

Krazz found this so amusing he did not bother translating it for the guards.

"I like you, Vulcan," he said at last, wheezing a little. "Even if you're ugly. You amuse me. So, you're industrious, are you? You're concerned with the cleanliness of your cage? Excellent. I will put in a requisition for the items you desire, and in addition to scrubbing this room from top to bottom you will act as my servitor as well."

"If you wish it," T'Shael replied. "The exchange is equitable."

Krazz and the guards were not quite out the door when the Deltans turned on T'Shael.

"Oh, delight!" Jali clucked, clapping her hands in frustration. "Mops and brooms instead of decent clothing! Soap instead of better food. Sheets and towels instead of the freedom of the air. Strange, your priorities, strange!"

"A softer tone, cousin," Resh admonished. "Though you could have consulted us first," he told T'Shael.

"One must begin somewhere," she replied levelly. "If you had requests I am certain our captors would have found them as entertaining."

"Well, I for one do no housekeeping for Klingons!" Jali declared heatedly.

"None have asked you to," was T'Shael's reply.

Cleante said nothing to anyone. She sat on her bunk alternately fingering the fastenings on the ugly convicts' uniform and stroking the fabric of her soft pastel blouse. It was rumpled and soiled from so many days' wear, ripped from Krazz's attack, but it was her favorite and she did not wish to part with it. She seemed indifferent to the controversy raging around her.

Then little Krn spoke.

"I will help you in your cleaning, Friend T'Shael," he piped up in his native tongue, drawing as close as he dared to a Vulcan except for his moment of panic on the Rihannsu ship; he was a little in awe of the pointed-eared ones. "I am not fearing hard work," he said with a meaningful glance at his cousin Jali. "And it will help to pass the time."

T'Shael looked at him solemnly.

"My gratitude, Krnsandor L'am," she said, also in Deltan and with a formal bow. "You are an honor to your forebears and to all your loved ones."

This formality tickled the child greatly, and he swung to his upper bunk with simian alacrity, stripping off his Deltan clothing and donning the Klingon uniform, giggling to himself.

There had been a discussion of privacy from the very first.

"This custom of hiding the body from the eyes of others is unknown to us," Resh said as spokesman for his cousins. "Nevertheless, we understand its place in your cultures."

Cleante shook her head, rousing herself at last. Jali's cure had taken her mind off the encounter with Krazz. She had felt no fear when he marched into their cell moments before. However, the constant eyes of the guard beyond the transparency were unsettling.

"I don't care anymore, Resh'da," she said. "We're all in this together. I just wish *they* didn't stare so."

Resh helped her take the blanket off the bunk that had been meant for Theras and together they hung it between the bunks as a sort of privacy screen. Cleante's eyes shone with gratitude, and she slipped behind the blanket to change.

Resh contemplated T'Shael. He shared Jali's belief in the hidden fire of the introverted, but would never offer uninvited.

"The Vulcan holds that a well-conditioned body gives no offense," T'Shael said, perhaps reading his thoughts. "It is a body, nothing more. But I will not be approached."

Resh nodded.

"Our pleasures will remain for each other," he said, indicating his cousins with either hand.

Jali came to stand beside him and he squeezed her hand hard, as if in warning. Jali fluttered her eyelashes invitingly.

"Perhaps later," Resh put her off vaguely. "We will be here a long time."

The hairless ones simply could not remove their clothing without some improvisation, however, and within moments Krn had tumbled down from his perch to join his elder cousins, his Klingon uniform discarded. The guard beyond the transparency peered in with renewed attention, gaping and gnashing his teeth in frustration.

T'Shael turned her gaze inward and, without bothering with the privacy screen—it was a body, nothing more— slipped out of her somber Vulcan garb and into the ice cold shower.

Cleante's human curiosity overcame whatever sense of propriety she possessed. After all, if they insisted upon doing it in public, why shouldn't she watch? She observed the Deltan choreography until it began to pall on her. Certain Deltan techniques required prolonged periods of immobility; humans might find these pleasurable in participation but they were boring to watch. Cleante sighed and began to gather up her human clothing. She did not mean to look at T'Shael, had meant to respect her privacy, but the Vulcan was spending too long in the icy water and the human was becoming concerned.

"I don't think I can," Cleante had said that day at the hot spring, embarrassed at her own embarrassment.

T'Shael's hand had paused at the closure of her Vulcan tunic.

"Then I shall forego it also," she said.

"No," Cleante said, upset. There was no graceful way out of this. "You go ahead. I'll sit here and read, or take a walk. I don't mind, really."

"There are many days for swimming," T'Shael said,

turning without hesitation and starting up the slope away from the steaming sulfur spring.

But never enough for a friend, she thought but did not say.

"Funny, aren't we?" Cleante said later on the telpher going home. "Humans, I mean. So free about sex, most of us, but funny about taking our clothes off for any other reason."

"It is part of your sense of privacy." T'Shael suggested. She had been puzzled by the human's hesitancy toward the traditional nudity of the hot springs. "To the Vulcan, the body observed is simply the body. It is the body touched and, through it the mind accessed, that is a matter for privacy."

"I don't understand it myself," Cleante admitted. "Maybe it's because humans are so dissatisfied with their bodies. No matter what we look like, we're unhappy about our weight, the shape of our legs, our noses, whatever. Vulcans accept their bodies. There's such a serenity in that."

T'Shael considered.

"Perhaps. And perhaps it is for this reason—" once again, as ever since her first contact with the human, she marveled at the words she found. "—I may observe quite objectively that you are beautiful and I am not; yet if I speak this it evokes instantaneous protest from you. This I do not understand."

Cleante opened her mouth and clamped it shut on the protest. It would not do to become too predictable.

The human in the Klingon cage could not help but be drawn toward the Vulcan in the frigid shower, transfixed by a sight that made her own body ache with cold: that thin, gracile body beneath the streaming water, all bones and angles.

How fragile looking for all your Vulcan strength! Cleante thought, realizing all in a rush how T'Shael had carried the weight of all their sorry behavior—Theras's madness, the Deltans' hysteria, her own tantrums—these many days without respite.

And Cleante understood why T'Shael had engaged Mastery of the Unavoidable yesterday in the courtyard, realized that her present behavior was perhaps some ritual atone-

97

ment enacted through the cold so anathema to the Vulcan. T'Shael stood unmoving in the streaming water, arms upraised and head thrown back, eyes closed and face unreadable, even her obvious state of trance no match for the tremors that shook her.

The human leaped off her bunk, snatching the blanket down and wrenching the shower off. She threw the blanket over T'Shael's shoulders and wrapped it around her, without touching and without a word, and without being able to look into those burning eyes.

Breathless from the cold, T'Shael abruptly broke her trance. The icy water streamed off her lank hair and down her plain face like tears. Clasping the blanket about her with one hand, she reached toward the human with the other. The gesture was not completed before Cleante turned to face her.

"I'm sorry—

"Forgive me—

both said in the same voice. "I misunderstood you."

"In your place and in your honor," Cleante began in Vulcan, trying to take the bucket and cleaning utensils from T'Shael. The Vulcan shook her head.

"There is still danger to you in the Klingon quarters," she said gently. "Krn and I will manage there. Perhaps you can persuade Resh to assist you here. Then Jali will participate out of fear of exclusion."

Cleante nodded. Both had learned to use the Deltan's whims against her.

"All right," she acquiesced. "But you be careful, too."

Gently she touched the scar that ran across the Vulcan's face. T'Shael had forgotten about it. Now, strangely, it began to throb, and she engaged a light healing trance.

"No danger to me," she responded to the human's concern with a touch of irony. "Lord Krazz assures me that if he has a craving for sheep there are enough on his father's farm to gratify him."

"He has no right to talk to you like that!" Cleante flared, clenching her fists.

T'Shael's demeanor indicated that it was of no importance.

"His aversion assures my safety and provides me with

98

welcome opportunity to study his language." She contemplated the youngest Deltan, who was entertaining himself with handsprings along the open space between the bunks. "If you would assist me, Krnsandor."

"I'm coming!" he crowed, shouldering his mop and standing at attention before her.

Cleante smiled and resisted the urge to hug him; he was a never-ending source of brightness in their long days and longer nights. Even a Vulcan was not immune to his enthusiasm, and it was possible that T'Shael's somber gaze softened as she contemplated him. She signaled to the guard to unseal the transparency and she and her assistant crossed the compound to Krazz's quarters.

Their days devolved down into a kind of routine of long days and longer nights. Supplies were beamed down every few weeks from passing ships, whether Klin or Rihannsu none could tell, but no one left the planetoid. The ships left only enough to be consumed within the time that they were gone, as if to prepare for sudden escape and the need to erase all traces.

The frequency of the ships was also noteworthy. They were not marooned at the far edges of the galaxy, then, but somewhere on the main Klin-Rihannsu trade routes, perhaps in the very heart of either Empire. The thought was a chilling one.

The captives were permitted to exercise outside in the compound at the height of the twin suns under the ever-watchful eyes of Kalor or one of the guards. They studied what little they could see of the planetoid's surface beyond the heavy electrified fence. It consisted of a vastness of barren plain dotted with scruffy underbrush fading off to a low range of ragged hills a few kilometers distant.

It neither rained nor snowed; there were no clouds in the rust-colored sky. A murky yellow fog hugged the ground every morning, obscuring the landscape until the ugly red suns burned it away. There was no freshness in the air; a lazy wind, baffled by the gravimetric pull of two suns, churned the dust half-heartedly by day. At night it found courage and howled about the captives' cage.

They had no work except their self-imposed housekeeping, to which even Jali soon acquiesced as T'Shael had predicted she would. But walls and floors could only be scrubbed so much, bedding and spare uniforms hand-laundered with harsh soap only so often, and no matter their industriousness the captives managed to complete their work before the midday meal. The time might have hung heavier were it not for the agility of their minds.

"We are agreeing that there is no escape for us," Resh began one evening in a kind of impromptu conference he had called over their monotonous supper, the dried meat and biscuits varied for T'Shael's sake with legumes and various unidentifiable reconstituted vegetables.

"That we must remain here for however long. Therefore we must refrain from personalities."

Jali rolled her eyes as if she could not imagine what he meant; T'Shael was impassive.

"And try to make our captivity as pleasant as possible."

"Agreed," T'Shael said, taking his meaning, though only a Deltan could apply the word "pleasant" to their circumstances. "We are teachers and students here, as at T'ling-Shar. Our deprivation will strengthen us, and the lack of books and teaching aids will challenge our ingenuity."

"To be grateful for a lack of things is Vulcan-peculiar!" Jali addressed the ceiling. Even her cousins ignored her.

"We can take turns sharing what we know. Teach each other stories and languages and songs," Cleante suggested, coming alive. "We can reminisce about the good times and plan for the future, share our dreams. We must! These things will keep us going. We mustn't let the boredom get to us, or the thought that we might never . . ."

She shuddered and left her thought unfinished.

"And no quarrelling!" Krn piped up, anxious to dispel the gloom. He lay with his head in Jali's lap, alternately picking his teeth and gnawing on his nails; their captors had yet to provide them with such decadent amenities as grooming aids. "If two have a difference, a third must settle it."

Cleante gave him a playful poke.

"Maybe you should be the arbitrator, Fresh Face. You get along with everyone."

"Oh, yes!" the little Deltan crowed, clapping his hands. "I am liking this!"

They sustained each other. There was an abundance of conversation, an exchange of cultural and linguistic and musical traditions, classes in exercise and meditative techniques, jokes and games and anecdotes. What time human and Vulcan might use for sleep or meditation the Deltans used for sex. There was energy and enthusiasm and even, from all but the Vulcan, occasional laughter. The Klingons watched and grew increasingly annoyed.

Alone in his quarters late into ship's night cycle, Spock of Vulcan knelt in meditative posture, slipped the datadisc Uhura always had prepared for him into the viewer, and refolded his hands into one of their myriad contemplative configurations. Item by item, the galaxy's tragedies and disasters passed before his deep and depthless eyes.

Prolificomm Intergalax, the official UFP "wire service" (Spock had always found curious the enduring use of that antiquated term), made its news releases available in a variety of forms. There was the ultra-condensed version, which was really no more than a string of easily-digestible headlines for the impatient or the harried. There were the in-depth analysis versions for diplomats, students and the merely obsessive, covering every conceivable topic from dilithium mining to ion warfare to extinct species to legalized brothels, complete with exhaustive statistics, local color, and commentary by every available expert in the field; Spock himself had occasionally been asked to contribute to these on a number of scientific topics over the years.

For the squeamish and faint of heart, there was a special Purge code to fast-forward past anything suggestive of blood and/or guts. Alternatively, for the jaded and the thrill-seeker, there was the sensory-enhanced version, complete with augmented sounds and smells, appropriate background music, and 3-D tactiles and special effects.

But there were those who took their news precisely as it had transpired, straight and unvarnished, and Spock was one of them. Ever since his return to the realm of humans from the abyss of *Kohlinahr,* his Achilles heel—if a Vulcan could be said to possess such a thing—had been his Mastery of the Unavoidable. To accept with resignation, if not with serenity, that which one could not change, without falling prey to the human extremes of hardness or bleeding of heart, had always been difficult for him. He had evolved a meditative discipline so deeply personal even Jim Kirk did not know about it, and it was this he practiced now.

The sufferings of the universe passed across his viewscreen, and Spock reached out for them and embraced them, reached into them and took them into himself, became one with them.

"A renewal of hostilities between two worlds in the Congeriis system leaves over one million dead and an estimated three million near starvation owing to the inability of supply ships to get through . . ." the commentator's synthesized and androgynous voice said, almost soothingly.

(Spock reached within and found hunger, acrid in the mouth, knifing in the gut, and he embraced it.)

". . . the precipitous cooling of a star in the Moldavi Nebula designated Z-Micron III and the estimation that populations in excess of thirteen billion have died with it . . ." the voice droned.

(Spock found unending cold and dark and plunged into them, became them, became one with the thirteen billion dead and dying.)

". . . the unearthing today of one hundred and four mutilated bodies, many of small children, tortured to death in the latest religious uprising on Andros IV . . ."

(Spock opened himself to depths of pain and fear as only a child can experience them, became that child, became all children, and the soul behind the Vulcan mask cried for the children.)

Plague, famine, war and cataclysm, the deaths of stars and the deaths of children, all that fueled the insatiable human need for sensationalism, became surfeit to a Vulcan perhaps too sensitive to the sufferings of others ever to perfect his Mastery, and yet he must. He had no choice. Ultimately he would come to accept what was beyond his control, giving instead everything that he was to those matters where he could say, "Let me help."

The larger horrors had run their course across the viewscreen and smaller ones replaced them. Minor assassinations, an occasional localized mass murder, the latest statistics on the Orion slave trade—these too Spock learned and embraced. And, there was one thing more.

". . . and on Earth this week, Ambassador Sarek of Vulcan delivered a speech before a specially convened session of the Federation Council, in which he asked . . ."

Spock focussed, slightly breathless, returned from the realms he explored in ever increasing intensity. He knew of the content of his father's speech. Perhaps here there was something he could do.

". . . The representative of the Empire of the Rihannsu acknowledges awareness of the whereabouts of the six known as the Warrantors of the Peace," Sarek was saying in those measured organ tones which could by turns mesmerize, entrance, calm, persuade, dissuade or freeze one in one's tracks. "That one of the six has died is also fact. To act upon either fact at this time is, we suggest, precipitous. Until we know the reason or reasons for the taking of the Warrantors, we would ask most especially that our colleagues of Andor, despite the death of Theras *shoor*Shras, reconsider their threats and the emotions which prompt them . . ."

Theras. Son of Shras, Andor's Chief Ambassador and Prelate of the state religion. Shras of Andor, who had journeyed to Babel aboard *Enterprise*. This was disquieting.

Spock could understand Jim Kirk's restiveness where the matter of the Warrantors was concerned, could almost envy him the privilege of acting it out. He, of course, had not that privilege. Not that it really did the Admiral any good to rant and pace and wring his hands, except for the emotional release it gave him. There was nothing any of them could do, it would seem, but wait.

Spock deactivated the viewer and refolded his hands into one of their myriad contemplative configurations. They also served who only . . .

"Tolz Kenran's latest dispatch," Lord Krazz announced, tossing it on his desk as if it smelled. "Somehow the Feds have learned of the blue one's death. Kahless knows how, but then the Rom system is riddled with spies. This is what comes of their subtlety, Kalor, mark my words! It turns out he was the eldest son of Shras of Andor, their chief diplomat from that world. Some sort of religious figure as well. Superstitious claptrap, but he carries a lot of weight. There have been the usual threats and counter-threats and Andor's mobilizing for some sort of action. Deliver me from Fed politics! All it means to us is that we're stuck at our sheepherding that much longer. Monstrous!"

"Our sheep are remarkably healthy, considering the length of their captivity," Kalor observed, watching them moving about the compound beyond Krazz's window. "Fifty-seven days, yet they show no sign of debility or disease or disaffection—"

"Disaffection!" Krazz snorted. "You tell me they sing and laugh like children." He never went near the captives at all now, but left that to his underlings. "What gives them the right to enjoy themselves while we perish of boredom?"

"That could be remedied, my Lord," Kalor suggested.

Krazz was sorely tempted. His mood had been darker than usual lately. He fingered Lord Tolz's dispatch thoughtfully.

"We will see the outcome of this Andorian business first," he decided. "If there is to be a standoff, I want living prisoners for leverage."

He got up from the desk and joined Kalor at the window. Together they watched the Deltans, who stood in a circle with hands linked, communing on some moderately titillating wavelength which always reduced them to giggles afterward.

"They do this all the time?" Krazz demanded.

"Several times a day, my Lord." Kalor timed his next statement carefully. "It would be interesting to see what would happen if they were separated."

Krazz looked at him shrewdly. He was as anxious to get off this rock as Kalor.

"Contain yourself for a while, Kalor. Let's not liquidate our stock before we're sure of the market."

T'Shael left the scrub brush in the bucket and sat back on her heels, drying her chilblained hands on her coveralls and tucking her lank hair behind her delicate ears. Even a Vulcan could permit herself an occasional respite from such labor.

It was not so much the monotonous, dirty work that wearied her (Klingons without their servitors were slovenly at the best of times, but in her advent seemed to be outdoing themselves), but the endlessness of Krn's chatter. T'Shael did not want to dampen the little Deltan's fervor, but his tongue was never still, and she was endeavoring to absorb every word uttered by the Klingons.

She could ignore Krn, but that would not be Vulcan. Further, much of his monologue was studded with questions, which T'Shael as a teacher felt compelled to answer. She tried to apportion some of her mind for Krn and some for herself.

". . . in which case I shall be among the most educated of Deltans!" Krn chattered, half to himself, half to T'Shael. She had set him to washing windows; he loved to climb, and the yellow dust from the compound covered everything. "Think you, Friend T'Shael, with all the instructions you are giving me, if our time here lasts long I shall return home a scholar!"

"Then all honor to you, Scholar L'am," T'Shael replied patiently. "But consider that the scholar knows the value of silence."

Krn's hairless face puckered into a pout.

"Am I talking too much?"

"Would it offend you if I said so?"

He tilted his head like a bird, thinking it over.

"Yes," he replied.

"Then I shall refrain from saying so." T'Shael fished the scrub brush out of the murky water and resumed her work.

Krn leaped down from his perch on the windowsill and spun into a cartwheel, coming to rest crosslegged in front of the Vulcan, who regarded him mildly.

"I wish you weren't a Vulcan," he said fervently. "Then I could give you a hug."

T'Shael stopped her scrubbing. Again she dried her hands on her coveralls.

"Would it please you to do so, Krnsandor L'am?"

"It would warm my entire afternoon!" the youngster said sincerely.

T'Shael considered. He was only a child, a child who might have to spend much of his life in this desolate place

105

before this matter was resolved. If it would be of service—

Were these a Vulcan's thoughts, or were they due to her contact with the human?

"It would be my honor, Friend Krn," T'Shael said slowly. She found that his carefully pheromone-free embrace was not distasteful. The child finished his work and scrambled off to rejoin his cousins; he could not be without the touch of others of his kind for long.

In his absence T'Shael was free to continue her linguistic study.

"Espionage!" was what Kalor called it, coming upon her suddenly and, he thought, soundlessly. The Vulcan had heard him coming and did not give him the satisfaction of reacting as he had hoped. "What do you think you're doing?"

"Studying the language of my captors," T'Shael replied in fair Klingonaase; she had mastered that much of it already. "To understand one's enemy is to render him no longer an enemy."

It was not precisely what she had wanted to say; "enemy" was far too strong a word for her, but her captors' conversations were not given to nuance. Her reply infuriated Kalor.

"I don't want your 'understanding,' sheep!" he snarled, kicking the heavy bucket beside her, making the water slop over the sides.

T'Shael did not so much as move aside as the filthy water splashed her. Something in the Klingon's voice puzzled her. She forced her retiring gaze up to meet his cold eyes, and almost caught the glint of fear in them.

T'Shael's knowledge of Klingon ways was limited, yet were it broader she still could not have understood Kalor's predicament. Possibly she could comprehend the weight of shame he carried from his father's treason, but the reasons for it within the *komerex tel khesterex,* the orthodox expansionist philosophy of his kind, would have struck her as illogical, wasteful, if not incomprehensible. Yet, therein lay Kalor's fear.

If his father had bequeathed him anything, it was that "sideways analytical squint" Krazz had cautioned him about. Mertak *epetai* Haaral had presumed within the confines of his own home and in the presence of friends to disavow the *komerex*, to suggest that conquest and subjugation need not be the only answers. A servitor overheard, and reported his treason.

And Kalor, for all his circumspection, had been infected with his father's disease. He was obsessed with the study of the species his race conquered and enslaved or merely slaughtered. He participated in the slaughter to ensure his own survival within the system, and it could not be said that he did not savor it, yet there lingered in the charnel darkness of his soul the insight of Kor *epetai* Zareht, his father's comrade, who had been to Organia. Kor had told of the Organian prophecy that someday Klingon and human would join together toward a new tomorrow. In that tomorrow it would be he who had the most knowledge of other races and the least of their blood beneath his talons who would best survive.

But this was today, and each dawn that Kalor's cold eyes beheld was proof that he had not yet been discovered for what he was: traitor's seed and traitor in his own right. No one must know his secret. The Vulcan and her curiosity threatened him by her very existence.

Kalor tried to bully her, but she was unmoved. He might have kicked her as easily; T'Shael knew this and did not respond. This infuriated Kalor further.

"We will see what becomes of you when Lord Krazz is informed of your spying!" he said, his triumph almost hiding his fear.

But Krazz's response was less than gratifying.

"So the ugly one spies on us? What harm can she do? Who can she tell?" Krazz chuckled evilly, watching his second carefully. "She's not unlike you, Kalor. She understands the value of analysis."

Kalor took this as a warning and stayed clear of the Vulcan, though he was not through with her yet.

Jim Kirk paced. It seemed all he ever did any more was pace. Uhura tried to ignore him, but he was literally inches from her chair and blowing a gale every time he passed. She watched him out of the corner of her eye. Three paces to the left, hard about, six to the right, hard about and back. Uhura sighed, put down her clipboard and turned toward him.

"Admiral, sir," she said sweetly. "Is there something I can help you with?"

Kirk was startled by a voice that was coming from somewhere other than inside his own head.

"What? No, nothing, thanks. Just restless." Uhura waited for him to finish. "How long has it been?"

"Since the Warrantors were kidnapped, since the Rihannsu issued their ransom demands, since they withdrew those demands, or since Scotty found out the Klingons are also involved?" she asked patiently. "Sixty-one days, fifty-eight days, forty-six days and twenty-seven days respectively."

Kirk laughed mirthlessly.

"You're beginning to sound like Spock. I meant how long have we been out here chasing ourselves?"

"Forty-nine days, off and on," Uhura said. "Not counting the medical runs and the mapping expedition."

"I'm almost beginning to believe the scuttlebutt you've been feeding the Romulans," he said. "Nobody loves us."

Uhura offered him no sympathy. She would not bother to mention that for every one of those forty-nine days as well as during the side trips she had sat here, sometimes on double shift, transmitting false information for the Rihannsu to pick up, simultaneously reaching out to all her contacts Federation-wide in the hope of finding a thread, a crumb, a molecule of hard information they could use. There had been precious little.

And at all times, onshift or off, she kept a special channel open for news of a Rihannsu Records Clerk named Lel. There had been none at all for some time.

The early weeks of their mission-within-a-mission had been fruitful. Sulu had been in place only a few days when the coded reports started trickling back. He had leaked the news of Theras's death before the official sources could even confirm that any of the Warrantors were still alive. Before the uproar died down he had hailed in to say he was going further underground, checking supply ship runs to see if he could spot any unusual activity, any special consignments of food or medical supplies, anything that might indicate where in an entire Empire four humanoids and a Vulcan might be being held.

The death of the Andorian had been rampant Court gossip; anyone who listened, even a servant or a humble Records Clerk, could have picked that up. But the trade routes, especially those that intersected with the Klingon Empire, were medium security classified and would take some deeper burrowing. That would take time. Sulu had logged his intention and signed off. They'd heard nothing further for over thirty days.

It could mean he was simply doing his job, was so deeply engrossed in scanning thousands of consignment lists and lading runs that he had neither time nor opportunity to check in. It could simply mean he hadn't yet found anything worth writing home about.

Or it could mean he'd been captured. Interrogated. Tortured. Executed. Uhura's hands had gone suddenly cold on the controls and she glared at the special channel indicator, willing it to light up. It didn't.

Please, Hikaru, be all right! she prayed, shivering involuntarily. Please let us know where you are.

Kirk noticed the shiver.

"You all right, Freedom?" He always called her that when they were alone. "Want me to dial up the thermostat?"

"It isn't that, Jim. I was thinking about Hikaru."

"I know," Kirk said grimly. "I hated letting him go over. I hate sending any of us off alone, but he and Nogura had this one negotiated over my head before the tea cooled. And he's like a kid. He has to do these daredevil things."

"As if you of all people couldn't understand that particular need!" Uhura said fondly. How many times had *she* had to stand by, waiting and wondering, while *he* went off on some breakneck expedition? Now he knew how it felt.

Kirk smiled wistfully.

"Reprimand noted," he said, looking past her at the stubbornly unlit indicator. "Wherever Sulu is right now, I hope he at least knows he's helped tip the balance in our favor. He may be instrumental in ending this thing that much sooner. We'll just have to trust his instincts to get him back."

Montgomery Scott's instincts, as well as his *modus operandi,* had been somewhat different from Sulu's.

"You never could hold your liquor, Earther," Admiral Korax slurred at him through the bottom of a Saurian brandy glass. "I owe you a broken jaw from the last time."

"Ah, stow it and pour us another, ye bump-headed freak," Scotty slurred back affably. "I'll drink ye under slow or I'll clobber ye outright and get it over. Which d'ye prefer?"

Korax snorted into his brandy, got it in his beard and dribbling down his chest.

"Ye're a braggart and a blowhard, Muntgohmurrhee," the Klingon chortled; he could still imitate the burr as well as he had during the celebrated donnybrook on Station K-7 half a Klingon's lifetime ago. "An' I almost believe ye."

Scotty's first reaction to the sight of his old fisticatory nemesis had been pure shock. Korax had gotten so *old.* He'd been only a youngster the last time they'd tangled—something to do with the Klingon's calling the *Enterprise* a garbage scow—but in the intervening years he had grown suddenly ancient. Scotty had forgotten the age differential that made a Klingon of thirty-five venerable. Korax must be close to thirty now, and in that respect he was older than Scotty. He was a scarred, wrinkled, iron-haired, and much-decorated admiral in the Klin Navy, nearing his retirement.

Of course, Special Section had briefed Scotty on all of that before they set him up at the Intra-Empire Free Station to spout his disaffection with Starfleet where it could be overheard by Klingons, Rihannsu, or any other unsavory characters who might take an interest. Still, actually seeing what had become of Korax had given him a turn. Intimations of mortality, indeed.

" 'Muntgohmurrhee,' " Korax was mumbling, pouring more brandy on the table than in their glasses. "Kahless, why can't you have a decent name, y'old drunk? Something I can pronounce, at least."

"Muh friends call me Scotty," the human said dourly.

" 'Skhottih.' " The Klingon tried it on his tongue. "Better. Still not civ'lized. But better." He shook the empty brandy bottle speculatively. " 'Nother?"

"I *said* muh *friends* call me Scotty," the human repeated sententiously. "Who's buyin' this time?"

"*I* am. Just because you bought the first two, you tight-fisted—"

"All right, then. Ye can call me Scotty."

Korax just growled and ordered another.

"*Doch*," he said after a while. "I hear they threw you out. 'Medical rest leave.' A joke."

"It's only temporarar—temperamentarry—temper—only for awhile," Scotty assured him solemnly. "Overwork."

"Testicles!" Korax shouted, making the Sulamid waiter jump and get its tentacles tangled around the fresh bottle of brandy it had fetched. "Man like you—have his own command. Disgrace! Stuck in the vowels of Kirk's rust bucket all these years. No wonder angry. Would've busted up whole planet, never mind pub, I had to serve under that—"

"Bowels," Scotty muttered into his mustache, trying not to laugh.

"*toH?*" Like most elderly Klingons, Korax was more than a little deaf.

"Nuthin'. Y're right, though. Passed over. Can't tell you how many times. Kirk gettin' the glory, me breakin' my—testicles—down below. Makes a man wonder what it's all for. If ye take my meaning."

"Aye," Korax commiserated, pounding him on the back, hard.

It was Scotty's turn to choke now, cough and splutter and add to the miasma of Saurian brandy saturating them both. They were really swilling in it by now. The other patrons had gotten bored with watching the novelty of a human and a Klingon getting drunk together and paid no attention.

"Won't take you back, you know," Korax said with sudden confidentiality. "Starfleet. Finished. Kirk's got powerful friends. Know that for a fact."

"Do ye, now?" Scotty squinted at him, interested. "An' what else d'ye know?"

"Be surprised," Korax said with an air of importance. He'd been trying to rest his chin on his hand and his elbow

111

on the table for some minutes without success; he somehow couldn't get all the moving parts coordinated. "An', come right down to it, what's difference? Politics! Engineer's an engineer, an' you're the best either side of the Zone, y'old sot." His ancient face took on a crafty look, as if he were about to reveal a great secret. *"Khest* it, we could use you!"

Scotty contemplated the bottom of his glass.

"Helluva recruitin' pitch, that."

"Best I can offer," Korax said, giving up on the elbow trick at last. "Offer you a ship. Handpicked crew. Command of your own. Think of it!"

He was overcome by a sudden wave of patriotic fervor; stood abruptly, listing dangerously.

"Glory of the kill, Skhottih. Think of it. A place in the Black Fleet, *Kahlesste kaase!* We can get drunk together for all eternity." Korax tried to salute; couldn't do that either. *"Kai,* Klingon! *Kai,* Skhottih!"

"Korax. Korax, lad, easy now!" Scotty helped him back into his chair, looked around to see if anyone was listening; no one was. "This offer of yours, now. It'll take some serious thinking."

Korax didn't seem to have heard, had lapsed into a sudden stupor. His head sagged onto his arms in the swamp on the table and he started to snore. Scotty was about to give up on him when the snoring broke off and the Klingon roused himself.

"Kle'tih'bach!" he snarled in *'aase,* forgetting where he was.

"Huh?"

"Politics!" Korax repeated impatiently. "Reminds me. You want ship, I'll give you one. Even tell you her name. Former commander got himself *khest.* Babysitting. Gaggle of Fed civvies. Roms stole 'em. Right out from under the Vulcans." Korax was giggling, silly. The hair on Scotty's neck prickled. Was the payoff going to be this easy? Korax had begun to babble. *"His* commander—old enemy. Like to snatch ship from him. Settle old score. Tolz is mortal enemy. Not like you, Skhottih old enemy, old drunk. Old friend."

He went on babbling, half in Standard, half in *'aase,* fell

112

forward and began to snore again. Scotty leaned over him, shook him gently, whispered in his ear.

"Korax, lad, tell me. These civvies. Ones the Roms took. Have any idea where they're keepin' 'em?"

Korax's head shot up suddenly and he glared.

"toH?" he asked slowly, dangerously.

"The—the ship, lad," Scotty said quickly. "I was askin' you about the ship. What'd ye say her name was?"

"Can't—can't remember," Korax muttered, and passed out.

Scotty breathed slowly, listening to the hammering of his own heart. Well, half a loaf. He finished his brandy and was about to pour another when two razor-honed young Klin sergeants stalked over to him. Scotty's flesh crawled. Shore Patrol in any uniform made him twitch. He held his ground. The Klingons ignored him, went straight to Korax.

"Admiral Lord Korax, sir?" one of them inquired formally of the sodden mass snoring on the table. When there was no response he and his companion each grasped an arm and lifted the comatose admiral out of his chair. One of them murmured something under his breath; Scotty didn't need to know any *'aase* to understand the word "senile."

"Best put him to bed, lads," he advised them judiciously, pouring himself yet another in the glare of their yellow eyes. "He's had some rough sailin'. Reminiscing'll do that to ye."

When the two had trundled the admiral out and the Sulamid waiter arrived to wipe the table, clucking fastidiously, Scotty tossed a few Credits into the mess and walked stiffly toward the Gents' (the only such facility in a Sulamid-run establishment). Once inside he rolled up his sleeve, selected the proper blade on his vintage Scout knife, and removed the tiny subcutaneous transceiver-recorder from the fleshy part of his forearm, slipping it into a hidden pocket. Then he dug deeper to retrieve the ethanol-inhibitor capsule McCoy had concocted to keep him sober through this encounter. This latter item he flushed down the tubes, chuckling to himself.

Korax, ye poor dolt, he thought. It was the brandy was the tipoff. If ye've ever seen me drink aught but Scotch ye'd know I wasna taking my drinking serious.

Stone cold sober, Montgomery Scott emerged from the

113

Gents' under the goggling eyes of the Sulamid waiter, sidled up to the bar and ordered a double.

He was tall even for a Vulcan, and strikingly handsome. More than one human female had stopped to admire him as he strode among the colonnades of the settlement at T'ling-Shar, and the Deltans were beside themselves. He paid no heed to any of them, but continued on his way with a purposefulness bordering on urgency.

Now he knelt in the presence of Master Stimm, but with a demeanor that indicated he was not accustomed to kneeling.

"Live long and prosper, *Sim're'At—*" he began, a breach of etiquette excused him in view of the expediency of his mission, but Stimm motioned him to silence with a gesture.

"Thee are called Stalek," he observed. Urgency served no purpose; there was nothing the Master could do to solve the younger Vulcan's dilemma.

"Yes," the one called Stalek replied, then waited as was proper for the younger in the presence of the elder. He could not but wonder how long he would be required to wait. Were he not Vulcan, he might almost be thought guilty of impatience.

Master Stimm sensed the handsome one's urgency from the depth of his wisdom, but allowed him to wait and consider his reasons for coming here. There could be no satisfactory outcome to their meeting.

"Thee seeks the one called T'Shael," Master Stimm said at last. "Surely thee are aware of what has transpired."

"Perhaps to a greater degree than any other, Master," Stalek replied, his proud, almost arrogant face revealing for a moment that something beset him deeply. "Excepting those who presently hold her captive."

Were he not a Master, Stimm might have betrayed his surprise. The old one had not had cause to consider the matters of male and female for many years; it was possible he had forgotten what knowledge a Vulcan's betrothed could possess where no other could.

"Thy mind is linked with hers," Stimm said, more to remind himself than to invade the other's privacy. His rank permitted him this leeway. "Thee knows for certain, then, that she still lives?"

"I do," Stalek replied, and had he been less preoccupied with his own concerns he might have caught the flicker of relief as it passed across the old one's face. That his deepest student might be restored to him was cause for satisfaction even to one so disciplined.

The younger Vulcan did not lower his gaze as was proper, but fixed the Master with an arrogant stare that perhaps held a trace of pleading.

"The Master knows what will happen to me if she is not returned."

Stimm caught the nuance of pain in the younger one's voice and looked at him sharply.

"And what would thee have the Master do?"

Stalek rose from his knees to pace the Master's cell in most unVulcan restiveness.

"What can anyone do?" he asked. "What discipline of mind can avert what awaits me if she is not restored at the appointed time? I despair of any, Master. I do not wish to die!"

"Kroykah!" Master Stimm cried sharply. The younger one must not disgrace himself by continuing this outburst. "This is unbecoming! If it is thy fate to meet death in such a manner, what can be done? Return to thy work and to thy meditations. Even a Master is powerless against the first *pon farr.*"

The words had been spoken, and hung between them like a threat. None but a Vulcan could understand the weight of shame those words implied. Stalek bowed his proud head at last.

"I ask forgiveness, Master," he said with something like sorrow. "There is so much I desired to do with my life. To have it taken from me so soon, and in so shameful a manner—"

"There is yet time," the Master suggested. He was not unmoved by the plight of the handsome one, and even a Master could question the illogic of Vulcan biology. He thought also of the introverted one, and wondered at her fate. *"Kaiidth!* None can know the future."

Six

"TERRA'S POETRY IS eloquent on the topic of love," T'Shael had said to Cleante in her rooms at T'lingShar, framed in the windowseat by a moonless Vulcan night, her treasured *ka'athyra* at her side, her words carefully chosen. "You as a human have experienced this emotion on a number of levels. I would learn from you."

And Cleante had laughed her brittle laugh and refused.

"I don't know anything about love," she had said, her Byzantine eyes acquiring a sadness the Vulcan could not help but see. "Sex, yes, but that's not what you mean. I can tell you what it's like to live without love. But tell you about love? I can tell you nothing, T'Shael!"

That was when the Vulcan, for the first time and with extraordinary boldness, turned the human's words against her.

"That is not good enough, Cleante alFaisal. You know far more than you choose to acknowledge."

And Cleante, as amazed at T'Shael's words as the Vulcan was, told her what she knew.

"Oysters!" Jali sighed, referring to the Deltan equivalent. Cleante recognized the word; Jali had practically lived on them at the settlement. "There is nothing equalling them!"

116

"Are you meaning them or their effect, cousin?" Krn wanted to know. "The word in Standard is what—aphrodisiac?" One of his extracurricular courses here in the Klingon cage included vocabulary improvement. He turned to T'Shael. "Aphrodisiac. I am liking this word. How is it said in Vulcan?"

"There is no equivalent in Vulcan," T'Shael said and, as Krn's face puckered, "I am sorry."

"So am I," Krn said sympathetically.

They talked about food often, particularly at mealtimes. The Klingons had not varied their monotonous diet after all this time, and only the memory of past culinary delights gave them any appetite at all.

"Remember the mushrooms, T'Shael?" Cleante asked excitedly. She became almost childlike during these fantasy sessions, in contrast to a growing melancholy otherwise. The Vulcan had noted these mood swings with concern. "Remember the first time I had them? Mushrooms big as dinnerplates, and so pretty I didn't want to eat them!"

"Indeed," the Vulcan said remotely. She seemed to be listening to something inside herself.

Cleante sat forward on her bunk, reaching across to take Resh's hand and Jali's in her own. She seemed to crave contact as much as the Deltans lately, and T'Shael wondered at this also.

Such thoughts were an invasion of privacy, T'Shael reminded herself. Further, had the human engaged in intercourse with any of the Deltans she would have known; the lack of privacy in this place assured that.

There were always the times when she and Krn were in the Klingon quarters, T'Shael reasoned. Of course, interaction with a Deltan or Deltans caused profound changes in human behavior, and surely she would have noticed.

Stop! T'Shael told herself forcibly, amazed at the trend her thoughts were taking. She had read the literatures of a dozen species, including their erotica, with at least an objective understanding but without any stirrings within herself. What did such abject voyeurism mean?

The Vulcan consulted her innate timesense. It was difficult to know the exact date it would be on her homeworld now because of the unknown number of days they had spent in the Rihannsu ship and the irregularity of days and nights in this place. But she knew enough to understand why her thoughts tended increasingly toward the sexual, toward the things Vulcans did not speak of among themselves.

Stalek, parted from me and never . . .

T'Shael kept her silence, listening to something within herself as the others chattered on about food.

"—this big across," Cleante was explaining, letting go of the Deltans' hands to demonstrate with her own. "And the colors! Pinks and purples and some with silver stripes. We'd gone climbing in the hills and T'Shael knew where they were hidden in a little valley near a spring . . ."

How to capture that moment and bring it alive for the Deltans? Cleante wondered—the pristine air and crystalline silence of the Vulcan dawn, the sound of windchimes announcing the sunrise as they left the settlement, her heroic human efforts to keep up with T'Shael in the mountains. The Vulcan could climb like a goat, agile and purposeful until she realized her human companion was falling behind.

"Forgive me," T'Shael said, an apology for her superior strength, for the differences between them.

She extended one strong and elegant hand, slightly less reluctant to touch than she might once have been, to help the human effortlessly up the crag. They came at last to the remarkably fertile hidden valley with mosses and lichens cushioning jagged Vulcan rock, minuscule flowers loud with color and fragrance, and soft spray from the spring misting over everything. And the mushrooms . . .

"These are why I suggested we bring no provisions," T'Shael said, perhaps allowing herself the smallest trace of pride in the secret bounties her world could provide. "Each has its own unique flavor and a high nutritive value. They are one reason we were able to forego the need for animal flesh."

Cleante said nothing. She had tried Vulcan vegetarianism and earned herself a severe case of dysentery. T'Shael had since convinced her that the difference in physiology made it unwise to attempt so rigid a dietary regime without proper acclimation.

Now T'Shael took a small knife from her carrybag. Like all Vulcan tools, it was compact and functional yet strangely beautiful, folding out of itself to produce an incredibly sharp blade. T'Shael cut the top off one huge purple mushroom with a single stroke, leaving the stem whole and still rooted in the soil. Cleante watched in awe, expecting a ritual. She was not disappointed.

T'Shael touched her fingertips to her tongue, then to the raw stump of the mushroom where it oozed slightly. She gently stroked the wounded-looking thing in a circular motion, chanting softly under her breath until the oozing stopped and the stem sealed over. She looked up to see the human watching her.

"This enables another to grow in its place," she explained. "The Vulcan takes nothing without return."

With that she took her knife to the huge purple mushroom cap, slicing it like good, rich bread.

"How did it taste, Cleante? Oh, tell us!" Krn pleaded, breaking the spell of her narrative with his enthusiasm.

Cleante tried to find words to describe the taste. What could she compare it to? There had been a suggestion of Terran lobster, of pomegranates, of the wild figs she had stuffed herself with as a child. Each bite had suggested something different, and something exclusively Vulcan and eluding description. Yet how much of that savor was the result of the clarity of the morning and the rigorous climb, of an unbroken fast and undemanding companionship? As Cleante sought words to gratify Krn's curiosity, T'Shael suddenly sprang up from her place on the floor.

"Get down!" she cried. "Under the bunks and cover your heads. Tremors."

The others did not understand her at first, did not know about or had forgotten the Vulcan ability to sense earthquakes. The sudden heaving of the floor beneath them was reminder enough. The captives scrambled for cover.

The quake lasted only a few seconds, but it was damaging. One of the heavy bunks toppled over directly where the captives had been sitting; great chunks of hastily-cast thermoconcrete cracked loose from walls and ceilings and slammed dustily to the floor. The very face of the barren plain beyond was altered; great fissures gaped where the ground had been unbroken moments before.

T'Shael found Resh huddled beside her under one of the

bunks; the final aftershock threw him against her and she was unable to shield in time against his churning thought impulses. His immediate fears about the quake and the safety of his cousins she could cope with, absorb them as if they did not exist, for the Vulcan accepts the possibility of imminent death and knows no fear. But even in terror Resh'da could not curb his sexual impulses.

Filtered through his general desire to unite in sexual ecstasy with all of the universe, T'Shael encountered in Resh's mind a distinct and specific longing for her! In the split second before she could block reception, she experienced the expected violent aversion coupled with a rush of reciprocal desire!

What was happening to her? Stop! she commanded herself, withdrawing as far into herself as she could and still remain conscious.

When the quake was over and Resh slid out from under the bunk with Deltan grace, he encountered the briefest glimmer of pure horror in the Vulcan's eyes. It was horror at herself and not at him. Then she locked her mask into place. Gentle Resh began to hold out his hand to her, to help her up, to attempt to ease her distress. He would never understand this race, never! T'Shael withdrew further. Resh's cousins' scrambling from their hiding places to cling to him made it unnecessary to explain his overtly aroused state.

"T'Shael? Are you all right?"

It was Cleante, covered with plaster dust as they all were, concern in her voice. The Vulcan's demeanor puzzled her.

"Undamaged," T'Shael replied, hugging herself as if experiencing a sudden chill. "And you?"

"I'm fine," the human said. She touched the Vulcan's arm and was astonished at how violently she flinched. "T'Shael, are you sure?"

The human's voice drew her away from the encounter with Resh. Further, Jali was watching, surmising with a fluttering of eyelashes more than T'Shael thought she needed to know.

"Indeed," the Vulcan said with what she hoped was conviction. She locked her gaze with Jali's until she had succeeded in staring the Deltan down.

For the first time since their capture, T'Shael knew the

desperation the others had felt all along. They had been held in this place for seventy-three of its days. Before an equal number had passed, perhaps sooner, she must return to Vulcan. She must!

In the Klingon quarters, where they had had no Vulcan to warn them, damage was more severe. One guard had broken an arm; Kalor had gashed his head on the scanner console. Furniture had toppled and crockery smashed; half of Krazz's store of ales and fruit nectars was destroyed. Doors had warped against their frames; the power source had malfunctioned, erasing half the computer tapes and sending sparks out of the transformer for the electrified fence, nearly killing the second guard. As for Krazz, the only damage was to his already wounded pride.

"This is the final insult!" he roared, watching over Kalor's shoulder as he tried to steady the scanners and get a full reading on the extent of the quake. "Even the planet conspires against us! Could my Lord Tolz have thought of a more idiotic place to strand us? Or is that part of his plan, to sacrifice us with our prisoners and throw a spanner into the Roms' works all at that same time? I will not stand here waiting for the ground to open and swallow me! I'll outthink Tolz Kenran yet!"

Kalor said nothing. His head ached; he wished Krazz would stop shouting. The time might be ripe to suggest alternatives or it might be dangerous to speak out of turn. Let Krazz reach a point where he was open to suggestion, desperate for it.

"Have you read the latest dispatch, Kalor?"

"Not without authorization, my Lord," Kalor lied.

"Well," Krazz grunted, not believing him. "To condense it for you, the Feds have refused to negotiate with 'pirates and terrorists,' their turn of phrase for the Roms, just as I predicted. They demand immediate return of the Andorian's carcass. What will they do when they learn it was dissected, I wonder? And positive proof that the remaining sheep are alive and well. I surmise from the conspicuous silence on our side, though you would have had to read carefully between the lines in the dispatch you haven't read—" Kalor did not so much as blink "—that we are once again at odds with the Rom Praetor. We were never meant to mix in it with these slithering freak-ears, Kalor, and nothing good will come of it. What I cannot determine from this distance is whether this turn of events shortens our sheepherding or prolongs it. I'm half-tempted—"

Kalor shut off the scanner, satisfied that the aftershocks were over and they were safe for the moment at least. He watched the familiar crafty look steal over Krazz's face.

"This experiment with the Deltans, Kalor. The one you outlined for me some time ago. You're convinced you could turn it to our advantage, even if they did not survive it?"

Kalor gestured that this was of no importance.

"My Lord has said himself that a dead witness is no witness. We now have to contend with the added danger of unstable seismic conditions. If a quake severe enough to kill our prisoners and perhaps the guards—"

Krazz chuckled at what to him bordered on genius.

"Very good, my—analytical—lieutenant." The word was no longer as offensive as it might have been. "You'll have your little experiment in . . . what was it you called it?"

"Xenopsychology, my Lord."

"Xeno—yes, whatever. I'm a soldier, not a scientist. This should prove entertaining. What will you need?"

"Only the storage shed," Kalor nodded in the direction of the windowless structure across the compound. "And a strong lock."

Records Clerk Level-4 Lel em'n Tri'ilril moved cautiously down the endless maze of corridors in the lowest level of the Citadel, certain he was alone, but no less uneasy. All of his senses were in overdrive, and he was sweating. He remembered the security monitor at the juncture just in time and flattened against the wall to sidle out of its range, leaving damp handprints in his wake, cursing himself for such an obvious, traceable human giveaway.

Gods, he thought. Gods, gods, if I ever get out of this one I swear I'll never cross another border. I'll stay safe on *Enterprise,* take battlecruisers and supernovae and doomsday machines in my stride and never get closer to a Rihannsu than a thousand kilometers for the rest of my life. Assuming there is a rest of my life.

They were onto him, he was certain; they were just waiting for him to blow his cover and save them the trouble of hunting him down. Of course, in the general paranoia following the blunder with the ransom demands, the sudden disfavor of the faction who sided with the Klingons and the high-level purge that followed it (including, he had just learned, the ritual suicide of the Praetor's nephew Dr'ell; that could be worth something if he could get it out), everyone was suspect, but Sulu had seen an increasing number of suspicious looks leveled at him. They were onto him, and they were after him. He had to get out of the Citadel, whether over the side or deeper in, but away.

His original timing had been perfect. He'd slipped into the Capital in the general influx of returning end-of-season leave-takers, had had himself installed on the staff of the Winter Palace—ostensibly as a temporary replacement for one Trajal m'ra Pael'naarkhoi, who had gotten embroiled with a colonial governor's housemaid and a paternity suit and was expected to be tied up in the settlement courts for months—and assigned Trajal's place in the Records Section barracks bloc just before the waste matter started hitting the ventilators.

Barracks living had not proved to be the best of arrangements. Aside from the temporary hardship of bunking with six others in a single room (so much for a private life, Sulu had thought, tossing and turning on the spartan sleeping mat), he had always talked in his sleep, and under the circumstances, that could get him killed. He'd had several sessions of hypnotherapy to ensure that he would dream in Rihan, but that didn't assure him. Still, as an unbonded male of his class he was barred from any other housing within the Capital, and he'd had to make the best of it.

He had at his disposal several identity changes and escape routes, some of them quite ingenious, but it was a question of when to jump. There was still so much he had to do, but if he let himself get boxed in . . .

A noise at the juncture ahead froze him and he doubled back, dodged another monitor, listened. Footsteps, echoes of footsteps, echoes of echoes down the endless corridors. Gods! McCoy had equipped him with aural enhancers and infrared implants to mimic Rihannsu hearing and sight; now if he'd only arranged for green blood and a trebled heart-beat . . .

No problem with that last, Sulu thought grimly. *Much more of this and my heart may never slow down.*

He glanced to either side, swallowed hard, pushed away from the wall with his sweaty hands, and hurried back in the direction he had come. If he could hot-wire one of the aircars in the Royal Armory's auxiliary hangar and at least get out of the Citadel . . .

"Speak to me of love," T'Shael had said. "You as a human have experienced this emotion on a number of levels."

"What makes you think that?" Cleante demanded too sharply, suddenly defensive. "Just because I've slept my way from Earth to Colony Seven to Vulcan?"

She saw a hardness come into the Vulcan's eyes and stopped. *Oh, T'Shael, why must I do this to either of us?*

"Such words are unworthy of you," T'Shael said evenly. "I refer not to such fleeting gratification, which is at any rate not my concern. I refer to deeper things."

Cleante did not answer. She got up from the sleeping couch and began to roam restlessly about the small flat that spoke so eloquently of its inhabitant. She thought of her own suite, which also reflected the taste of its owner, though perhaps to her disadvantage. It was much bigger than these rooms, much more cluttered, filled with mismatched, over-stuffed furniture and worn mementos of the childhood she had yet to outgrow, clothing and jewelry flung about everywhere, one entire wall naturally dominated by the latest in audvid equipment for instant sensory gratification.

The Vulcan's flat had no audvid screen and no clutter. It was bare without being barren. Aside from the intricately carved doors of the cabinets containing her vast collection of linguatapes, there was little ornament of any kind. There were a few exquisite examples of the renowned Vulcan glasswork ("A logical craft from a world blanketed in silicates," T'Shael had said the first time Cleante admired them, offering the guest any one of her choosing as was proper. Cleante, knowing the protocol by now, had as politely declined); the expected IDIC print on one wall (as ubiquitous in Vulcan households as a crucifix in a Terran nunnery); and nothing more. The floors were not carpeted as most interiors were, but covered with soft mats woven of fragrant grasses. Glassless casements allowed the breezes in; unobtrusive sensors set into the window frames regulated temperature and warned off insects and night-flying birds. It was a peaceful, harmonious setting for a like individual.

But was T'Shael as peaceful as her surroundings? Cleante wondered. Would she be asking such questions if something weren't troubling her? Cleante stopped her restless prowling and looked at her companion, who had returned to the restringing of her *ka'athyra* as if to mask the human's embarrassment and perhaps her own.

"If you prefer not to answer—" T'Shael began at the same time Cleante said, "When you say 'deeper things'—"

"Forgive me," the Vulcan said, and waited for the human to continue.

"I'm not sure what you mean," Cleante said. "But if I can tell you anything at all, I'll try."

It was all anyone could ask. T'Shael fastened the final string at the neck frets of her instrument, stilling all of the strings with her hand so that they would not resonate in sympathy with her voice.

"You were once a teacher," she began. "Such service as you offered on Gamma Erigena—"

Her celebrated year among the aboriginal inhabitants of what had come to be known as Earth Colony Seven, Cleante thought wryly, and also wistfully. It had been a strange year in a lifetime of strange years.

A lush and unspoiled world, Gamma Erigena was inhabited primarily by an utterly non-belligerent, childlike species who welcomed the more advanced Terrans, eager to learn their ways. Teachers were needed, and Cleante had been quick to volunteer.

She was only a student teacher, another of her reckless career changes, and she had volunteered for Earth Colony Seven partly to escape from her mother, who was not yet High Commissioner but no less overbearing, and to extricate herself from a series of love affairs that would culminate in her fling with Rico Heyerdahl.

She found herself becoming more attached to these primitive, gentle aborigines, especially the children, than she could have believed possible for the daughter of Jasmine alFaisal, holder of the patent on cold professionalism. They were so totally non-aggressive, found joy in the smallest things, sharing that joy so readily with others. They were extremely tactile, embracing their teachers constantly, superlatively grateful for the instruction they received. Cleante had left them when their attentions became cloying. She could not be tied down to anyone, anything, for too long. Yet she had wept as Gamma Erigena spun out of sight of her port on the starliner going back to Earth. She often wondered what might have happened to these gentle, uncomplicated beings had Klin or Rihannsu stumbled on them first. But had she really loved them?

She had spoken to T'Shael about them, particularly about the grammatical structure of their language, which had no distinguishing pronouns, only a universal "we." The Vulcan had listened with great interest, but neither had spoken of any emotional attachment. It was not like T'Shael to jump to conclusions. What did her question mean?

Or was she not talking about the Erigenians at all?

Their world had also been where Cleante had first encountered Rico Heyerdahl, but she had never mentioned him to T'Shael, had she? Randy Rico with his ready laugh and come-day-go-day manner, who with his patched and jury-rigged scout was on layover for an overhaul—

Rico! Cleante thought with a pang, scarcely listening to what T'Shael was saying. Rugged, wonderful Rico, scion of an old Argentinian family by way of a Nordic freighter pilot, possessed of the Latin fire of one and the insatiable starlust of the other. Green-eyed, brown-skinned, flaxen-haired and wonderful in bed, though not much for talking either before or after; he was just literate enough to pass the pilots' license exam and proud of his ignorance. Rico, Rico, I had to leave you before you left me, Cleante thought. It was that simple. And I haven't thought about you since, but all this talk of love—

T'Shael was watching her curiously. Allah only knew what emotions were playing havoc with her face. Cleante tried a little Mastery of the Unavoidable and forced herself not to apologize.

"I wasn't listening," she managed to say.

T'Shael, thinking she had been misunderstood, attempted to clarify.

"The Way of the Vulcan is based upon duty. From duty springs service, and the Vulcan considers this sufficient. But as I understand the human way, service—such as your service to the inhabitants of Erigena—may sometimes evolve into that which, for want of a better term, I shall call dedication. And from such dedication, I believe, can sometimes spring love."

Cleante shook her head, all thought of Rico forgotten, grateful for once that she was not Vulcan. Such tortuous reasoning to arrive at a conclusion about that which humans came by naturally.

"Are you asking me if I loved my students?" Cleante asked, and before T'Shael could answer, "Maybe I did. I've never stopped to think about it. But I never said anything to you. How did you know?"

"In the same way that I am aware of your love, despite ambivalence and a strong desire to deny it, for your maternal parent," T'Shael responded hesitantly, dropping this particular bombshell with inordinate softness.

Cleante's eyes widened as she understood several things at once: understood why Vulcans in general were so standoffish, and why T'Shael in particular was so reluctant to touch; understood why they had not gone to the ruins together since the storm; and understood, or thought she did, T'Shael's reasons for asking such questions.

"The day we were caught in the rainstorm," Cleante said slowly, all her fears about that day suddenly realized, "you read my mind, didn't you? You know everything there is to know about me, yet you can still—"

"Do not misunderstand," the Vulcan said. "No one can know 'everything there is to know' about another. To learn the depths of another's soul requires prolonged mutual sharing in mind-link, not so brief an encounter as my mind had with yours."

"You seem to have gotten an awful lot from your 'brief encounter,' " Cleante said ironically. Like most humans, she did not entirely understand the Vulcan telepathic gift, and it frightened her.

"I merely read those thoughts uppermost in your mind at the moment of danger," T'Shael explained carefully. "At such times one is drawn toward that which one most values. In your case it was toward your work on Erigena, and toward she who is your mother. In the first instance I sensed pride of accomplishment, a warmth of reminiscence, and a sadness at departure. In the latter I sensed what I can only describe as a great sorrow. An incompleteness. A need for that which she could not, or would not, give. I believe this need was love."

T'Shael stopped, a little breathless, as if it had cost her as much to relate the experience as it cost Cleante to live it. Her next words were tinged with something akin to embarrassment.

"I ask forgiveness for my intrusion into your mind. I return your knowledge of yourself to you, as if it had never passed to me."

Cleante crossed the room and drew quite close to the Vulcan. She was about to risk a great deal.

"T'Shael, this—mind-link. How does it work? Can a Vulcan have such a link with . . . with another species? Say a human?"

"It is possible," T'Shael said honestly, wishing she did not have to be so honest. Knowing what the human desired and knowing she could not give it. "But it is reserved for instances of very close friendship."

"I see," Cleante nodded. "And of course that's not possible for us."

"Regrettably, it is not."

"And why not?" the human demanded, as she had demanded before without getting a satisfactory answer.

"It is not to do with you," T'Shael said almost gently. "It is that I am one who cannot aspire to such friendship. I must remain alone, that is all."

"And the *why* is not for me to know?"

"Precisely."

With that T'Shael withdrew into herself and began to tune the *ka'athyra* as if she truly were alone. Like most of her race she was possessed of perfect pitch, and had intrigued Cleante with this ritual before. But the human was not to be distracted this time. She sat uninvited beside the Vulcan in the windowseat and took her hand away from the strings, holding it firmly in her own.

"T'Shael, you can't just give a human back the knowledge of herself." The strings of the instrument, unconstrained, set up a plaintive resonance to her voice. "I won't accept it. You have to offer me a fair exchange."

The Vulcan gently but firmly extricated her hand from the human's.

"I do not understand," she said. The *ka'athyra* responded to her voice in melancholy tones until she stilled it.

"Oh, I think you do!" Cleante said sharply, and before the Vulcan could close in on herself she went on. "I want to know as much about you, T'Shael, as you know about me. You've taught me a great deal about Vulcans, but precious little about the one Vulcan I'm most interested in. The Vulcan I choose to be my friend."

"Perhaps you choose unwisely," T'Shael suggested, not meeting her eyes.

"I don't happen to think so!" Cleante flared, then forced her temper down. "I will be your friend, T'Shael. Whether or not you choose to be mine."

The noise assailed T'Shael's sensitive ears before she was halfway across the compound. It was the cry of a Deltan in the throes of despair.

"They've taken Resh away," Cleante explained above Jali's frantic wailing.

T'Shael put down her cleaning implements and contemplated the two remaining Deltans clinging to each other in a corner of their cage. Jali's cries were piercing to human ears; to the Vulcan they were excruciating. T'Shael blocked them as well as she could. Her concern was for Krn.

"There was much activity between Kalor and the guards all morning," she observed. "And the small one seemed to sense something which made him most uneasy. It was why I dispensed with his assistance and sent him back here. Where have they taken Resh'da, and for what purpose?"

"I don't know!" Cleante said, clenching her fists at her temples. The wailing was driving her to a despair of her own. "A little after you went to Krazz's quarters, they simply marched in with their blasters and took Resh away. They wouldn't let us near the windows to see where they were taking him. Naturally poor Resh offered no resistance. He only gave Jali a look, as if he couldn't bear to be parted from her. As if he knew he would never come back. She's been carrying on like this ever since; I can't do anything with her. Since Krn's come back it's gotten worse. I can't make them stop."

"They must be persuaded to stop," T'Shael said. "Or Resh'da will die."

Seven

"TAKE THE SMALL one," T'Shael said abruptly to Cleante.

The human extricated Krn from his cousin's embrace and let him wrap himself around her. His cries subsided to whimpers. Cleante thought of the last time he had done this, of the Rihannsu ship and Theras. She shuddered and began to soothe the small one with soft words as T'Shael dealt with Jali.

She took the Deltan by the shoulders and shook her hard. Startled into silence, Jali glared at her.

"You are knowing where they are taking your brotherlove," T'Shael said intensely in flawless Deltan, looking hard into the eyes whose fluttering lashes held back great pools of tears waiting to follow those already streaming down the hairless face. "Speak it me!"

"A place, a darkness-place!" Jali moaned, twisting her body frantically, trying to free herself from the viselike grip. "A loneliness-place, no touching and thus—oh!"

She began to wail again, her wails becoming shrieks. T'Shael gathered herself and struck Jali hard across the face with the flat of her hand.

Cleante jumped as if she had been struck. She had never seen the Vulcan resort to violence before. She watched transfixed, wondering if T'Shael had gone mad.

"They were not using the shuttlecraft and thus," T'Shael continued relentlessly in her perfect Deltan, focusing in on Jali as if they two were the only beings in the universe. "Resh'da is therefore near and thus. It is having hope. Sense out your brotherlove and tell it me!"

Jali's eyes lost their focus for a moment and she seemed to search for something. She let out a small cry and clambered up on one of the bunks, pointing out the high window in the direction of the storage shed.

"There!" she cried. "This place of storing things, darkness-place. No-windows place." She slid to the floor and seemed to crumple in on herself, rocking inconsolably. "No-sunlight aloneness place—oh!"

She made to shriek again, but T'Shael merely raised her hand and she subsided.

"Hear me!" the Vulcan said, reverting to Standard for emphasis. "There is no bond between you and me, Jali'lar Kandowali. But Resh'da is of value to me and I would do all in my power to save him were it my place. You are his kinswoman and his lover. If you cannot reach your mind into his and sustain him he will pine for lack of physical contact as is the way of your people and he will die. The choice is yours, Jali'lar."

Jali had known this all along, but the Vulcan's putting it into words forced her to acknowledge it. She struggled to control herself.

"I will try to reach and thus, but I despair—oh!"

"Then your despair will communicate itself to Resh'da," T'Shael said sternly.

Hearing this, small Krn let go of Cleante and took Jali by the hand, pulling her with him.

"We must try, cousin," he said with a grave and sudden maturity.

Together he and Jali crouched by the wall nearest the storage shed and began their mantra.

"Do you think it will work?" Cleante asked, drawing quite close to T'Shael, seeking some comfort for herself, though she knew better than to ask.

"Unknown," T'Shael said remotely.

She was more concerned with the reasoning behind Kalor's dragging Resh away than with the event itself. What could it mean? Kalor the analytical one—T'Shael had read this in him from the beginning—would know that a Deltan bereft of touch can die of loneliness. What gave Kalor the power to endanger his Empire's captives with impunity? Had something happened in the galaxy beyond that had altered the captives' fate without their knowing it?

"Will Resh die?" Cleante was asking.

"If his cousins are unable to sustain their link with him . . ." T'Shael's voice trailed off. There was a thing that she could do, but as the time drew closer and her need to return to Vulcan grew stronger, it held considerable danger. "I also have a tenuous link with the gentle one. It may be possible for me to be of service."

Having said this to the human, T'Shael acknowledged that she was committed to it. But she was not prepared for Cleante's reaction.

"*You* have a link with Resh—with a Deltan?" There was hurt in her voice more than incredulity, hurt that T'Shael would reject a link with her and yet—Cleante remembered the earthquake. "I see."

"It was not my desire to sustain it, nor do I desire to use it now," T'Shael said, allowing herself something as extraordinary as personal preference. "Nevertheless, if it is all that will save Resh'da—"

There was a long silence, punctuated only by the Deltans' mournful chanting.

"T'Shael?" The human's voice was soft, controlled, without self-pity. "What's going to happen to us?"

The Vulcan turned and, as if it were a gesture natural to her, brushed a lock of tangled hair from the human's brow.

"I do not know," she said.

"Analysis, Bones?" the Admiral said to McCoy. "How do you read her?"

"Who? You mean the High Commissioner of United Earth?" McCoy asked innocently, giving the title the high-falluting tone it deserved. He had definite opinions about Jasmine alFaisal, all right, but would keep them to himself while Spock's ears were in the vicinity. "I'll reserve judgment for the time being, Jim."

"That is most unlike you, Doctor," Spock commented

drily. "Such restraint from one who is noted for his ability to reach what he himself would call 'snap judgments.' "

"Yes, I'm surprised at you, Bones," Jim Kirk chimed in. "You're not going mellow on us, are you? Have you noticed, Spock, how he seems to be mellowing in his old age?"

"Indeed, Admiral, his characteristic vitriol has recently become tempered with—"

"If you two are quite finished," McCoy grumbled, pretending to be more annoyed than he was. "I was about to say that I think the High Commissioner is a damn fine actress. Either that or she really is as cold as a witch's—"

Kirk and Spock exchanged glances.

"Predictably hyperbolic," Spock said.

"Yes," Kirk said thoughtfully. "But his assessment happens to coincide with mine. The lady is quite an iceberg."

Some kinds of stress were easier to deal with than others. The Red Alert mentality of a genuine emergency left one no time to think. One *did,* and left the qualms and second thoughts, the trembling hands and collywobbles, for later when things calmed down. Their present assignment, ferrying a delegation of VIPs on what was probably a fool's errand and keeping them entertained in transit, with Scotty "recuperated" and back on board but Sulu still unaccounted for, left one little to do *but* think. And get the collywobbles. Kirk had been off his feed since they'd picked up the last contingent on Delta IV; McCoy and Spock were sparring just to take his mind off it.

The relatives of the kidnapped Warrantors, led by Jasmine alFaisal, had taken it upon themselves to initiate contact with the Romulan Praetor. While the Federation Council, having already refused to negotiate with the Rihannsu on their own terms, could not officially sanction such activity, it also could not permit so many important government officials to go sailing off on their own. The *Enterprise* had been pressed into service to escort the delegation to and from its meeting with the Praetor's representative, and to provide the necessary show of force to prevent any misunderstandings on the part of the Rihannsu or their allies.

Enterprise's sudden "rehabilitation" would throw the Rihannsu a curve, and Uhura could still continue her misinformation blitz ("throwing tinfoil in the radar," she'd called it; only Kirk, student of old Earth wars, got the joke). Still, command under such circumstances would give anyone the collywobbles.

"If I understand your metaphor completely, Admiral, might I suggest that an iceberg presents less than one-sixth of its surface to the casual observer?" Spock said quietly as the three wended their way to yet another evening reception, the last before their arrival at the highly classified neutral world where the Praetor's representative was to meet with them.

"Meaning you think there really is a woman under that stone facade?" Kirk asked.

"Meaning she is here in a personal capacity, not an official one; therefore she is far more concerned about her daughter's welfare than her 'public' demeanor might indicate," Spock, who knew all about stone facades, observed.

"Since when did you become an expert on the human psyche, Spock?" McCoy demanded, still groping for a comeback to the accusation of hyperbole. "Next, you'll be hanging out a shingle."

"Doctor, I submit that twenty-eight-point-seven-three years of continuous exposure to the species has provided me with at least a working knowledge—"

"Gentlemen!" Kirk said testily, and they ground to a halt. "Laying it on a bit thick, aren't we?"

When they both looked properly contrite, he continued.

"What I want to know is why there was no representative from Vulcan. Spock?"

"Vulcan abides by the official Federation position, Admiral. As a consequence no representative was sent."

"But the Vulcan Warrantor must have someone to speak for her, in an unofficial capacity at least. Who's her relative on the Council?"

"T'Shael of Vulcan has no living relatives. She is a volunteer Warrantor, in place of one whose services are required elsewhere. It is a not uncommon practice."

"And typically Vulcan," Kirk mused. "Do you know whose Warrantor she is, though?"

"Indeed," Spock said, stepping aside to permit the Admiral to enter the reception first. "She is Warrantor for Vulcan's Ambassador-at-large, in the place of his only son."

It took a while for it to sink in. Kirk turned sharply to stare at Spock.

"She's Sarek's Warrantor—in your place?"

"Precisely."

"Then why the hell aren't you or Sarek going with the others?" Kirk demanded heatedly. "Certainly somebody should! Why didn't you tell me this before?"

"Because it was never my intention to meet with the Rihannsu, Admiral. Neither my government nor T'Shael herself would expect it. This meeting can only serve to exacerbate the Warrantors' captivity. Vulcan abides by the official Federation position, and so do I."

"And you said the Romulans wouldn't succeed in creating dissension among us!" McCoy butted in. "You've just contradicted yourself right there!"

"Doctor, I submit—"

"Bones—"

"Admiral Kirk!"

The voice was Jasmine alFaisal's, and while it was not loud, it was piercing enough to carry across a room filled with other voices. The High Commissioner herself was making her way toward them under full sail.

"We'll continue this discussion in my cabin, later, Mr. Spock," Kirk said shortly before the formidable personage descended upon them.

"As you wish, Admiral," Spock said, and even Kirk couldn't read the expression on his face.

Stone facades indeed.

"Starbase XI, this is *Enterprise;* come in, please. Personal Theta Z-36B, Uhura here. Tamerlane, are you still awake, honey?"

Static and the beginnings of a picture. Uhura sat back in her chair and waited for it to settle in.

"Tam here, *Enterprise*. Sitting up with a teething baby. How are you, Nyota?"

Mai-Ling Hong's husband and small son materialized on the screen. The baby was chewing his fist and fussing.

"I'm fine," Uhura responded sympathetically, watching the little face pucker unhappily. *"Qir'lal* root."

Static. Or a clumsy Rom intercept wave.

"—didn't get that last, Nyota. Say again?"

"Qir'lal root. Vulcan import shops carry it. Rub some on his gums and it'll take the sting out. Poor baby! How's Mai?"

They chatted for a while, Tam soothing the baby and the Rom wiretap making snow around the edges of the picture the entire time. If only their technology matched their rapacity, Uhura thought almost sadly. The baby eventually fell asleep, snuggled against his father's shoulder, one tiny fist clutching Tam's luxurious Tatar beard.

"So where're you guys headed now, or can't you talk about it?" Tam asked sociably.

The snow at the edges of the screen fluctuated nervously.

"Well, I really shouldn't," Uhura confided. "But Code 4's still safe, isn't it?" More fluctuations. "We're in charge of bringing the VIP's to their meeting with the Romulans."

She hoped the term "Romulans" singed their pointed ears.

"No kidding? Sounds halfway important. But boring."

Uhura laughed musically.

"Boring? I've had to have three new gowns made up. Formal receptions every night. I'm only on the bridge tonight because I begged off with a hangover. And there's this one delicious type attached to the Deltan delegation—"

She went on in some detail while Tam and the Rihannsu listened attentively.

"Some fun!" Tam said a little enviously. "Some of us get to party all night and the rest of us sit home with the baby. No justice in this man's universe."

He paused, and their eyes met despite distance and static. Here it comes, Uhura thought.

"Still, I bet it's dull without Hikaru around," Tam said. "You think he's happy since he's gone civilian?"

Between them they could almost hear the Rihannsu operatives scurrying through their files to find Sulu, Commander Hikaru, Retired.

"The money's certainly a whole lot better," Uhura said,

hoping Starfleet Command was getting this as well as the Rihannsu. "But I think he misses the excitement."

Ironic, she thought, considering any one of a thousand possible scenarios Sulu could be embroiled in at that very moment. She called upon all of her considerable acting talent and put on her best smile for Tam's sake, and to lull the Roms.

"Speaking of old friends, Tam. As in the type who go by the book? Has anyone heard from our mutual friend D'Artagnan? The Admiral's been asking for him."

She pictured the Rihannsu scrambling through their dossiers and wondered if any of them had ever read Dumas; they might actually enjoy it. Not that they'd appreciate the reference; they were nothing if not literal minded. Good! she thought. Keep them busy.

"Funny you should ask," Tam said deliberately. "Because a lot of people at this end have been asking too. But no, nothing. Not a word."

Damn! Uhura thought. Damn, damn, damn!

"But I'll keep an ear to the wind, as they say," Tam promised.

"Okay, honey," Uhura said cheerily, fighting to keep the smile in her voice. Oh, Hikaru, where *are* you? "I'd better go or the Admiral'll be on my tail for personal calls again. Give the baby a kiss for me. And don't forget the *qir'lal* root."

"Thanks, Nyota. I'll look into it."

"Enterprise out."

The Rihannsu decoding clerk glanced up from her linguanalyzer into the discontented eyes of her superior.

"We come to the conclusion that it is probably worthless, Centurion," she reported obsequiously. "Another meaningless social broadcast, just as the female aboard *Enterprise* stated."

"Show me," the Centurion said tersely. "Call up the suspect elements. I want to see them for myself."

The decoding clerk did not dare object. She punched up the transcript of the dialogue between Uhura and Tam, extracted the terms the linguanalzyer deemed worthy of study. The Centurion read aloud.

" '*Qir'lal*—a benign, edible-fruited thorned succulent indigenous to System Eridani, roots used for medicinal—'

"All very well," she snapped, interrupting herself. "Or perhaps an oblique reference to the Vulcan prisoner, *Ie?* Or to her representative among the delegation?"

"But, Centurion—"

"Silence! The question was rhetorical and did not require your opinion."

The decoding clerk subsided into silence and the Centurion read on.

" '*Guys*—a colloquial collective referent which may include female as well as male.' Well. Typical of this androcentric species. What else?

"The reference to Code 4 is probably innocent," she answered her own question. "We'll leave it at that."

Will we? the decoding clerk wondered. If it were me, that's the first thing I'd suspect. But since both the linguanalyzer and my Centurion concur, and I am *only* a decoding clerk—

"I surmise its naivete because of the direct mention of the former crewmember, this Hikaru Sulu," the Centurion explained off the clerk's skeptical look. "Surely they would not reveal his whereabouts so freely if they suspected we had broken their code."

"Surely not, Centurion."

"Well. The references to gowns and to the sexual prowess of Deltans are probably just what they seem, typical humanoid hedonism, but we'll double-check them anyway."

Yes, of course, the clerk thought. *We* will.

"And what, kindly tell me, is a 'hangover?' "

The decoding clerk explained. The Centurion snorted in disgust.

"Hedonism!" she repeated. "Orgies in deep space. *This* is how seriously they take their mission?"

The decoding clerk did not answer.

"And what is this expression about 'keeping an ear to the wind?' Well?"

The decoding clerk became suddenly animated.

"I researched that one most especially, Centurion. It is a colloquialism native to Earth, particularly to the geographic area whence the male at the starbase derives his origins—"

She stopped, hoping for a crumb of praise; that last item had required considerable work, and she was inordinately proud of it. But praise was not forthcoming.

"It is sometimes varied as 'an ear to the ground,' " she went on, resigned. "Referring back to a time when the race employed certain herbivarous quadrupeds as war machines and the sound of their hooves could be discerned by an enemy over some distance by means of—"

"Ie, Ie!" the Centurion barked impatiently. "Have you Vulcan blood? What *is* your point?"

The decoding clerk blushed green. She did not have to sit here and be insulted.

"Only that the reference to 'ears' might be a code word for us, Centurion," she said, recovering herself. "Considering humanoids' preoccupation with such superficialities and their own stunted aural appendages," she added hastily.

"Well!" the Centurion said after some thought. "But what does the reference mean? 'An ear to the wind.' Well, what?"

"I am still working on that, Centurion," the clerk said long-sufferingly.

"Well. Work, then." The Centurion stared at the linguanalyzer, dissatisfied. "D'Artagnan. D'Artagnan. The 'analyzer at least states it is a proper name. But whose? You are certain there is no such person in any of the personnel files?"

"Negative, Centurion. Not in Starfleet. Not in Special Section. Not among known civilian operatives."

"Well. Or not well. We will study it further." The Centurion was visited with a sudden fit of manic laughter which made her subordinate glance at her in alarm. "I like the importance they place on the delegation's meeting with 'the Romulans,' as they insist. If only they knew who we were sending!"

The decoding clerk looked up at her hopefully, waiting for an explanation; mere decoding clerks were not privy to Court gossip. But the Centurion did not deign to explain.

"Code this and send it back to Cryptoanalysis," the Centurion said, restored to her normal discontented self. "Let them run it through one more time. Well?"

"At once, Centurion," the decoding clerk said dispiritedly, anticipating another day's work at the least.

Defense Minister Lefv and the Foreign Minister were gossiping behind their hands in a safe corridor well beyond the Holy. Each had survived in the Praetor's party long enough to be spared intracranial listening devices.

"—the very fact that he is a eunuch should make it self-evident that he is nobody," Lefv was saying. "But of course one cannot expect humanoids to appreciate such subtleties."

"Obviously not," the Foreign Minister tittered. "But the Praetor's chamberlain, sent to speak to the delegates as His Representative! How too original!"

"The thought of them speaking their heartfelt pleas to him who draws His bath and picks up His soiled linen—oh, spare me!" Lefv giggled, then grew grave. "It's the only thought that's given Him any pleasure recently."

"Well, considering *that one*'s suicide—" The name of Dr'ell, once heir apparent, would never be spoken again. "—one *can* understand."

"That's nothing to do with it," Lefv said knowingly. "It is this: *He* is displeased with the disposition of this hostage business because the Consul is displeased, and *She* is displeased because the Emperor, All-Glory-to-His-Names, has condescended to acknowledge its existence and *He,* All-Glory-to-His-Names, is displeased. Therefore—"

"It is time," the Foreign Minister interrupted, indicating the wall chronometer. Such talk made him uneasy, and the Praetor expected them to be punctual.

They descended the aisle into the Holy to find the Praetor, in the foulest of humors, awaiting them. He had not even bothered with Unseen this time, but lay stretched out on his couch, his chamberlain massaging his temples.

"Leave us," the Praetor said, his voice reduced to a tired croak. "Oh, and—" he raised one long-nailed hand in a languid afterthought, "have her sent for at once. Direct shuttle from her flagship if necessary. If anyone can redeem us from this—detritus—it is she."

"At once, Excellency," the chamberlain said, but the

Praetor had already turned his attention to Lefv and the Foreign Minister.

Kirk almost wished he hadn't insisted Spock come to his quarters after the reception, which had seemed to go on forever. The Deltan delegation—there was an entire flock of them, all interrelated in some intricate consanguinity only a Deltan genealogist could fathom—had pestered him with endless questions which of course he couldn't answer, and Jasmine alFaisal had latched onto his arm with an aggressiveness even his celebrated charm couldn't deflect.

"You know more about this than you're telling me, don't you, Admiral?" she had asked pleasantly enough, a drink in one hand and fairly glittering with as much jewelry as she could comfortably carry around; there was something, too, about the High Commissioner's personality that glittered, eclipsing her jewelry when she wanted it to. "More than you're telling any of us. Military secrets? Espionage? How much am I allowed to pry out of you?"

"As much as you think you can, Commissioner," Kirk had replied, equally pleasantly, though this woman set his teeth on edge. "I'm certain someone in your position knows as much as I."

"And what makes you think they didn't clamp a security lid on the entire matter before they took the trouble to wake me and inform me that Cleante was missing?" she demanded.

Her voice was not entirely steady; the glittering armor seemed less bright than at first glance, possibly vulnerable in spots. Perhaps Spock's iceberg metaphor had been accurate.

"I used to think I had considerable influence," she went on, almost to herself.

She was staring vaguely past Kirk's shoulder, her drink forgotten, the reception forgotten, her stone facade all but forgotten, even her auditor forgotten except that she needed him to justify the sound of her own voice.

"I used to be confident that there were people I could call upon in a situation like this. Suddenly everywhere I turn I find a wall of silence." She blinked, looking at him. "And can we stop this 'Commissioner' nonsense, or must I really call you 'Admiral' for the rest of the evening?"

"Jim will do. If that's what you want—Jasmine."

"What I *want,* Jim, is to have my daughter returned to me—safe and whole and if at all possible untouched by these events. Somehow that seems to have been forgotten in all of this talk of 'hostage situations' and 'non-negotiable demands.' It's as if as public officials the beings in this room have somehow relinquished their rights to be parents."

"A very wise friend of mine once said that the purpose of diplomacy is to prolong a crisis," Kirk observed. "It's one thing to bandy the terminology about in the abstract. Something else when it involves a loved one."

Jasmine looked as if she might hit him, and Kirk wondered why he'd had to be so calculatedly cruel. Until he saw the armor drop completely.

"Cleante is everything I have!" Jasmine breathed. "If my entire career has meant nothing more than a threat to her life . . .

She did not finish. The hand that held the drink shook visibly; she put the glass down in a clinking of jewelry lest she shatter it. Kirk watched her regain her composure; it was a masterful performance.

"Odd," she said, avoiding his eyes. "I've never told her that. Perhaps that upsets me more than anything." She turned on him, intense. "But if I have to get down on my knees before the Praetor's Representative in order to get her back, and on my terms—"

The improbability of such a scenario or her ability to pull it off strengthened her. When Kirk looked at her again the armor was locked into place, steelier and more glittering than ever.

And he hadn't been able to pry loose from her all evening. He'd spoken briefly to the Deltans, had had no chance at all to speak to Shras of Andor, though Spock had covered for him there.

Of the entire delegation, the Andorian was the most tragic figure, for he was going to the Rihannsu not to appeal for the return of a living Warrantor, but to plead for the remains of his eldest son. The ancient one's face and deceptively frail arms still bore the scars of the Andorian blood-mourning rite, and his once fierce eyes were sunken behind rivulets of gelid tears.

His soft voice was beyond anger, held only a great bewilderment. What had he done to anger his gods that they should seek such retribution? he asked again and again of anyone who would listen. No one could give him a satisfactory answer. He retired to his cabin ahead of all the others, to slash his flesh again with the razor-sharp *flabjellah* and renew his mourning.

Kirk had excused himself at 2400 hours for a tour of the bridge with no intention of returning to the reception. The delegates might be too keyed up to sleep, but he had a starship to run. He had just stepped out of the shower and was thinking of contacting Spock to tell him not to bother when the doorchime sounded.

"Come," Kirk said, knotting the sash of his robe loosely about his waist and running his hands through his still-damp hair.

"If you are fatigued we can pursue this another time," Spock suggested, still in uniform, still buttoned down and impeccable.

"You're not getting off the hook that easily," Jim Kirk grinned. "Sit. Where've you been?"

"Seeing our guests to their respective quarters," the Vulcan replied, seating himself and casually making a premeditated move in the perpetual chess game the two old friends kept going by their own particular rules. "And offering condolences to our old acquaintance Shras. These events rest heavily upon him."

"Mm," Kirk said thoughtfully. "Any way you look at it, it's an ugly situation. If the surviving Warrantors turned up on our doorsteps tomorrow, there are still repercussions that may not be resolved in our collective lifetimes. And the longer it goes on . . . do the Rihannsu actually think they can salvage anything at this late date?"

"Difficult to ascertain," was Spock's opinion. "Unless and until the Warrantors are recovered."

"Unless and until . . ." Kirk mused, remembering why he'd asked Spock to come here. "You knew about this—T'Shael—from the very beginning, didn't you? Why didn't you say something?"

"I did not have all the facts until quite recently, Jim. The privacy of volunteer Warrantors is considered sacrosanct.

Only through my access to Starfleet confidential files was I able to ascertain that T'Shael was in fact my particular Warrantor. My years among humans have taught me to manipulate Vulcan integrity to my own advantage."

Kirk made a move on the board and decided to do a little manipulating of his own.

"I don't see how you can not go with the others tomorrow," he said incisively. "I can't believe your conscience hasn't been eating at you all this time. Knowing an innocent party is being held prisoner, under who knows what duress, in your place. Spock, you can't just do nothing!"

The Vulcan contemplated a move, his face unreadable. He touched a piece tentatively, withdrew his hand.

"Jim, I cannot do otherwise. My government's position—"

"—is no different than Earth's or Andor's or Delta's. You'd be going not as a government representative, but as a private citizen—"

"—who is also a member of Starfleet. No, Jim. I cannot separate the two and neither will the Rihannsu. I am not at liberty to take an action which would admittedly relieve me of a considerable burden of Vulcan responsibility."

Such an admission was rare even between two as close as these. Kirk could read the distress in the solemn brown eyes.

"You could have shared your feelings with me at least," he suggested helplessly, wishing he hadn't broached the subject at all. "How's the saying go? 'A sorrow shared is half a sorrow?' "

"Perhaps that is true for humans," Spock said, completing his move at last. "The Vulcan does not burden others with his own concerns."

"What are friends for?" Kirk asked, making a reckless move he regretted the instant he let go of the piece. "I'm sorry I brought it up."

"I, too, have considered accompanying tomorrow's delegation, perhaps to take some overt action against the Rihannsu," Spock said out of nowhere and not completely casually. His eyes did not leave the chessboard. "However, there is far more at risk here than the lives of five innocent beings, and this restrains me. As I hope it restrains you also, Admiral. Checkmate."

Jim Kirk tried a weak smile. It was no use. Spock knew what was on his mind before he did sometimes. The two of them might have outfoxed the Rihannsu once before, stealing their cloaking device and living to tell about it, but this was not their operation, not directly. Scotty had done his share and come home, Sulu was still missing in action, and the stakes were just too high.

"You win," he conceded on all levels, setting up the board for another game. "Tell me about T'Shael. I knew Shras's son, and Jasmine told me all about Cleante. As for the Deltans, I can never tell them apart. But the Vulcan is an enigma. If it wouldn't be a breach of privacy—"

"She is by training a linguist," Spock began, making his opening move. "And a deeply private person. She is also offspring of extraordinary parents. Her father Salet was conceivably the greatest musician-composer of his day, and a particular hero of my youth. T'Pei her mother was at one time provost of the Science Academy, and chief scientist aboard the *Intrepid*."

"My God!" Kirk said, awed at the significance of that. "Small universe! How many Vulcans are there—about fourteen billion?"

"Fourteen billion, seven hundred fifteen million, three hundred eighty-four thousand, five hundred nine, according to the last census."

"And the odds against your life's crossing T'Shael's or either of her parents'—"

"—are astronomical. Nevertheless, all things are interrelated, Jim."

Jim Kirk was awed into silence for a long moment.

"I'm just thinking," he said at last. "If she accomplished nothing else in her entire lifetime, T'Shael has given us our friendship. And given you to Starfleet and the safeguarding of the galaxy at large."

"Jim, I hardly think—"

"No, let me finish. She's done these extraordinary things simply by being what she is, and offering her services. I'd like to think we could somehow be—instrumental—in seeing her, and the others, safe home again."

"As would I, Jim," Spock said solemnly.

*   *   *

Cleante was about to disturb T'Shael's meditation, but hesitated.

The Vulcan's trances had become deeper and deeper of late, and Cleante wondered at this. Was it only to escape the clamor of the Deltans that T'Shael withdrew so far, or were there other reasons?

The captives had tried everything to have Resh freed, but to no avail. They pleaded with the guards with what little Klingonaase they had; they were met with drawn weapons and stony silence. They began a hunger strike; Kalor threatened to kill Krn and they stopped. Finally, T'Shael went to the Klingon quarters to speak to Krazz. She found her way obstructed by Kalor.

"The Deltan merits no punishment," she stated. "One can only assume you have isolated him for another purpose."

"It's none of your business, sheep!" Kalor snarled at her. "Tend to your slop buckets and practice one of your celebrated Vulcan silences."

"I offer myself in Resh'da's place," T'Shael said, knowing it was futile.

"Your offer doesn't interest me!" Kalor sneered. "Your species thrives on solitude, just as it is death for the hairless ones. I will find out why."

"My species has other weaknesses which might suit your experimentation."

Kalor's hard face might have betrayed a momentary surprise. Again he was reminded of how well the Vulcan understood him, and how she threatened him. He drew very close to her, gently entwining his coarse fingers in her hair before yanking her head back hard.

"Don't be in such a hurry to die, Vulcan!" he hissed in her impassive face. "You'll get your chance!"

The link between Resh and his cousins was gradually deteriorating. Cleante did not want to force T'Shael to take up her link with the gentle one, but there was no choice. She touched the Vulcan's shoulder lightly.

"T'Shael?"

It took some moments for the Vulcan to surface from the depths of her meditations. She did not need to ask Cleante what she wanted. She had been preparing for this. She rose

147

from her meditative posture and went to stand by the wall nearest the storage shed where the Deltans huddled disconsolately. She looked at Cleante for a long moment.

"If I am successful in taking up the link, there will be a certain—overlapping of personalities. For a time Resh and I will be as one. Words may be spoken, matters revealed of great intimacy to each of us. It is important that you understand this."

"If you want, I won't listen," Cleante offered, ready to shut her ears, ready to do anything that would save Resh without embarrassing her friend.

"It is imperative that you listen, that you witness," T'Shael said. "If I am unable to break the link, you must bring me back."

"All right," Cleante said, her heart pounding as she realized the weight of responsibility this entailed.

Krn and Jali scrambled aside as T'Shael drew nearer, splaying her delicate fingers and touching them to the cracked and gritty concrete. She closed her eyes and scarcely seemed to breathe.

"I am T'Shael," she began, whispered. "I-am-T'Shael. Resh'da Maprida'hn, I reach for thee. Reach to me, Resh'da. Your sisterfriend awaiting is."

There was a silence, T'Shael's breathing, nothing more. The Deltans and Cleante clung to each other, watching the solitary Vulcan. Even the ubiquitous guard, though he had no idea what was going on, stood filling the transparency, transfixed by what T'Shael was doing.

"I-am-T'Shael. I-am-T'Shael," she repeated patiently, doggedly. Her voice took on a lyric quality, became the voice of the gentle one. "I-am-Resh'da. I-am-Resh'da . . .

"Loneliness my fate and darkness, oh! I am wanting touch and touching. Touching minds is not enough. Touching am I or dying. My body-soul aching is for touch of gentle cousinfingers, oh! Pain of aloneness unbearable empty is . . .

"T'Shael Vulcan sisterfriend, oh! Wanting was I your passion awakening! She who all inside is, burns with whitehot flame when opening! T'Shael-love, your mind and mine reaching, oh! Grateful am I, but it is not enough. And you a special burning soon, oh! . . .

"I fading am, my cousin-loves, without your touch and touching. . . . All is darkness cold aloneness . . .

"Farewell, Jali'lar sisterlove! Farewell, Krnsandor more-than-cousin, gentling plaything and my sustenance! All our loved ones my warmth remember-bringing . . . Farewell, then, Resh'da, too much of aloneness, oh!"

The Resh-voice ended in a soft moan, and T'Shael was thrown away from the wall as if by an unseen hand. Cleante rushed to her, found her breathless and trembling.

"He has broken the link!" the Vulcan said, and there was pain in her eyes and in her voice. Cleante had never heard such pain, not even when they stood beside the bloodstone in the ruins at T'lingShar. She helped T'Shael to her feet. Pray Allah she could draw some of that pain away! "He fears pulling me down into his despair and so forces me away. Gentle Resh has chosen death. I can do no more."

If she heard Jali's wails or Krn's whimpering, T'Shael gave no sign. Profoundly distressed, she withdrew into herself, leaving the human to cope with the surviving Deltans. She had done all she could, and it was not enough.

And Kalor, who had told the guard to call him should anything untoward happen among the prisoners, stood at the transparency unnoticed, his teeth bared in a cold, feral smile.

It took Resh'da Maprida'hn, gentle Resh whose life was love, over a week to die. Then the guards came for Jali.

"Nooo!" she shrieked her ear-splitting shriek as they held her, twisting and moaning and clawing for Krn, whom Kalor wrenched from her grasp and threw against the far wall.

Krn scrambled to his feet unhurt, seeking T'Shael's eyes for a moment as if to draw some courage from her, then locked his eyes with Jali's. Jali shrieked again and again. She was pouring out negative pheromones at a prodigious rate, but the guards seemed to have built up an immunity. Her eyes faltered away from Krn's.

"Small one, I cannot!" she shrieked. "One cousin here and one on the otherside, I alone in neither place being. Such Aloneness I Can Not!"

It was over in an instant. One moment she was violently

alive, thrashing and shrieking. The next she inhaled sharply, withdrawing her life-forces as only a Deltan can. She went limp. Utterly lifeless. Even T'Shael could not block a reaction of sheer horror.

The guards released Jali as if such instant death could be contagious, and she crumpled to the floor. Kalor seemed momentarily stunned, robbed of his prey, though he recovered himself quickly. He took a step toward Krn as if to take him in Jali's place.

The little Deltan stood paralyzed with shock, staring at his fallen cousin. Both Cleante and T'Shael moved to stand between Kalor and the last remaining Deltan. But Kalor had a better idea.

"Leave this one," he ordered the guards. "We'll see how long it takes!"

They took away what was left of Jali'lar Kandowali to the place where awaited her brotherlove. She whose eyelashes could seduce a Klingon would flutter those lashes no more.

Small Krn died in his sleep in Cleante's arms. Even a direct mind-link with T'Shael could not save him.

"I am not fearing, T'Shael-friend," he said mournfully. "It is only that I am so sad!"

"Your cousins have each other," Cleante pleaded with him. "They're together where they are. Surely they can wait for you awhile yet! Who will stay with T'Shael and me if you die, Krnsandor?"

The small one put an arm around each of them and looked at both with a wisdom far surpassing his years.

"You two will have each other," he said knowingly. "There is a special word in Vulcan, T'Shael-friend. A word meaning more-than-friend. A *deep* word. Tell it me!"

"The word is *t'hy'la*, Friend Krn," T'Shael said without hesitation. Was this love, this emptiness at knowing the child would die? What a fool she had been to presume to scientific inquiry concerning such a phenomenon!

"*T'hy'la*," Cleante whispered, her Byzantine eyes sparkling with the tears she would not let Krn see. "What a beautiful word! Why didn't you ever teach it to me, T'Shael?"

"You did not ask," T'Shael said remotely, illogically. If

150

this was love—small wonder humans had expended such agonies over it down the centuries!

She had long since abandoned her reluctance to touch in the face of Krn's need. The small one was dying, and if it was of comfort to him to spend his last hours entwined about her or the human, what right had she to refuse?

"T'hy'la!" Krn sighed contentedly. "I am liking this word, for both of you. I will sleep now, Cleante-love."

Cleante held him tightly, as if her life as well depended on it. She had not slept for days, but lay awake listening to the small one's breathing, dreading the moment it would stop. When at last it did, it was so gradual and so still she barely noticed.

"You're certain there are no marks on the bodies, Kalor?"

"None to speak of, my Lord. A few minor lacerations on the eldest one's hands. Broken fingernails from clawing at the locked door. Nothing on the other two."

"Excellent!" Krazz initialled the report slate with a flourish. "So. Two reports. The official one, which our superiors will of course share with our pointed-eared allies—assuming they're still speaking, and that's anyone's guess—will read as follows:

" 'Disposition of the Hairless Ones:

" 'Subject One evidenced disruptive behavior and was separated from the others for purposes of crowd control. Despite the best of treatment, succumbed to unknown ailment which was probably the result of an innate weakness of the species since there were no physical symptoms. See attached report, etc., etc.

" 'Shortly thereafter, Subject Two committed suicide. See attached supplement. Subject Three succumbed to unknown ailment believed to be that which caused the death of Subject One. Etc., etc.' "

"In other words," Krazz concluded, looking at Kalor under his eyebrows. "They just died. Let the Roms play at dissection all they want with these three; it earned them nothing with the blue one. And there's nothing here either they or the Feds can pin on us. Let them both puzzle over it, eh, Kalor?"

"It should keep them guessing, my Lord."

Krazz was in a magnanimous mood. He poured the dregs of last night's liquor on the floor and kicked the bottle unceremoniously into a corner, pleased when it shattered. Give the ugly one something to do when she arrived with her scrub bucket. Krazz yawned, stretched, scratched his stomach and belched prodigiously, opened a fresh bottle and poured the first drink for his lieutenant.

"Now for the second report," he wheezed contentedly, smacking his lips over the first drink of the day. "The one we will encode and smuggle out directly to our own security people—the few who are not in Tolz Kenran's employ. I trust you have given it the full benefit of your analysis, Kalor?"

"My Lord may judge for himself," Kalor said, handing it to him with an absence of overt reaction that would have done a Vulcan proud.

He had found uncanny satisfaction in compiling this report, in the painstaking thoroughness with which he had documented each phase of the Deltans' deaths, the behavior of the human and the Vulcan. He was particularly intrigued by the Vulcan's telepathic intervention; the *tharavul* enslaved on Klin planets had their psi-centers excised, and he'd never had opportunity to observe their telepathy firsthand. The study had absorbed him more than anything else he could remember.

He watched his lord poring over the report. Krazz was a slow reader; he mouthed the words as he read, pausing from time to time to grunt or chuckle or pour himself another drink. When at last he had finished he grinned like a fat, malicious baby.

"Excellent, Kalor. Excellent! Every contingency covered. A step on the road to your own command, perhaps a military governorship. Who knows—perhaps they'll give you Delta once we've conquered it."

Krazz laughed at his own joke until he was in danger of toppling out of his chair. Kalor allowed himself a moment of stiff amusement, then grew serious. As far as he was concerned, his experiments had only begun.

"With my Lord's permission, there are the two remaining prisoners. I have been studying their responses to the deaths

152

of the hairless ones, but there are a number of further experiments—"

"Yes, there are, aren't there?" Krazz grunted, an evil glint in his eye as he thought of Cleante without the Deltans and their strange chemicals to interfere. His pleasure was shortlived. He handed Kalor a freshly-decoded dispatch. "Unfortunately, they'll have to wait. It seems our Rihannsu allies are due to pay us a visit."

Eight

THE HUMAN WAS having another of her nightmares. She sat
bolt upright in her bunk as she often did now, eyes fixed on
some unseen horror in the enveloping darkness. Before the
scream left her throat the Vulcan—who scarcely slept at all
anymore—was beside her.

"T'Shael!" the human gasped as if she were suffocating.

"Here," the Vulcan said.

The human drew several deep shuddering breaths before
she could trust herself to speak.

"It was there again," she said at last. "The emptiness, the
falling. I was free-falling through endless space. It was cold
and I was alone and there was nothing to hold onto. No
stars, just nothingness. And then, then I heard Krn. He was
crying and I was trying to find him and I felt so empty. More
alone than ever." She stopped, wrapped her arms around
her knees, defenseless. "T'Shael, I don't know how much
more of this I can take. If it keeps up, I swear I'll go mad!"

"This would seem a normal human response to the events
of our recent past," T'Shael suggested. Consciously or not,
she began to stroke the human's tangled hair, which hadn't
been combed in months. With a sudden pragmatic purposefulness—though as a student of xenopsychology she would
not deny its therapeutic value—she began to rake her long
fingers through the tangles, unknotting them patiently strand

154

by strand where the matting was extensive. "It will perhaps lessen with the passage of time. I profess, however, that I do not understand this human fear of solitude. This almost metaphysical terror which—"

"Oh, T'Shael, I'm so exhausted! No philosophy tonight, please?"

"Forgive me," the Vulcan said, pursuing her task in silence.

The two surviving Warrantors were a sorry looking pair. Their hands were raw and roughened by the endless drudgework. It took two far longer to complete a task once undertaken by five. T'Shael, despite the events of their recent past, continued to clean for the Klingons, for a Vulcan will ever keep a pledge, regardless of to whom it was made. Their feet were callused by months without shoes, their frequently-washed uniforms stained and threadbare from the same harsh soap that coarsened their skin and turned their ragged unkempt hair to tangles in the human's case and a limp lustrelessness in the Vulcan's. The monotonous diet also took its toll. Cleante's lips were cracked and covered with cold sores; her gums bled. And T'Shael, though she did not speak of it, had forgotten what it was like to be warm.

"Oh, why don't they kill us and get it over with!" Cleante cried suddenly, pulling free of the Vulcan's ministrations, infuriated beyond reason.

She rushed at the transparency, pounding it with her fists and startling the dozing guard, who grinned at her stupidly.

"Damn you, Kalor! Why don't you kill us and get it over with?" she raged. "We know it's your doing! Krazz is too stupid to be as . . . as *evil* as you! You're a monster, Kalor! We don't want to live in the same universe as you! Why don't you finish the job you started?"

She was out of breath, powerless, beating her fists against the unyielding transparency. But the diplomat's daughter realized the futility of her actions, saw what a sad ridiculous figure she presented, turned away from the door and the staring guard, hugging herself and sobbing helplessly. She had half expected T'Shael to restrain her somewhere during this outburst and would have welcomed it. She was surprised and disappointed to find her unmoved and merely watching.

155

"I—can't—stand it anymore!' the human sobbed, collapsing on the bunk, folding in on herself. "I want it to end. I don't care how. Even death is better than this!"

T'Shael said nothing, but resumed her task as if there had been no outburst, no interruption. The guard grew bored with watching and resumed his dozing as she had known he would. What little privacy the captives could salvage had always been won by virtue of the guards' predictability.

The Vulcan's hands were deft and steady. Having untangled the last strand of the human's hair to her own satisfaction, she began to braid it into a number of neat intertwining plaits which somehow stayed braided without benefit of hairpins or other fastenings. The effect was aesthetically pleasing and seemed at last to have calmed the human; T'Shael wondered why she had not done this before.

"Do you truly wish death?" she asked when she thought Cleante was calm enough to answer. She heard Cleante sigh.

"Not really. Not in the sense that our Deltan friends chose it," she said. "I just get so—so *angry*. Don't you ever get angry, T'Shael?"

"Anger at injustice is natural to all intelligent species—" the Vulcan began.

"—but to give evidence of anger is not the Way of the Vulcan," Cleante finished for her, almost laughing. It reminded her of the old times, the getting-to-know-each-other times, the safe times, before all this. She grew serious. "Do I wish death? No. I have a little more courage than Jali—I think. Do you miss them, T'Shael?"

"Yes," the Vulcan admitted. No need to burden the human with the depth of her mourning. Nor with her knowledge of the extent of Kalor's intentions, of the odds against their survival.

"Do you think Kalor will try to kill us now?" Cleante asked, and the Vulcan's hands faltered against her susceptibility to well-placed questions.

"None can know the future," she said evasively.

Cleante turned to look at her as she completed the last braid.

"That's not good enough, T'Shael."

The Vulcan looked at her gravely.

"She who asks the question must be prepared to accept the answer."

"I see," the human said after a long moment. "T'Shael, have you ever been afraid?"

The question caught the Vulcan offguard, and she examined her soul carefully before she answered.

"Not for myself," she answered truthfully.

"But for someone else?"

The question was a direct invasion of her privacy. Salet, my father, T'Shael thought, overcome by an old memory. He whose soul was music, whose fate was chronic illness and an early death—

Stop! she commanded herself, and answered the human's question.

"Sometimes."

"If I were in danger—if you thought I might die—would you be afraid for me?"

"Need you ask that?"

The human took the Vulcan's hands between her own.

"How cold your hands are!" she marvelled. "Are you ill?"

"It is cold here," T'Shael said vaguely. She knew what the human would say next, and she could not—

"I wouldn't be afraid of anything, T'Shael, if I knew you were there to be strong for me. If you and I were *t'hy'la*."

Cleante felt the Vulcan flinch and tightened her grip on her hands so she would be constrained by politeness at least and not pull away.

"I understand what it means now, T'Shael," Cleante said intensely. "Remember when you said 'The concept of love is written large in Old Vulcan literature'? I went to the ancient sagas and read as much as I could. You know my Ancient's less than perfect even with computer-assist. It was a struggle, but I kept at it. And I kept coming across that word.

"*T'hy'la!* It sang! The texts around it cried out with beauty, and I had to know! I searched for it in every lexicon and couldn't find it. I thought it might be one of the Unspoken Words and asked my professors. I got that *chilling* Vulcan silence and the old dodge: 'The Vulcan understands.'

157

The other side of which, though your people are too polite to say so, is 'The outworlder need not know.'

"I didn't dare ask you; I didn't know how I'd react if you refused to tell me. So I put it out of my mind. Until Krn said it.

"T'Shael, I understand now! And if we're going to die at Kalor's hands it's going to be horrible, I know it! He'll think of everything he can to make us suffer, but I can accept that, T'Shael. Even torture. Even death. If only I knew you were there to be strong for me. Oh, T'Shael, *please!*"

She was on her knees on the floor and T'Shael, who of all the captives had ever been most successful at ignoring the guards, glanced quickly at this one and found him slumped against the transparency, mouth gaping, quite asleep. Were she human, she might have been relieved. She turned her gaze on Cleante and something wrenched inside her. The time grew closer. How could she explain?

"Cleante, please!" she whispered hoarsely, she who never asked anything of anyone. "Do not ask this of me now, I plead with you! I cannot—"

"T'Shael!" the human almost screamed, remembering the guard just in time. "The reasons you gave me back on Vulcan don't make any sense now! We may both die, T'Shael. No reason outweighs that!"

"The reasons I gave you on Vulcan are as nothing compared to the reason I cannot give you now!" T'Shael said.

"It is that I am one who cannot aspire to such friendship," T'Shael had said to Cleante on Vulcan during the safe times, the getting-to-know-each-other times. "I must remain alone, that is all." (The fact that I harbor the potential for terminal illness is not for you to know, my human companion.)

"I will be your friend, T'Shael," Cleante had said despite all deflections of her overtures. "Whether or not you choose to be mine."

And the Vulcan had continued the tuning of her *ka'athyra* while the human sat quietly and watched, the intensity of her emotion slowly dissipating, the soft sounds of the harp restoring the tranquility of the moonless Vulcan night.

"Your hands are never still," Cleante said at last with a kind of wonderment. "Play something for me?"

It was a request she had made often before, as often as T'Shael had asked her to sing some old Earth ballad or other. Neither was self-conscious about her gifts in the presence of the other. But this night the Vulcan had refused.

"No," she said, a word abrupt and uncommon to her, putting the *ka'athyra* back on its shelf with finality. "I must consider what you have asked of me. Perhaps tomorrow I will begin to show you something of what you wish to know."

T'Shael would say no more. Mystified, Cleante had walked back to her own flat through the silent streets of the settlement, watching the soft streetlights activated by her body readings lighting the way before her and extinguishing themselves in her wake in silent fanfare. She was too excited to sleep, wondering what new mysteries of the Vulcan, and of one Vulcan in particular, were about to be unfolded to her.

They were in a part of the city Cleante had never seen before. New architecture blended harmoniously with some quite old, all of it seeming to rise organically amid tranquil parks and airy meditation halls, broad softstone pedestrian streets, museums and art galleries, shops and libraries. It was typical of any Vulcan metropolis, with one significant difference. This part of the city of T'lingShar radiated music.

Countless small shops displayed row upon row of Vulcan and outworld instruments, sheet music and synthesizers; subdued notices announced a seemingly endless series of concerts and recitals in public theaters, gardens and private dwellings. There were odors of exotic woods and resins, a Vulcanly muted cacaphony of instruments being tested and tuned, stray arpeggios escaping from porticoes and open casements. The very windchimes, melodious throughout the city, were here refined to an exquisitely lyrical quality. Where elsewhere they might simply announce the hour, here they sang it.

Cleante was not aware that she was holding her breath, drinking everything in. She was aware that she was smiling, something she tried not to do in unfamiliar Vulcan situations. But none of the Vulcans they passed in the streets seemed to notice, nor to engage that particular non-noticing mode that so irritated the human under other circumstances. They were simply too absorbed in their work to concern themselves with the blatant emotionalism of one lowly outworlder.

A change had come over T'Shael as well. It could not be called excitement or anticipation, surely; there was no sudden spring to her long, easy stride, no lightness in the expression on the familiar somber face. But there was some intangible difference in her manner. It was as if she, melancholy pilgrim, were one with this place. As if here, as nowhere else, was where she belonged.

"You are of course aware that all of our world's manufacturing and heavy industry have for centuries been conducted in the asteriod belt which surrounds the mainland," T'Shael was saying. "Only that which neither despoils the environment nor disturbs the tranquility of our world is permitted onworld. Music crafting is one such exception."

With that she led Cleante down a narrow cul-de-sac and through a side door of one of the shops.

It was actually one huge, high-ceilinged room, with every available space utilized in some aspect of the manufacture of the *ka'athyra*. Cleante marveled as always at the purring silence of Vulcan machinery. What in a human workshop would be the racket of robots, clatter of hand tools, insistent hum of computers and noisy banter of human voices, were here reduced to a soft whirring, the gentle rasp of minute handplanes against raw wood, the occasional murmur of subdued Vulcan voices. There were computers here, incredibly complex ones, and robots for the rough work of cutting and shaping, but the final workmanship was the product of the expertise of deft and meticulous Vulcan hands.

Perhaps a dozen crafters, mostly female, from young adults to the very ancient, labored over individual instruments in various stages of completion. As T'Shael entered the workshop, though she made no sound and in no way drew attention to herself, all activity ceased, and the crafters looked to her in silent acknowledgment. The eldest, a whitehaired female bowed with age, whose gnarled hands seemed incapable of the delicate work they had that moment set aside, came to greet the newcomers.

"Peace and long life, child of the Gifted One," she said to T'Shael in a voice so soft Cleante could barely hear her, her ancient hand suddenly graceful as she raised it in greeting. Her dark eyes glittered with a special light.

"Live long and prosper, Crafter T'Sehn," T'Shael replied solemnly and with a suddenly augmented dignity such as the human had never seen about her usually retiring person. It was as if she were some offshoot of royalty returned to the family estate to visit her retainers, Cleante thought, banishing the thought in the same instant. Vulcans made no such class distinctions. All were equal in the All. And yet—"We have come to observe only. If the time is inconvenient—"

"To her whose father was Salet?" the ancient one asked incredulously. "Never, T'Shael-*kam*. As your father honored us with his presence, so you and your guest are ever welcome."

Unobtrusively and as if by some hidden signal, the others had returned to their work. T'Shael brought Cleante forward.

"This is Cleante alFaisal. She seeks to study our way." She glanced at Cleante to indicate her confidence that the human would do nothing to disgrace her. "This is T'Sehn, most gifted of the crafters of T'lingShar, as T'lingShar is most gifted in music of all the Vulcan. She alone was crafter to my father throughout his life, and crafter to the renowned Senor before him."

The ancient one neither shied from the praise nor took any glory from it. She had done with her life only that which it had been given to her to do. Her glittering eyes fixed on the Terran with quiet curiosity.

"I am honored, Crafter T'Sehn," Cleante the diplomat's daughter said formally.

"Our place is yours," T'Sehn replied, her ancient hands describing the all-encompassing gesture that was uniquely Vulcan and which Cleante had seen T'Shael make so often. "You are free to observe and question as you wish."

She then motioned the two to accompany her. With perhaps the slightest trace of pride she took an obviously quite new *ka'athyra* from its place beside her workbench and placed it reverently in T'Shael's hands.

"That the daughter of the Gifted One may be the first to try its worth," she said.

T'Shael sat at the crafter's bench without speaking, positioned the *ka'athyra,* activated the resonancer, and began to play.

Cleante listened. It was a fairly simple melody, if anything about Vulcan music could be considered simple, which she had heard T'Shael play before on her own *ka'athyra,* and she was struck by the difference in tone between the two instruments. T'Shael's *ka'athyra* had sounded pleasant enough in itself, but it paled beside the mellow richness of this instrument.

It was obvious that T'Shael appreciated the difference as well. She stilled the strings with her hand and rested the fragile curving neck of the instrument against her shoulder for a long, contemplative moment.

"It surpasses your best, venerable one," she said to T'Sehn, handing it back to her as if it were a living thing.

"As with all my craftings, it is yours if you desire it," the ancient one said, and this was not formality.

Again her ebony eyes sparkled with their strange light, which was almost a kind of affection. Cleante sensed a long and deep-running bond between these two and began to drift away, feigning absorption in the work transpiring around her that she might remove her intrusive human presence from the specialness of this encounter. She saw T'Shael refuse the proffered gift.

"The performer must be worthy of the instrument," she said quietly, rising from the workbench. "I am not my father."

For as long as the child T'Shael could remember the healers had come to the house.

"Your father's sickness knows no cure," one of them said not unkindly, taking her aside in her seventh year. She was an adult by Vulcan standards and considered capable of accepting such information with maturity. That the plain-faced somber child already knew her father's fate, that it had become part of the fabric of her being, was neither within the healer's knowledge nor his jurisdiction. "It will weaken him over a period of years and inevitably bring about his death."

"My gratitude for your aid, Healer," T'Shael answered carefully, bidding him farewell in her mother's stead—T'Pei the master scientist was attending an academic conference in the city of ShiKahr—in the visitors' foyer as was proper. The healer's skilled hand might have rested for a moment on the small dark head, though none witnessed it.

Salet's affliction was still called by its ancient designation *plak s'ran*, "the blood killing." Its medical specification was *leukokupricytosis*, a progressive disorder in which hemocyanic blood cells became deformed and lost color. These color-stripped cells massed in major blood vessels and blocked the flow of oxygen, causing edema in the lungs. Bone marrow deterioration made the replacement of new cells inadequate, and as deformed cells accumulated in joints and spinal fluid, the victim's initial shortness of breath and chronic fatigue were replaced by severe joint pain, debility, wasting and death.

L-Kc was genetically linked, but undetectable by the most sophisticated antigen scan. Offspring of its victims carried a 50 percent risk factor. Once contracted, the disease was always fatal.

In ancient times it had been considered a form of retribution for certain transgressions of decorum, notably overt emotionalism, whose rapid breathing and ensuing exhaustion mimicked the disease's symptoms. There were still those who could not deny some residual credence in this superstition.

The victim was not offered sympathy, for that was not the Way of the Vulcan. Nor were inquiries made as to his health, for such was a breach of privacy. The sight of the healers coming and going with the transfusions which sometimes offered a temporary reprieve was enough to inform the curious.

But Salet the Gifted One was a public figure, renowned not only on his home world but throughout the galaxy for his composition and performance on the *ka'athyra* and other instruments, though such notoriety did not carry the same weight on Vulcan as "fame" in human societies. To offer praise to the individual for innate gifts is illogical, though considerable honor attaches to one's *use* of such gifts. It is a fine distinction which few but the Vulcan understand. Though he was not a "celebrity" in the human sense of the word, Salet was known to many, as was his affliction.

"His life might be prolonged if he were to desist from

public performance," one of the healers said to T'Pei the musician's consort on another occasion, after a particularly harrowing night. "His auditors make excessive demands upon him, which he, as his duty, fulfills to the utmost. It drains him."

"What is the logic of a long life without purpose?" small T'Shael piped up, breaching two rules of etiquette—speaking unaddressed in the presence of her elders, one of whom was a guest in her parents' home, and interrupting a private conversation—in a single breath. "Is it not better to live a shorter life which is full of meaning?"

T'Pei her mother froze her with a glance. Whatever else might be said of T'Pei—that she was among the most brilliant scientists in her field, that she was efficient, logical, in short a model Vulcan—it could also be said that she was as cold as she was beautiful. Plainly her offspring drew no resemblance from the maternal side.

"Your rudeness is unaddressable," T'Pei said icily, her black eyes blazing. The child was old enough to know better! "You will go to your room and consider what atonement will expunge this disgrace to our household in the presence of a visitor!"

"I ask forgiveness," T'Shael said, addressing the healer and not her mother. As a further disobedience, she went not to her own chamber but to her father's sickroom, though not before her sharp ears heard a final exchange between her mother and the healer.

"It is not unlike the very words the Gifted One said to me," the healer said. "He knows his music kills him, yet his life is music. It is an irrefutable logic."

"The child is offspring of the father," T'Pei said distantly, and T'Shael knew it unwise to linger further.

She went to where her father lay pain-wracked and silent in the shuttered room, his lips drawn back from his perfect white teeth in a soundless grimace that was the only evidence of the agony his illness visited upon him. The extraordinarily gifted fingers which the night before had flown over the strings of the *ka'athyra* in the presence of thousands were now knotted with spasms into bundles of useless twigs. The cabinet tops were littered with transfusion paks and triox hypos; a gentle floral incense, which sometimes soothed the great musician, smoked softly in a brazier in one corner. The great musician himself, shivering silently and gasping for breath, was another bundle of twigs beneath a coverlet.

T'Shael said nothing. She took a cloth from a basin on the bedstand, wrung it out in cool scented water, touching it to her father's temples and wrists in turn. She took a flagon of mineral water from the wall servitor and poured some into a cup which she held to his lips; when the acute phase of the sickness was at its worst it was the only sustenance he could take. In a day or two, when the transfusions had taken their temporary effect, Salet would be up and about, hobbling a little on painful knees, but pretending he could block the pain, resume his work, his passion, his music. For now, only his fever-glazed eyes moved, and they fixed upon his small daughter with a more than Vulcan fondness.

"Your mother will be displeased," the musician managed to gasp. "She prefers you attend your studies."

"I have completed my studies," T'Shael said softly, knowing he could not bear sounds above a whisper. She longed to sit beside him on his pallet, but knew the shifting of her small weight would add to his pain. Instead, she knelt on the thick carpet beside the sickbed. "And as she who is my mother is always displeased with me, there is no new reason for concern."

Were her father not Vulcan, he might have smiled. As it was, he found himself better able to control the wracking pain in the presence of the small one. That she visited him with a different kind of pain—the knowledge that she too might one day succumb to his illness—he did not speak of.

"Let us consider now," he began with mock solemnity, unable to untwist his fingers enough to count upon them. "You have completed your academic studies. And have you practiced your music?"

"Yes, my father." T'Shael held out her hands, already long and beautiful, to show him the newformed scars where the heavy strings of the *ka'athyra* had cut into the flesh of her as-yet-unhardened fingertips. "And I have been to the crafters' shop in your absence. Crafter T'Sehn assures me

165

the new consignment progresses on time and to your specifications."

The musician was gratified. How quietly animated this
bright child was, before the events of her life began to
envelop her in ever deepening levels of silence! Salet felt
some of his elusive strength returning.

"And your meditations, child?" he chided gently. "Surely
you have not found the time to cross the path of Master
Stimm this day?"

"I have spent my required time with the Master, my
father, and have just now returned," T'Shael replied dutifully.

"Have you opportunity to eat or sleep with all of this
activity?" the musician wondered, teasing a little, as even a
Vulcan father was permitted with the flower of his bleak
existence.

"Not while you are ill, my father," T'Shael said with
fervor, and her eyes burned into his.

Salet was humbled by her intensity.

"Then we must remedy at least part of that, my child," he
said, and though it cost him considerable pain he extended
his arm to her, indicating that she was to lie beside him on
the pallet and rest her head upon his shoulder.

"I cannot, my father. My mother has instructed me to
remain in my room. I have committed a serious breach of
etiquette which—"

"I shall heal the rift between your mother and you," Salet
promised. His breath came shorter now; he could not block
the pain forever. "Your presence soothes me. Would you
deny me that measure of comfort?"

"Never, my father!" T'Shael cried, and lay beside him,
curling herself up as small as possible so as not to jar him.

She barely rested her head upon his shoulder, determined
to add no pressure to his inflamed joints, though it made her
neck ache to remain in so unnatural a position. But the
incense and her father's labored breathing, the safety of his
embrace lulled her, and soon she was asleep.

As her daughter had predicted, T'Pei was not pleased. She
stood in the doorway of her husband's sickroom, hands on

her hips, surveying the scene with cold lips pressed hard together.

"You indulge the child, husband," was all she said.

While the small one was deep in slumber, the musician would not sleep as long as his sickness raged. Nevertheless, the small burden resting on his thin shoulder was of comfort to him.

"Perhaps someone should, my wife," Salet gasped.

T'Pei turned on her heel and left them, father and daughter, to each other's companionship. Within the month, such casual intimacy would be forbidden them, forever.

Within the month, T'Shael was formally betrothed to the handsome, arrogant Stalek by standard prearrangement with his parents, and all her child's ways were put behind her. While she might tend her father in his sickness, she was henceforth forbidden to touch any male relative except in ritual circumstance.

On the day following the betrothal ceremony, T'Pei the master scientist departed as science officer on the maiden voyage of the first all-Vulcan Federation starship, whose name in Standard was *Intrepid*. As the best in her field, she had been recruited by Starfleet to oversee the operation of what at that time was the most sophisticated computer system aboard a starship. As a premiere scientist among a race of scientists, she understood the value of such a position, and accepted it with alacrity.

"Your plans have come to fruition, my wife," Salet said with some color to his voice on the morning of her departure.

He was at the synthesizer console in his studio, harmonizing certain arrangements he had composed in his head months ago but had lacked the strength to complete until now. Were this not Vulcan music, it could be called melancholy. Salet in his heart of hearts had dedicated it to his daughter, whose plain face he had been unable to watch as she dutifully went through the motions of yesterday's betrothal ceremony.

"Do you truly think this prideful boy a suitable match for our quiet one?"

"Two of such quietness would bore each other to death, husband," T'Pei said with a touch of impatience. Her shuttle departed in a matter of minutes; she had hoped this leave-taking would be brief. "That would be illogical. Stalek is of good family and has already been accepted into the Academy of Engineers. I know not what else you expect. Further, his people carry no trace of the sickness as far back as any reckoning." T'Pei let this sink in, not cruelly, but to emphasize that his affliction was stamped on his daughter's genes as well. "If she intends offspring, our quiet one may come to thank me for that."

Salet let the melodies die away and switched off the console that he might devote full attention to his wife. Today was one of his strong days; nevertheless, his breathing was labored.

"I sometimes question the logic of keeping to the old ways in everything," he mused. "One has only to consider a marriage such as ours to wonder at the betrothal of unconsenting children. We are so unlike, my wife."

"And what would you have preferred? Another quivering aesthete like yourself? With all respect for your gifts, husband, you did well to acquire a pragmatic mate, or if nothing else, you would have starved to death." T'Pei drew on her travel cloak to signal her departure. "You spend too much time among outworlders. It has made you unorthodox."

Salet gave no answer. That his musicianship had led him to study many cultures and to make the acquaintance of many from other worlds was not, to him, a disadvantage. But to T'Pei, the Vulcan was the only way, and her spouse lacked the stamina to debate her on this occasion. He only looked at her steadily, unblinkingly, his eyes burning a little, not unlike his daughter's.

"Give my farewells to the quiet one when she returns from school," T'Pei said, drawing up the hood of her cloak. "No doubt you two will create better harmonies in my absence."

She held out the first two fingers of her right hand, and Salet crossed them with his own. They would not see each other for five years, and in that amount of time Salet could well be dead. The thought seemed to trouble neither of them.

*　*　*

"What you're trying to say is that you can't be friend to anyone because someday you might get your father's sickness?" Cleante asked when at long last she and T'Shael left the crafters' shop.

She could not believe it was already nightfall; the time had simply flown. It had been an incredible day, though tomorrow promised to rival it in incredibility, for tomorrow she, an outworlder, had been invited to attend one of the most sacred of Vulcan ceremonies.

But that was tomorrow. Right now she must concentrate on getting a straight answer from her stoic companion.

"You don't want to become too attached to anyone, or have anyone mourn you—is that it? T'Shael, that's not only absurd, it's illogical!"

"It is one reason," was all T'Shael said.

She could not be drawn out further no matter how Cleante challenged her, and finally the human gave up, thinking instead of everything she had learned this day, and of everything she was to experience on the morrow.

"The reasons you gave me back on Vulcan don't make any sense now!" Cleante cried, on her knees at T'Shael's feet on the floor of the Klingon cage. "We may both die, T'Shael. No reason outweighs that!"

The first of the ugly red suns peered over the horizon, slowly burning away the turgid morning mists. Another dreary day was beginning; for all either captive knew, it could be their last. Oh, why couldn't T'Shael do what she asked? Cleante wondered. For both of them!

"The reasons I gave you on Vulcan are as nothing compared to the reason I cannot give you now!" T'Shael said.

The *Enterprise* was on night cycle. Diurnals had dimmed, the helm and most other bridge stations were on automatic, the relief engineer had just reset her controls and gone to bed. The labs were empty; only an occasional monitor hummed or hissed or silently took its readings. In the herbarium, artificial moonlight shone on dormant leaves and tightly furled blossoms, the recorded sounds of night birds echoed distantly, and butterflies slumbered on the undersides of branches, their wings folded serenely.

The corridors were quiet and all but deserted. Most ship's personnel, except for the insomniacs and the innately nocturnal, were asleep or recreating or doing whatever it was humanoids did when their time was their own. An occasional fragment of music or laughter or more intimate sound drifted out of the Rec Dec and some of the cabins. All was well.

Quietest of all were the guest quarters. The delegation was returning to Earth after its abortive mission to the Praetor's Representative, and while none were guaranteed to be sleeping, all were quiet—whether brooding, praying, planning the next course of action or silently mourning. Here, all was not well, but it was quiet.

On the bridge, only Sciences and Communications were occupied. Spock worked silently, engrossed in calculations of some unspecified nature. Uhura was at her post, weary and resigned, not because she had to be, but because she could think of nothing better to do.

She had given up counting the days, had checked the relays to the special channel indicator a thousand times hoping to find a short that would explain its dogged unlit silence. She had stared at it so often and for so long she no longer saw it. That was why, when it finally did flicker and beep softly, she gave a little involuntary shriek and pounced on it, breaking several fingernails in her urgency.

Spock glanced up from his console to see her holding her breath, listening with her entire being.

". . . *Enterprise*, come in *Enterprise* . . . Gamma 7 Floater calling *Enterprise* . . . come in, please . . ."

The signal was faint, full of gaps and heavy with static, and the voice was not Sulu's. Uhura boosted and filtered as much as she could, prepared for the worst. She was unaware that Spock was watching her.

"*Enterprise* here," she said crisply; she'd been play-acting for the Rihannsu for so long it came naturally by now. "You're very faint, Gamma 7. Can you boost your gain? I can barely read you."

"Negative. This frequency too risky. Can't hold channel long. We have a priority data feed."

"Stand by."

Uhura flipped coders and decoders, scanned for Rihannsu

bugs, found none, put the whole thing on Code 5 Descramble.

"Go ahead, Gamma 7."

The floater's relays fed in a whole string of numbers and Uhura's pulse began to race. These were the trade route coordinates Sulu had promised just before they'd lost contact! It meant he was alive and still free to move about. Or had been, at least long enough to broadcast his findings to a floater.

The numbers stopped as abruptly as they'd begun.

"That is all, *Enterprise*. Indications possible followup later. Will reroute through Outpost 3 when received."

"Roger, Gamma 7, and many thanks. Can you verify source?"

"Negative. Data received irregular intervals, source unidentified. Can give you directional fix, however."

"Relay directional, please, Gamma 7," Uhura said, breathless. If Starfleet and Special Section knew Sulu's whereabouts, they could—

"Confirmed vicinity ch'Havran, Rihan Empire," the Gamma 7 operative reported. Good Lord, Uhura thought. That's Remus, right in the heart of the Empire. If Sulu can't get out on his own steam, they'll never be able to retrieve him. A violent burst of static made her clutch at the transceiver and she almost lost her connection. *"Enterprise?* One thing more."

"Go ahead, Gamma 7."

"Source relays this message: There's a joker in the deck."

Hikaru, you devil! Uhura thought. *Now what is that supposed to mean?*

"Floater—say again, please."

"All we have. Quote: There's a joker in the deck, unquote. Moving out of range, *Enterprise*. Floater 7 out."

The frequency terminated with a snap, as if the floater had sensed a pickup about to be locked on and had parabolaed out of its grasp. They took their lives in their hands every time they broadcast, these floating communications stations. Uhura began to breathe normally for the first time and glanced over at Spock.

"You heard?"

"Indeed."

She raised Kirk on the intership.

"All right!" Kirk said as soon as he'd sent for them. His clothes looked thrown on and his hair was tousled from sleep, but he was wound up like an antique clockspring. "We know he's alive. He's passed us six Klin-Rom trade routes, any of which could have a stopover in some isolated spot where a group of valued prisoners might be sequestered, and according to the floater there may be more. Spock, can you run these through and pinpoint every planet of any size along these routes that might be a strong possibility?"

Spock handed him a computer tape without a word; he'd read the numbers off the comm con over Uhura's shoulder while she was getting Kirk out of bed, had them cross-referenced and analyzed before Kirk asked them to report to his cabin.

Kirk looked at his First Officer sheepishly. When would he learn?

"Thank you," he said quietly, slowing down just a little. He hefted the tape in his hand and looked at Uhura. "We can work with this. But the message about the joker—what in God's name does it mean? Could it be a code Hikaru had pre-arranged with Special Section?"

"I've already contacted Special Section, Admiral," Uhura said primly. "Expecting a comeback within two hours."

Kirk opened his mouth but nothing came out. Time was his command crew would at least have pretended to wait on his orders instead of anticipating them. Was he being paranoid? He looked at these two he cherished—the solemn one, the animated one—and recognized that they too felt helpless in the face of Sulu's galloping around the Rihannsu cosmos and Nogura's insistence that they stay put. Here at last they had a chance to help. Could he blame them for being over-eager?

"I don't know what you people need me for at all anymore," he said, with the air of a martyr. He got no sympathy.

* * *

As soon as Uhura got her answerback from Special Section, he found out exactly what he was needed for.

"You were right, Jim," Uhura reported, several hours later; it had taken Special Section that long to get through to her. She hadn't slept—none of the three had; if they were planetside it would have been just before dawn. "It *was* a code. The Rihannsu hierarchy as a deck of playing cards. Read Emperor for King, Consul for Queen, Praetor for Jack, and so forth."

"And the Praetor's Representative—" Kirk prompted hopefully.

"—was to have been designated Ace," Uhura answered.

"Then who's the Joker?"

Uhura took a deep breath.

"Ordinarily Special Section would have accepted the delegates' meeting with the Praetor's Representative on face value, especially since the Federation Council never gave it official sanction," she explained. "But when I gave them Sulu's message they ran a voiceprint on the individual purported to be the Praetor's Representative."

"And—"

"And for one thing, they determined that he's a eunuch—"

Kirk swallowed a laugh.

"That's a—titillating piece of gossip. But what good does it do us?"

Uhura and Spock exchanged glances. It *was* a little subtle, unless one knew Rihannsu culture.

"By tradition, no Rihannsu who cannot mate and continue a clan line is permitted a political career," Spock explained. "Castration is considered tantamount to execution in some instances. It is employed upon conquered political enemies. And upon Court servants, to eliminate their aspirations to power."

"So the man the delegation spoke to is a ringer," Kirk said.

Uhura nodded.

"Special Section got a positive ID on him from the voiceprint. He is identified as Garefv m'kh, and has no clan name. He serves as the Praetor's chamberlain, a glorified body servant."

"Those *bastards!*" Kirk exploded into the silence.
"Those calculating, arrogant—" He stopped, calmed himself. "I'll have to—break it to Jasmine."

The High Commissioner's rage was no less explosive than
Kirk's, and lasted considerably longer. But because she was
who and what she was, it also had some effect.

She received Kirk in her cabin after he'd ordered Spock
and Uhura to their respective beds and left a time-delayed
message on her intercom. He barely had time to shave
before she indicated she would like to speak with him.

Her face had been carefully made up to hide the ravages of
the past few months, or possibly only last night's sleepless-
ness; her jet black hair hung loosely about her shoulders,
and she wore an opulent blue-green dressing gown that
shimmered like peacock feathers. Kirk recognized Tiburon
pseudosilk, knew what it cost with shipping charges and the
import tax. Or perhaps diplomats waived such considerations. At any rate, if Jasmine had intended to impress him,
she had succeeded.

She offered him a cup of tea. He refused it, stood with his
hands clasped behind him just inside her sitting room while
she fussed with cream and sugar and the elegant argent tea
service she never traveled without.

"The key to always having to sleep in a strange bed is to
surround oneself with enough personal paraphernalia so that
one can pretend it is one's own," she said in an attempt at
lightness, holding the teacup delicately and looking at him
over the rim. "Your news is not critical, but it is certainly
unpleasant," she observed with a diplomat's instincts.

Kirk told her what they'd just learned.

"It's *indecent!*" she managed at last, after she'd paced
and ranted in several languages, flinging against the bulkheads whatever came into her hands (though only, Kirk
noted, unbreakable or easily replaceable items; the tea service in particular emerged unscathed). "To think that they
would make such a mockery of what we were seeking! I am
offended for Shras most of all, though by now none of us
knows if our children are living or dead. The *indecency!* Bad
enough the swine kept us waiting for nearly two weeks, then
sat there cordoned off in his specially designed chair with his

specially subdued lighting so that none of us ever got a clear look at him! Worse that he let us plead with him for days, then minced and demurred and said he couldn't help us! And now this is the worst of all! Oh, give me five minutes with the Praetor and I will leave him in similar condition to his chamberlain!"

"I don't doubt that for a minute," Kirk said, suppressing a smile, picturing it. "May I make a suggestion?"

Jasmine threw up her hands in despair.

"Why not?"

"This piece of information was obtained by one of our operatives in the very heart of the Empire. Unless he's since been caught—" Don't think about that! he told himself grimly, "—there's no way the Rihannsu can know we've blown the chamberlain's cover."

Jasmine weighed this, letting her diplomat's instincts have full play.

"Our confronting them with that could mean a serious loss of face," she said slowly. "And there's no greater advantage in dealing with the Rihannsu. They will *have* to begin real negotiations now in order to square it with their gods."

" 'ch'Khroi mrerlel'lu fv'chril,' " Kirk said, quoting the old proverb. John Gill had introduced his seminar on Romulan History with it back at the Academy. " 'All is permissible unless one is caught.' "

"Exactly!" Jasmine said, triumphant. She hesitated. "But we don't want to endanger your man on the inside."

"We're in the process of trying to get him out," Kirk explained. Come on, Hikaru, he thought. Cut the heroics and come home. Enough is enough! "At least hoping he has the good sense to know when to jump. And he's given us something else."

He explained to her, without going into specifics, about the trade route coordinates. Jasmine listened intently, seating herself for the first time since her tantrum.

"And if you succeed in determining the exact location—" she said slowly. "What are you suggesting? A commando raid?"

Kirk shrugged.

"Why not?"

"*No!*" she said adamantly, on her feet again. "This *must*

succeed at the bargaining table. There must be no further loss of life, no further deterioration in relations. I must talk to Shras and the others. How soon can your communications people get me through to the Federation Council's Special Session at this distance?"

Sub-commander Tal surveyed the dusty, grassless compound from the window of Krazz's quarters. The Rihannsu officer grimaced with distaste. He loathed Klingons; their predatory stench offended his aristocratic nostrils. Nevertheless, he was not in a position to question his Empire's choice of allies.

"You say the Deltans succumbed to an unknown ailment?" he asked Krazz over his shoulder, not taking his eyes away from the limited view afforded by the window, his cultured voice rife with suspicion. "Why did it not affect yourselves or the other prisoners?"

"How should I know?" Krazz growled. Tal turned on him sharply and the Klingon softened his tone. "Maybe it doesn't affect species with hair. I'm a warrior, not a nursemaid. It's all in the report."

"*Is* it?" Tal inquired incisively. He had read the report, ambiguous and Klingon illiterate though it had been. "*All* in the report?"

"Are you accusing me of deceit, *Ri-hann-su?*" Krazz demanded. "If so, spit it out! Stop stepping around it as if it were excrement. Don't make me forget we're allies!"

It is something I would gladly forget, Tal thought with silent rage.

"My Commander will also read your report," was what he said, giving no indication of the murderous fury he held inside. "And also conduct an inspection of the surviving Warrantors and of the conditions under which they are being held. But for now I will conduct a preliminary inspection. You will escort me to the prisoners at once."

Krazz muttered something unintelligible in an obscure dialect and bellowed for Kalor.

"My *subordinate* will escort you," Krazz managed between clenched teeth. His beady eyes fixed on Kalor, as if to warn him to watch his step. "Show *Sub*-commander Tal our—detainees."

"Immediately, my Lord!" Kalor said, saluting smartly.

Had Krazz been less preoccupied with keeping the Romulan in his place, he might have wondered at Kalor's promptness. A more astute commander would have known his lieutenant had been loitering just outside the door, absorbing every word. In Kalor's universe, opportunities were for seizing.

Nine

A STREAM OF murky red sunlight shot through the transparent door of the Klingon cage, illuminating the two captives in their sad tableau. Cleante continued to kneel at T'Shael's feet and would not be persuaded to rise.

"Perhaps—" the Vulcan began with difficulty, "—perhaps a brief mind-touch to allay your fears. I cannot offer more at this time, Cleante. Please try to understand!"

Cleante looked up at the somber face, the burning, troubled eyes. Something was terribly wrong, but what? What could be more wrong than their captivity, their helplessness at Kalor's hands? What was it that was so dreadful a Vulcan could not speak of it? Cleante got up at last and sat beside T'Shael on the bunk, still holding her hands. To her knowledge there was only one thing so shameful to Vulcans that they would not speak of it.

"T'Shael, when you had the link with Resh, he said something to you. He·said 'And you a special burning soon.' What did he mean?"

Even a Vulcan's restraint had its limits. T'Shael wrenched her hands free of the human's insistent grasp.

"Do you wish the mind-touch or not?" she asked, her voice gone hard.

"I'm sorry," Cleante said, avoiding the burning eyes. "Yes. Please."

The Vulcan might have sighed. She touched her fingertips together and gathered herself. Then she looked at Cleante incisively.

"Relax your body and compose your thoughts," she instructed. "Do not attempt to block your thoughts from me or to move them in any particular direction. Will you trust me?"

Cleante nodded.

"Then leave your thoughts open. And do not attempt to speak until the touch is completed."

The human nodded again and the Vulcan touched the fingers of her right hand to the reach-centers of her face. Cleante closed her eyes and heard the unspoken words in her mind.

"Control," the Vulcan's mind thought to hers. "What is, is. Beyond our ability to alter it. Fear is illogical. Fear heightens suffering, accentuates pain. Control conquers fear. Control transcends. Pain is fleeting, suffering temporary. They are as nothing in the All. Tranquility is strength, control—transcendence . . ."

The sensation was peculiar at first, like a knife blade so thin it entered unfelt, to probe, to search out and to excise the turbulence in the untried, never-before-reached human mind. Eye of the storm, Cleante thought, fixing on the image. She could almost feel her heart rate slowing. She would not be afraid of anything, if only—

I am here, the Vulcan thought to her, and the disciplined mind began to withdraw. Cleante bowed her head and sighed, beyond the reach of fear.

T'Shael, in a deeper part of her mind than she had allowed the human to know, wondered by what right she spoke of control, in view of what was soon to become of her.

That was when an unfamiliar double shadow cast itself across the red glaring light from the transparency, the shadow of a single being doubled by the twin suns. The shadow shoved the snoring Klingon guard aside with its superior strength, the ugly red suns just over his shoulder sharply silhouetting his clearly Rihannsu profile.

* * *

Sub-commander Tal stood framed in the transparency absolutely livid. Krazz had refused him authorization to enter the cell. He rounded on Kalor in disbelief, the incongruously old and knowing eyes in his still youthful face flashing dangerously.

"This is an outrage!" he stormed. "These are not criminals or slaves you intern here but valuable Federation detainees, political prisoners of the highest order! More is hanging in the balance than you realize. This is not one of your slave planets! You have caged them like animals!"

"It's wasteful to hold prisoners unused. We either train them for service or we kill them," Kalor said, his voice devoid of inflection. That he personally would reserve Cleante for the harems and T'Shael for the experimentation labs he did not mention.

He also gave the Rihannsu officer no rank designation, though technically Tal outranked him in either of their services. It was to Kalor's purpose to remain unimpressed by Rom status or Rom tantrums.

Tal's eyes narrowed to slits. Most Klingons were easy to read, simple brutes with one-track minds. This one baffled him. He stalked across the compound.

"There must be changes, and at once," he fumed. "These primitive living conditions will be altered. The prisoners' diets must be improved, medicines and nutritional supplements provided. And these uniforms, the lack of proper sanitation! Not to mention the total lack of diversion, reading material, simple amenities. These conditions are appalling!"

Kalor shrugged, implying that if the Romulan thought these conditions primitive he had obviously never visited a slave planet.

"Before our flagship leaves this place, such matters may well be taken out of inept Klingon hands!" Tal raged.

Kalor shrugged again as if it were all one to him, and followed at a discreet distance as Tal stalked into Krazz's quarters unannounced.

"I will interview the prisoners," he said imperiously.

"*Will* you?" Krazz snarled, his heavy eyebrows lowering. "Not while I command!"

It was an impasse. Tal forcibly reminded himself that these

bipedal beasts were his Empire's allies; he also reminded himself that while he was outnumbered here, it was his Empire's flagship that orbited above.

"That may be altered sooner than you think," was his retort as he signalled the flagship to beam him aboard.

He went directly from the transporter chamber to his commander's quarters to make his report. The Commander heard him out without comment until he got to the actual disposition of the prisoners.

"The two surviving females appear to be in reasonable health, Commander, the Terran of course being more susceptible to minor ailments than the Vulcan—" Tal heard the Commander's sharp intake of breath and knew she would finally rotate her overstuffed chair to face him.

"A Vulcan!" she hissed, and Tal saw the old familiar turmoil, the cold anger warring with unquenched passion, on her strongly beautiful face. "A female?"

"Yes, Commander," Tal said evenly, watching her face relax.

"Well, it could be worse," she said, shaking her soft and burnished hair off her shoulders with an impatient gesture. She swung the big chair idly, smiling for the first time. "We're very formal today, aren't we, Tal? 'Commander'?"

"This *is* an official briefing, is it not, Commander?" Tal asked a little archly. "Further, I cannot remove the Klingons from my mind. They infuriate me! They're so bestial. I find them offensive under any circumstances, but this arrogant indifference to our purposes—"

The Commander allowed herself a laugh then, a rich, breathy sound that ended as abruptly as it had begun.

"You're such an aristocrat, Tal. I've always liked that about you." She came around the desk and put her arms about his waist. "Have a drink with me? We'll wash the taste of Klingons out of your mouth."

"Perhaps later," Tal said, softening a little.

She could still captivate him after all this time. He had passed up endless preferments, a command of his own, to remain with her. To remain in her shadow, actually, since she would always exceed him in command ability. It was one of many complex reasons why she had been able to regain her flagship after the debacle with the Federation spies and the cloaking device. Unless he extricated himself from her orbit he would live and die a sub-commander.

Nor was hers the only shadow across Tal's life. There were the myriad small shadows of her many casual lovers, but he was not disturbed by them. They were by definition temporary, and none could prevent her from returning to him as she always did. But there was one other shadow, perhaps the longest of all, most difficult to dispel, the shadow of a Vulcan who had presumed to touch her heart. To the best of Tal's knowledge no one else, not even he, had succeeded in doing that.

He stroked her soft and burnished hair, a slight smile playing across his aristocratic lips. He marveled that there wasn't so much as a single strand of gray in her hair. His had started to gray when he was still quite young; it had always made him seem older than he was. She had always found it appealing. Even now, her small fingers twined about one of the curls at his temple. Tal felt her sigh as she broke the embrace.

"You're right, of course," she said. "Duty first."

Again she tossed the soft hair off her shoulders, galvanizing herself.

"If this Klingon requires a show of force—" Her voice was hard now, steely, the voice of a Rihannsu Fleet Commander. "Set the fore phasers for tight range and lock onto his quarters. We will see how he cares to deal with me!"

Changes were being made. Krazz growled and foamed and gnashed his teeth and turned colors, but even he would not defy a flagship's phasers aimed between his beady eyes. He acquiesced.

The Rihannsu ignored him.

Tal supervised the repair of walls damaged by groundquakes, the installation of private sanitary facilities complete with a sonic shower, the provision of luxurious Rihannsu toiletries. There was a food synthesizer programmed for Terran and Vulcan cuisine, a rich carpet for the cold floor, soft new civilian clothing to replace the drab uniforms, even a small library computer. The Rihannsu flagship had very little in the way of tapes security-cleared for Federation prisoners, but for two who had had no such diversion for over one hundred days this much was an extraordinary boon.

While Krazz sulked, Kalor supervised Tal's supervisions. He had orders not to let the Romulan out of his sight, and for once he did not chafe under his lord's paranoia. If Sub-commander Tal moved like a shadow, then Kalor was the shadow's shadow.

It was T'Shael who thanked the Rihannsu sub-commander. Cleante was strangely quiet in the presence of these newcomers, as if puzzling out what their arrival could mean. T'Shael also presumed to make two requests.

"If it is permitted," she addressed Tal in her careful manner. "There are perhaps additional computer tapes to which we might have access. These are so few."

Politics aside, Tal had no particular loathing for Vulcans, and he had noted this one's quiet dignity from the first.

"These are all we have in your Standard language," he said, not unkindly.

"I am a student of other tongues," T'Shael said in flawless High Rihan, and the aristocratic Tal was both startled and impressed. "Comparative study would be of great value."

"I shall mention this to my commander," Tal replied in the same tongue. He suspected she had more to say, but reverted to Standard to keep Kalor from fingering the weapons at his belt. The Klingon had begun to glare and shift his feet the instant he heard a language he did not recognize. "There is something else?"

"Our gratitude for your provision of additional clothing," T'Shael said, giving Cleante a warning look before she finished her thought. The soft Rihannsu-style garb lay neatly folded on one of the bunks; with the constant traffic of the repair crew neither prisoner had had opportunity to change. "But with all due respect, we prefer to retain our prisoners' garb."

Cleante opened her mouth to protest that she had not been consulted in this, but T'Shael's look silenced her. The exchange was not lost on Tal, who wondered at it.

"And why, may I ask?" He reverted again to High Rihan, ignoring Kalor, curious to see how much of this esoteric and difficult tongue the Vulcan knew. "Our Empire will continue to hold you until a satisfactory conclusion has been reached with your Federation. But you are not criminals and should not be treated as such. If the styles are not pleasing—"

T'Shael lowered her eyes slightly to indicate that this was of no significance.

"We are still prisoners," was her answer to Tal's question. "It is illogical to pretend otherwise."

"I see," Tal replied, not entirely pleased with the answer.

If the looks exchanged between human and Vulcan were not lost on Tal, neither were they lost on Kalor. He made a mental note for his xenopsychology file and continued his shadowing of the shadow.

"Would you invite Krazz's attention with such colorful and attractive garments?"

Cleante's Byzantine eyes stopped blazing. Of all the amenities the Rihannsu had brought with them, she had been most eager to discard the coarse, threadbare uniform for bright civilian clothing. Now she understood T'Shael's logic.

"I didn't think," she said, smiling a little now that her cold sores were healing. "Typical human hedonism, I guess. I'm sorry."

"Do not disparage your humanity," T'Shael said distantly. "It may be of more advantage than you know."

Tal watched his Commander rise from their couch as if in a dream. He lay back among the cushions in the same position in which they'd finished. Even in love she needed to assume the dominant position; Tal understood and made no objection. It pleased him that she occasionally consented to give herself to him, regardless of the terms she chose.

She had slipped into a diaphanous gown which served to enhance her ripe beauty, and Tal studied her through half closed eyes, trying to muster enough passion to pleasure her yet again. It was impossible. He was sated, exhausted, close to sleep. She, on the other hand, seemed to have acquired new energy from their encounter, as if she had taken his strength and added it to her own. Where moments ago she had floated aimlessly about the room, sipping at her drink from the corner of a square goblet and shaking her hair idly off her shoulders, now she quickened her pace, electrified.

"I've worked it out, Tal," she said, her voice sharper than it need be in the intimate half-dark. "The Klingons have given me an opening to pin this whole matter on them and save face for the Praetor yet again. Let us hope this time he appreciates it." She looked at her sub-commander, her sometime consort, who was drowsing. "Tal, pay attention!"

"Yes, *Commander,*" he said with sleepy irony. His aristocratic fingers hid a yawn. "Perhaps before this is over the Praetor will have overreached himself for the last time," he suggested, knowing that to voice this in public was high treason, but confident that here he was entitled to his opinion. "The Consul's displeasure is no secret. And the Federation's response to this stupid ploy with the chamberlain—The opposing factions had begun to close on him while we were making our departure. I half expected someone to stop us."

"The factions are still only factions," the Commander said, dismissing them. "None is strong enough to act alone, and they will never resolve their differences long enough to join forces. The Praetor will somehow manuever around the Consul and restore himself in the Emperor's favor as always, and perhaps it's just as well. At least we know what to expect from the Praetor. Let us be grateful he is still the Praetor."

"And we are still his pawns," Tal said, propping himself up among the cushions. "How I wish we were shut of this business!"

"As do I," she admitted, sitting beside him on the couch, letting her eyes and then her hands stray over his long-muscled body.

Like most males of his caste he had an old fencing scar across one shoulder, a mark of honor, and her small fingers traced its familiar contours with uncharacteristic gentleness. There were newer scars across his chest and back where her nails had scored him in their love-play; whether these were marks of honor or not none could say. They would heal quickly, leaving no evidence of whatever other marks she might have left upon his soul.

"Tell me," she said now, conversational, stroking him. "Do *you* believe this nonsense about the Deltans?"

"Of course not!" Tal snapped, rousing himself from

among the cushions to throw a richly brocaded dressing gown—a gift from her—over his shoulders; her touch made him shiver sometimes. "Treacherous Klin butchers! They dispatched the Deltans as handily as if they'd done it with table knives. They were bored with looking at each other and sought diversion in torturing their zoo specimens. You know the sort of experiments they conduct on their slave planets! They'd have found a way to kill the other two as well, barring our arrival. They have no concept of the political implications, none! How can even Klingons be so abysmally stupid?"

"Regardless, both their superiors and ours accepted their version," she said.

"I take it the encounter with Tolz *epetai* Kenran was a distasteful one?" Tal suggested with some irony. "You have not spoken of it since your return."

The Commander, known for the usual restraint of her language (angry she might be and frequently was—enough to keep her crew constantly on the alert; the proper degree of unrelieved tension gave her the results she wanted—and as strident as she was angry, but she was never profane), uttered a single vicious curse, one of the most vile she could have chosen. Tal, surprised, had not even known she knew that one.

"If you don't wish to elaborate—" he tweaked her, risking her anger; he had always found it stimulating.

"Oh, 'elaborate!' " she mimicked him. "I shall elaborate. The Klingon may be half again my size and so much the louder, but he has lost this match and does not yet realize it!"

She had spun away alone in her personal scoutship the instant she'd finished reading Kalor's report on the Deltans, intent on bearding Tolz Kenran in his den, demanding to know what manner of handpicked incompetents he had selected for this assignment and what exactly he proposed to do about the indiscriminate destruction of sixty percent of their bargaining chips. To his credit, Lord Tolz did hear her out before attempting to bite her head off. To her credit, the Commander did not give him time to bare his back teeth.

"These things happen!" Tolz roared at her. Not an excuse, not an explanation, a statement of fact. "They happen!" he roared again for emphasis.

At least it sounded like roaring. The Commander, having never dealt with Tolz Kenran before, having guided her scout into his vessel's shuttlebay only moments before and marched in unannounced to see him, could not know that this was his normal decibel level. Nor had she been quite prepared for his appearance. He was possibly the ugliest thing on two legs—gnarled and knobbed, grizzled and rheumy-eyed and missing most of both hands; she'd seen her share of Klingons in the years since the Alliance, but it was all she could do to look at him.

He, on the other hand, did not look at her at all, but pontificated out of the side of his slack and slobbering mouth, his attention taken up by an audvid screen on which the Year Games were being broadcast. They were a rerun, especially for her benefit, the Commander was certain, of last year's match where the visiting Allied team, comprised mostly of Rihan, had been so badly beaten. Tolz had positioned the screen so that she could not look at him without having it always in the corner of her eye; he had the final freestyle battle sequence on ultra slo-mo and the screen was awash with green blood and falling, twitching bodies.

"My Lord—" the Commander began again. Her first tirade had dried her throat, and the sight of him casually sipping chilled fruit nectar when he had offered her nothing (not that fruit nectar would have helped her; she was in need of something far stronger) taxed her to the limit of her patience.

"Seems to *me*—" Tolz cut her off, riveted on the screen, gloating as the Rihan team took yet another casualty, "—seems to *me* it was *your* ones made the first kill. What's a few more after that?"

"That is not the issue here, my Lord!" she said sharply, trying at least to remain civil. Tolz had also insisted they speak only in 'aase and without translators. It was the only language he knew. Why bother learning those of other worlds which would someday be crushed by his own? Unfortunately, it was one she found more difficult than Terran Standard. "The one was accidental. The three were deliberate and calculated murder!"

"We are Klingons!" Tolz Kenran roared, and this time it was a roar. His clawlike prostheses gripped the arms of his chair and propelled him half out of it. "Not babysitters, not errand boys. Get that straight! I acquiesced to this because I was promised a substantial portion of the ransom! Now your ones have *khest* me out of that. So tell me why I'm still involved?"

"You *are* involved in this, my Lord—implicated, as we all are—in ways you cannot begin to understand!" she said loudly against his deafness and the roar from the audvid screen, facing him down, though she had to look up at him to do it. "The first one's death has been appeased, in ways it makes me ill to contemplate. But the deaths of the three will fall upon your head, unless—" She waited until he had resettled in his chair, fumbled for the audvid control with his mangled, fingerless hands, trying to shut her out again, "—unless we can find a . . . a scapegoat."

Tolz fumbled and cursed and dropped the audvid control, glowered at it where it lay just out of his reach on the carpet. Before he could summon a servitor to fetch it for him, the Commander stooped with a singularly graceful movement and retrieved it, holding it where he would have to reach toward her to get it.

"What the *khest* are you talking about?" he slobbered at her, slack-jawed and baleful. "A scapegoat? What?"

"I'm not gifted in your language, my Lord. Perhaps that's not the word I want." She held the audvid control out toward him, tantalizing. When he refused to reach for it she flicked the screen-off mechanism, deliberately. "But you take my point. Someone must be found to exonerate both our Empires and satisfy the Federation. As I understand Klin philosophy, he who dies for the honor of his Empire automatically earns a place in the Black Fleet."

"Rom breast-beating," Tolz mumbled. "Exoneration. Keep it to yourselves!"

"Your functionary on the planetoid, this Krazz," the Commander persisted, pretending she hadn't heard him. "Consider him forfeit. You may execute him yourself or permit me the honor. Or perhaps we will just leave him to the Federation."

"Never!" Tolz roared at her, snatching the control mechanism away from her at last.

Could she tell he was laughing at her, laughing at the universe for the tricks it played on one in one's old age? Hadn't eliminating Krazz been his object from the beginning, an old score to settle, part of a malodorous plot fermenting in his brain from the moment his superiors handed him the sealed orders to assist the Roms in this silly kidnapping caper? Could she tell he was laughing at her? Probably not. Roms had no sense of humor to begin with, and could never distinguish among Klin moods because all of them had teeth.

"Never!" he roared again, reactivating the audvid screen, addressing himself to it. "You will not dictate to the disposition of my officers, I don't care what your rank in your Empire. Go away!"

He signalled for a servitor to bring him another fruit nectar and shut the Commander out completely, chuckling evilly at some sadistic slapstick transpiring on the screen in a dialect she could not understand. The servitor, of unknown species and indeterminate gender, fluttered and squeaked about its nervous ministrations. The Commander waited for it to finish and scuttle out.

"He is forfeit," she repeated, loud enough to be heard above the mayhem on the screen. "Either that or it falls on you!"

"Hah!" Tolz *epetai* Kenran roared, though whether at her or at the screen the Commander couldn't tell.

"So. That's my story," she said to Tal, shaking the soft, burnished hair off her shoulders and pouring herself another drink. Now it was she who must wash the taste of Klingons out of *her* mouth. What must the crew think of their less-than-secret assignations, knowing that she and Tal were cross-caste and could never mate? Did she care? She came and sat beside him again, her small hands soothing him as before. "And what is yours? The care and feeding of our remaining prisoners. They are in good repair now? Healthy? Contented with their captivity?"

"Hardly 'contented,' " Tal answered, and it was he who

mimicked her this time. "But better off than they were. And safe from predators for the present."

"That's the best we can hope for, isn't it?" She studied his face carefully. "You're concerned about them, aren't you? Why?"

"It disturbs me when these things affect innocents," he said honestly. "They've done nothing. I don't see—"

"No one is an innocent, Tal," she said pointedly. Poor Tal, all aristocratic sensibilities! Would she ever succeed in hardening him to life's little realities? "No one. Accept that, or you'll never be more than what you are, Sub-commander."

"I know my place, *Commander*," Tal said coldly, and she drew back as if he'd slapped her.

"I see," she said, taking her hands away and wondering how he'd react to what she was about to say. "The entire abduction party was implicated in the Andorian's death, you know. Commander Delar and his guards were executed. Garroted."

Tal gripped her shoulders fiercely, forgetting himself.
"No!"

"You were close to him, weren't you?" she asked, not without sympathy.

"We were brought up in the same regimental unit, from boyhood," Tal said distantly, his hand going to the scar on his shoulder. "He was always my better; it was why he rose higher than I." He smiled bitterly. "Only to come of this!"

He leapt off the couch then, knotting the dressing gown about his waist and pacing restlessly.

"And why?" he demanded, rounding on her as if it were her fault. "Executed! For what reason? For the accidental death of a crazed and dangerous prisoner? And not so much as a choice of means, but garroted like a common criminal? *Why?*"

"For bungling the abduction," she said indifferently. "That is the official word handed down from the Praesidium. The dispatch that returned to the Federation with the Andorian's remains was worded somewhat differently."

Tal stopped his pacing. He no longer asked her how she knew such things. She was closer to the Praetor than either of them ever acknowledged aloud.

"That dispatch," the Commander went on, "was apolo-

getic in the extreme. The gist of it was that the abductors were a splinter faction acting in collaboration with the Klingons but without authorization from the Praesidium. Once that little untruth was let fly, the negotiations with the Federation were begun in earnest. They have just been informed of the Deltans' deaths. It is incumbent upon us to blame that on the Klingons. It would be the first intelligent step in this entire terrorist charade.

"As for the garroting. It's an accepted form of execution on Andor, I'm told. Appeasement, reparations, whatever one wishes to call it—little short of groveling, if you ask me. Now it is my task to somehow hold the two remaining prisoners safe from Klingon depredations, though without setting foot on the planetoid, until the Praesidium can find a way to relinquish them without further antagonizing the Klin and without further loss of face. Situations like this, Tal, make me embarrassed to be Rihannsu."

Tal looked at her in some alarm, and she laughed her breathy laugh.

"Come, Tal, if we can't be honest with each other . . . besides, I said as much to the Praetor the last time we—before we left the home port. It was why he gave me the task of somehow setting this mess to rights."

She rose from the couch too, slipping her small hands inside his dressing gown to embrace him.

"It is my final test. My last atonement for the loss of the cloaking device. Our Praetor has a long memory. This will be the final proof that I am worthy of my flagship and his trust. And perhaps, one day, higher things. Will you still be by my side on that day, I wonder, Tal?"

She saw that he was brooding, though whether over the death of his comrade Delar or over her constant references to the Praetor she could not tell. She stepped into the sonic shower, returned moments later to don her uniform.

"We're in a precarious position, Tal," she said at last. "We have several dimensions in which to operate. We have our official orders. I also have top-security discretionary orders for which I alone must take responsibility. And then we have the Klingons, whose orders frequently contradict ours, and whose perversities present an ever unpredictable variant. I shall be glad when this is over."

She glanced at her chronometer.

"Get some sleep before you go on watch," she said, making it an order. "I must find a way to relieve the universe of at least one Klingon."

Tal watched her go. He was tempted to ask permission to accompany her, but knew better. There were some things she must do alone.

The desolate planetoid revolving around its twin suns beneath her flagship was to solve the Rihannsu Commander's problem with Krazz, though it would rob her of the satisfaction of personally sending him to the Black Fleet. It had already chosen another destination for the short-tempered Klingon.

"What's going on?" the Commander demanded of the last of the repair crew, who had formed a hasty honor guard to greet her personal scoutship when it touched down in the dust of the barren plain just beyond the compound. She vaulted out of the scout, which had made a particularly rough landing, to find the ground beneath the hatch ramp she stood on rippling so violently it nearly knocked her off her feet.

"Groundquakes, Commander," one of the guard reported, saluting sharply as he too struggled to remain upright. "The planetoid's surface appears quite unstable. This is why our initial repairs were necessary. We have been experiencing intermittent tremors all morning, Commander!"

"Wonderful!" the Commander grimaced, steadying herself. The ground beneath her small craft shuddered into stillness at last and she stepped off the ramp with Rihannsu dignity. "Escort me to Lord Krazz. I will have words with him!"

The journey was unnecessary. Krazz was coming to her.

"I've had enough of Rom meddling!" he roared, storming out of his headquarters with the entire Klingon contingent at his heels and heading in her direction. "I have my orders, *Kahlesste kasse!* Put up with your comings and goings . . . interference . . . my prisoners . . . my orders . . . had enough!"

Half of what he said was lost in the distance between them

and the rumbling of the ground far off, but still he kept coming. The Commander waited, trying not to smile at the ludicrous figure, his short legs churning up a great cloud of yellow dust that half obscured and nearly choked him for all his roaring. Let him bellow, she thought haughtily. He won't have sufficient wind to spit by the time he gets here.

Krazz never reached his destination. The ground beneath him first rumbled as if in warning, then began to heave. Krazz's legs shot out from under him and he pitched forward onto his face. Kalor, only a step behind him, shortening his long stride to match his lord's, grabbed for him and also fell. Krazz shook him off with a murderous glare and got to his feet on his own power. Before Kalor could rise, a great fissure split the ground, and Krazz disappeared as if by sorcery.

He never had time to scream his terror or bellow his outrage. As quickly as it had opened, the ground buckled and groaned and slid shut again with a sickening grinding sound. Krazz was gone.

And with him, for he had fully intended to smuggle it out on the next supply ship whose commander he could trust and therefore kept it concealed at all times upon his person, was Kalor's report on the innate weaknesses of the Deltan species and how best to utilize them for purposes of conquest and the glory of the Empire.

Kalor gnashed his teeth and tore at his mane and slobbered in his rage, which the Rihannsu mistook for grief and wondered at. How else did a Klingon rise in the ranks except through the death of his commander?

Kalor eventually calmed himself, both because the Rihannsu were watching and because it finally dawned on him that Krazz's taking the report with him to his eternally unmarked grave could only be to his advantage. He could certainly piece the report back together again from memory, if he ever got off this miserable rock, and perhaps the arrival of the Roms would expedite that. Further, he could now explain that the Deltans' deaths had been Krazz's doing and that he, Kalor, had only been obeying orders.

"I'd like to believe you," the Rihannsu Commander said, sitting behind what had been Krazz's desk in the headquarters. Her repair crew was once again inspecting the buildings, which thanks to their previous work had sustained little damage this time. They would be leaving soon. She looked fixedly at Kalor, who stood in his customary place, at attention, but just barely. "Unfortunately for you, Klingon, I don't. Not entirely. There is a grain of truth in what you say, but no more. Unfortunately for me, I haven't the leisure to investigate more thoroughly. My flagship is too well known to Starfleet; it draws too much attention to linger too long near the border. Nor can I so much as leave one of my officers here to keep an eye on you. You are in charge here, for the present. But I will tell you one thing—"

She leaned forward, resting her elbows tentatively on the desk, half expecting to encounter some noisome Klingon slime there, but she did not. Only then did she notice how immaculately clean the room was. Some influence other than Klingon had been at work here. The Commander thought about the two prisoners, whom she still had not seen, much less spoken to. The sight of a Vulcan, even a female, after so long—

"If it were up to me," she said to Kalor, focusing herself on the matter at hand. "I would relieve you of command and intern you aboard my flagship until I could learn the truth of this sordid affair. At the very least I would assign some of my own hand-picked guard to keep an eye on you. Unfortunately, I am not at liberty to do that."

The fact being, she thought but did not say, that the Praetor wants to be certain there are no Rihannsu in evidence in the event that talks break down and the Federation comes seeking its orphans.

"So I must leave you here, alone. I'm taking your guards with me as surety in case your Empire becomes . . . recalcitrant. You needn't bother to object. I'm sure you can manage two unarmed females without recourse to guards."

"I was not going to object, Commander," Kalor said slowly, speaking for the first time. His eyes were a lizard's in his inscrutable face. "It is the Klingon's duty to obey."

The Commander looked at him contemptuously.

"Let me make one thing clear to you," she said, getting up and confronting him with the desk between them. "When I return, I will find two living, healthy, unmolested prisoners. Either that, or I will find one very dead Klingon. I promise his death will not be an easy or dignified one. Do you understand me?"

"Perfectly, Commander," Kalor said, his reptilian eyes glinting with grudging admiration.

"All that negotiating with the Romulan to get the extra tapes and you've scarcely looked at them!" Cleante teased T'Shael, trying to break her unblinking stare.

Both had weathered the quake unscathed despite the strange fact that T'Shael had given no warning this time, and Cleante had actually had to pull her to safety. Neither had yet been informed of Krazz's death; they were only prisoners after all.

The human had noticed the Vulcan staring at a single frame on the computer screen for an inordinate amount of time before abruptly switching it off. Now she sat staring vacantly into space—alarming behavior for one who was never idle. Cleante teased her to mask her own uneasiness.

"What are you doing, making the tapes last longer?"

There was no response.

"Or is it against your principles to admit you enjoy them?"

Still there was no response.

"T'Shael, for the love of Allah, what's wrong?"

The Vulcan's eyes, when at last she turned them toward the human, made Cleante pale. Where they had always burned with her internal fire, now they were unnaturally bright, febrile, all but incandescent. Cleante thought of the ever-deepening trances, of Resh's dying words in the link, of the coldness of T'Shael's hands and the seeming coldness of her heart in refusing her friendship, and began to understand.

"Your eyes are feverish," Cleante observed carefully. "You *are* ill!"

The Vulcan shied from her concerned touch, raising a warning hand that trembled uncontrollably.

"Yes!" she acknowledged at last, her voice strangely husky as if it, too, like the tremor in her hands, was beyond her ability to control. "It is a form of sickness. The time is past when I was to have returned to Vulcan. Now there is no recourse."

Cleante knew that whatever she said now must be phrased with the utmost care.

"T'Shael—it's not your father's sickness, is it?" she asked, knowing it was not.

"No." T'Shael bowed her head, her voice damping down some great reluctance, some powerful shame. "No, it is not."

Cleante said nothing. She crossed to the transparency, still unaccustomed to the absence of guards, and looked across the compound. It was what she had thought it was as far back as the link with Resh. Something to do with the immutability of Vulcan biology and their strangely illogical betrothal customs, some overpowering mating urge which, left unconsummated . . . There were so many questions she wanted to ask, but knew she could not.

"Maybe," she began after a small eternity. "Maybe now that the Romulans are here, maybe if we explained—"

She did not have to turn to know that the Vulcan's eyes burned into her.

"I'm sorry," the human said.

"It is too late for that," T'Shael said with a desperately Vulcan resignation. "*Kaiidth!* And it cannot be spoken of." She paused.

"Cleante, if I might presume to ask a thing of you . . ."

"Anything!" the human cried, and T'Shael faltered, awed at the trust that single word implied.

"It will be a sickness, and a madness, and a great shame. I will do things no sentient being should do, powerless to prevent myself. I ask your forgiveness in advance, for my behavior."

"T'Shael—"

"I beg of you, let me finish! While there is still time, while I still retain some measure of rationality. If you would assist me. Do whatever I ask, no matter how bizarre—"

"Anything!" the human said again.

Ten

"NOW THE WRISTS," T'Shael instructed once she had finished binding her ankles to the foot of the bunk with braided strips torn from an extra blanket. Cleante stood testing one with all of her feeble human strength; it seemed to her to be strong enough to hold anything. "Secure them to the support posts as tightly as you can."

The Vulcan lay with her arms outstretched above her head as if in supplication, wrists passive beside the support posts of the bunk to make it easy for the human to tie them there. Cleante clenched her fists at her temples and shook her head in despair.

"It's such an indignity," she whispered. "T'Shael, I can't!"

"If it were possible, I would lock myself away where I could not be seen and could not cause you harm," T'Shael explained, her voice strangely harsh and edged with impatience. "Soon I shall become a mad thing, beyond my ability to control. I do not wish to harm you! Cleante, please, there is not much time! And you have given me your word."

"Yes, I have, haven't I?" the human sighed, fumbling the makeshift cords around her companion's wrists with clumsy, reluctant fingers.

"Tighter!" the Vulcan commanded through clenched teeth.

Her body tensed suddenly in a kind of seizure and it was some moments before she could regain control. When at last she did her eyes accused the human.

"Spare me your human delicacy! Mastery of the Unavoidable, as I have endeavored to teach you! Pull the cords as tight as you can. I must not have opportunity to free myself!"

Cleante gritted her own teeth and wrenched the cords tight, forcing herself not to react as they cut into the flesh of T'Shael's wrists.

"Excellent," the Vulcan said, straining against the bonds and finding that they held. "Now the final one. Quickly!"

There was a single length of cord left, enough to loop around T'Shael's waist and the entire bunk, lashing her fast to it. Cleante coiled it nervously around her two hands.

"If you have another seizure you could strain yourself, damage something inside," she said. "You're secure enough this way. I won't do it!"

"There will be further seizures and far stronger. It makes no difference," T'Shael said, and Cleante began to realize exactly what she meant. "Cleante, please!"

The human did as she was instructed, tears running silently down her face and splashing onto the cords as she knotted them.

"Oh, T'Shael, *why?*"

"Because I am linked with Stalek." The Vulcan's voice was hollow and remote, as if she spoke from a great distance within herself. Her incandescent eyes were as far away. "If the male's need is not fulfilled, he must die. When the male dies, she who is linked with him, if her need is not fulfilled, also dies. As it was in the dawn of our days, as it will be for all tomorrows. This is our way."

Her eyes fixed on the human as if for the last time, and not a little fondly.

"One thing more?"

"Anything!" Cleante whispered, wiping the tears away with the heel of her hand, not thinking of what that word had required of her so far.

"Speak of this to no one, neither Klin nor Rihannsu. I

cannot ask you to conceal my condition, for it will soon become impossible; I ask only that you spare me its shame for a time. No Vulcan should be seen at this time, but there is no help for it. None can spare me what is to come; you alone can spare me its shame, for a time at least."

"I'll try!" Cleante sobbed, wanting to touch her, to offer some comfort, knowing any attempt would only make it worse. "T'Shael, I'll try!"

It was all anyone could ask. The Vulcan nodded without speaking, clamping her eyes and throwing her head back as another seizure took her.

"A betrothal ceremony!" Cleante had cried with a child's delight when she and T'Shael had stepped from the music crafters' shop into the warm velvet darkness of a Vulcan evening in the safe times, a small eternity ago. "I didn't think outworlders were permitted."

"You attend as my guest," T'Shael explained, implying that this was no small honor. "The honor is extended to me because of he who was my father."

"He must have been a wonderful person," Cleante said, thinking of the father she had never known.

Her invitation to the betrothal ceremony had been but the final event in a day filled with events.

"The performer must be worthy of the instrument," T'Shael had said, finishing the simple melody and handing the *ka'athyra* back to Crafter T'Sehn as if it were a living thing. "I am not my father."

That was when Cleante began to drift away, to remove her intrusive human presence from the specialness of the moment between these two. She backed up and almost stepped on a small, sleek animal that shot precipitously across her feet, hissing irritably. Cleante crouched to investigate and was amazed at what she found beneath one of the workbenches.

"It is indeed a Terran feline," said an even male voice. "Though having been born on Vulcan, it has a Vulcan name."

Cleante scrambled to her feet to encounter the most attractive Vulcan male she had ever seen. He seemed quite young, perhaps younger than she, though it was impossible to tell with Vulcans. He was slight and not very tall; his eyes were at a level with her eyebrows, and they were the color of amber and Vulcan serious. Cleante smiled; she could not help herself.

"I am called Sethan," he said. "The cat is called I-Letyah. Despite her birthplace, she is quite Terran. Quite given to emotion."

If he weren't Vulcan, Cleante might have thought he was joking. She could not take her eyes off him.

"She's beautiful," she said of the cat, whom Sethan had retrieved from under the workbench and was stroking gently. "Is she yours?"

"She belongs to this place," Sethan said, putting the cat down on a table, where she picked her way among tools and wood shavings with great delicacy. "Some years ago, Salet the Gifted One was presented with an Earth feline by a human, who also had the gift of music. I-Letyah is a descendant of that feline. You will see many in the street of the crafters. The Gifted One had a fondness for them. He said their dignity was worthy of a Vulcan."

You must have been a child when he died, Cleante thought. If you were even born. Yet you speak of him with such reverence. What an extraordinary being this Salet must have been!

"You're very friendly—for a Vulcan," she blurted out before she could stop herself. She did not apologize as she would have with T'Shael.

"I am accustomed to the ways of humans," Sethan said cryptically. "Would it please you to have a guide as you observe our work here? She who is my grandparent would desire it."

He indicated the ancient T'Sehn, who was still deep in communication with T'Shael.

"If you're not too busy," Cleante said, enjoying the moment. She held her breath, knowing exactly what the young Vulcan would say next.

"The Vulcan knows there is a time for everything," Sethan said by reflex, and Cleante tried not to laugh.

"The varieties of wood we use are several," Sethan

explained, beginning with the first step in the crafting of the *ka'athyra,* which was logical. "In ancient times only *shaforr* or Eridanian teak from the polar forests was used, its rarity making the *ka'athyra* a costly and highly valued creation possessed only by the most distinguished, and by the innately gifted such as Salet, who had such treasures bestowed upon them by virtue of their performance.

"As a result of our commerce with other worlds, of course, the crafters began to experiment with other kinds of wood, though the backboard is still fashioned almost exclusively of our precious *shaforr.* Salet the Gifted One introduced the use of Terran birchwood for the soundboard. It is the principal wood used in the crafting of your Earth's violin, if I am not mistaken."

"I wouldn't know," Cleante said dreamily, her inquisitive fingers caressing the silken grain of the unfinished teakwood as she savored its raw, heady fragrance. "Is that why your grandmother's instruments sound different from anyone else's?"

"It is one reason," Sethan said, his eyebrows expressing his surprise. "You are most perceptive—"

"—for a human," Cleante finished for him. How did one go about seducing a Vulcan? she wondered whimsically.

"I meant no offense," Sethan said gravely.

"None was taken," Cleante smiled at him. "I was only teasing."

"Indeed," was Sethan's reply as he led her to the computer complex in one corner of the shop.

"After the initial cutting of the components and after each crafter has completed the preliminary finishing, the sonic integrity of the soundboard is tested here," the young Vulcan explained, indicating any number of complex readouts which Cleante could not begin to interpret. "Each soundboard, having been cut from the living wood, has its own unique molecular structure which affects its vibrational potential. This may sometimes be compensated by altering the thickness of the backboard or the correlative positioning of the anterior chord-pegs, and it will ultimately determine the adjustment in disposition of the resonancer, which is the true mark of the crafters' art. The tensile quality of the strings, the purity of the lacquers used in finishing and the number of coatings of lacquer are of course other variables which . . . I am boring you."

Cleante was startled out of her reverie.

"No," she protested. "Not at all. I'm anything but bored; I'm—overwhelmed. It's so complex. And each of you crafts your own individual instrument from beginning to end, no piecework. I'm amazed at that kind of skill. And you seem so young!"

"I am twenty-one-point-sixteen Standard years," Sethan said without the usual Vulcan demur on matters of personal privacy. "And merely an apprentice. I have studied the crafters' art since my seventh year, but am not yet permitted to begin a *ka'athyra* of my own."

Cleante was not sure how she felt about that.

"Then what *is* your place in the scheme of things?" she asked him, wanting to listen to his voice, wanting of course to learn as much as she could about Vulcan music and its instruments, but wondering at the same time if Crafter T'Sehn or any other were her guide, would she be as interested?

For the first time in her nearly two years on Vulcan, Cleante realized how little she knew of the basic facts of life on this cryptic world. She had had glimpses of family life— staid, elegant couples walking with their one or at most two offspring in the museums and public gardens, conversing softly, side by side but never touching, the children if anything more solemn than their parents. Only the very smallest, infants under the age of two or so, behaved like human children—chattering and animated and endlessly inquisitive. Something indefinable happened to them after this age to transform them into miniatures of their parents.

If there were courting couples, Cleante had never seen them. She had never noted their absence until now. She had observed the deference paid to all elders, whether stranger or close relation, as if great age automatically incorporated the venerable into some vast extended family. She had seen an occasional sloe-eyed graceful female heavy with pregnancy, somehow rendered more graceful, more dignified in her fecundity. And was there anything more aesthetically pleasing than the sight of a Vulcan female with her newborn at the breast, unashamedly providing nourishment for her child wherever and whenever it was required, seated beside a hot spring or beneath a shade tree or walking the tranquil pedestrian ways, the child cradled in a soft sling over her shoulder and a look of perfect serenity on her genteel face?

But where did it begin? Why was there never any mention in Vulcan literature, or at least the literature Cleante had read, of courtship customs or marriage rites? How did Vulcans choose their mates?

One could hardly imagine them forming casual liaisons; the very concept of a love partner was incongruous. How then did they choose a life partner, someone with whom to procreate their lithe, delicate-eared, inquisitive offspring? Why was it never spoken of? One could only assume the choice to be grounded in logic. Some form of genetic selection, perhaps, in which the individual was computer matched with the eugenically optimum partner? Cleante shuddered to think of it. Perhaps that was why she had never asked.

How *did* Vulcans choose their mates? And could a Vulcan choose a human?

"Then what *is* your place in the scheme of things?" Cleante asked Sethan, wanting to hold his attention, to learn more about him.

"The computers are my responsibility," he said. "Also, it is the duty of the apprentice to keep the workplace clean and in order."

"Sweeping wood shavings can't be much of a challenge to someone as talented as you," Cleante said. "Someone who is of a crafters' family," she added, trying to put it in a Vulcan perspective instead of an egotistical human one.

"All here have done as much in their apprenticeship. There is no shame in such labor," Sethan observed with a touch of pride. "Further, I have one other task which supersedes all else."

Cleante bit her tongue and followed him to a part of the workshop she hadn't noticed before. It was a separate, soundproof room plentiful with tools and dusted with wood shavings like the main room, in the center of which, not quite completed, stood an obviously Terran keyboard instrument.

DWELLERS IN THE CRUCIBLE

The human studied it. An old-style manual piano? No, the shape was wrong, and amateur though she was Cleante noticed the double keyboard. She knew as much as the next person about contemporary Terran instruments, most of which were computertronic and practically played themselves, and as an archeology student she knew the really ancient ones. But this fell somewhere between. What was it, and what was it doing in a Vulcan crafters' shop?

"It is a harpsichord," Sethan answered her puzzled look. "This particular model being styled after those of your Earth's sixteenth century, Old Calendar."

"Of course," Cleante said, as if it had merely slipped her mind. She most especially did not want to appear human-ignorant in his presence.

"There is a common misconception that the *ka'athyra* is somehow akin to Terran stringed instruments such as your harp or violin," Sethan was explaining, familiarly caressing the harpsichord's flank as he had stroked the cat. "It is often referred to by those who do not understand as the 'Vulcan harp.' Because of its association with extemporaneous music it has even been compared to the guitar, a much inferior instrument. The outworlder does not understand that the Vulcan does not differentiate between 'classical' and 'popular' music. It is all music. And if the *ka'athyra* has Terran relatives, they are the sitar, and the harpsichord. The dynamic principles are the same."

"I see," Cleante said, though she did not. She peered inside the instrument, baffled by its complexity of strings and plectra. "And you're constructing this yourself?"

"It is my third," Sethan said, his voice devoid of any self-aggrandizement; the Vulcan does only that which it has been given to him to do. "Though it is only a simple eight-foot. The Gifted One was master of the sixteen-foot. I have not yet that gift."

"I see," Cleante said again, out of her depth. "You can build something like this from the ground up, but you're not permitted to construct your own *ka'athyra*."

"Of course not," Sethan said reasonably. "That is far more difficult."

Neither was aware of T'Shael's silent presence; she seemed to materialize suddenly before the near-finished harpsichord. Sethan stood to one side in deference, much concerned with her opinion.

"If I may—" the introverted one began, her long and elegant fingers poised over the keyboards.

"The honor would be mine," Sethan said formally.

T'Shael played a rapid series of arpeggios and nodded her approval.

"Your skills progress, Sethan. The Gifted One would be pleased.

"Sethan's maternal parent learned the crafting of the harpsichord from Salet," T'Shael explained for Cleante's benefit. "Sethan himself has studied the craft on Earth, among those few who still practice it."

"That's why you get along so well with humans," Cleante smiled at the young Vulcan, watching out of the corner of her eye to see how T'Shael would react.

"Terrans seem to prefer computer-linked instruments almost exclusively at present," T'Shael addressed Sethan as if the human had not spoken. "Strange that it is the Vulcan's duty to preserve the dying art form of another world."

"All honor to the Gifted One for his perception of this," Sethan said deferentially, and T'Shael lowered her eyes in acknowledgment.

Cleante found herself growing restless. She'd forgotten the Vulcan penchant for becoming absorbed in a single topic to the exclusion of all else.

"It is still preserved in its place of honor," she heard Sethan say and wondered what he could possibly be talking about. "Though she who is my grandparent would have it returned to the dwelling of the Gifted One, perhaps as the centerpiece of some manner of shrine."

"Such is the devotion of the venerable one," T'Shael acknowledged.

Cleante thought if this exchange of courtesies went on much longer she might scream.

"I should like to see it," she heard T'Shael say.

Sethan nodded and led them up a winding staircase to a kind of balcony just under the rafters of the high-ceilinged shop where, sheltered by a rich velvet-colored arras as if it were in fact part of a shrine, stood another, completed harpsichord.

This must have been Salet's, Cleante realized as Sethan reverently swept the arras aside. She had only to look at T'Shael's face to be certain.

The introverted one placed her long and elegant hand against the sounding board in the sign of the *ta'al*, communing with the instrument if not with its creator. Neither Cleante nor Sethan made a sound.

"My father is dying," T'Shael said to T'Pei her mother, rising from the couch where the healer had advised her to rest after her donation of blood for her father's transfusions. Her voice was edged with something heretofore unknown to her; a human would have called it anger.

T'Pei said nothing, but came and sat in her daughter's place, awaiting the healer who had hurried off to tend to Salet in this latest crisis of his disease.

"The healer's prognosis gives him less than eleven-point-two months of life at his present rate of deterioration," T'Shael continued. "Yet you who are his wife abandon him."

T'Pei had deigned to remain at her husband's side for slightly more than a year following *Intrepid's* first voyage, if only because *pon farr* made it necessary and because the starship was in drydock for refitting for that amount of time. The master scientist had resumed her position as provost of the Vulcan Science Academy in the interim, but both the starship and its science officer were due to depart on a second voyage within days. T'Pei had been offered personal leave to remain with her dying husband and had refused it. Her duty aboard *Intrepid,* as she saw it, was the greater good.

Now she sat erect on the couch, her cold black eyes impaling her adolescent offspring with the intensity of her disapproval. T'Shael returned the look without flinching.

"Neither my presence nor my absence will alter Salet's fate," the master scientist said in measured tones. "At least give the pretense of subscribing to logic, my erratic offspring! I have fulfilled my biological duty as wife, though little good it did the Gifted One in his present illness—"

T'Pei stopped herself; such intimate matters were not for her daughter's ears.

"It is at any rate none of your concern."

The healer arrived then to draw blood from T'Pei for additional transfusions, curtailing further conversation. The master scientist departed on *Intrepid's* final voyage, and the child of the Gifted One returned to the care of her father.

She could have consigned Salet to an infirmary where his care might have exceeded what she could provide, but she did not. He was Salet the Gifted One, and he must remain within the context of his creativity, of the crafters' shop, of the constant flow of distinguished visitors—musicians and composers and crafters and musicologists from his world and others—or what life remained to him would be devoid of meaning.

T'Shael was adept now at giving her father the medications and transfusions he required; it was no longer necessary for the healers to trouble themselves. She supervised the crafters' shop, that the name of Salet might continue to be attributed only to instruments of the highest quality.

She took care of her father's physical needs, feeding and bathing him when he could not manage for himself. She screened his visitors and made them welcome when he was strong enough to receive them. She transcribed his compositions when he was too weak to do so himself, and when he found sleep impossible she sat in the darkened sickroom amid the odor of incense and played softly on her *ka'athyra* that he might at least find peace in meditation. She was daughter, nurse, companion, hostess, housekeeper and secretary—all but wife, in all areas save one.

In addition she continued her studies, earning two graduate degrees in linguistics before her sixteenth year, continuing also her meditations with Master Stimm, though only because this pleased her father. Already she was visited with the hunger that was to culminate in her reaching out to Cleante—the hunger to know the ways of other beings, and to examine the Way of the Vulcan in light of that knowledge.

It was the reaction of a visitor to her father's wasting illness that first evoked the curiosity that was to become the hunger. The visitor was a Terran, a distinguished musicologist from the United States of Africa whose melodious voice and elegant mannerisms had intrigued T'Shael from childhood.

He had taken her aside when she was a small one, using her innate musical ear to teach her Ibo and several other tonal languages from his part of Earth whenever his travels took him to T'lingShar. It was he who had brought Salet the gift of the cat who was to become ancestor of Sethan's I-Letyah. He was the first human T'Shael had ever encountered, and he fascinated her.

The African came away from a visit with the Gifted One, knowing it would be his last, with tears coursing unashamedly down his dark face.

T'Shael had never seen tears before. Her first concern, powerful enough to make her presume upon the Terran's privacy, was that her father's honored friend had been taken ill.

"*T'Kahr* Anekwe?" she asked, addressing him with the Vulcan word which among other things meant "teacher," for such he had been to her. "Are you ill? What remedy can be offered for what afflicts you?"

"There is no remedy, child," the musician told her. "My affliction is known as sorrow. I look upon your father whom we all cherish and who is soon to be taken from us, and my heart overflows with grief."

T'Shael wondered at this. Vulcans understood that death is but a passage from one mode of life to another, and surely her father would be free of suffering in the mode he approached so nearly. Yet perhaps what the African described was akin to the aching hollowness she experienced but could not give voice to whenever she looked upon her father.

T'Shael experienced no such aching hollowness when T'Pei her mother died, when the starship *Intrepid* and the four hundred Vulcans aboard were consumed by a massive intergalactic virus. She awoke before dawn one morning to the far echoing sound of a harpsichord, and followed it to her father's studio.

Salet had been helpless to move for weeks; the healers, assuming his illness to be in its final stages, had shaken their heads and gone away. He had long since outlived the limits their knowledge of the disease had given him, clinging to life beyond all known medical parameters, none could determine how. He should not have been capable of dragging himself from his sickbed to his studio, much less of sitting upright at the keyboard or of engaging his mind for composition; nevertheless he had done so. T'Shael observed him from the doorway in a kind of awe.

He was the skeleton of a Vulcan, skin stretched taut over protruding, pain-wracked bones and rendered a mottled green where countless broken capillaries formed spidery traceries between skin and bone; there was no muscle tissue left to speak of. His concaved ribs heaved mightily with his efforts to draw breath; his noble face, plain and austere as his daughter's was and now so wasted, was thrown back in a kind of trance as his knotted fingers plied the double keyboard. But he was not so far removed that he could not sense the introverted one's presence.

"Your mother is dead," Salet said, and T'Shael did not question how he knew. She waited while he drew breath enough to finish. "She and—three hundred ninety-nine others. The scream of incomprehension, incredulity. Death was swift but somehow—unjust. Yet her life had meaning, while she lived it."

T'Shael examined her soul and found there was nothing there, not so much as ritual mourning. T'Pei, my mother, she thought. Living or dead, it does not signify to me except in that it affects he who is my father.

"My father," she began, seeing that he would return to the keyboard. Its ivory surfaces glistened virescently; his flesh was so deteriorated that the pressure of his fingers against the keys tore and ravaged it. Yet he played on. "You will overtax yourself."

"I have done so long since, my child," the Gifted One responded, his eyes burning, as hers did. "I shall find rest enough soon enough, T'Shael-*kam*. Permit me, while the gift is still mine to use."

It was the only farewell he could offer her; nothing further was permitted between father and daughter in the Way of the Vulcan. T'Shael moved away out of the room to the sharp, definitive sound of the harpsichord, ironic tribute to her mother, who scorned all things Terran, leaving her father to his mourning and his privacy, knowing that when she returned she would find him slumped over the keyboard, dead, knowing that unlike the musician Anekwe she did not own the luxury of tears. Nevertheless, she carried her mourning for her father in her heart, as she carried the potential for his sickness in her blood.

Having completed the cremation rite for the Gifted One and the memorial service for the master scientist *in absentia,* the introverted one relinquished claim to her parents' dwelling and all her inheritance and, in her sixteenth year, committed herself as Warrantor to the settlement at T'lingShar. If she had neither her father's gift nor her mother's brilliance, if she was an orphan in a society where family ties were strong, if she was precluded from attachments to others by the disease she carried and her own moral code, she could at least be of service.

"He's very handsome," Cleante said when they left the crafters' shop, ruminating over the day's events and wondering if she would have a chance to see Sethan again tomorrow at his cousin's betrothal ceremony.

"Your pardon?" T'Shael asked. She had been quieter than quiet since she had once again sheltered her father's harpsichord behind its arras with an air of finality.

"Sethan," Cleante explained breathlessly, trying to keep up with her companion's long stride, stumbling a little on the cobblestones in the dark. Only those parts of the city where outworlders predominated had streetlights; the Vulcan's acute night vision made them unnecessary elsewhere. "I think he's very handsome."

"Indeed," T'Shael said thoughtfully.

"Well, don't you think so?" Cleante demanded, sensing that the introverted one was in danger of introverting herself into extinction unless a little human teasing could prevent it. Why must Vulcans always be so serious? "Of course, he's probably too young for you, and you've known him all his life, but—"

"There is a certain aesthetic harmony to his person," T'Shael acknowledged, as if it had only now occurred to her. She studied the human's face in the darkness. "Doubtless, she who is his wife will come to appreciate this in time."

Cleante turned her ankle on the cobblestones, but the sharp pain went virtually unnoticed in her dismay.

"He's *married?* But he's so young. I wouldn't have thought—"

"He was betrothed in his seventh year. As T'Peli his cousin will be in tomorrow's ceremony. As all Vulcans are."

Cleante digested this. She suddenly had answers to all of her questions about Vulcan marital customs. Or did she?

"But how is it done? Who decides for a seven year old?"

"It is by parental arrangement," T'Shael said. "In ancient times it served to prevent wars and to strengthen ties between neighbors whose ancestral lands adjoined."

"But that's so unnecessary nowadays!" Cleante protested. "It's so—primitive!"

"It is our way," T'Shael said simply.

"But how can it possibly work? Who can tell what two children will be by the time they're adults? Suppose they're completely incompatible?"

"It does not signify," T'Shael countered, perhaps thinking of her own parents. "Personality conflict cannot exist in the absence of emotion."

Cleante wanted to argue that, wanted to argue with the entire concept, almost wanted, except for her overwhelming curiosity, to back out of tomorrow's ceremony. How could she enjoy it if she was too embarrassed to speak to Sethan?

A sobering thought made her stop walking. She had a stitch in her side and her ankle did hurt; she steadied herself against a garden wall, smelling the rich night fragrance of *kleshameen,* hearing the windchimes announcing the hour. She studied the Vulcan she had known for nearly two years and until a moment ago, had thought she knew quite well.

"T'Shael, is there—someone for you?" she asked carefully, knowing she risked being told in no uncertain terms to mind her own business. "Were you also betrothed when you were a child?"

The Vulcan stopped and turned toward the human, eyes hooded, face unreadable at any rate in the thickening darkness.

"It is our way," she said, defying debate.

The human caught up with her. They were almost at the settlement; Cleante would have to ask all her questions before T'Shael retreated to her austere flat and her deepening silence.

211

"Tell me more about it," Cleante asked softly, trying very hard to view the matter through Vulcan eyes. "About him. Your betrothed, I mean. And what it means to you. I suppose once you've gone through the ceremony there's no changing it, no going back. It's as binding as marriage?"

"Correct," T'Shael said.

"But what if you don't like each other?" the human asked plaintively.

The Vulcan did not condescend to address such emotionalism.

"Tell me what he's like, at least," Cleante persisted into the silence. She wanted it to be romantic. This was better than eugenic selection, wasn't it? Certainly parents would have their children's best interests in mind when they chose. "Is he a musician or a crafter? Does he live in T'lingShar? I've never seen you with anyone."

"He is by profession a gravity-control engineer," T'Shael replied, nodding a formal greeting to several passersby as they entered the settlement and walked beneath the colonnades of the academic halls. There were lights here for the benefit of outworlders, but Cleante found she could read no more in her companion's face than she could have in the dark. "He makes his dwelling among the asteroids. There is much new construction in the Belt, and that is where his skills are needed. He is called Stalek."

They stood in the archway of Cleante's apartment complex; it was a matter of moments before T'Shael would excuse herself and vanish into the night. There were so many unanswered questions.

"You haven't really answered me," Cleante said. "You tell me what he does but not what he's like. How he feels about this 'parental arrangement.' How he feels about spending his life with you, and you with him. How you stay in touch when he lives so far away. I want to know—"

"I will answer no question which in politeness ought not to be asked," T'Shael said tightly. It was as close as she could come to telling the human to mind her own business. Neither spoke as a boisterous knot of Tellarites stormed past, jostling and quarreling and perhaps a little drunk. Tellarites were like that. "If this will gratify your curiosity: Stalek and I are mind-linked as a result of our betrothal.

212

Beyond that, we have had no communication in the intervening years. Yet when he summons me, I will go. The rest is not your concern."

Cleante opened her mouth. There were no words. The wonder of the day was tarnished somehow; the morrow held little enticement. If she'd known the ceremony was for children she would have refused the invitation, no matter the breach of propriety. She could still do so. None of it made sense to her.

"Just one more question," she dared, perhaps a little too loudly, when she saw that T'Shael was about to walk away without so much as bidding her goodnight. "You've been betrothed to this stranger since you were a child. What happens now? How long do you have to wait—according to the Way of the Vulcan, of course; I'm sure it's all written down somewhere—before you're permitted to communicate with each other? Before you can get down to the business of making little Vulcans, or whatever you choose to call it. Or are you going to tell me there's a more logical way of doing that?"

T'Shael studied the human for a long moment before she spoke.

"It is to your advantage that your invitation to the betrothal comes from Crafter T'Sehn, whose wishes I honor above my own," she said coldly. "Otherwise I would question the merit of your attendance. Do not judge too easily what you cannot understand."

What is the price of understanding? Cleante wondered, holding her breath and tensing her own body as T'Shael had another seizure in the confines of their Klingon cage. If I had known this was what it meant, what lay behind the ritual and the parental arrangement and the distance your people attempt to put between yourselves and your biological drives I would never have been so human-flippant about Sethan, would never have presumed to criticize your way of dealing with this thing. Must you die, T'Shael, for this? And must I stand here, playing at Mastery of the Unavoidable though I no longer believe in it, helpless and near hysteria, watching, listening—

They had gone to the betrothal ceremony after all, she and

T'Shael, though only after the Vulcan had come for her in the early morning to dictate what she was to wear and how she was to comport herself. Cleante chafed at being treated like a child, then realized that the smallest Vulcan child needed no such instruction and engaged what little humility she possessed. She most especially wanted to win back T'Shael's approval after her disgraceful behavior the night before.

The ceremony itself was pristine in its simplicity: a brief processional of the intended couple and their respective parents accompanied by a number of priestesses chanting in an obscure Ancient dialect Cleante could not understand. There was an aura of incense and of flowering plants, the sound of a multiplicity of small bells.

The ritual seemed dominated by females, and Cleante wondered at this, though she knew she would get no answers if she asked. She watched in silence, stealing a glance from time to time at Sethan, who stood with his grandmother and a large family grouping, some of whom Cleante recognized from the crafters' shop. Sethan might never have known the human he had entertained so graciously yesterday. Cleante turned her attention from him to T'Shael, who had retreated into herself, present in body only.

Thinking of your own betrothal so many years ago, my Vulcan friend? Cleante wondered. Thinking perhaps of the stranger you must one day consign your life to? When it's time, does he come to live with you at the settlement? Or do you abandon your place as linguist and Warrantor to float among the asteroids, a forced-grav belt dictating to your every movement, an arrangement made without your consent dictating to your entire life? Oh, T'Shael, how can you simply accept this?

But there were no answers, and the human contained herself, playing the objective observer, ignoring the pang she felt when the two small ones stepped up to the ritual dais to perform the mind-link that would join them for life. She looked at Sethan's small cousin and saw instead T'Shael so many years ago, plain-faced and vulnerable, and closed her eyes against the sight. If T'Shael noticed, she gave no sign.

There was a banquet following, and there was dancing. Cleante could almost enjoy this, losing herself in the intricate and mesmerizing choreography, wondering how so many could move so rapidly past each other through winding circles within circles, following the complex rhythms without ever touching or so much as yielding to the ghost of a smile. How strange Vulcans were after all!

The music was ancient and evocative and almost savage, the instruments strange and exotic, their sound compelling, and the combined effect to her human ears was at once elevating and vaguely erotic. Yet the dancers spun and patterned and clapped their hands to the everchanging rhythms, their bare feet soundless on the cool granite floor, their faces as stolid as ever.

Cleante focused on T'Shael, now whirling past Sethan, now spinning off into a figure of her own both acrobatic and effortlessly beautiful, her lank hair flying, her spare body transformed into a fervid instrument of movement, her face as unreadable, her eyes as hooded as if she were meditating or quietly instructing her students at the settlement.

Perhaps it was a form of meditation, this dancing, Cleante thought; there were precedents aplenty on Earth and elsewhere. But on those worlds such ritual inevitably evolved into some form of religious ecstasy. Not here. Ecstasy was illogical.

If Cleante came away from the betrothal ceremony quieter than usual, if her depression was deep enough for T'Shael to remark upon it, it was because she had come to an impasse where Vulcans were concerned. She was no longer sure she wanted to live on this world for another two years. She had managed to antagonize her human companions long ago, and she despaired of ever understanding T'Shael. She was feeling quite alone and friendless when she received a terse commpic from Jasmine announcing her intention to run for a second term as High Commissioner. Cleante's depression was now complete. If her mother won the election she would have to stay on Vulcan for six years instead of two. It was more than she could stand.

She had wanted to pour all of this out to T'Shael on the morning they went to gather the herbs for the Masters' tea, to beg for another chance at understanding, to evoke some consideration for her humanness, but the diplomat's daughter had her pride. She also reminded herself, there was no escaping the Vulcan influence now, no matter her mood, that it was selfish to burden another with her private concerns.

Well, Rihannsu and Klin certainly solved my dilemma for me, didn't they? Cleante thought, trembling with contained hysteria as she paced before the transparency, staring across the dark compound to where a light shone from the Klingon quarters. Maybe I should be grateful to them, she thought bitterly, for giving me such a unique opportunity to learn the Way of the Vulcan in all its ramifications!

She and T'Shael had been left relatively alone since the Rihannsu had completed their repair work. The food synthesizer made it unnecessary for any of the Klingons to burst in on them with their unappetizing rations, and there had been no guard for weeks. Cleante had watched any number of Rihannsu coming and going from Krazz's quarters, including a female, strongly beautiful, obviously a figure of authority. It occurred to the human that she hardly saw Kalor at all any more, and she hadn't seen Krazz since the groundquake over a week before. Were the Rihannsu taking over their captivity? What did it mean?

She was strangely indifferent, reduced to torpor and despair. Under any other circumstances she would have been overjoyed, certain that even if their captivity endured indefinitely Kalor's reign of terror at least was over, and Rihannsu could be reasoned with. But it made no difference now. Nothing could get T'Shael back to Vulcan in time, and she was going to die. Not even the Rihannsu could remedy that.

Or could they? Vulcans and Rihannsu had a common ancestry; perhaps she could make them understand what was wrong and they could do something. If she could attract the powerful female's notice, surely the universal bond of womankind could be called upon to outweigh race and politics.

T'Shael's condition had worsened in the past several hours, in ways that threatened to drive the human mad. The seizures were almost continuous, each more prolonged and violent than the last. The Vulcan's wrists were raw and bloodied from straining at her bonds, and Cleante had had to force a gag into her mouth to keep her from swallowing her tongue.

Before that, the Vulcan had kept up an almost continuous stream of incoherent ramblings, obscure words that Cleante had never heard but somehow knew were sexual words, companions of fevered erotic hallucinations. These had given way to horrible feral growls and now an impassioned moaning. The hair on Cleante's neck prickled and she shivered in empathy; she had heard such sounds from her own throat in the embrace of a particularly skilled lover. She felt as much a voyeur as if she were actually witness to T'Shael and her ill-fated Stalek in the throes of their passion. The distance that separated them made this an obscenity; Cleante could not continue to watch, to listen.

And T'Shael knew all. Her eyes were open and lurid with shame. She could see and hear what she had become. If the physiological symptoms did not kill her, surely the shame of them would. Cleante turned away in a futile attempt to lessen the Vulcan's shame, retreating to the furthest corner of the cell, eyes squeezed shut and hands clamped over her ears, refusing to witness.

She remained that way for only a moment. Then she steeled herself suddenly and crossed to the transparency, pushing on it though she knew it was probably locked. She could not look at the Vulcan, whose eyes pleaded where her voice could not.

T'Shael, I'm sorry, Cleante thought to her. I only said I'd try; I never said I'd succeed. I'm only human, my Vulcan friend. Please forgive me for what I'm about to do.

Cleante clenched her fists at her temples, threw her head back and—as she had wanted to do from the moment of their capture, as only T'Shael's presence had prevented her from doing for all these harrowing months—screamed at the top of her lungs.

Eleven

THE HUMAN'S SCREAMS brought Tal and two of his vanguard, with Kalor pulling on his boots and loping across the compound to keep up with them. He had abandoned his round-the-clock watch on his pointed-eared allies to catch a few hours' sleep and this had been his reward. Where the Roms went, he would go. This was still, nominally, his command.

Tal entered the cell first. He was met by Cleante who, praying she had read some compassion in his ancient and knowing eyes in their few encounters, threw herself into his arms and upon his mercy. The diplomat's daughter would use her talent for histrionics, would use anything she had, to save her friend.

"I must speak to your commander!" she said frantically. "My friend is ill; she will die without assistance. It is a matter for females. Let me speak to your commander, please!"

Tal quickly appraised the Vulcan's condition, then hesitated. Kalor was trying to push his way past the guards when an imperious voice froze them all in their tracks.

"Stand aside!" the Commander ordered sharply, and Klin and Rihannsu alike fell away instantly.

She had not gone near the prisoners, had not so much as

218

looked at them for her entire stay here. She had been prepared to depart with the morning suns still thinking of them in the abstract, as two anonymous entities whose fate she could dictate from afar. She did not want to set eyes on the Vulcan, on any Vulcan, for the remainder of her days. Yet the human's screams had piqued her curiosity.

She quickly sized up the human as quite attractive for one of her species, then forced herself to look at the Vulcan. A female, plain of face and no more nor less like the Vulcan she had known than one Rihan was like another. Any number of strong emotions flooded her complex soul, but none was the loathing she'd expected. She took T'Shael by the shoulders and locked her eyes with her own.

T'Shael burned. The touch of the Rihannsu was like a current arcing through her. She writhed beneath it, arching her back and gnashing her teeth despite the gag, straining against her bonds and growling in her throat. Her eyes rolled up in her head and she frothed at the mouth, and all the while she was conscious of what she did, helpless to prevent it. The *shame*—

"I think I know what afflicts this one," the Commander said at last, taking her hands away. Her voice was almost tender, but reverted instantly to the voice of authority as she turned to Tal. "Instruct my physician to beam down with his strongest sedatives. And clear this place at once!"

"Ordinarily I would not remind you of our departure date—" Tal said a full day later.

"Then don't do so now!" the Commander said shortly. "We will stay until I know if the Vulcan lives or dies. Now go away, Tal. Go back to the ship and leave me in peace!"

She spoke as if to a lap pet whose presence she suddenly found irksome. Tal stiffened under her condescension. Subordinate he might be, but never subservient.

"Commander, we are under orders—"

"—to arrive at the Decian Outpost on such-and-such a stardate," she finished for him. "We can still do so if we delay our departure for a day or two or even three."

"Only if we risk overtaxing our engines," Tal said incisively.

219

"Then we will risk it!" the Commander almost screamed. "Tal, you are out of line and treading dangerously close to disciplinary action. Don't push me!"

The sub-commander chose his next words carefully.

"It seems I don't need to. You are pushing yourself. Or the Vulcan is."

T'Shael had been under heavy sedation for a full day, and her survival was still uncertain. The Commander had once done as much research as was possible on Vulcan biology for a very specific reason, and it was her opinion that if the introverted one could be kept unconscious and unable to respond to her drives until her distant male counterpart succumbed to his, she would live. It was Tal's opinion that something more expedient could have been done, and he said as much.

"I can't believe you would suggest such a thing!" the Commander said when she had heard him out, her voice hard and dangerous.

"In her present state will she know the difference?" Tal asked practically. "Any male will serve to quench her fire, fulfill her need. I don't suggest consigning her to a brute. Choose someone yourself from among your junior officers. One who is handsome and sensitive. One who writes poetry, perhaps, and has not yet killed. She might find pleasure in it. Certainly it would solve all of our problems."

The Commander gave him a frigid look.

"Perhaps you would like to volunteer your services, Tal," she said acidly. "Though I wouldn't have thought she was your type."

Tal's response was a bemused smile. The Commander was reminded—as if she, female officer in a warriors' society, could ever forget—what a philosophical chasm lay between male and female in some things.

"Try to understand," she said, her voice softer. "She is a Vulcan. It is different for them, almost sacred. For all that she is my prisoner and I hold discretion over her life or death, I cannot do what you suggest. And I can't believe you would respect me if I could."

She turned away from him, lost in her own thoughts as if he weren't there. Tal dared approach her.

"She reminds you of him, does she not?" he asked gently, prepared to understand.

"Of course not! She's just another Vulcan. Contrary to the old saw, they don't all look alike—" She stopped, giving him a long-eyed look. "You don't seriously believe I still concern myself with . . . with that other, do you?"

Tal's old and knowing eyes spoke for him. The Commander sighed.

"If he had a younger sibling, would I avenge myself on him through her?" she mused. "Wait, Tal. There is a method to my madness. You will see. For now we stay, until I say otherwise."

Unable to sleep with the intermittent sound of orbital thrusters aboard her ship, never able to sleep onworld, the Rihannsu Commander crossed the compound and entered the Klingon cage. The human, who sat on the edge of the bunk where the Vulcan lay drugged and unmoving, seemed not to notice her.

The Romulan Commander, she whose Name of names was one of the galaxy's better kept secrets, studied the only other females on this ugly, forsaken world. Human and Vulcan, she studied them. She had been indoctrinated in a hatred for humans all her days, and had reason enough to find bitterness in the sight of a Vulcan. Yet why did this simple scene move her? She touched the human's shoulder lightly and was met with those Byzantine eyes, which were dulled with fatigue.

"Leave us," the Commander said shortly. "Get some sleep. You are on the verge of collapse. We have no expertise in curing human ailments, and I won't have you endangering your health while you are under my command."

Cleante eyed her suspiciously, instinctively drawing closer to the comatose Vulcan. T'Shael was no longer gagged, no longer bound except by the cord around her waist, and that only to prevent her from falling out of the bunk. The human held the long and elegant hand between her own as she had done since the Vulcan had first been sedated. The Commander took this in, weighed it.

"I have not spared her life thus far in order to forfeit it

221

now," she answered Cleante's suspicions. "I have my orders, and a respect for our common ancestry. And I have other reasons."

Something in the tone of her voice made Cleante wonder. As fatigued as she was she could hear the almost-tenderness, incongruous in the mouth of this hard, disciplined female. She had heard the same voice when the Rihannsu first determined the nature of T'Shael's affliction. Cleante rose unsteadily from her place at the Vulcan's side, stumbling a little on the suddenly uneven floor. The Commander caught her by the shoulders and Cleante was startled at the fierce strength in those deceptively small hands. Of course, the Rihannsu kinship with Vulcans—

An exhausted human stumbled to her bunk and fell immediately into a deep, dreamless sleep. The Commander took up the vigil.

Why do I bother with this exercise in futility? she wondered, loosing the last of the Vulcan's bonds; she would not awaken now, and at any rate the Rihannsu's strength was an easy match for hers. Why not let your race's perverse rutting cycle destroy you as it surely would have if I hadn't intervened? I have discretionary orders from the Praetor himself to kill you both and end this ridiculous affair, blame it on the Klingons if I choose, and it may come to that yet. I have reason enough to loathe the very sight of a Vulcan. I am a warrior, hardened against mercy. Why do I continue to keep you alive?

Is it because I see your merit in the way the human cares for you? No one has ever cared for me in that way, nor I for anyone. Is it because despite what I told Tal you do remind me of that other, of that one who could have cost me my career if not my life but who spared me, leaving me instead with a wanting that—

Spock! The only thing in this universe I ever wanted and could not have, could not win by powerplay or subterfuge or simple sensuality, and because of that the only thing I wanted and continue to want with a longing that will never be entirely stilled.

Spock! What were you that you could do this to me?

That wasn't exactly just, of course, she forced herself to

admit. He had never actually misled her, never made a single overt move. It was she who had pursued him, drawn to his alien magnetism panting and rabid as a she-bitch while he was ever cool, remote, only "carrying out his duty." Had she stopped to truly listen to any of his words she would have found the truth beneath their subtlety, but she had succumbed to the dark richness of his voice and the electrifying almost-touch of his fingers and had not heard.

"I hope that one day there will be no need for you to observe any restrictions," she had said to him, meaning that she would win him over to herself as well as to her Empire.

"It would be illogical to assume that all conditions remain stable" had been his reply. And from that cold phrase she had mistakenly assumed her passion reciprocated.

What a godforsaken fool she had been! How humiliating to find her own emotions used so handily against her! It was why she had found it so easy to contemplate his execution once she discovered his true intent.

She was confident even now, so many years after her fury had cooled, that she would have had him executed without hesitation, could have garroted him with her own small hands without remorse to assuage the injury to her pride. Yet would that have succeeded in ripping him out of her heart?

Spock! Is it only because I cannot have you that I continue to want you? Spock the Unconquerable. Once conquered, would you hold as little interest for me as the countless males I have devoured and cast aside as empty husks since I encountered you?

She had contemplated innumerable variations on such conquest over the intervening years, as a way of keeping her sanity as she postured and smiled and served aboard others' ships as prelude to re-winning her own. The lonely hours in her empty cabin aboard her flagship, regained finally by dint of ferocious determination following the debacle with the *Enterprise,* were filled with evil fantasies of taking him captive, injecting him perhaps with some of the drugs her people used to augment sexual desire, or perhaps merely waiting, holding him until his next *pon farr* and watching with vengeful pleasure as he suffered something akin to the agonies she had suffered in his wake. But these fantasies had left her as unfulfilled as the males she had used as substitutes for him in the long months following her repatriation from the Federation. They resolved nothing.

It was all of a piece, really: her humiliation at his hands, the shame of being taken prisoner by the *Enterprise*, the theft of the cloaking device. She might have taken her own life. It was standard procedure among her kind in such circumstances; she had almost done so in the guest quarters on the *Enterprise*. Only Spock had prevented her. She would forgive him for that least of all.

"Such death would be a waste," he had said to her, and she had glared at him without speaking.

The guard in the red shirt stationed unobtrusively outside her quarters reported that she was refusing food and all attempts to see to her comfort; she forbade anyone to so much as cross her threshold. They were three days from the starbase where she would be held for interrogation when Spock dared defy her restriction. He stood in the open doorway, respecting her space but making his presence felt.

She would not respond to him, would not give him the satisfaction of admitting that he knew enough of her—their minds had touched but briefly in their encounter aboard her ship, but she had yielded up to him far more than he to her— to know what she was contemplating.

"You were not searched as a matter of courtesy," he said. "Nevertheless, it is known to us that every Rihannsu officer carries a suicide capsule. I would advise against its use."

"Why?" she spat at him, coming alive for the first time. "Don't you realize that if I get back my command—assuming I am not executed for bringing disgrace to the Praetor by losing the cloaking device—I will use every cell in my being to destroy you and your precious Federation? Before this I was opposed to the Federation as a matter of duty, like any loyal Rihannsu. But you have inflamed that duty into fervor. I will destroy you!"

"Will you truly be in danger once you are repatriated?" he asked, seeming not to hear the rest of what she said or, knowing it already, choosing to disregard it. "Our intelligence reports indicated you were highly placed in the Praetor's favor. If you do in fact face the possibility of punishment—"

"Oh, don't worry about me!" she said bitterly, tossing her soft burnished hair off her shoulders. "I still have the Praetor's favor. He finds me beautiful. I have used that to advantage before, and I will do so again."

Spock looked thoughtful.

"It is unfortunate that this must be the way of your people," he said sincerely.

"Unfortunate?" She came toward him, her gray eyes flashing. If she could trust herself to get close enough to him . . . the wanting came over her despite her rage, bringing a warm flush to her flesh, a fever to her body. If she took one more step she would be unable to stop herself from tearing at his clothing, seizing him to her. "We all have our gifts. Why not use them? Do you find the idea distasteful?"

He did not answer immediately.

"It is disquieting that one so gifted must permit herself to be used in such a manner," he said at last.

"But you don't find it—personally—upsetting?" she demanded.

"No," he said, not quite honestly, and she saw the briefest flicker of something in the deepness of his eyes, remembering what he had said to her in the turbolift on the day of her capture. *Had* she underestimated her effect upon him? Had she reached some part of him after all?

"I would have had you killed, you know," she said.

"I have no doubt of that," he replied.

"Yet you care what becomes of me?"

"Yes."

"If I decided—in a moment of pure insanity—to seek political asylum in your Federation—" She hesitated. It was not in her to beg. "It would change nothing between us, I suppose?"

She knew, for their minds had touched, what his answer would be before he uttered it.

"I think not, Commander," he said somberly. "I believe we both recognize that."

"Of course." She turned her back on him, shaking her soft hair off her shoulders in resignation. "You have my word that I will not attempt my life. But I do not wish to see you again. Ever!"

"Understood," he said, and was gone.

Gone but never gone, the Commander thought, keeping her vigil at the bedside of the plain-faced one. *If he had a younger sibling, you might have been she. If you live, how shall I use you for my purposes?*

On the planet Vulcan, in the metropolis of T'lingShar, in the place of the Masters, a messenger waited.

Master Stimm contemplated the messenger, a priestess of the betrothal rite. Her message was contained in her very presence, yet the Master would permit her to speak out of deference for the distance she had traveled to bring it to him personally.

"The one called Stalek is dead," she said in her honeyed voice. They all had these voices, these keepers of the betrothal rites; the Master had always found them unsettling. "Before his ordeal ensued he requested that you be informed, out of respect for your place in the life of his betrothed."

The Master nodded. It was not required that he express gratitude for information he would prefer not to have received, information that could mean only that his deepest student was also dead. The priestess acknowledged the Master's silence and took her leave.

The Master entered a state of deep trance, for what could have been days or only a moment. The meditative reaches that were his owned no time nor place; they were as fluid as eternity.

The Vulcan knows that there is a time for everything. The Master was an old one. There was no longer anything to sustain his tenuous link with this reality. With no noticeable ripple in the continuum of the universe he made his choice. *Kaiidth!* What was, was.

But even a Master is not omniscient.

T'Shael did not so much as open her eyes. By every logic she understood she should be dead; nevertheless she lived. She dared to move her hands and found them no longer restrained, felt tentatively for the cord about her waist and found it also had been removed.

She reached inside herself and found only silence. Her longtime link with Stalek, a kind of chronic undertone in her consciousness transformed in recent months into a cry and then a roar and at last an agonized scream, was gone. How was this possible, and she still alive?

T'Shael turned outward at last, listening. There was the sound of her own heartbeat, and the quiet breathing of another. Someone sat beside her on the narrow bunk; she became more aware of the presence as her senses were restored to her. She raised one enervated hand, reaching without quite touching.

"Cleante—" she whispered hoarsely, her throat constricted.

"She sleeps," said an unfamiliar voice. "As you should."

Baffled, T'Shael opened her eyes at last to seek out the human, who slept the sleep of the dead in the bunk across the cell. She tried to prop herself up on her elbows and was restrained by a small, strong hand.

She had thought she'd dreamed a Rihannsu female, thought her part of the bloodlust and febrile hallucinations that had assaulted her so utterly she knew nothing else. Now she focused intently on this obviously real being.

"It appears you're going to live," the Commander said drily. "Are you hungry? The human tells me you haven't eaten for some time."

"I have no hunger," T'Shael said weakly, fighting a wave of nausea at the very thought. But weakness was no excuse for impropriety. "It is apparent that I owe you my life. My gratitude for this."

The Commander gave her a wry look.

"Spare me your gratitude. You are my hostage. I can take your life as easily as I have saved it. As the situation stands at present you are more valuable to me alive, that's all."

"Nevertheless, while I live it is your doing," the Vulcan said carefully. "With all due respect, I am certain you know my name, yet I have no name to call you."

"Nor will you," the Commander said abruptly. "My name is private to me."

"I ask forgiveness," T'Shael said, lowering her eyes.

"No need. It's an idiosyncrasy of mine. You could not know. I am known for all practical purposes as the Commander. It serves."

"I shall obey your restrictions, Commander," T'Shael said solemnly.

She did not see the Rihannsu blanch at the familiarity of her words, their emulation of another time, another Vulcan. The Commander gave her a piercing look, almost as if she suspected her of some form of mockery.

"When I tell you my reasons perhaps you will rethink your gratitude."

"I've allowed you to live so that you may be of use to me," the Commander said.

She had brought the Vulcan into the Klingon quarters so as not to be overheard by the human. Her crew was preparing to leave orbit; there was little time remaining to make clear to the Vulcan why she had been pulled back from the brink of death.

"I owe you my life," T'Shael said yet again. "I will serve your purpose."

She was stronger now—up and about, showered and rested; she had even eaten something. There was a haunted quality to her that might never go away, and her unwavering willingness to be used by one who was her ideological enemy and potential executioner almost swayed the Commander from her intent. Almost. She was still the Commander.

"Tal tells me you speak High Rihan," she said as if making idle conversation. "Is this so?"

"Some scant knowledge of the tongue is mine," T'Shael replied.

"Typical Vulcan understatement!" the Commander remarked. "Well then, you know something of our languages and perhaps something of our ways. How well do you know our ancient culture—our martial arts, for example?"

"The ways of violence are of no interest to me," T'Shael replied. "Though my present captivity has been most instructive."

Could a Vulcan be sarcastic? The Commander ignored the irony, intended or not.

"We have a kind of dagger in our ancient tradition," she

228

began, as if giving a lecture. "More of a short sword, really. Small enough to be concealed on the person if one is resourceful, yet of sufficient length to run an adversary through."

Her small hands described the motion in the air as if from long practice, and T'Shael's being might have shuddered. She was not yet fully recovered from her ordeal.

"It is called a *dirhja*," the Commander went on as if she hadn't noticed. "A beautifully designed thing, often with a jeweled hilt; some are quite valuable. It is unique in that it has three perfectly equilateral edges rather than two, and it is of course incredibly sharp. Its advantage over an ordinary two-edged sword is that, wielded skillfully, it enters painlessly and with little loss of blood. What follows depends upon the victim.

"If the victim has courage he will make no move, and the *dirhja*, depending upon the wielder's discretion, can then be withdrawn—though not quite painlessly. The wound can be cured, though it leaves a most unusual scar. On the other hand, if the victim is craven or a fool he will struggle against the blade, and it will disembowel him with varying degrees of thoroughness."

The Commander studied the still weakened Vulcan, perhaps a little cruelly. T'Shael's face betrayed nothing.

"Can you—" the Commander said at last, "—you who abhor violence, possibly appreciate the beauty of such a weapon?"

"Doubtless there is a logic in your telling me of this," T'Shael said evenly. The taste of blood, taste of death, lingered in her mouth; such talk visited her with revulsion, yet in deference to her rescuer she must listen.

"Of course!" the Commander said, shaking her soft hair off her shoulders imperiously. "You are to be such a weapon for me. You are to serve as my *dirhja*, my three-edged sword."

"I do not understand," T'Shael said carefully, a wave of something that was not nausea washing over her, threatening to engulf her.

She had sensed the complexity of this Rihannsu, this warrior female, from the very beginning, and understood that whatever she had in mind must be worthy of her complexity, her warrior's need to command, to control. T'Shael thought of her lecture to Cleante on the ripple effect of one individual's actions against the face of existence, and was appalled at her own naïveté. How far removed she was from that now, dragged by circumstance into situation after situation that rippled outward from her very being no matter if she acted or remained passive, circumstances that she was helpless to affect by logic or moral stance. Stalek's death was but one instance, and it was profound enough. What followed now?

The imagery of the three-edged sword visited the Vulcan with a sudden, chilling metaphysical terror. She who had never been afraid for herself stood transfixed at the permutations the Rihannsu Commander had at her disposal. The Commander had said she would use her, but how? And how would her usage ripple out into the universe? T'Shael allowed herself the indulgence of wishing she had died when Stalek did.

"I do not understand," she said to the Commander, who at any rate owned her life or her death.

"Two edges of my sword are fairly obvious," the Commander began. "You and the human both will serve me in these. It will be upon my authority that you are returned to your Federation, if and when the tangle of details is untangled. I will tell you at least that negotiations have resumed—"

She waited for some reaction from the Vulcan, who could not have known for all these many months that any such negotiations even existed. Whatever she expected—hope, relief, gratitude at least for this much information—she saw no change on the austere face. She might have known better.

"So," the Commander went on wryly. "Upon your return, you and the human will testify that it was the Klingons who abused you and killed the Deltans, that your treatment at the hands of Rihannsu was consistently deferential, non-threatening and in accordance with intergalactic treaties on the disposition of political prisoners.

"By your testimony my Empire's honor is salvaged, my Praetor saves face, and I personally can only profit. That is the first edge of my sword.

"But it cuts another way, and the second edge is this:

230

There are those within the Federation who will demand retribution, who will seek to embarrass our Empire, provoke a confrontation, perhaps threaten war. Your testimony will have the effect of neutralizing these recidivist warmongers, rendering them impotent. They can't touch the Klingons in any event thanks to the Organians, damn them!"

T'Shael considered. The Warrantors' abduction by the Rihannsu, their sedation aboard the starship were reprehensible acts, crimes against their persons certainly. But no permanent damage had been sustained, and Theras's death was a result of his own madness. It would be no untruth to fulfill the Commander's dictates here, and the ripple effect would be the prevention of further hostilities. This was unquestionably a good. T'Shael nodded her silent acknowledgment; this much she would fulfill, and willingly.

"Your sword has a third edge," she said quietly, masking her intellectual terror, knowing that this edge would be sharpest of all.

"That is for you alone," the Commander said. "The human will have no part in it. Only a Vulcan merits it."

There was the briefest flicker of emotion across the austere face. The Commander knew something of Vulcan friendship bonding, remembered the human's unsleeping vigil. She waited.

"The human has great value to me," T'Shael said unashamedly. She knew she risked much in revealing this, but trust must begin somewhere. "I would spare her whatever ordeals I might."

"I thought as much," the Commander said, pleased, allowing herself the ghost of a smile. "This also serves my purpose. You will do much to assure the human's safe return to her loved ones."

T'Shael gathered herself for what was to come.

"There is a certain Vulcan," the Commander began, watching the plain face carefully. "He is a high-ranking officer in your Federation's Starfleet. One of the terms of your repatriation will be that his commander's starship must retrieve you from this place when the time comes. His name is Spock."

Spock, son of Sarek, whom I have never met and yet whose Warrantor I am, T'Shael thought. What would the

Rihannsu do with that piece of information? The austere face betrayed nothing.

"This Spock and I have encountered each other before." The Commander's face was less adept than T'Shael's at concealing her emotions for all the intervening years. Her voice took on a sharpness that seemed on the verge of a great anger or perhaps tears. "He was on an espionage mission to infiltrate my flagship and abscond with a priceless military secret. In so doing, he betrayed my trust in a manner both personal and humiliating. For this he has earned my unmitigated enmity."

"With all due respect, Commander," T'Shael presumed to interrupt. "If this is a matter of personal privacy, I do not wish—"

"Oh, don't worry," the Commander said archly. "I have no intention of telling you anything more. That is for Spock, if he has the courage."

T'Shael drew upon herself and decided something. She would not be the instrumentality of any more death. She would not endanger the one called Spock or any on his starship—if it meant her own death or even Cleante's.

—Cleante! My friend, my would-be *t'hy'la*, you who have interceded for my life against all odds, you whom I have not even had opportunity to speak to since my ordeal—I have no right to speak for your life, yet if I give my own and you must remain here alone . . .

Forgive me, my more-than-worthy, but if the third edge of the Commander's sword means death it will only be for me. The ripple effect must end here—

"If it is your intention to use us as a lure, to entrap the starship and the one called Spock."

"Of course not!" the Commander said, amused at how ruthless she must appear to this introverted being. Hadn't she considered this as one of the possibilities open to her from the first—a way to end this sordid mess in a kind of glory and purge her soul of Vulcans for all time? "That is the approach of the battle ax, not the *dirhja*. The *dirhja* is subtle. It uses the victim's own weaknesses against him. And it always leaves a scar.

"When you are repatriated you will seek out the one called Spock. You will presume upon his Vulcan privacy, his

Vulcan pride. You will require of him that he tell you the tale of his betrayal of a Romulan. You will be living proof that a Rihannsu has sometimes more honor than a Vulcan. You will require this of him because I have saved your life, and he will tell you on his honor as a Vulcan. If he has that honor, that courage—the courage to face the *dirhja*."

T'Shael was silent, weighing what she had just been told. If the one called Spock had indeed done these things, surely as a Vulcan he would accept their responsibility. Nevertheless, such an invasion of his privacy was dimensioned by levels of meaning which—

"You style yourself as a Warrantor of the Peace," the Commander said, again wondering if what she was doing was just. Surely it was not this one's fault she had been born a Vulcan. "I have made you the Warrantor of my vengeance. Oh, don't trouble your Vulcan soul about it," she said almost tenderly as she sensed T'Shael's inner shying from the choice of words. "It is a good vengeance, a noble vengeance. To know that Spock has the courage to admit what he has done to one other—a disinterested stranger and one who abhors the ways of militarism—assuages my lust to destroy him. Can you understand that?"

"Perhaps," T'Shael said carefully, but without hesitation. "I accept your charge, Commander. I will do what you require of me. On *my* honor as a Vulcan."

The Commander allowed herself a bitter smile.

A slight, athletic figure, treading lightly to compensate for the psychic weight of the information he carried (certain death if he was more than peripherally searched; he might as well have it tatooed across his high-cheekboned face), braved his way through the RihanFed Border Station toward the helmeted and heavily armed sentry at the single airlock. The next few minutes would make him either a free human or a dead Rihannsu.

They would not take him alive. He had decided that hours ago as he carefully concealed the microcoded data chips on various parts of his person. It wasn't cowardice, his decision, nor fear of their methods of interrogation; it was his certain knowledge that once they started asking their questions they would get the answers. Spock had warned him the

233

Rihannsu had certain techniques to which even Vulcans were not impervious. He knew he wouldn't have a chance. And there were so many others involved. . . .

Okay, Sulu thought, eyeballing the sentry from his place in the queue with the other departees. If he tries to stop me I'll either make a grab for his blaster and hope he's got it on full charge, or I'll throw myself out through the airlock and jam the mechanism behind me. By the time they get the atmospherics operating my lungs will have burst in the vacuum. *Sayonara*, Lel em'n Tri'ilril. Better luck in the next life.

Gods, he thought. I've been playing Rihannsu too long; I'm beginning to think like them. Suicide as Viable Option? Have to bounce that little paradox off Spock when I get back. *If* I get back.

The queue moved forward.

Wake up, Hikaru! Three hundred meters beyond that airlock lies freedom. Pretty stupid of you to screw up now.

The border station, which the Rihannsu called ch'Mrelkhre ("the small end of the funnel" was the nearest Standard rendering, implying that only the chaff got through) and humans called simply Omega, had been set up on the Federation edge of the Neutral Zone by the terms of the Earth-Romulan treaty at the end of the Wars over a century before. An uneasy agglomeration of Rom-human space architecture, constructed more in a spirit of competition than cooperation, it perched precariously half in, half out of the Zone, constantly patrolled by ships from either side. As many as several hundred passed daily through the no-man's-land of the umbilical between the two halves of the station after being carefully screened by the sentries on either side.

Sulu, waiting in the queue with the appearance of a calm he did not feel, occupied his brain with searching for some analogue to this place. Checkpoint Charlie, he thought. The Berlin Wall, Old Earth. How childish all that seemed now, in the enlightenment of a United Earth. Maybe someday this station would also seem childish, obsolete, in a time when Rihan and human embraced as brothers and border sentries were an endangered species.

He had come close to believing that possible over the past few months, rubbing elbows with the Rihannsu in the street—living with them, working with them, sharing a meal, a card game, the company of a woman. Perhaps the day would come when he could call them friend.

He was the next save one in the queue; in front of him an elderly Tellarite struggled with a cumbersome musical instrument in a sealed case. The sentry was insisting the case be opened despite its showing clean on his scanner rod. The Tellarite was protesting loudly, attracting a crowd of mixed Rihan and humanoid types.

Gods, Sulu thought, beginning to sweat. Just what I need!

"Enough, grandfather," the sentry said at last; whatever else might be said about them, the Rihannsu had a certain respect for age. "Either you unseal the lock now or I'll blast it open."

The Tellarite grumbled and grudgingly opened the case. A hands-on search revealed a tiny packet of illicit stimulants cleverly concealed in the instrument's reed box.

"I have a heart condition!" the Tellarite pleaded. "I can't get those drugs on the other side. Excellency, please!"

The bribe passed from hand to hand so quickly Sulu almost missed it; anyone standing behind him would have seen nothing.

"Only because I'm in a generous mood, grandfather," the sentry said magnanimously, pocketing the drug pouch anyway, pulling the Tellarite out of the queue to stand by the airlock while he resealed the case. "You could be detained for a lot less."

The crowd lost interest and began to drift away. Sulu stepped forward, his identicard at the ready.

"They'll try anything, won't they?" He nodded in the direction of the Tellarite, to be certain the sentry knew he had seen.

"Destination, Clerk Lel?" the sentry barked. Sulu's heart skipped; the confidentiality might have been unwise.

"Earth Outpost 3," he said with equal terseness, tapping the carrycase under his arm importantly. "New list of contraband."

The sentry eyed him skeptically.

"Missed my transport," Sulu explained, hoping it sounded casual. "Thought I'd slip through with the civilians."

Still the sentry said nothing.

"Like to get back by twelfth hour. Got a lady waiting for me."

He said something else in an obscure dialect he'd picked up in his travels, and elicited a quick leer from the sentry.

"If she's worth it, she'll wait," he said at last, his suspicions dissipating. He ran the scanner rod over the carrycase perfunctorily and jerked his head in the direction of the unhappy Tellarite. "Escort the old one through, will you? Better he has his heart attack on the Fed side."

Sulu laughed at what could only be called a Rihannsu joke. The sentry activated the atmosphere inflow and opened the airlock. Records Clerk Lel em'n Tri'ilril took the disgruntled Tellarite's arm and tried to hurry him down the umbilical.

It was a sterile place, gloomily lit, the atmospherics hissing ominously, the clearsteel walls cold to the touch. In the event of all-out war the two ends of the station would be sealed off and the umbilical literally pulled apart as each side scrambled to retreat as far inside its own territory as possible before the shooting started, and woe betide anyone caught between the airlocks at such a time. A few years back, when a Rom bird of prey had slipped invisibly out of the Zone to disintegrate Earth Outposts 2, 3 and 4 before being stopped by *Enterprise,* the station had gone on All Alert and severed the umbilical for the first and hopefully last time, propelling six civilians—three from each side—out into space.

The three outposts and the border station had been rebuilt at Rihannsu expense as part of their reparations following the bird of prey incident, and the terms had almost brought the Praetor down. Perhaps somewhere in the back of his long memory he had thought that snatching the Warrantors of the Peace would somehow make amends for the incident.

But when it came right down to it, no one knew what was in the Praetor's mind except the Praetor, and it made no difference to those walking down the endless length of the umbilical (another 250 meters, Sulu told himself, another two hundred, another—), the sound of their own footsteps echoing off the frigid clearsteel walls.

Was it Sulu's imagination, or had the Tellarite begun to quicken his pace? The old man's stiff-kneed shamble had been replaced by the stride of a much younger being. As they passed through the airlock on the Fed side at last, Sulu gave the Tellarite a stunned look. He had somehow shed a generation in the minutes they'd spent in the umbilical.

"Special Agent Gadj," the Tellarite reported, flashing his ID at the bewildered Sulu. "Specializing in creating diversions so the real stuff can get through. Welcome home, Commander. Buy you a drink before we phone the Ice Man?"

"Think I'd like to use the head first," a delighted Sulu said, grinning deliriously.

"Understood," Gadj grinned back.

Twelve

THE RIHANNSU FLAGSHIP described a low departure orbit, appearing as a small unblinking light moving steadily across the unfamiliar starfield above the barren planetoid. Cleante knelt on an upper bunk and peered out one of the high windows, watching it go. She thought of what the Commander had said to them before she left.

"We Rihannsu are reared in the military as a matter of course," she had explained, standing in the hatchway of her scout in the dusty compound, armed and in full regalia, an impressive figure, strongly beautiful. Was it possible her attitude toward her prisoners had softened somewhat during her stay here? "Though some of us have other talents. I pride myself on being no mean diplomat. I will do all in my power to see that the remaining obstacles to your repatriation are put down. It will be a matter of weeks, in my judgment, perhaps less."

She actually smiled at Cleante, though it was a calculated smile, a diplomat's smile, meant to reassure without necessarily having any substance behind it. Cleante was reminded of her mother's professional smile and had to force herself to smile in return.

The look the Commander gave T'Shael was cryptic and almost challenging—a reminder of her pledge. The Vulcan acknowledged it with silence; she required no reminder.

"I dislike leaving you in the custody of that two-legged animal," the Commander said, her eyes narrowing in the direction of what were now Kalor's headquarters. "But my orders are exact on that point. Worry not. He knows what will happen to him if either of you are harmed."

She stepped into the scout with no further farewell. Cleante suppressed a shudder, wondering if even the Rihannsu's authority could control Kalor's sadism from such a distance. It would be an uneasy few weeks at best.

The small moving glow across the night sky flickered and vanished as the flagship broke out of orbit and headed toward deep space. Cleante dangled her legs idly over the edge of the bunk as Jali had been wont to do; she caught herself doing this and slid down. Better not to think too often of those who had died.

She had not said a single word to T'Shael since her recovery, not knowing how to break the silence. Would T'Shael hate her for breaking her promise, for seeking help? It was a chance she had had to take. Anything to save her friend. Anything.

The human was startled to find the Vulcan contemplating her from across the room with an expression of uncharacteristic warmth. T'Shael's eyes no longer burned with their febrile incandescence; that had been replaced with a deep and possibly ineradicable sadness. But where Cleante had expected reproach she instead found acceptance, even—affection?

"I thought you'd hate me," she said simply.

T'Shael shook her head.

"Not possible."

"Why? Because hatred is an emotion?"

"Because my logic was flawed and you dared correct it, even at the risk of destroying our friendship. To take such a risk is to confirm the value of such friendship. I am honored."

Cleante puzzled over this, abandoning it with a shrug.

"That's too Vulcan for me," she admitted with a small laugh.

She felt suddenly euphoric. They were both alive, T'Shael's crisis was past, and there was hope that they would soon be freed. Most of all, T'Shael was not angry with

239

her. If only Kalor were somewhere across the galaxy instead of only across the compound! She would not think about that.

"How do you feel?" she asked T'Shael, then quickly rephrased to spare herself the standard lecture on emotion. "I mean, what are you thinking? It must be very strange for you."

"Indeed," the Vulcan said. "It is strange to find an emptiness where for so long there was the presence of another consciousness. Stalek and I knew nothing of each other, yet our minds were locked together in this way. I am aware that I was powerless to prevent his death; nevertheless there is this emptiness . . . It is much like what I experienced when Resh'da and Jali and Krn died—a helplessness to prevent, which logically implies Mastery of the Unavoidable, yet—"

She stopped, looked at the human with frank bewilderment. How to explain the essence of emptiness, the realization that she, melancholy pilgrim, was for the first time in her life totally alone, completely severed from all connection with her species or any individual therein? Assuming she ever returned to Vulcan, what awaited her? What would be her place? She was an unwed female with no living kin, sole survivor of the inferno of *pon farr*. T'Shael knew of no precedent to her situation. Yet why burden the human with this?

"I do not know what I think, nor how I feel," she said. "Your original choice of words was perhaps more accurate—I *feel* this thing, inasmuch as I am unable to rationalize it, reduce it to logic . . . I begin to understand why my people have suppressed all emotion for over a millennium."

Cleante had no answer for this. Would T'Shael do the same, withdrawing from all she'd hungered to learn in their time together? Was the human responsible for this? A long and fragile silence ensued.

"I broke my promise to you," Cleante dared at last.

"It was a promise you should never have been called upon to make," T'Shael said at once. She took a deep breath, gathering herself. "Your breaking of it has spoken more to me than any logic I know. It has spoken to me of love."

Cleante smiled, suddenly shy.

"You asked me to do that back on Vulcan. I'm sorry I took so long."

She saw T'Shael's eyes flicker with distress and hastened to reassure her.

"I'm only teasing. Oh, please don't take everything I say so seriously! Listen to me. I said back then that I'd be your friend, whether or not you chose to be mine. Whether you carried your father's sickness or not. Whether either of us was struck by lightning or swallowed by the ground or lived to the next millennium. Through Klingons and Rihannsu and *pon farr* and all our differences, through life and through death if necessary, T'Shael. I meant it then and I mean it now."

"What you speak of is beyond the standard, human concept of friendship," the Vulcan said slowly, gently. Cleante held her breath, dared not speak. "What you ask will not be easy—for either of us." T'Shael found the words less painful than she might have thought. "The Vulcan friendship mode is a crucible. There is that in it which can purify, refine, strengthen. There is also that which can immolate, destroy."

"It hasn't exactly been a barrel of laughs so far," Cleante said with a wry smile. "Although I have to admit it's been . . . interesting."

"And you have endured," T'Shael said, more open than she had ever been before. "And continue to endure. Through life and death and all our differences, then, Cleante alFaisal, my more-than-worthy. My *t'hy'la.*"

"*T'hy'la,*" Cleante repeated softly.

Kalor and a sea of troubles might have been transported to the far ends of the galaxy.

But Kalor was still very much with them.

The first thing he did in his new role as commander of the prisoners' encampment was to leave their cage unlocked.

"He couldn't have forgotten," Cleante said, watching the door swing open at her touch. "What do you suppose he's up to?"

"Unknown," T'Shael replied. "But in view of Klin sexual taboos, you might do well not to venture outside."

"I'd forgotten!" Cleante clapped her hand over her mouth

in horror, remembering her first encounter with Krazz half a lifetime ago. Then she laughed, a shadow of her old nervous laugh. "Oh, well, it's sort of a built-in safety factor, isn't it? As long as Kalor can't lure me outdoors . . ."

"Perhaps," T'Shael said vaguely, not at all certain that this was Kalor's reasoning.

She had no doubt he was still formulating experiments to try on his remaining prisoners despite the Rihannsu Commander's dictate. If she and Cleante were now confirmed as *t'hy'la*, the strength of their bonding would no doubt soon be tested.

The test came sooner than even T'Shael could have anticipated.

She and her scrub bucket arrived on Kalor's doorstep the morning after the Rihannsu had left, ready to resume where she had left off. As far as the Vulcan was concerned, her pledge to serve the Klingons was still in force.

Kalor had celebrated the end of the pointed-ears' governorship by smashing the neck off a fresh bottle of liquor and drinking himself to the verge of a stupor. But only dead drunk could he turn off the machine that hummed endlessly in his brain, plotting and planning. He would not allow himself the luxury of getting that drunk. The machine continued to hum, and the Vulcan's arrival clicked several diabolical calculations into place. Kalor's lizard eyes glinted at her coldly.

"Get out of here, Vulcan!" he slurred. "If I see one more thing with pointed ears I'll puke!"

"As you wish," T'Shael said. She was halfway across the compound when Kalor came roaring after her.

"You, Vulcan! Stand where you are!"

T'Shael turned on her heel to see him tightening his weapons belt and stalking toward her. She saw to her relief that Cleante had not come to the door of the cage; she had not heard, and need not witness whatever was about to happen.

The Vulcan shifted her housekeeping tools into one hand, readying herself. She could defend herself against an unarmed Klingon, but not if he drew his disruptor. She did not consider retreating to the relative safety of the cage; to remind one such as Kalor of his species' taboos might be incentive enough for him to break them.

Kalor might be drunk, but he wasn't stupid. He knew what hidden strength lay in that fragile form, and whipped out the disruptor while he was still several meters from T'Shael, his lizard eyes promising her no quarter if she resisted. T'Shael stood unwavering. In the wake of *pon farr* her senses were abnormally acute, her skin hypersensitive; she did not wish to touch or be touched by anyone. Cleante had understood, had not so much as come near her since her ordeal. If Kalor were to discover her weakness he would exploit it to the fullest. T'Shael locked in her Mastery of the Unavoidable and waited.

Kalor wasted no time. He grabbed the front of her uniform, twisting it hard across her chest with one rough hand, pressing the disruptor against her ribs with the other. He towered over her, his breath hot and foul with drink.

"Say you're afraid of me, Vulcan!" he hissed. T'Shael did not answer. Kalor wrenched the fabric of the uniform tighter until another female would have cried out. "Say it!"

"It would not be true," T'Shael said evenly.

The Klingon thrust her away from him into the dust, scattering the cleaning utensils, then grabbed her by the hair and forced her to her feet again. He pressed himself against her from behind, the disruptor hard against her spine, his voice harsh in her delicate ear.

"That was quite a show you put on for our visitors," he hissed, caressing her cheek now with the muzzle of the disruptor. "You Vulcans are not the sexless monoliths you pretend. If your freak-eared cousins hadn't been underfoot I would have matched your lust with mine."

T'Shael's Mastery faltered for an instant. Her shame had been witnessed by this one, then. She gathered herself. The Klingon preys upon the weakness of others.

"If it is your desire to take me you have the power to do so," she said flatly. "The histrionics are unnecessary."

Kalor released his grip on her, though he kept his weapon ready.

"You would go with me willingly?" he demanded, Klingon-suspicious.

"Never willingly," T'Shael replied. She did not so much

as brush the dust from her uniform, yet she had dignity. "But I am powerless to prevent the exercise of your will. The Rihannsu Commander's dictate notwithstanding."

She had him there. Rape constituted permanent damage to the prisoners, and would cost Kalor his life. He slung the disruptor into his belt with a disgusted gesture.

"I might as well seek pleasure from a block of ice," he sneered, a lifetime of abrupt, brutal gratification snatched mainly by force suddenly sticking in his craw, clinging to his charnel soul, gagging him. "I won't give you the satisfaction!" His lizard eyes glinted evilly. "The human will be far easier to persuade."

He did not take a full step toward the cage before T'Shael threw herself across his path.

"Will you risk your life against the Commander's orders?" she asked, rapidly calculating what little real bargaining power she had against him.

"I take no orders from Roms!" Kalor roared.

He was loud enough to bring Cleante to the transparency. Only a small pleading gesture from T'Shael prevented the human from rushing across the compound to intercede for her friend.

T'Shael realized that Kalor was more crazed then drunk, that the Rihannsu's prolonged stay had tipped him over a kind of edge, that he would continue his sadistic experiments though it meant the death of his prisoners and subsequently his own. Was there a logic she could use to deflect that madness, at least for a time, to save Cleante?

"The human will not acquiesce to your demands," she said quickly, calculating. "You will have to force her, and I suspect that would be incompatible with the nature of your experimentation."

Kalor's eyes narrowed and his fist came up instinctively.

"What do you know about it?" he demanded, taking a step toward her, menacing.

"I caution you: the human is watching," T'Shael said quietly, noting his nervous darting glance toward the transparency. He did still value his own safety, then. "If you intend to continue your research despite the Rihannsu dictate, you will require a voluntary subject."

"Meaning you." Kalor said slowly. It was all too simple, too treacherous. "But you said you'd never go with me willingly. Now you're contradicting yourself. Explain!"

My words were that should you desire sexual gratification I would go with you, but never willingly. You cannot expect me to feign pleasure any more than you can elicit fear where none exists. I will serve your purpose, in whatever manner you decide, on one condition."

"You dare to bargain with me?" Kalor roared. "I could kill you where you stand!"

"And in so doing condemn yourself to death," T'Shael replied.

Some small part of her mind marveled at the words that came out of her mouth. She who had been known for the quality of her silences was transformed by her own rootlessness and her need to save one other.

Kaiidth! She would bargain with the Klingon and she would win, though the winning kill her. The crucible of the *t'hy'la* could also immolate.

Kalor seemed to be wrestling with some monumental decision. His savage face twisted under the strain of his intellectual battle. Since when did the prisoner bargain with her jailer, the subject with her keeper?

"Just out of curiosity—I don't say I'll agree—what is this 'condition' of yours?"

"That your experiment begins and ends with me," T'Shael said without hesitation. "You will give me your word that you will not harm the human, neither lay hands on her, nor subject her to duress either physical or mental, nor force her to do anything against her will, and that the Rihannsu will return to find her exactly as she is now."

"You'd accept the word of a Klingon?" Kalor was incredulous.

"A Klingon also has honor," T'Shael said. "When it serves his interest in xenopsychology."

If the human hadn't been watching, Kalor might have struck her again. Instead he contained his anger. It would work its way out in his experiment, which would be a diabolical one.

"All right," he nodded slowly. "I'll accept your bargain.

But I, too, have a condition. I want to know what you'll tell the Roms when they return. Assuming I don't arrange for your accidental death before they do.''

"I shall tell them that my actions were voluntary. That much is true. Extenuating circumstances are of no matter."

The Klingon weighed this, still smelling treachery. He whose ideology was rooted in deviousness was at a loss to deal with such relentless honesty.

"Go back to your cage," he growled at last. "The door will remain unlocked. Return to my quarters at nightfall and we will seal our bargain."

"As you wish."

"I remember the Vulcan aboard the border ship," Kalor mused almost to himself. "I was very young. My first deep space voyage."

He stopped. Such personal details were none of the Vulcan's business, unless of course he were to give her a graphic description of exactly what he and his crewmates had done to her compatriot. He would enjoy that, if he thought he could get a reaction out of her. Well, she'd have enough to react to before this night was over, *kai* Kahless!

"I remember how high they kept the temperature control in that vessel; we were all in a sweat by the time we were through with her. I learned later how hot it is on your planet, how sensitive you green-bloods are to cold."

T'Shael said nothing. The blanket she had thrown over her shoulder to make the brief trip across the compound was eloquent proof. She was beginning to understand what Kalor had in mind.

"What did you tell the human?" Kalor demanded. "I'm sure I would have heard her screeching and carrying on if she knew why you were here."

"I told her you required some task of me," T'Shael said evenly. "Since you were unwilling to have me complete my housekeeping this morning. It is the truth in either case."

Kalor grinned like a crocodile.

"I'm beginning to like you, Vulcan," he said with admiration. "You're learning to think like a Klingon."

*   *   *

T'Shael did not tell him that Cleante hadn't accepted her story from the beginning.

"Just what the hell was that all about?" she had demanded the instant T'Shael returned to the cage. "I saw what he did to you. You're covered with dirt. Are you all right? What happened out there?"

"I am undamaged," the Vulcan reported. "Kalor's ethanol intake has increased with the departure of the Rihannsu, and apparently he felt a need to exercise his authority. To do so he found it necessary to knock me down. It is of no matter."

"But what did he say to you?" Cleante persisted, her fists clenched, her Byzantine eyes blazing. "What did he want?"

"Nothing of consequence was said," the Vulcan said vaguely, wondering if that was a lie. The ripple effect of one's actions upon the face of the universe—

"That's not good enough, T'Shael."

"His subject matter was racist and not particularly coherent," T'Shael said with a touch of impatience. "Would you have me repeat his words? They were neither interesting nor especially original. I would prefer to utilize my time more fruitfully."

The subject was closed. T'Shael sat at the computer console and inserted one of the linguatapes Tal had ordered for her, absorbing herself in a research project she had begun as soon as she felt strong enough after her ordeal.

Her concentration was High Rihan and its phonemic linkages with Ancient Vulcan. Previous researchers had theorized that both could be traced back to a common preliterate matrix, incontrovertible proof of the kinship between Vulcan and Rihannsu. But their data was incomplete. T'Shael picked up the thread where her predecessors had left off. She would contribute what she could in the time remaining to her. If Kalor meant to kill her, and she had no doubt that he did, her final hours would not have been wasted.

When the moment came for her to cross the compound to whatever fate awaited her, she looked at Cleante, who was more than a little hurt at being ignored all day. There had been no alternative; the most aimless of conversations might have let slip the true content of the dialogue between T'Shael and Kalor. T'Shael was visited with a sudden pang of pure dismay. She could not so much as say farewell without revealing the nature of her journey! The trouble with being a Vulcan was one fell prey to well-asked questions.

Cleante sprang to her feet as T'Shael tried to reach for a blanket and slip away without drawing attention to herself.

"Where do you think you're going?"

"Logically there are few places for me to go," T'Shael said drily. "Kalor requires that I complete the morning's tasks."

"At this hour? Why wait till after dark?"

"Perhaps his inebriation made him desire solitude," the Vulcan suggested, trying to make the human believe her. How else was she to keep her end of the bargain?

Cleante looked at her for a long moment. Something was seriously wrong here; she could sense it.

"T'Shael, if you're lying to me—"

"Cleante," the Vulcan said gently, then paused. She must make this work; she *must*. "*T'hy'la*, I trust my exposure to outworlders has not so corrupted me. Try to remember that a Vulcan cannot lie."

Cleante tried to laugh, but the foreboding lingered. She hugged herself, suddenly cold.

"I just have this feeling," she began.

"Kalor values his life," T'Shael pointed out. "He will not harm me."

He may take my life, but he will not reach what I am, the Vulcan thought as she crossed the compound with all deliberate speed, knowing the human's eyes were upon her. When I say he will not harm me, this is my meaning. In being imprecise, *t'hy'la*, am I in fact telling a lie?

"Leave the blanket," Kalor said harshly, his rough hand ripping it out of hers.

T'Shael understood. His experiment would be to consign her to the cold of the planetoid's nighttime surface, barefoot, without shelter, wearing only her worn prisoner's uniform. His reasons were known only to himself.

"Does your experiment include my death?" she asked, remembering the Deltans.

248

"Does the laboratory rodent question its keeper?" Kalor snarled. He relented a little; there was an almost lascivious pleasure in having the Vulcan at his mercy after so many months of being threatened by her very existence.

"You don't want to prejudice my experiment, do you? All right, I'll tell you. For this night at least I probably won't let you die. I only want to test your species' tolerance for cold. If you can still walk when the suns come up, you may return. As for subsequent nights. . . ."

He indicated the door on the far side of his quarters, the only one in the encampment that led away from the compound toward the barren plain where Krazz had died and the scraggly hills beyond. The night wind moaned dismally; a turgid ground fog undulated across the plain, obscuring thorny scrub and innumerable sharp stones. It was already below freezing, and the long night had just begun.

T'Shael gathered herself and passed outside without giving the Klingon so much as a backward glance.

Two courses of action lay open to her. She could keep moving, forcing her circulation with carefully paced jogging and controlled breathing; it could be done under desert night conditions as every Vulcan child learns by the age of seven. But there was no succulent plant life here to provide fluids; exhaustion and exposure would claim her long before sunrise. She must find shelter, or make it.

There would be caves in the hills, but one did not seek shelter in a cave where seismic disturbances were so frequent. On Vulcan, one could scoop out a shallow depression in the sand, but here the ground was hard-frozen; T'Shael had already tried it. She weighed all of this without slowing her purposeful, energy-conserving pace.

Reaching the foothills at last, she found enough loose rock to build a partial shelter in a crude semi-circle against the cliff face. The labor was exhausting but it kept her warm.

When at last she had finished, T'Shael braced her back against the barely sheltering curve of the unyielding cliff face and slid first into a fetal position, deliberately slowing her breathing. Then, as she felt the circulation returning to her lower extremities, she was able to curl her feet under her in a way most humans would find contorting, if not impossible.

The soles of her feet were gashed and bloody from her headlong journey across the rock-strewn plain, but no matter. Their throbbing assured that they weren't yet frostbitten. T'Shael wrapped her arms tightly across her thin chest, tucking her long and elegant and now totally numb hands under her arms to try to restore them. At last she curled up into herself, curving her back until her forehead touched her knees.

Her lank hair whipped against her face in the raw wind that still got through the chinks in her rock wall, frost-stiffened into stinging needles. She welcomed the pain; it would keep her alert. The nape of her thin neck, exposed by the inadequate collar of the uniform and her flailing hair, lay naked to the wind, vulnerable. She locked her jaw to stop her teeth from clashing together, but nothing would stop her body's trembling. She engaged the lightest of trances; anything deeper would slow her heart rate and she would freeze all the more quickly. She had only to endure until the first of the twin suns appeared, bringing with it some semblance of warmth.

Nothing in her disciplined life or all her Vulcan training had prepared her for this. Like all Vulcan children she had undergone *Kahswan,* the ten-day trial in the desert, but the dry cold of nights on Vulcan was as nothing compared to the raw, damp, murderous cold of this nameless place. No natural thing could kill a Vulcan faster than the cold.

I must not die! T'Shael thought, realizing as she had not before that Kalor's pledge might not apply to a dead Vulcan. Until the Rihannsu return, for Cleante's sake, I must not!

The thought gave no warmth, yet it focused her, gave meaning to her suffering, and each minute survived was a minute she need not live through again.

T'Shael endured.

Kalor sat in the comfort of his quarters contemplating his sensors, which showed a Vulcan reading several kilometers off in the hills, at low ebb but still functioning. If the readings still registered in the morning he would fetch the Vulcan back, thaw her out, and repeat the process the next night, and the next and the next. Then he would implement the next phase of his experiment.

Kalor smiled his crocodile smile. He would teach Vulcan and human and even Romulan the parameters of a Klingon's honor.

Cleante awoke with a start. She'd promised herself she'd stay awake until T'Shael returned, but as the night wore on she'd succumbed to sleep.

The first of the red suns was already up and the Vulcan's bunk had not been slept in. Cleante bolted for the transparency without thinking. She was in time to see T'Shael crossing the compound slowly and with some difficulty. Careless of her own safety, Cleante rushed to her side.

She threw her arm around the Vulcan's shoulders, half supporting, half dragging her, feeling how cold she was through the fabric of the uniform and the blanket clutched carelessly about her as if she couldn't get her hands to work. T'Shael's eyes were closed; she seemed to feel her way across the compound, her feet dragging in the dust. The Vulcan mask could not hide the fact that she was in pain.

Kalor watched from his window and found the scene amusing.

Cleante led T'Shael to her bunk, sat her down, removed the blanket, and assessed the now bloodless lacerations on her hands and feet, the evidence of exposure and possibly frostbite on her hands and face and the tips of her ears.

"What did he do to you?" the human said, nearly choking on her rage. "That animal! That vicious animal! Oh, T'Shael, what has he done?"

T'Shael shook her head, unable to speak at first.

"He has done nothing," she whispered hoarsely, her voice almost gone, "Nothing to which I do not acquiesce. We have made a bargain, Kalor and I."

She would say nothing more, and she was so weak Cleante did not have the heart to question her further. She programmed the food synthesizer for the herbal tea T'Shael favored; the Vulcan refused its fragrant, steaming comfort though her eyes expressed her gratitude.

"I will require a healing trance, or the frostbite at least will exact its price. If you would watch over me until I call to you—"

Cleante merely nodded, helping her lie flat and pulling extra blankets off the other bunks to cover her.

The human spent the next hour pacing the length and breadth of the cage, once again keeping the Vulcan's vigil, trying to understand what this new form of torture could mean. What kind of "bargain" could Kalor have exacted from T'Shael? And how could she, mere human, make him stop torturing her friend? How?

"Why?" Jim Kirk demanded. "Why us? Why an unarmed, unescorted shuttlecraft? And why did the Romulans insist upon the two of us—you and me—specifically and unconditionally?"

By rights the Admiral should have been pleased at the genuine breakthrough in the final negotiations with the Rihannsu. He should have been further pleased that he and the *Enterprise* were to recover the two surviving Warrantors from their as yet unspecified location. But the terms of that recovery smelled fishy to him, and he didn't mind saying so.

"You suspect a trap," Spock suggested. "A trade-off. Two civilian hostages exchanged for two high-ranking Starfleet officers, against whom the Empire has a considerable vendetta."

Kirk made a face. Old memories . . .

"Wouldn't you?" he asked. "Suspect a trap, I mean? They've tried everything else to save face. Their demands for ransom and release of political prisoners were rejected outright. They were forced to execute three of their own officers to appease the Andorians. Their rift with the Klingons continues to widen. What's to stop them from salvaging a little glory by snatching us? What a *coup*— capture and summary execution of the thieves who stole the cloaking device. And no maneuvering room. It makes me twitch."

Spock said nothing. Sometimes it was necessary for Kirk to do his thinking aloud.

"It's too pat," the Admiral admitted at last, rubbing the back of his neck where the muscles knotted. "They wouldn't risk it at this point. They're as anxious to end this thing as we are. But why don't I feel right about it?"

He got no answer, and threw up his hands in resignation.

"Paranoia, I guess. I just wish Special Section would finish debriefing Sulu so we could get his perspective. They've refused to give us a crack at the last set of coordinates he brought through with him. Afraid we'll jump the gun."

Spock looked at him mildly.

"I know, I know," Kirk admitted. "The thought has occasionally crossed my mind. I don't like having my terms dictated to me by Rihannsu. But I've held out this long—with a little help from my friends." Spock acknowledged this with his silence. Kirk relaxed at last. "I haven't heard your opinion, old friend."

"In my opinion," Spock said deliberately. "Where Command dictates, we will go. If it means two of the Rihannsu's most desired targets journeying alone in a shuttlecraft to the edges of the quadrant as some test of honor, of good faith, then so be it."

Jim Kirk grinned.

"You're right. Although you forgot to remind me that I asked for this."

"Gratuitous, Jim."

Kirk fastened the flap of his tunic and checked his chronometer.

"Looks like as soon as we get destination orders I'll get what I asked for. Sacrificial lamb is not a role I'm comfortable with. Or is it Judas goat?"

Thirteen

"I ONLY HAVE one thing to bargain with," Cleante said to Kalor, trying to keep her voice steady. "Bring T'Shael back. Leave her alone. I'll do whatever you want."

"I'm not interested," the Klingon lied, lolling back in his chair, studying her.

His powerful legs were stretched out in front of him, crossed at the ankles, his coarse hands folded over his stomach in an attitude of total relaxation, total command. He had the Vulcan, and now the human, completely at his mercy.

For three more of the desolate planetoid's long and glacial nights he had consigned the Vulcan to the cold. Twice she was able to drag herself back to the compound at dawn; on the third morning Kalor had had to set the Kzantor for surface skim and fetch her back from the hills.

He had carried her into the cage, semi-conscious and near frozen, dumping her unceremoniously on the carpet at the human's feet. The Vulcan's resistance lowered with each exposure to the cold; the human's was destroyed anew each time her companion went off into the night.

For three days Kalor had watched as Cleante hounded T'Shael with questions to which she got no answers. This seeming rift between them pleased him inordinately. For three nights he had forced the human back into the cage at

254

disruptor point as the Vulcan departed, locking the transparency against her reasoning, her pleading, her rages and tears.

This night he had returned to unlock the door, leering at her, his breath pluming out around him like dragon spume in the frigid air.

Cleante watched him swagger back to his quarters. She knew exactly what he expected of her, but she would do it anyway. She had made the decision as soon as she'd seen what he was doing to T'Shael. All she had needed was this opportunity.

She found the clothing the Rihannsu had left behind, choosing a shimmering, lowcut tunic over soft trousers that accentuated her figure. With steady fingers she unbraided her long, luxuriant hair, letting it cascade over her shoulders and down her back. She found among the exotic Rihannsu toiletries a vial of scent—an ironic joke in this place—of a kind that enhanced the body's natural chemistry.

The next best thing to Deltan pheromones, Cleante thought, with homage to Jali. She applied the scent liberally, running her perfumed fingers through her hair at the last and, steeling herself, started across the compound.

Kalor studied this new aspect of the human, his relaxed posture belying his ravening desire. It had been a long time since he had had a female under any circumstances; he could not ever remember any female so frankly sexual offering herself with so little pretense. If he did not seize the moment her loathing might overcome her desperation to save the Vulcan. Still, Klingon perverse, Kalor toyed with her.

"I'm not interested," he said, as if dismissing her.

He pretended great interest in the scanner readout at his elbow, though it showed him the same thing it had for four consecutive nights: a solitary life form in the far hills, slowly cooling down toward death.

Cleante dared not look at the screen. If that single life reading should fade or suddenly flicker out . . . she glared at Kalor, who knew what she was feeling and reveled in it.

"All right," the human nodded.

She had one ploy left. She wrenched open the door that led to the hills before Kalor could stop her.

"What do you think you're doing?" he snarled, slamming the door shut, planting himself between her and it.

"I'm going to die with my friend," the diplomat's daughter said with all the grandeur she could muster. "It's the only way I can guarantee the Rihannsu give you exactly what you deserve!"

Her Byzantine eyes blazed at him. Kalor scowled, licking his lips, feral.

"Why do you care what happens to her?" he demanded, frankly puzzled. "She's not of your species. There can be no kinship. Your death won't do her any good. It's meaningless!"

Cleante looked at him with pity. What could friendship, love, possibly mean to him?

"You're an idiot, Kalor," she said sadly and without fear. What more could he possibly do to her? "You don't understand anything. Now get out of my way! I'm going to be with my friend."

The fire in her eyes challenged the Klingon, fanned the flame of his desire. He seized her face in one rough hand and forced his mouth onto hers, remembering at the last moment not to bare his teeth. Cleante did not struggle, nor was she passive. Kalor felt a resistance in her, which suggested it could be overcome with the proper technique. He stepped back, still holding her chin in his hand. Her lips were bruised, but her eyes continued to dare him.

"Bring T'Shael back," she whispered, breathless, seductive. "Bring her back and I'll do whatever you want!"

It was too tempting, too easy. It's a trap! Kalor's Klingon soul shouted, almost in the voice of Krazz. He thrust the human away from him, wiping his mouth with the back of his hand.

"You're very beautiful—for a human," he breathed. "And full of fire . . . I like that . . . But we both know it's only to save the Vulcan. I know you hate me. You say you will do anything? I want to see you beg. I want to know that though you loathe me you will come to me on your knees and beg."

Cleante went rigid. Humility had never been her strong suit. No one would degrade her in this way, no one!

The wind moaned about the compound. The crucible of

the *t'hy'la* could strengthen, refine, purify, T'Shael had said. Anything for you, *t'hy'la,* anything!

The diplomat's daughter took Kalor's coarse hand in her own, kissed it tenderly, brushed it against her cheek and the luxury of her hair, cradled it between her breasts so he could feel the beating of her human heart. Slowly, her eyes never leaving his, she sank to her knees at his feet.

"Please, my Lord Kalor!" she begged softly. Anything, *t'hy'la!* "Please!"

Kirk hovered over Spock's shoulder as the science officer decoded the coordinates Command had just relayed to them. He could not hope to make sense out of the complexity of figures with anything like the Vulcan's speed, but thought maybe being there could somehow make things happen faster. They'd been given the final go-ahead to retrieve the Warrantors, and Kirk's adrenaline had just kicked into overdrive.

Spock finished decoding and called up the correct star-chart. Kirk leaned in and squinted at it.

"Practically off the edge of the quadrant," he remarked. "Which one specifically?"

"This one." Spock's delicate finger pinpointed an undistinguished dot in the center of the starfield. "One of a group of predominantly uncharted small planetoids clustered around a number of Class N variable stars, approximately midway between both Neutral Zones and in disputed territory. The nearest Federation parameters would be the Minara system and Outpost One on the Rihannsu border."

Kirk looked to Sulu. Freshly debriefed, he had returned to the *Enterprise* via Special Section VIP courier. He had refused to part with his Rihannsu ears and seemed to relish the stares of the crew. Ever eager to do his share, he was not about to interrupt these two for whom it might be said that Genius at Work was no hyperbole.

"Does that jibe with what you brought back?" Kirk wanted to know.

Sulu leaned over Spock's other shoulder, studied the chart for a moment as if recalling something he had committed to memory, and nodded.

"It's for real, sir. No question." He traced an invisible line of planet hops with one finger. "The Klin ships cross the border here, then diverge here, make three colony stops along this route, refuel here, rendezvous with the slower Rihan transports here, then double back. This one—" his finger stopped where Spock's had, "—is the only uninhabited stopover. As far as I know."

Kirk nodded, satisfied.

"Not exactly a day trip," he mused. "Scotty says he can give us Warp eight to Rator. That's where we have to leave *Enterprise*. How long?"

Spock calculated in his head.

"Fifteen days, four-point-zero-six hours at optimum warp."

"And then we cut loose in the *Galileo*." Kirk grimaced, still unhappy about it. "Lame duck in a shooting gallery. How long will we have to be a target out there?"

Spock looked thoughtful.

"Difficult to be precise over such a distance in uncharted territory. However, barring unforeseen obstacles . . . an additional two-point-seven-six days."

Kirk rubbed his lower lip absently.

"And as many days back with possibly sick or injured passengers. If only we could bring a medical team . . . damn diplomats!" He rested a hand on Spock's shoulder as if to borrow some of the Vulcan's imperturbability. "All right, let's go!"

T'Shael opened her eyes to darkness.

The last thing she remembered was a slow, helpless slipping into the final sleepy stages of hypothermia. She analyzed. Kalor had come for her as he had the night before, but this time he had not brought her back to the cage. Her eyes accustomed themselves to the imperfect darkness, her acute night vision picking out starshine through flaws in the roof of the tremor-damaged structure. Kalor had locked her in the storage shed. But why?

T'Shael shivered involuntarily; she had been unconscious and unable to engage the healing trance and her body was making a slow recovery. There were sharp stabbing pains in her extremities and the bones of her face and she couldn't flex her fingers, but these things would remedy themselves now that she was out of the killing wind. The shed was unheated; it was cold here, cold enough to be uncomfortable, but not cold enough to kill.

Kalor arrived at dawn, leading Cleante into the shed.

"Not long," he warned her, locking the door behind him.

Cleante did not say a word. She took T'Shael in her arms and held her for a long moment, rocking her like a child. T'Shael found herself returning the embrace. Awkwardly with her damaged hands and her inexperience in such matters, she returned it nevertheless, finding it strangely curative.

"Thank God, you're all right!" Cleante said, breaking the embrace at last, blinking back tears.

She had brought food and blankets, and busied herself setting things up on crates and containers stacked about the shed. Kalor apparently intended T'Shael to remain here indefinitely. The Vulcan watched the human cautiously, not misled by her industriousness.

The dim light in the shed could not disguise how haggard Cleante looked. Not that the events of the past few days had lent themselves to restfulness, but there was something more here.

"You look unwell," T'Shael observed gently, charily, noting that after her first carefully orchestrated embrace Cleante shied from her touch, her very proximity. "Has something untoward happened in my absence?"

Cleante laughed her nervous, high-strung laugh; T'Shael had not heard it for some time.

"Whatever gave you that idea?" the human asked, her voice laced with heavy irony and not a little hysteria. "What could possibly have happened? I spent another night not knowing if you were dead or alive, another night pounding on the door begging Kalor to listen to me. Nothing unusual."

"Forgive me," T'Shael said, made more uneasy by the human's answer. She who could not lie was unable to prove untruth in another. "These past few nights must have been most difficult for you to bear."

More than you can know, my friend, Cleante thought, though her face was almost Vulcanly controlled. More than I can ever burden you with knowing. I must not let slip the slightest clue as to how I've spent this past night.

"I'll live," she said airily. "We both will, T'Shael, and that's what matters. Kalor has decided to keep you here. Even he's not stupid enough to let the Rihannsu find you half-frozen."

T'Shael received this information with deepening concern.

"Is that truly his reason?"

"How should I know?" Cleante demanded irritably. "We're only prisoners; we don't get answers." She began pacing restlessly, hugging herself. "Maybe he got tired of listening to me scream. What difference does it make? The only important thing is that you're here, you're safe, and we're one day closer to rescue. We've got to hold onto that, T'Shael, no matter how."

Something in the way she said this gave T'Shael pause. She dared invade the human's privacy enough to take her by the shoulders and seek the depths of her eyes.

"Cleante, if you have interceded with Kalor in any way—"

Cleante pulled out of her grasp.

"Don't be ridiculous! What could I possibly do? There's only one thing he could possibly want from me."

She stopped. She had rehearsed this scene all night, planning it even as she lay in Kalor's fevered embrace. The diplomat's daughter must draw upon every bit of her acting talent to mislead the one person in the universe who knew her best.

"You don't actually think . . . T'Shael, I'm amazed! How could you think that of me?"

The Vulcan bowed her head, ashamed.

"It seemed a logical possibility in view of our captor's appetites and his persuasiveness. I ask forgiveness for the very thought."

"I'm really surprised, that's all," Cleante went on, playing her role to the hilt. "If I were going to do anything like that I'd at least insist he bring you back to the cage where you could be warm, where I could talk to you."

I tried, T'Shael, the human thought. I pleaded with him all night but he refused me, knowing if you and I were together

260

too long you would learn the truth. These visits are all he will allow.

"Besides," there was no pretense in the shudder she experienced, "he disgusts me!"

T'Shael looked at her for a long moment. There was an undefined tension here.

"If you are certain—"

"Have I ever lied to you?" Cleante demanded, trying not to sound too aggrieved.

"Never," the Vulcan acknowledged, but she was not satisfied.

Night after night she spent alone in the cold and dark of the storage shed, wrapped in a blanket and her meditations, wondering why Kalor had spared her. Was it only to protect himself from the Rihannsu or was this some new aspect of his experimentation? Could a Klingon be merciful? Or was Cleante lying to her?

Day after day Cleante came to visit her, staying only a short while, bringing food and nervous conversation and a renewal of T'Shael's uneasiness. The lie that human could not admit to and Vulcan could not prove began to form a barrier between them. Cleante's mood swings in these brief visitations were alarming. At times she was almost manic, chattering away about their impending rescue as if it would happen that very day. At other times she was listless, enervated, lapsing into an uneasy silence long before Kalor came for her. She would not let T'Shael touch her nor even come too close. T'Shael noted these things somberly and without remedy.

Meanwhile, Kalor was fairly intoxicated; intoxicated with the success of his experiment, which he would entitle, in the report he need not entrust to anyone this time: "Honor and Friendship: Exploitable Weaknesses in the Vulcan and Terran Species"; intoxicated, too, with the discovery that pleasure need not always take the form of debauchery and slaughter; intoxicated with the discovery that certain human females could be extraordinarily gifted in the love arts.

When did it stop being brutal gratification and begin to evolve into interest and concern and a kind of sharing? As one night followed another, on which night did Kalor ex-press concern that Cleante might be too fatigued to con-tinue? On which occasion did he begin to evidence that he could give pleasure as well as take it? In which instance did Cleante cease to close her eyes and clench her teeth and force her mind back to Rico or the boy from Deneva and accept the reality that this was Kalor—Klingon and mur-derer, but also a being who was not entirely insensitive? One might as well try to determine at what moment Kalor ceased to be a total brute and began to become an intellectual. His venture into xenopsychology had begun to operate on a level he could never have anticipated.

"Cleante," he would whisper (tenderly?), at any rate softly, as she lay with her head on his broad, vestigially scaled chest, no longer pretending relaxation but experienc-ing it, as he tangled his no longer quite so coarse fingers in the luxury of her hair. "Kleant. It could almost be a Klingon name."

"But I could never be a Klingon," Cleante murmured. "I could never kill to earn adult status, and call it a game."

She could hear her voice trailing off. How could she possibly allow herself to feel drowsy? She thought of T'Shael alone in the cold and was suddenly alert.

"Tell me more about the Games. About the *komerex tel khesterex,* the Expanding Empire. And about you, Kalor. I want to know."

At first she had started him talking to keep his sexual demands bearable, but as he talked and talked she found herself taken up in his narrative. Was this any different really than her study of the Vulcan through T'Shael?

Kalor was inordinately pleased. No one had ever taken an interest in him in this way before. He told Cleante about his father, about his obsession with rehabilitating the family name, about the cunning and the compromises and the sacrifices necessary just to stay alive in his society. Cleante began to understand, and her horror at a being who could execute his own father, then kill the friend who had assisted in the execution turned to pity.

Sad, twisted Kalor, Klingon who never should have been. If he had been born anything else . . . if, when she and

T'Shael were rescued, she could intercede for him, ask that he be re-educated within the Federation, explain that—

Explain what? That he had killed the Deltans, had almost killed T'Shael, could no doubt kill her as she lay in his arms?

Cleante was confused, more confused than she had ever been in her life. She thought of the philosophical "crises" that had beset her on Vulcan and had to force the laugh back in her throat lest Kalor hear her. How trivial all that seemed now! Here in this place that didn't own a name she walked a tightrope of indeterminate length—daily lying to her closest friend, nightly making love to her worst enemy, while awaiting the arrival of friend or foe to set things right again. If she did not go mad . . .

"The shuttlecraft has left the Federation mother ship," Tal reported to his Commander.

"You are certain it's the *Enterprise?*" she asked without looking up from her reports.

"We are monitoring from a considerable distance, Commander," Tal reminded her. "Its call-signal is definitely that of a Constitution-class heavy cruiser. We cannot identify it precisely, but we have no reason to believe the Federation would renege on its pledge at this point."

"Nor shall we," the Commander said, putting down her writing implement and looking at her sub-commander for the first time. "How many life forms do you read in the shuttlecraft? They do have their screens down?"

"As promised," Tal affirmed. "They have left themselves open to our scanners. We read two: one human, one Vulcan."

"Good," the Commander said without reacting, knowing Tal was watching her closely. "Set course back to the planetoid at maximum speed. I want to be there and gone before that shuttlecraft arrives."

Tal frowned.

"For what purpose, Commander? We have been instructed that the Klingons will retrieve their own."

The Commander looked annoyed.

"To ascertain the final status of the prisoners, of course. I argued myself hoarse before the Praesidium about the inadvisability of leaving that *thrai* alone with the prisoners and for once I lost. I would not put it past him to have interfered with our purposes, even at this late date."

"Are you certain that is the only reason?" Tal presumed to ask, wondering what scenarios would transpire on the desolate planetoid if she and the Vulcan from the shuttlecraft should encounter each other by her design. "And, more to the point, will we be able to depart in time?"

"Leave that to me!" the Commander said dangerously, trying unsuccessfully to wilt Tal with her glare. "In the meantime, amuse yourself with giving me hourly status reports on the whereabouts of that shuttlecraft."

"Of course, Commander," Tal said. If there was irony in his voice, there was none on his face.

Cleante grew careless, and T'Shael discovered the truth. She who could not lie learned at firsthand how many cutting edges a single lie could possess.

"I'm sorry I'm late," Cleante said a little too lightly as Kalor locked the door behind her on this particular day now slipping into night. Did T'Shael only think she saw a glance exchanged between human and Klingon? "I seem to have slept most of the day. I've been so restless lately!"

"Perhaps you are ill," T'Shael suggested, probing. "Does the tension of our captivity weigh on you so greatly now that it is almost at an end? Or is there something more?"

Cleante laughed her nervous laugh, fidgeting with the food containers she had brought.

"Will you stop cross-examining me? Come and eat this while it's still hot."

"I have no hunger," the Vulcan said, her eyes deep with perplexity. The human's tension was almost tangible. "I had thought you might not come."

Cleante stopped her fidgeting and looked into the hooded eyes, taking T'Shael's statement as an accusation, realizing how much she must depend on her visits.

I'm all she has now, the human thought with a pang. All the more reason why she must never know the true cause of my restlessness, my exhaustion.

"I'm sorry, I—" she began, but T'Shael interrupted her.

"It is of no matter, except that I sense further groundquakes, perhaps soon. I wished to warn you."

"Oh," Cleante said, relieved that minor things like deadly groundquakes were the only cause of T'Shael's concern. "Well, for the next few nights I'll have to sleep under the bunk instead of in it, I guess. What about you?"

"I can make shelter here," T'Shael said, dismissing it.

"Should I—should we tell Kalor?" Cleante asked after too long a pause. "Or should we let him suffer through it?"

T'Shael gave no answer. She drew closer than Cleante found comfortable, assessing the sleep-heavy eyes, the bruised lips, the fact that Cleante had absentmindedly worn the Rihannsu clothing instead of her uniform. Cleante realized this too late and her hand went to the neck of her tunic. It was a high-necked one, but not high enough to completely cover her throat.

With a sudden quick aggressiveness T'Shael seized her by the collar, wrenching it back to expose the human's throat, which was covered with love bites. The Vulcan's hand trembled, the thin fabric tearing under the ferocity of her grip.

Cleante tugged at her hand, trying to make her let go. She felt exposed, violated, more soiled by T'Shael's penetrating gaze than by anything Kalor could do to her.

"T'Shael, let go of me! For the love of Allah, don't accuse me! And don't be angry. I can't bear it!"

Never had she seen such intermixed pain and anger ripping through the Vulcan mask. T'Shael's voice was anguished.

"Why?!"

"To save your life, damn it!" the human shrieked. "What else could I do? Was I supposed to sit there night after night waiting for you to die? What right do you have to ask me to do that? What makes you think you're the only one capable of sacrifice?"

T'Shael released the human from her grasp, withdrawing, trying to gather herself, soul-sick with what she suddenly comprehended, what she had been too blind to recognize before. She could only imagine the degradations Kalor had visited upon Cleante night after night while she remained safe and inviolate in this place. The injustice of it, the evil of it, should have screamed across the compound to her, but she had not heard. The ripple effect of one's actions upon the face of the universe: first Stalek's death, now Kalor's evil and her *t'hy'la*'s sacrifice be upon her soul. This must not continue!

"It's the only way, T'Shael," Cleante was saying dreamily, standing near the door as if she actually anticipated Kalor's arrival with some kind of pleasure. "It's the only way for both of us to remain alive and whole until they come for us. Can't you see that? You have to admit it's logical.

"Besides, it isn't so bad. Kalor's quite sensitive, sometimes. I never would have expected that. I've convinced him that I want him for himself now, not just to save you. That can be a great advantage. For both of us."

And I'm not being totally honest with you, my *t'hy'la*, Cleante thought. The truth is my feelings are so jumbled I don't know the truth anymore. I started out just trying to save your life, pretending, going through the motions. But now I find I almost welcome Kalor's touch. It's been a long time since I've held someone in my arms, responded to him, felt him responding to me. I can't say I love him, not after what he did to the Deltans, what he's done to you. But is it possible I'm no longer pretending, possible I actually find pleasure in him? Oh, T'Shael, I'm so confused! The only thing I'm sure of, the only thing that's real and true and honest is what I've told you—that this is the only way I know. It's the only pure and unselfish thing I've ever done, the only sacrifice I can offer you. Is it somehow less pure if it's no longer a sacrifice?

She was so totally absorbed in the confusion of her thoughts that she did not sense T'Shael's approach, could not have heard her at any rate because of the Vulcan's feline stealth. The long and elegant fingers moved like lightning to the precise spot on the human's shoulder as T'Shael's other arm broke her unconscious fall. The Vulcan picked up her human burden effortlessly and placed her gently, gently on the floor of the shed, sheltering her with crates and boxes against the eventuality of groundquakes.

No, my more-than-worthy, it is not the only way, T'Shael thought, composing the human's limbs as if in sleep, cover-

266

ing her tenderly with her own ragged blanket. My way may not be logical, but it is final.

As she could have done for all these many nights but had foreborne because she had taken Cleante at her word, as she would blame herself for the rest of her life, she gathered her Vulcan strength and forced the flimsy lock on the door of the shed. With a purposefulness she had not had before—her task all these months had been to remain with the other prisoners, draw on her resources to try to keep them all alive; she had failed with the Andorian and the Deltans, and must not fail this time—she found the power source that electrified the fence about the compound, ripped it loose in a shower of sparks, and scaled the fence.

Within moments, her long and effortless stride carried her in the direction of the hills, toward where her sixth sense told her would be the locus of the next tremors. If the cold did not claim her, the maw of the planet would. If Kalor came seeking her, she would force him to kill her. He must no longer use her to manipulate Cleante. The human would be free of him until the Rihannsu returned, and they must return soon. They must!

T'Shael stopped only once, just as the compound was almost beyond range of her acute night vision. She turned and looked back, no longer feeling the vicious wind. She swept the lank hair out of her somber eyes with one hand and raised the other in the *ta'al*.

Live long and prosper, Cleante alFaisal, my more-than-worthy, she thought. If it could have been otherwise, I might have deserved to be your *t'hy'la*. Forgive me my failure. *Kaiidth!* As I have endeavored to teach you, and as you have succeeded in teaching me—

Tears stung into the Vulcan's eyes, but it was only the wind. She turned her back on the compound and loped purposefully toward the hills.

Jim Kirk rubbed the sleep out of his eyes and adjusted his seat to an upright position. He looked across at Spock, who was exactly as he had been when the Admiral began to doze, piloting the shuttlecraft at maximum speed, unerring and tireless.

"A matter of hours now, Jim," Spock replied to the

unasked question. "And, Jim—" Would the information he was about to impart alleviate the Admiral's uneasiness or exacerbate it? "We are being scanned, at regular intervals, by a vessel which remains beyond our sensor range."

"They know we're out here," Kirk mused.

Out here and at their mercy, he thought but did not say.

Back home on *Enterprise*, five pairs of eyes watched Sulu's monitor until the blip that was the shuttlecraft disappeared.

"Out of range now, Mr. Scott," Sulu, restored to his customary place at the helm, reported unnecessarily.

"Aye," Scotty sighed, shifting his weight in the command chair. "Looks like it's us that does the waiting now."

"Some of us have done the waiting all along, Mr. Scott," Uhura reminded him softly, leaving the comm con at last to sit on the steps behind him.

"Aye, lass, that's true enough," Scotty acknowledged. "And none of us are denying that's sometimes the hardest of all."

"Dammit, I should've been allowed to go with them!" McCoy exploded into the silence, pounding the guardrail he was leaning against and making Saavik jump. "I'm just as much implicated in that cloaking device business as they were, and there might've been something I could do!"

"You've done what you could, Leonard," Scotty tried to assure him, nodding in the direction of Sulu's ears, clapping a hand over his own arm where McCoy had implanted the ethanol-inhibitor. "And I'll swear in my case you did too good of a job. I haven't gone on a tear since."

"That's the thanks I get!" McCoy grumbled. "I just wish I could get a look at the two survivors before Jim and Spock have to bring them all the way back here. What if they're sick or injured? What if—?"

His voice tapered off. For one thing there was no one around to argue with him, for another he was merely voicing what all of them were thinking.

"Funny, isn't it?" Sulu had said when he'd first gotten back. "Funny, how we've all gotten involved in the lives of people we've never met."

He had by now shed most of his Rihannsu mannerisms

and the thinking that went with them, though he still affected the ears, and he might continue to dream in Rihan all his days. His return to the human realm had been a kind of culture shock.

He'd been lionized by the Prolificom media (though all requests for interviews had been answered with anonymous press releases in order to preserve his cover), showered with accolades *in absentia* by the diplomatic community and the public at large. He'd received a commendation and a hand-shake from the head of Special Section himself, then had slipped back into his uniform and his place at the helm to become just Hikaru Sulu, Commander Reactivated, helms-man extraordinaire and something of a swashbuckler, but in all other respects just one of the crew.

No one on *Enterprise* had made a fuss over him; he hadn't expected them to. Heroism was the norm for these people, and Sulu had accepted their business-as-usual attitude as the best welcome he could ask for.

The others had murmured their agreement, all but Uhura, who spent her life getting caught up in the lives of people she'd never met, and in worrying about the people she saw every day who insisted on trying to get themselves killed in one fashion or another.

She had put the comm con on automatic at last. Nothing of significance would come through at this distance until Spock hailed in from the shuttlecraft three days from now, and her usually mellifluous voice was hoarse from thanking all those people, from the ones she knew personally like Tam and Mai-Ling to the anonymous voices of the Floaters. She needed to rest now. She sat on the steps of the command well, warming her soul at the metaphorical campfire, know-ing Jim and Spock and the Warrantors would come home safe because they must.

"Funny," Sulu had said, having shaken off the Prolificom reporters at last, a little dazzled at the larger-than-life figure they'd made of him in "Operation D'Artagnan" as they'd headlined it.

And if Scotty didn't answer him right away, it was be-cause he was more preoccupied with people he *had* met, and with how they had changed.

Unlike Sulu and his VIP courier, Scotty had slipped back

aboard weeks ago with no noticeable fanfare and had gone back to his engines and the routines around which he'd built his life, but the encounter with Korax still haunted him. Whatever concrete value his small role in the larger operation might have led in aggravating the friction between the strange bedfellows that were the Empires, its residual effect on him personally had been profound.

He found himself studying his face in the shaving mirror of a morning, counting the age lines, wondering what it must be like to be a Klingon and have it all past you by the time you were thirty. No wonder they were rapacious, violent; it was all over for them so quickly. It was a strange and uncanny feeling, this sudden duality, this ability to see through the eyes of a Klingon.

And Saavik, silent Saavik, no stranger to duality, sat at her post as navigator dunsel, unneeded really while they idled at station-keeping off Rator, which was as far as the Rihannsu would allow them to go. She had had the least active role of any here, yet she, too, had not been unchanged by events. For one thing, she had never had to listen to so many anti-Romulan slurs in all of her brief life.

Most humans knew nothing of her background. They saw her in the Starfleet uniform and took her for Vulcan, forgetting how well she could hear when they occasionally felt free to make disparaging remarks in her presence. These remarks had always been rare, originating from those of narrow mind and unexamined opinion whom one might suspect of bigotry in any event. But with the tensions created by the Warrantor situation, the slurs seemed to be on everyone's lips, even if they only went so far as, "Well, what else can you expect from a Romulan?"

Saavik had gritted her teeth and become all the more Vulcan, fighting the urge to judge as she and hers were being judged, to return bigotry for bigotry. Insults are effective only where emotion is present, Spock would say—Spock, who all his life had borne the bigotry of human and Vulcan alike, invoking the personal mantra he had bequeathed Saavik from the beginning: Tolerance. Tolerance is logical.

Indeed, my mentor, Saavik thought in his absence. But it is difficult.

So deep was she in her personal thoughts that she hadn't

realized the others were talking around her, joking the way humans did when they were anxious, when a silence had gone on too long and threatened to engulf them.

" . . . and not another day goes by without we do something about those ears, D'Artagnan," McCoy was saying. "You're attracting entirely too much attention."

"Aw, Doc, do I have to?" Sulu fingered them nostalgically. "You have to admit I've grown sort of—attached to them."

The others groaned, and Saavik glanced at Sulu quizzically, to find him grinning at her, inviting her to share the joke. Humor, she thought. It was a difficult concept, but one that could warm the heart in the dark night of space.

Fourteen

THE FIRST OF the tremors brought Cleante around. She tried to sit up, but the room spun around her, and the pounding in her head—

Memory returned slowly. She had been arguing with T'Shael in the storage shed, trying to make her understand. A sense of falling . . .

What had T'Shael done to her, and where was the Vulcan now?

Cleante sat up in spite of the headache. She was in Kalor's quarters, on his cot, still fully dressed, but— Her hand went to the collar of the tunic where T'Shael had torn it. She looked up to see Kalor standing over her.

He had been drinking, still held the bottle in his hand. He seemed not to notice that the room swayed with tremors, perhaps thinking his inability to keep his feet was a result of the alcohol and not external events. His mood was surly.

"Your green-blooded friend has finished me," he slurred. "Escaped, *khest* her! Don't ask me how. She dies and the Roms kill me. Some bargain! Treachery and deceit—from a Vulcan. The universe *has* gone mad!"

"We can still find her!" Cleante said, springing off the cot. "She may still be alive. If we can bring her back—"

Kalor squinted at her. The drink may have clouded his

vision. There might be two of her. Which one could he trust? The floor beneath him bucked again and he struggled to keep his feet.

"You and I as allies?" he growled, Klingon suspicious. "The universe *is* askew! Or is it you and the Vulcan in connivance against me? That I would sooner believe!"

"What difference does it make?" Cleante demanded, thinking fast, "As long as T'Shael is alive when the Rihannsu return. Think, Kalor! Once we've found her you can make her stay, but if you leave her out there she'll certainly die. And so will you!"

Kalor's lizard eyes shifted uneasily. He could tell the Roms the Vulcan had committed suicide. Would they buy that after the Deltan business? Or was it better to say she'd escaped? How could they believe that after he'd managed to hold her all this time? Panic was new to Kalor; he didn't like it.

The drink had certainly clouded his wits; he could see no clear plan of action before him. Only one thing was certain: the human was still here, still desirable. If he must die for the loss of a Vulcan, let him snatch what pleasure he could from his final hours.

"I have to think about this," he said, taking a final swig from the bottle, slamming it on the table. A tremor sent it crashing to the floor; the room reeked of the vitriolic stuff. Kalor ignored it, wiping his mouth on his sleeve and looming over Cleante. "First things first."

"All right," Cleante acquiesced without thinking.

She did not take time to bargain, to exact his promise that they would search for T'Shael after. She might have insisted they find T'Shael first, so great was Kalor's need, but she did not. She would never know why. Was she afraid of pushing her luck and angering Kalor in his dangerous state? Could it be a fulfillment of her own needs as much as his? She did not analyze it; she simply began to undress.

You'll have to bear the cold a while longer, T'Shael, she thought, loosening her hair and slipping out of her clothes. I'm sorry. Or, maybe I'm not. I didn't force you to run away; the decision was yours. Maybe this is my experiment in xenopsychology now, my way of humanizing a Klingon—if that isn't a contradiction in terms. Maybe it's my final atonement, my hairshirt. Maybe I'm just tired of apologizing.

She shivered a little at the sound of the wind, hugging herself as she lay there waiting for him. The tremors seemed to have died away for the moment. Cleante looked up at Kalor, who could not know the turmoil in her mind and would not have cared, knowing only that she was here and she was for him.

The Commander preferred her private scoutcraft to the transporter for surprise visits. It made for a grander entrance, and its power dampers rendered it absolutely silent. It touched down in the darkness of the compound as if it were part of the night wind. If Kalor had not been otherwise engaged he still could never have anticipated what happened.

The Commander stepped out of the scout and moved about the compound soundlessly. Within seconds, she had assessed the situation, and acted.

Her hand was on her disruptor as she seemed to materialize in the doorway. She fired from the hip with deadly accuracy and Kalor crumpled without a sound.

"No Klingon defies me!" the Commander said in a voice that made it clear how she, female in a warrior society, had come to be what she was. She grabbed Cleante's wrist and yanked her unceremoniously off the cot. "You seem none the worse for wear. Get dressed. You'll have to lead me to the Vulcan."

Cleante allowed Kalor one stunned, incredulous glance before she stumbled into her clothes. Within moments she and the Commander were locked in side by side in the scout. There were no guards, no ideological barriers, only two females, born under different stars, united on a single point: the need to find the third, who held a different meaning to each.

"She would head for the epicenter, in the hills, there," Cleante said suddenly and with absolute certainty.

The Rihannsu acknowledged without question and pointed the scout's nose toward the ragged hills.

The ground had begun to rumble again as the scout set down in the last level place before the hills clawed their way upward. Loose rock from fist-sized chunks to great boulders rattled erratically down the slopes.

"Stay here!" the Commander ordered, clambering out of the scout's hatch and strapping on emergency climbing gear. "You're only a hindrance without boots!"

"I must go to her!" Cleante shrieked into the wind, and though the Commander knew it would slow her down, she consented.

They did not have to go far.

"There!" Cleante pointed, her other hand covering her mouth as she choked down pure horror.

T'Shael was pinned against an outcropping by a huge boulder, arms outstretched as if in supplication, unconscious if not dead. There was no way of knowing how long she had been like this. A trickle of blood from the corner of her mouth had almost congealed in the cold; her flesh was devoid of color and colder than any living thing Cleante had ever encountered. The human scrabbled frantically at the huge rock with her bare hands until the Commander pushed her aside.

"Heat flares!" she shouted, pointing in the direction of the scout. "And there's a portastretcher in the storage hatch. Quickly!"

Cleante stayed only long enough to see the Commander casually shove the boulder out of the way and catch T'Shael as she pitched forward before she fled down the slope.

The Commander laid the Vulcan on the semi-rigid portastretcher while Cleante struggled with the heat flares, watching as the Rihannsu performed a perfunctory examination, wincing as the small hands gingerly probed the thin, battered body.

"Broken ribs and clavicle, probable lung puncture. Possible pelvic damage as well; I can't be certain. Considerable internal bruising, at any rate," she reported matter-of-factly, strapping the portastretcher as tightly as she thought the Vulcan could tolerate. T'Shael was beyond the reach of pain. "And of course exposure. The price of self-sacrifice! She will probably live, if your Federation is punctual. We must move her back to the compound."

So saying, she hefted the portastretcher by the carry-straps and brought the Vulcan down the slope toward the scout, with Cleante holding a flare to light the way. The ground rumbled and pitched beneath them, causing both to stumble more than once. Somehow, they made it.

They lashed two of the heavy bunks together to form a makeshift shelter within the confines of the cage, "in case the quakes bring the roof down," the Commander said tersely. Together they padded the floor with mattresses and blankets, and Cleante crawled into the shelter to offer her body heat to the still-comatose Vulcan. She sat upright when she realized the Rihannsu was studying her.

"I must go," she said, crouching close to her two former hostages, almost protective. "I have already overstayed my escape margin."

Cleante touched her arm.

"Thank you!" she cried, frustrated by the inadequacy of language at such a time. If T'Shael were conscious she could at least say it in High Rihan, but it was still only words, insufficient. "From T'Shael and me, from Vulcan and human, thank you!"

The Commander looked at her wryly.

"Tell it to your gods, if you believe in any," she said shortly, and was gone.

The quakes continued throughout the endless night. Chunks of concrete broke loose from walls and ceilings, and more than once Cleante wondered if the entire planetoid would open and swallow them as it had Krazz. Her mind whirled with the events of the past few hours.

She finally understood that Kalor was really dead, that the Rihannsu were gone and that within a matter of hours, perhaps at any moment, a Federation ship would rescue them. T'Shael was alive, if barely; their ordeal by fire and ice was almost over. It seemed too much for her poor, exhausted human brain to fathom.

Kalor—dead! How did she feel about that? Cleante wanted to cry, to wash herself clean of him, but also to mourn him. She found that she couldn't. What might he have become if that embryonic intellectualism, that almost-sensitivity in him had had a chance to grow and conquer his Klingon need to maim and destroy? She would puzzle it all out later, after they'd been rescued. Maybe then she would be able to mourn him, to fit him into her past as she might have cause to fit him into her future.

Could a human be impregnated by a Klingon? Cleante wondered. Human children grew up on whispered horror stories of what happened to those captured and enslaved by Klingons. It hadn't seemed important before, when all that mattered was saving T'Shael. Now, with the promise of a return to a normal life, it suddenly became critically important.

Cleante huddled closer to T'Shael, who had begun to tremble, regaining consciousness, reacting to her injuries and the hypothermia. A strangled moan forced itself from the Vulcan's lips.

"T'Shael, be still! Don't move," Cleante whispered. "You're badly hurt but you're safe now. They're coming to rescue us, *t'hy'la*. Hold on a little longer!"

The Vulcan began to cough and Cleante quailed, thinking of the internal bleeding and the incredible pain. She held T'Shael's head while she coughed up an alarming amount of blood from damaged lungs and lapsed again into welcome unconsciousness.

Cleante began to weep then. Oh, don't let it end now! she pleaded, not knowing to whom. She's been through so much and I've failed her so abysmally. Don't let her die now! She wanted to wrap her arms around the Vulcan and infuse some of her strength into her, but was afraid to hurt her more.

How—unclean—you must think I am, Cleante thought, wiping the tears away at last. How weak and carnal and utterly human you must think me! I wouldn't touch you at all except that the could makes it necessary. I feel so dirty compared to you.

I've failed you, T'Shael. I let you flee to almost certain death while I jumped right back into Kalor's bed. I'm sorry! I'm so sorry!

With a great effort of will, T'Shael forced herself to the surface of consciousness. How much more preferable to stay down out of the reach of pain, but she must . . .

Her entire body was a mass of pain; were she human, she might have screamed. She was beyond the ability to suppress the pain, too weak to engage a healing trance. Though the light was a stabbing agony, she opened her eyes; opened them to meet the depthless gaze of one of her own.

Not Rihannsu, but Vulcan. T'Shael knew. A glance took in the deep red of his uniform, the glint of insignia. Starfleet? It was true, then. She had not imagined Cleante's voice pleading with her to hold on.

They were safe. They?

Cleante! T'Shael's mind screamed, but she could not make the words come. The Vulcan who held her—she could feel through the pain that he was carrying her gently, setting her down with infinite care inside some unfamiliar, low-ceilinged structure—read her distress.

"Do not attempt to speak," he cautioned in a voice deep with something T'Shael could not name. "All is well. Your companion is unharmed."

Had her distress been so apparent? T'Shael struggled to speak despite his warning, to ask forgiveness for her display of emotion before one of her own, but stopped. There had been no reproach in his voice, but, rather, a vast understanding. Who was this one, and why was his manner thus?

"You will jeopardize your life if you continue to struggle," he said and, reading her thoughts, answered all her questions. "I am called Spock."

T'Shael closed her eyes against a fresh pain. That it should be this one of all!

"I would advise that you neither open your eyes nor attempt to move," the one called Spock said. T'Shael felt his fingers at the reach-centers of her face. "Nor should you attempt a healing trance. You are too weak."

T'Shael thought an acknowledgment to him and he took his hand away. Another presence made itself felt—heavy male footsteps resounding on a metal floor. Not a building, then, but a vehicle of some sort. They had been rescued, would be transported away from this place. It was over. T'Shael fought the impulse to open her eyes, to ask where Cleante was.

"How bad is she?" demanded the voice of the second male, a voice of authority.

"Difficult to be certain, Jim. I can maintain her at certain levels of self-healing until we reach the *Enterprise,* but that is all."

278

"And we can't contact McCoy until we're back in our space," the one called Jim said grimly. "The sooner we get moving the better. Do you think it would disturb her if—"

"On the contrary, it may prove therapeutic," Spock said, again in that voice of vast understanding.

T'Shael heard other footsteps—light, quick bare feet against the metal deck. No need to open her eyes this time. With what little strength she had left she raised one hand. It was gently embraced by two human hands, and T'Shael's pain receded in the emanation of love from those hands.

Did she dare smile? If death were to claim her before she could let Cleante know the depth of her gratitude, her—yes, call it love—even in the presence of strangers—

For the first time in her life, T'Shael smiled.

"I'm here," was all Cleante said, and it was all that was needed.

Jim Kirk looked at Spock, who acknowledged the scene in silence before setting the controls for a gradual, low-angle liftoff that would avoid jarring the shattered body of their very ill passenger.

"Please understand, Ms. alFaisal, I have to ask you these questions. Those are my orders. If there were any other way—"

"I don't mind, Admiral," Cleante smiled. "I'm a little disoriented, that's all. I spent six months convincing myself that the cage was real. Now I have to do the same for the *Enterprise,* for all of you. It's strange being treated with such kindness after—after so long. And I'd feel much better if you'd call me Cleante."

Jim Kirk grinned his spontaneous, boyish grin at her. He had been struck by her beauty even in the chaos of rescue and had taken surreptitious pleasure in simply looking at her—covered with plaster dust, exhausted and near shock—on their two-day journey in the shuttlecraft. He looked at her now, safe aboard his ship, almost at ease with her return to civilization, her long hair brushed till it gleamed, flowing down her back, her Byzantine eyes more than a little sad, and found her breathtaking.

"Cleante," he acquiesced warmly, and she liked the way he said it.

They were seated around the table in the officers' lounge of the vast and, to Cleante, awesome starship—the Admiral, the one called Spock and herself, with the odd one named Dr. McCoy just arriving now after looking in on T'Shael. While his face showed only some of his concern, Cleante did not need to look at him to know that T'Shael's condition had not changed.

Cleante tried not to think about that. As T'Shael herself would only too readily point out, it was needless emotion over that which one was helpless to control. Cleante made a conscious effort to relax. She was back among humans and Vulcans again, safe at long last. Why was she still so uneasy?

"You've been very specific about the events of your immediate capture," the Admiral was saying now. "If you could tell us a little more about the rest—your internment by the Klingons, how they treated you—"

"How they treated us?" Cleante laughed her high-strung, humorless laugh. "At first they ignored us. Until they found out they could use us for experimental purposes, like lab animals." Oh, Kalor—sad, twisted Kalor! "Of course, that wasn't until months later. We were fed, sheltered and ignored for months. Until they took Resh away . . ."

Her voice faltered, and she looked slowly at each face around the table, not seeing them at first, but seeing the Deltans: Resh'da, Jali, Krnsandor, the gentle companions who were no more.

Cleante shook it off, concentrating on each pair of eyes that looked at her. The Admiral's hazel eyes were encouraging. The doctor's blue eyes were preoccupied; part of him was still with his patient. The Vulcan's eyes were deep and quietly receptive.

"That isn't what you want to know!" Cleante said, suddenly, unreasonably angry.

She had no right to be angry, she told herself. For the first time in months she knew for certain that there were still such things as normalcy and compassion in the universe. Everyone had been so helpful: the cadet who had gotten her settled in the guest quarters; the paramed who had treated her bruises and reconstructed her teeth where they had decayed through months without proper food or hygiene; Commander Uhura who had personally contacted her mother for her, and the rest of the crew who had welcomed her, taken her on a tour of the ship, invited her into their recreations, updated her on news and gossip she had missed in her absence . . .

And these three, who had saved her life and were trying to save T'Shael's. What right did she have to be angry with them?

It was only that she did not want to answer their questions, did not want to gratify their male curiosity about what was done to women in captivity and, most especially, did not want to answer any questions about T'Shael. They would find ways to make her tell them about *pon farr,* about her own involvement with Kalor, about things she wanted to lock away unexamined forever, and most especially did not want to discuss with men.

"That isn't what you want to know!" she lashed out at them, jumping up from the table wildly, turning her ankles in the unfamiliar shoes, struggling for control. "You want to know if we were tortured, beaten, raped. I hate to disappoint you, gentlemen, but we were not!"

"Cleante—" the Admiral began.

"Let her talk, Jim." McCoy interjected.

He recognized the cathartic value of her anger and knew she had a great deal locked inside that had to be let out. He also had a thousand questions following the physical he'd given her when she first came aboard, and had been counting on this debriefing to answer at least some of them.

McCoy had been the first to greet the shuttlecraft, barely able to contain himself while the hangar deck pressurized. Spock had raised him as soon as they'd crossed back into Federation space, and the doctor had been on tenterhooks until he could actually get his hands on his patient. He never felt completely comfortable treating Vulcans; their bodies were entirely too dependent upon their brains.

The first thing McCoy did was recruit Lieutenant Saavik as a blood donor; her type matched T'Shael's almost exactly. He couldn't help comparing the robust, vital young cadet with the pallid wraith in the diagnostic bed.

T'Shael's lack of response puzzled McCoy. His indepth diagnosis coincided almost exactly with the Rihannsu Commander's cursory one; T'Shael had extensive internal injuries, but nothing that a combination of the best medical technique and her own innate healing powers couldn't cure in time. But she either could not or would not engage the healing trance without Spock's assistance, and McCoy was at a loss to understand why. He tried talking to her the first time she regained consciousness.

He'd been doing a minor microsurgical procedure to repair her damaged lungs, afraid to risk anesthesia in her weakened condition. He cringed every time he was certain he had hurt her. T'Shael made no sound, but McCoy was suddenly aware of those dark, hooded eyes assessing him. Could anyone's eyes look as deep as a Vulcan's?

"T'Shael?" McCoy tried his best human smile, only slightly mispronouncing her name. "You're among friends, in the sickbay of the starship *Enterprise*. My name's McCoy."

The somber eyes acknowledged this in silence.

"I'm sorry if the procedure caused you any discomfort," McCoy went on, careful not to say "pain" to a Vulcan. "Your injuries were rather severe, but you're getting the best possible care. I realize it will be normal for you to remain unconscious for considerable periods of time. If you could assist us with a healing trance—"

The solemn eyes closed, a withdrawal. She was incapable of anything as vehement as refusal.

"Can't you tell me why you won't?" McCoy watched the deep eyes open again, saw something in them he didn't want to examine too closely.

"It makes no difference," she said in a voice that was barely a whisper, and withdrew again.

McCoy turned away from the bed to find Cleante, barefoot and silent, holding the doorframe as if uncertain whether she was allowed in. McCoy supposed he and his team had been rather perfunctory in hurrying T'Shael out of the shuttlecraft and into Sickbay, all but pushing the human aside, their concern for the physically injured perhaps unfair to her whose injuries were not as readily visible.

"Ms. alFaisal? Come in, please." McCoy got a chair for her. "It must seem as if we're ignoring you. We've been so preoccupied with your friend here."

Cleante stood by the bed looking down at the unconscious figure, tears glistening in her eyes. For the third time she must keep a vigil for the Vulcan. Was three truly a lucky number, or was that only an old Terran superstition?

"Won't you sit down?" McCoy fussed, recognizing symptoms of shock, chronic fatigue and all manner of delayed psychic trauma without having to look too closely.

Cleante shook her head. She did not take her eyes off the Vulcan.

"What's going to happen to her?"

McCoy hesitated.

"We're doing everything we can for her," he said, reassuring her without giving her false hope. "And wearing yourself to a frazzle won't do her any good. Why don't you—"

Cleante seemed not to hear. McCoy stood rocking on his heels, watching her. Finally, he took her gently by the arm.

"I'd like to do your examination now, if you don't mind. You can come back and sit with her as soon as we're through."

Cleante nodded and went with him, throwing a last wistful glance over her shoulder at the Vulcan. The look was not lost on McCoy, who had seen it far too often on another all too human face.

"There's something you should know before you begin, Doctor," Cleante said, settling herself a little warily on the examining table, which immediately began its welter of readouts. "There's a chance I may be pregnant."

McCoy nearly dropped his mediscanner, but he said nothing.

"I was due for an immunity booster when we were captured," Cleante was saying, looking at the ceiling and not at the doctor, "and my cycles became very irregular during our imprisonment. Then they stopped altogether for a while— nerves and poor nutrition, I guess. It wouldn't have made any difference, except—" She looked at him, a plea for understanding. "If I am pregnant, I don't want you to tell me, just yet. I have a special reason for asking, Doctor."

"I understand," McCoy said, although he did not. He patted her hand absently and went on with the exam.

He puzzled over it. If she was pregnant, it could only be

by a Klingon, probably the one Jim and Spock had found blasted in the compound. What did it mean? If the Klingons had sexually abused their captives, wouldn't they have eliminated all evidence before the prisoners were due to be repatriated? His examination of the Vulcan had shown her untouched. Why only the human? What did it mean?

On a larger scale, what sort of life awaited a child of human-Klingon parentage? McCoy was certain such inter-mix offspring existed within the Empire, assuming they weren't aborted or murdered at birth, but he knew of none within the Federation. Wouldn't Cleante want to know as soon as possible?

"It wasn't what you think," she was saying, her hand on McCoy's arm. "I wasn't forced. It was my own decision."

McCoy said nothing, pretending total absorption in his diagnosis. Was it possible—McCoy pushed his own preju-dices aside—that this beautiful girl could find something desirable in one of her reptilian captors? McCoy found himself not wanting to know.

"Ms. alFaisal," he said, covering her hand with his own. "I'm a doctor. That entitles me to medical opinions. When it comes to my patients' personal lives, I find it safer not to allow myself to think."

"Thank you." Cleante managed a pale smile. "I appreci-ate that."

As to whether or not she was pregnant, McCoy kept his findings to himself.

"Let her talk, Jim," he said now in the officers' lounge, watching Cleante closely, seeking any sign that she was on the verge of a breakdown. He didn't think she was. She seemed remarkably resilient. However, if she didn't exor-cise the horrors of her recent experience, McCoy was cer-tain she would break.

Cleante immediately sensed his monitoring; it was easy after six months of being constantly watched. She took deep breaths as T'Shael had taught her to do, and felt calmer.

"When the Klingons first arrived we were roughed up a bit," she began. She laughed her humorless laugh. "I was almost going to say 'manhandled.' Klingon-handled? I don't know."

She told them how Krazz had tried to molest her and how Jali had intervened. It began to pour from her now—the fear, the uncertainty, the long months of boredom and their efforts to stay active and cheerful, the slow, sad deaths of the Deltans, the groundquake that had killed Krazz and the arrival of the Rihannsu. She would stop there, she told herself, would tell them she was tired and couldn't continue and would return to the next session with some plausible lie to explain T'Shael's injuries. Wasn't she adept enough at lying by now?

"There really isn't much more, Admiral," she said, her voice grown hoarse from talking, or perhaps by design. "At first it was terror—terror on my part and the Deltans', never T'Shael's. Without her I don't think I could have—then when she became so ill, I—"

She stopped herself forcibly. Was she out of her mind?

"I'm tired!" she said crossly, like a child. "I have nothing more to say."

"She ought to rest now, Jim," McCoy cut in anxiously. He did not like the hysteria he could hear behind her abruptness.

"A little more, Bones," Kirk said, waving off McCoy's concern. He smiled at Cleante, activating his celebrated charm. "Continue, please, Cleante. A little more. You said T'Shael became ill. Tell us about that."

For once Jim Kirk's charm wasn't going to work.

"I won't answer any more questions!" Cleante nearly screamed.

Control! she told herself. As T'Shael has endeavored to teach you—Oh, T'Shael, I'm sorry!

"Cleante, we're trying to help your friend," McCoy said, taking over, redirecting her. "T'Shael's psychosomatic symptoms are all out of proportion to her injuries. She refuses to engage the healing trance. If she were human I'd say she were suffering from profound depression, but I can't say that about a Vulcan, can I? Unless you can tell us what went on back there, how she was injured, why she refuses our help—I'm stumped. If you're holding back information that might be of help to her—"

Kirk was about to add something of his own, but Spock spoke for the first time, interrupting both of them.

"Gentlemen," was all he said, and the others deferred to him. He seemed to weigh his words carefully before he went on.

"Ms. alFaisal, you are aware that it was necessary for me to employ mind-touch with T'Shael during our return journey."

Cleante nodded. She hadn't even thanked him for that. She remembered surrendering her place beside T'Shael to him several times, watching with quiet fascination as he touched the introverted one's mind with his own and sustained her tenuous hold on life.

"While the touch is not intended to intrude upon subconscious thought, when one is as ill as T'Shael certain barriers are lowered and certain predominant thoughts and memories emerge involuntarily."

"If you were able to read T'Shael's thoughts—" Cleante told herself she trusted him, but she wasn't sure, "—then you already have your answers!"

"The impressions I received were incomplete," Spock demurred. "You must help me to complete them."

Cleante glared at him. She could trust none of them, not even him! Surely, as a Vulcan he should understand why she couldn't speak of certain things! Men! They were all alike. She wanted to strike at him, to protect T'Shael from him, from the whole universe.

"Ms. alFaisal," Spock persisted, impervious to her glare. "You need not fear betrayal of a friend's confidence. The Admiral and Dr. McCoy are well aware of the significance of *pon farr*."

Cleante saw Kirk flinch slightly, saw McCoy look away and begin to fidget.

"Of course!" McCoy whispered, as if to himself. "Of course! She's of the right age. It would explain the residual symptoms of stress. But how could she have survived it alone, without the male?"

"That is for Ms. alFaisal to tell us," Spock said, his gaze never leaving hers, "as it is for her to explain T'Shael's injuries, and the death of the Klingon."

Cleante had thought only T'Shael's eyes could penetrate in that way. Whom was she protecting—T'Shael or herself? She had done what she had done in the expediency of the moment. If it had failed, was that her fault? What is, is, she told herself, unconsciously thinking like a Vulcan. What had come between her and T'Shael was none of their business, but the rest . . .

In one breathless monologue, Cleante told them. Everything.

The transparent well between the officers' lounge and the corridor slid shut, separating Cleante from the trio around the table. Jim Kirk watched her thoughtfully. She stood waiting for the turbolift, head bowed with thought or simple weariness, shoes held loosely in one hand. She looked so young, so vulnerable. Had they been too hard on her?

"She needed to get it out of her system, Jim," McCoy answered the unvoiced question. "We did the right thing."

Cleante stepped into the 'lift without looking back, and Kirk turned his attention to his two companions.

"Opinions, gentlemen," he said. "Spock—the Rihannsu Commander. Small universe? Coincidence or design?"

"Her involvement would explain many of the specifications of our retrieval of the prisoners," was Spock's opinion.

"But why?" Kirk wanted to know. "Just to make us twist in the wind? Some subtle form of revenge?"

Spock looked thoughtful. He had found more in the turmoil of T'Shael's thoughts than he had told Cleante, more than he intended to say here. That was between him and the introverted one.

"Doubtless there is some logic to her actions which we will come to learn in time," he said cryptically, and Kirk knew that was all they'd get out of him. He turned his attention to McCoy.

"Bones, about our repatriates. Will they be all right?"

"You want my official prognosis or my basic gut feeling?" McCoy asked laconically, trying to lighten the mood.

"Whichever sounds better." Kirk grinned his appreciation, then grew serious. "There hasn't been much work done on nonmilitary hostages recently, has there?"

"No, there hasn't, because we haven't needed it," McCoy said. "Generally, those who disappear into either Empire are never returned. But I've done a comparison between what we do know about the impact of long-term internment on civilian hostages and a preliminary profile of our young human friend. The transition back to normal life will be rocky for her at first, but I don't foresee any permanent damage. Of course, a lot depends on what plans the Council has for these two now."

Jim Kirk watched the galaxy go by through the vast port of the officers' lounge. He passed a hand over his eyes.

"There's been a lot of rethinking on the entire concept of Warrantors. Security at T'lingShar has been stepped up to a degree which Vulcan authorities find—" he glanced at Spock; "—disquieting."

Spock might have smiled. While Vulcans could not be "disturbed" or "upset," they could conceivably be "disquieted."

There's been some extremist talk of abandoning the idea altogether," Kirk went on. "The Deltans have withdrawn their remaining Warrantors from the settlement. They're demanding reparations from both Empires *and* the Federation Council, and they have a lot of people in their camp."

"Perhaps the Deltans should be made aware that such divisiveness was precisely what the Rihannsu intended," Spock pointed out.

Kirk laughed mirthlessly. Try explaining anything to an outraged Deltan.

"It's the diplomats' problem," he said. "Meanwhile it's been suggested that Cleante and T'Shael at least be released from their commitment. Whether temporarily or permanently will depend heavily on your findings, Bones."

McCoy greeted that piece of news with a scowl.

"I'd recommend they be released permanently, period. Returning to their former way of life could trigger all sorts of problems. Make them feel like they're sitting in the middle of a bull's-eye, waiting to be victimized all over again. Welfare of the galaxy be damned; I won't sanction it.

"Jasmine alFaisal's term runs out in a little over a year. It might take Cleante that long to get back on her feet psychologically. I'd insist she spend at least six months back on Earth. Give her a chance to sort things out in her mind, resolve any residual problems she might have. And she's by far the healthier of the two.

"As I understand it, T'Shael has committed herself as a

Warrantor for life. Now, I'm no expert on Vulcan psychic response, present company notwithstanding, but from what I can assess of that young woman's mental state, the sooner she's freed from what she considers her bounden duty the better. Whoever she's Warrantor for ought to be persuaded to release her at once."

"Ambassador Sarek has already done so, Doctor," Spock said quietly.

McCoy's jaw dropped.

"Bones, how bad is she?" Kirk asked. McCoy was still staring at Spock. "Bones!"

McCoy blinked, refocused. He'd jump on Spock later.

"Jim, I honestly don't know. It's like putting a puzzle together with some of the pieces missing. There's much more here than I can figure out. Physically she's mending already. That enviable Vulcan physique. But how do I go about measuring psychic trauma in a Vulcan? Between *pon farr* and blaming herself for her fiancé's death and her reaction to Cleante's involvement with the Klingon, the closest thing I can compare her experience with is Spock's encounter with V'ger—pure sensory and intellectual over-load, though over a much longer period of time. I will say this much: whatever happens to her depends in large part on Cleante. And vice versa."

Kirk gave him a puzzled look.

"Explain."

"Oh, come on, Jim! You've seen it as well as I have, and so has Spock. These two are forged together for life. They're almost a mirror image of you and Spock, both of them falling all over themselves with self-sacrifice. There's an old phrase in Latin—*amicus usque ad aras*. 'A friend in spite of all differences; a friend to the last extremity.' There's even a Vulcan word for it, isn't there, Spock?"

"The word, Doctor, is *t'hy'la*," Spock murmured, ignoring McCoy's obtuseness.

"That's it!" McCoy nodded. "That's what we're dealing with. They're both blaming themselves for what happened, both wallowing in guilt, and until they can resolve that . . ."

Cleante approached the bed and took T'Shael's hand. The Vulcan was somewhat stronger and had been propped up to a half-sitting position. Solemn eyes met sad ones and neither spoke.

"You can have it disinfected when I leave," the human said at last.

"I do not understand," the Vulcan said.

"Your hand. So you don't catch any of my germs. I feel so—dirty."

A flicker of pain passed across the gaunt face, and T'Shael tightened her hold on the human's hand in disclaimer.

"Do you think I could condemn what you have done?" she asked, bewildered.

"Why else did you refuse it?" Cleante asked plaintively. "Go off into the cold—try to kill yourself?"

"To spare you further shame. That you should do such for one so unworthy—" The Vulcan's voice was almost as plaintive. Then she gathered what little pride she possessed. "Nor did I 'try to kill myself.' "

"I don't know what you call it!" Cleante said sharply. "Any more than I know what to call what you're doing now!"

"I do not understand," T'Shael said, trying to withdraw her hand. It was Cleante's turn to tighten her grip.

"Passive refusal to live is the same as actively choosing death," she said fervently. "If you die now, you're as good as telling me what I did was worthless."

"It was never my intention—"

"But that's the way I'll look at it. For the rest of my life, T'Shael. If you die on me now, after all we've been through, I'll hate you for as long as I live!"

T'Shael inhaled painfully, and the readings on the panel above her jumped violently. Cleante cursed herself for doing this, but it was necessary.

"There is more to this than you know—" T'Shael began, thinking of Spock and her pledge to the Commander. If she should die before she could fulfill that pledge, the pledge of the *dirhja*—

"And there's more to it than you know, either!" Cleante countered, keeping her voice steady by main force. "I may be pregnant."

She winced as T'Shael's hand tightened so fiercely on

hers she almost expected to hear bones crack. She plunged on.

"And if I am, T'Shael, I'm going to need you more than ever, because as far as I know no human has ever borne a half-Klingon child and tried to raise it in our society. And if I am pregnant, I will bear that child, because it can't help being what it is, and it deserves a chance to live. But I'm going to need someone to be there for me, T'Shael. Someone to be strong for me. I'm going to need you."

T'Shael's hand went limp, and she withdrew it at last from the human's.

"If you carry such a child, the responsibility is as much mine as Kalor's," she said remotely, seeming not to hear the rest of what Cleante had said. "That I should be the cause of this—"

"T'Shael, listen to me," Cleante said intensely, taking her hand again. The Vulcan did not resist. "I don't want to hear your theory about responsibility and ripple effects. I don't want to hear any of that. I want you to answer something for me—quickly, without rationalizing it. Would you die for me?"

T'Shael seemed puzzled by the question.

"Need you ask that?"

"Not really!" Cleante said with tears in her voice. "I've always known the answer to that one. But there's a harder one, and I don't know the answer to it. Will you live for me?"

Fifteen

LIEUTENANT SAAVIK WAS on her way to Sickbay to see if Dr. McCoy required her for any additional blood transfusions. She found his insistence on using fresh whole blood as the growth medium for synthetic blood quite illogical. He could as easily use freeze-dried plasma; it was the accepted technique, but far be it from a mere cadet to question one of Starfleet's medical Brahmins. Besides, she was young and strong and healthy and could spare four times the blood of a human donor; from the look of McCoy's Vulcan patient she might very well have to.

With such thoughts in mind, Saavik was understandably surprised to see T'Shael standing shakily in McCoy's office, the doctor flapping about her like some distraught gallinaceous creature with a wounded offspring.

"You're not strong enough to be walking around!" he insisted, tugging at T'Shael's thin arm and finding her immovable, belying his statement. "You still have internal injuries. You could start bleeding again. I won't be responsible!"

"Then with all due respect, Doctor, I release you from your responsibility," T'Shael said in a tone of voice McCoy had heard entirely too often from another Vulcan.

He supposed he ought to be grateful his patient was showing so positive a response. It meant she had made up her mind to pull through. Still. . . . He muttered something incomprehensible and continued to hover, arms folded, glowering.

T'Shael turned her attention to Saavik.

"It is fortuitous that you have come here," the introverted one said softly, supporting herself unobtrusively with one hand on the back of a chair. Saavik had not heard her speak before and found her voice lower than she'd expected and pleasing to the ear. "I wished to thank you for your service to me, but I did not know what name to call you."

It was a Vulcan formality. One never asked another's name of a third party, but waited for its owner to offer it.

"My given name is T'Saavik," the young cadet said, strangely flustered in the presence of this one and the irascible human doctor. "Though among humans I am called Saavik; it is easier for them to pronounce. As for the transfusions, it would be illogical for me to refuse what you need and what I have in abundance."

The hooded eyes appraised her for a long moment, and Saavik's gaze almost faltered until she collected her wits.

"I do know something of logic," she said, perhaps a little archly. "Though I am half Romulan."

"It was not my intention to question your origins," T'Shael said evenly. "And my gratitude remains."

Saavik's gaze did falter this time.

"I'm often asked, that's all. The difference is apparent to other Vulcans, though I cannot—" She saw the introverted one sway slightly on her feet and caught at her before McCoy could. "If it was only to speak to me—"

"You're going back to bed this instant, young lady," McCoy began, knowing it was useless.

"I must speak with the one called Spock," T'Shael said purposefully, steadying herself and dismissing any reference to her health even as she refused assistance. She focused on Saavik. "If I could know where to find him, and at what convenience to him—"

Saavik looked at her chronometer.

"He will be off-duty now. I can ask him to come here,

293

or—" She could see that T'Shael did not desire this, and looked at McCoy as if daring him to refuse her permission. "I can bring you to him."

McCoy threw up his hands.

"Why not? By all means, let her go marching up and down the halls at her leisure. Maybe you'd like to take her to the gym for a workout—half-knit bones, damaged organs and all. The old saying is true: you can't win an argument with a Vulcan—much less two of them!"

Saavik's face might have betrayed a momentary amusement, and she and T'Shael were united for an instant in the fellowship of logic against the forces of human emotionalism. It was T'Shael who broke the bond, driven by something of greater import.

"If I might have more suitable garments than this," she said, indicating the disposable Sickbay robe.

"Of course!" McCoy said, suddenly finding something about this scenario to his liking. "Can't have you walking around like an advertisement for death, can we? Don't go 'way. I've got just the thing."

Saavik watched him disappear into an anteroom, her raised eyebrow implying that even for a human he was eccentric. T'Shael reacted not at all. In a moment, McCoy returned with a bundle of recently synthesized clothing, handing it to T'Shael with a mysterious smile. He watched her unfold each garment slowly and with considerable interest.

There was a pair of close-fitting dark trousers, cut in the unisex Vulcan style, that tapered softly to the ankles, and sandals almost identical to the single worn pair T'Shael had owned at T'lingShar—so far away, so long ago. T'Shael unfolded the knee-length tunic last of all. It was high-necked and flared of sleeve as she favored, and the color . . .

So far away, so long ago: the deep rich purple of the arras that sheltered Salet's harpsichord in the crafters' shop, the precise color which in the ancient frescoes in the ruins of the Old City symbolized fidelity and remembrance. Only one could have pored over every shade available in the synthesizer, selecting this one exactly.

"There's something else," McCoy said, grinning, avuncular. He handed T'Shael a small octagonal box he'd had hidden behind his back. T'Shael looked at him. Had she understood the reference, she might have said he was like a small boy at Christmas. "Go ahead. Open it."

Inside on a bed of some soft stuff lay a single ruby stud earring, identical with the one T'Shael had worn in her left earlobe since her betrothal, appropriated by the Rihannsu in the first drugged days of capture and then lost forever. Symbol of unwed female, gift of understanding. *Amicus usque ad aras. T'hy'la.*

Saavik, understanding the significance of the ruby if not of the clothing, studied the tips of her boots, allowing the introverted one her privacy. McCoy, human curious and less attuned to the nuances of Vulcan propriety, watched the solemn face for some trace of that deep-buried emotion he had studied for years on a kindred face.

"Cleante asked me to give you these when I thought you were ready," he said meaningfully. He did not know what words had last passed between Vulcan and human, but knew too well the agonies, the broken rules that this kind of relationship necessitated. "She also asked me to tell you she'd stay out of your way until you had reached a decision."

T'Shael's hand might have trembled so that she almost dropped the jewel box. She said nothing. With a Vulcan's indifference to the body she began to undress, causing McCoy to beat a hasty retreat, muttering something about tending to more cooperative patients.

Saavik led the introverted one down the corridors, close enough beside her without encroaching on her personal space to offer assistance should the unsteady pace falter, the battered body give way to minor inconveniences like fatigue or mere gravity. The rich purple tunic effectively hid the sharp outline of bones barely contained beneath taut flesh; the careful mask hid still-present pain, but nothing could hide the burning in those hooded eyes. Saavik, whose life had been short but not uneventful, wondered what manner of inner fire burned in this way.

She pressed Spock's doorchime, indicating to the introverted one that she was to enter first.

"Come," Spock said, as Saavik had known he would. He

never demanded the identity of visitors; it was as if no one, nothing, could disturb him.

The door slid open and T'Shael entered slowly but with dignity. Spock was at his desk, writing with an antique pen on real paper, though he put both aside when he saw who his visitors were. T'Shael had not seen anyone write in this manner since the Ardanan illuminators in their enclave at T'lingShar. So long ago, so far away.

Spock's eyes appraised the introverted one, then fixed on Saavik, who lingered just inside the doorway.

"You desire something, Saavik-*kam?*"

His tone was bemused. Saavik started slightly, chagrined at being found out. Her mentor knew quite well what she desired—to witness with her insatiable curiosity the dynamics of a conversation between these two. She drew herself up, military correct.

"Negative, sir. I shall be at my duty station until I am required."

"Very well, Ms. Saavik," Spock said, as correct as she, though his eyes might have smiled. None need instruct him in insatiable curiosity. "Dismissed."

He turned his attention to the introverted one.

Jim Kirk found Cleante walking in the herbarium.

He simply watched. The setting was perfect. She was a flower among flowers, a unique and exotic bloom in the midst of this plethora of blossoms from all the Federation's worlds. He did not know how he had known she would be here among the butterflies and the plashing fountains, but he had known. He who longed for a beach to walk on could understand her yearning for the scent of flowers and the smell of damp Earth after such captivity as had been hers.

Cleante sensed his presence, looked up from the lotus pool she had been contemplating and smiled at him. Jim Kirk felt something tug at his heart.

"There's a special holiday in my part of Earth," Cleante said. "It was begun in the twentieth century by the visionary leader Anwar el Sadat, but I suspect it goes back further than that, back to the Egyptian soul. We call it 'Smell the Breezes Day.'"

Jim Kirk grinned at her.

"I can appreciate that," he said.

Something in him wanted to reach out and touch her, to caress the luxury of her hair if only for a moment, but he refrained. The years were wrong, for one thing, and so soon after the Klingon . . . perhaps another, later time. The galaxy was wide, but not so wide their paths might not cross again. Rank hath its privileges; he could find her again if he wanted to.

"We'll be arriving at Starbase XI around 1200 tomorrow," he said, trying to be businesslike. "Have you spoken to your mother?"

Cleante shook her head.

"I could have sent a commpic once we were in range, but I didn't. I want to talk to her face to face. And, there are other things on my mind."

"It isn't easy being friend to a Vulcan," Jim Kirk suggested gently, knowing what at least some of those "other things" were.

"Especially when the Vulcan insists she's not worth the friendship," Cleante said softly, the sad look coming into her Byzantine eyes again.

Jim Kirk thought about that.

"It's a flaw in the species," he suggested. Who knew better than he? "That's why they excuse themselves with logic all the time, try to explain away how deeply they care. Why they need humans to argue with them, convince them of their worth. It's a lifelong struggle."

He said this last in a martyred tone calculated to make Cleante laugh. She did, covering her mouth with her hand, the old nervous habit. She liked this man, liked him very much. How wide could a galaxy be?

"What 'other things?' " he asked her suddenly, basking in the sheer enjoyment of the moment, but mindful too of McCoy's insistence that the captives exorcise their captivity.

"Oh—" Cleante moved away from him slightly, contemplating the lotus pool again. "For a while I thought I might be pregnant. False alarm, though."

Kirk digested this.

"Would that have been a problem for you?"

Cleante shrugged.

"Possibly. A lot depended, and still depends, on T'Shael."

Jim Kirk could resist no longer. He took her hand and kissed it, lightly, gallantly, in his best officer-and-gentleman manner.

"Stubborn lot, aren't they? Vulcans. Sometimes I wonder why we bother."

Cleante knew what years of struggle and persistence and sheer strength of will lay behind his offhandedness, knew as much awaited her, if T'Shael would only—

T'Shael must make the right choice; she *must*, or their captivity would have no meaning. And they would have the pattern of this man and his Vulcan to follow as they chose their own particular path.

Spock turned his attention to the introverted one. He offered a chair with a silent gesture and she, as silently, refused it. Spock made note of the particular color of the tunic, the single earring, and saw from these things that the human's influence still held T'Shael to this life, if only temporarily. Once she had unburdened herself of what she had to say to him, what would she choose?

Spock looked at T'Shael and saw, as if in her shadow, Salet the Gifted One. He recalled the composer's exquisite harmonies as they had saturated his own youth, the creative energies which belied the myth that Vulcans had no emotions, for that which did not exist could not have expressed itself in such music.

He looked at T'Shael and thought as well of T'Pei the master scientist, whose death in the death of *Intrepid* had reached him across the vastness of space. In what way could he honor these two unique beings in service to their offspring?

He looked at T'Shael and saw her pledge as Warrantor freeing him to fly between the stars, to explore the strange new worlds within as well as without, freeing him to be by Kirk's side.

Warrantor in place of Sarek's only son, Spock thought, what return can I offer you?

More to the point, could he who had witnessed the simple gesture between Vulcan and human in the shuttlecraft possibly stand detached? He who had faced a number of kinds of death must do what he could to shield another of his kind from its enticement.

"I owe you my life, *T'Kahr* Spock," T'Shael began, using the word that among other things meant teacher. "My gratitude for this."

"Does one thank duty, T'Shael?" Spock asked mildly, sounding not unlike his father. He would savor the debate needed to win her to the side of life. "It is I who owe you a debt of gratitude for being Warrantor in my place. It is a debt which I can never fully repay."

"It was not duty which continued mind-touch despite your awareness of the message I carried," T'Shael countered. She was driven, and the words came readily. "I would not be the instrument of shame to you, but in insisting that I live you leave me no choice. I have made a pledge which I must now keep."

Spock stood slowly and moved away from the desk, his hands outstretched as if to bare his heart to the Rihannsu sword he had read in T'Shael's mind.

"Speak what you have pledged, T'Shael-*kam*, freely and without reservation. None can bring shame to me but myself."

T'Shael spoke what the Commander had instructed her, her voice low, her words carefully chosen, her eyes downcast in respect for Spock's privacy.

"She said I was to be the Warrantor of her vengeance. 'Living proof that a Rihannsu has sometimes more honor than a Vulcan,' " she finished. "These were her exact words."

She felt strangely lightheaded, though whether as a result of her weakness or of some burden lifted from her soul she did not know. She felt the deck move beneath her and thought illogically of groundquakes. Perhaps a storm of some sort . . .

She swayed and would have fallen, but the hand of one of her own caught her and indicated with a gesture the eminent good sense of seating herself. Then, in a voice mellow with something T'Shael could not name, he told her the tale of a

Rihannsu and a Vulcan and a thing called a cloaking device.

"And how do you judge me, T'Shael-*kam?*" he asked when he had finished. "Do you find my actions dishonorable?"

"T'Kahr, it is not my place to judge," she began.

"But it is," Spock interrupted her. "If you are to fulfill the pledge of the *dirhja.*"

He watched her shy from the term, though she had not shied from the responsibility. She was almost free of that now. Whatever followed, he must tread carefully or he would lose her.

"Do not trouble yourself," he said gently. "What the Commander could not know is that she need not have used you. Whatever scars I bear are neither new nor are they of your doing. I have weighed this question of honor often since our encounter, yet I cannot say that I would not do as much again. But I must know how you judge me."

T'Shael studied him for a long moment. This was a deep one.

"I judge that I cannot judge," she said at last. "In your place I should have lacked the courage to attempt such, even for the safety of the Federation."

"Perhaps," Spock said with a suggestion of doubt. There were many kinds of courage, including that which considered death before the disgrace of a friend. "But one discovers different levels of meaning when one dwells among humans. As I need not tell one whom a human calls *t'hy'la.*"

He had deliberately broached the one topic which could cause her more distress than all the ravages her captivity had visited upon her.

"If she calls me such, it is to my shame," T'Shael said with difficulty. "Such cannot be for me. Not with this one, not with any one, for I have proven unworthy."

"Yet Cleante calls you *t'hy'la,*" Spock countered. "Why do you refuse her equal honor?"

T'Shael's eyes were deep with trouble and she did not answer.

"You fear the responsibility for one who would bind herself to you unconditionally," Spock suggested. "As I also feared once. However, it was easier for me."

"I do not understand," T'Shael said. From what his face told her, nothing had been easy for this one, ever.

"I am half human. I had some basis from which to begin. For you it is all unknown, therefore it will be more difficult. Death might be easier, for you."

T'Shael's silence acknowledged how readily she entertained this thought.

"But will you accept the responsibility for what it will do to the human?" Spock asked, knowing he would get no answer. "You must decide what you want."

T'Shael's eyes flew to his.

"What *I* want? And who am I to want?"

"You are neither more nor less than any other. Do not presume to too much humility, T'Shael. It dishonors that which created you and those who gave you life."

"*T'Kahr*—" T'Shael began, but he refused the title with a gesture, implying that he could not be teacher to her who would not be taught.

"Consider to whom you speak," he said, and T'Shael was silent. She whose mind he had touched understood what he had given and would give for a human *t'hy'la*. "It is of course your privilege to deny yourself the glories of *t'hy'la*. But by what right do you deny one who has sacrificed herself for you?"

T'Shael's eyes were deep with misery. Oh, that she were human so she could wash away this feeling with tears!

"The nature of her sacrifice, *T'Kahr*—" Cleante, my more-than-worthy, that you should do such for me!

"—was selfless in the extreme," Spock interrupted her, his voice gone suddenly harsh. "And how do you repay her?"

"I can never repay her, *T'Kahr!*" she said with acute distress. "This is the nature of the difficulty!"

"Is that how you define friendship, T'Shael?" Spock demanded. "As a balance sheet—one sacrifice equally repaid with another? Then perhaps you are right. Perhaps it is not for you."

T'Shael struggled with anger. He had no right to oversimplify the matter, to trivialize it. He had not suffered the crucible of their captivity, could not know—

Was he smiling? Smiling at her? For what reason? T'Shael forced her anger down. She was a Vulcan; she was in control. She tried to understand.

"You speak of my friendship as an honor," she said deliberately. "This I do not understand. What am I that she, that Cleante, should continue to choose me?"

"You are that which she needs," Spock suggested, his voice gentler. How familiar were these agonies! He wished he could spare her some of this, but it was necessary. "The other half of her soul, as the ancient poets of both your species have expressd it. Accept this from one who knows, T'Shael-*kam*."

T'Shael studied him for a long moment, and he permitted this from the depth of his serenity. She wondered what he would have become without his human counterpart.

"Perhaps High Master of *Kohlinahr*," he answered her unvoiced thoughts. "Or the hollowest of beings. Essence of emptiness. I have stood on the edge of such a precipice, T'Shael. It is no pleasant place.

"Perhaps you are unaware that your own Master has chosen death," he added after a moment.

Word had reached him through diplomatic channels a day or two earlier; he had taken it upon himself to tell her when he judged the time to be right. T'Shael gave no reaction, though this must have reached her. Necessary. Spock went on.

"Despite all logic, you will no doubt take the burden of this upon yourself, as you would the death of your betrothed, of the other captives, even of your captors. It is a heavy burden, T'Shael. Perhaps more than one can carry alone."

T'Shael did not answer. How could she?

"Perhaps you would also like to assume responsibility for my actions," Spock continued, relentless. Necessary. "You were, after all, my Warrantor. Does not your freeing me for Starfleet give you a share in my moral decisions? Perhaps you were instrumental in my betrayal of the Rihannsu Commander."

Even the introverted one could protest so wild a leap of illogic, yet she did not. Hadn't she entertained these thoughts?

She was on her feet, disregarding her weakness and her injuries, taken with a sudden trembling that was not physiological in origin. She turned away from him, hugging herself in unconscious emulation of a certain human.

Spock watched her. Her distress reached to him from across the room and he allowed it to do so. Necessary. There was no growth without pain.

"Consider that the Way of the Vulcan speaks of the suppression of all emotion," he suggested gently. If she would call him teacher, he must be worthy of the title. "Yet it also speaks of IDIC. Consider that Surak never met a human. Might such an encounter have altered his formulation of the Way? Is there not room for growth in any philosophy? And the concept of *t'hy'la* is more ancient than any philosophy.

"Why did Vulcans initiate contact with so immature a species as the human? Haven't you wondered, T'Shael? Our technology far surpassed theirs. Our arts, our philosophy, our commitment to peace—all that constitutes a culture—were superior. Why then our eagerness to comprehend these beings? Can you not use the example of your own experience as answer?

"Consider that you are free, T'Shael. You have fulfilled your pledge to the Commander with no harm to me. You are freed of mate, of kindred, of Warrantorship. The universe is vast and full of alternatives. You have nothing remaining to you but the human. How will you choose?"

He watched the struggle she could no longer suppress, watched with quiet recognition the familiar birth-pangs of emotion in one of his own. He who had been reborn in the rebirth of V'ger could officiate in this rite with no little appreciation.

"Listen to your soul, T'Shael-*kam*," he said tenderly. "It must be the final arbiter. You have passed through a portal through which there is no returning. Love for the human, once initiated, cannot be undone. Accept that you can never repay your *t'hy'la* for her sacrifice, and let this be the foundation of your love."

T'Shael found that her eyes had filled with tears. Overcome with shame she sought to hide them, blink them away, but the eyes of the deep one burned into her and she knew she could hide nothing from him. He had led her along a path where his own footsteps were plainly visible. She turned to him and he held out his hand to her in the *ta'al*. She responded, matching her hand to his. Spock brushed the tears from her eyelashes with gentle fingers.

"Go," he barely whispered. "Go and share your discovery with she who is your *t'hy'la*."

Cleante pressed the release on her cabin door almost before the buzzer sounded. She knew who would be there.

She saw the dampness on the plain, somber face, and before she could speak T'Shael took her in her arms—awkwardly, inexperienced, but willing to practice for the rest of her life.

"You do not carry Kalor's child," she whispered, sensing this and puzzled by it. "Why did you not tell me? Why keep this knowledge even from yourself?"

"To pique your curiosity. To try and hold you here," Cleante said through her own tears. "To find out if you still loved me."

They clung to each other like children.

Jasmine alFaisal began to materialize on the transporter pod while the Admiral was still shouldering into his uniform tunic. Spock, standing at parade rest beside the transporter con, buttoned down and impeccable as always, gave him a bemused look. Kirk secured the front flap of his tunic, cleared his throat, and braced himself as if for a hurricane.

But it was a very subdued High Commissioner, bereft of jewels and badges of office, her jet black hair pulled back severely from a face that wore no official mask, who followed the Admiral to the VIP lounge, stopping to thank as many individual crewmembers as she encountered for their part in the rescue, not in the well-practiced tones of diplomacy but in the simple, unrehearsed words of a mother who has had her child restored to her. Jim Kirk made note of the absence of glitter, of the real woman emerging from behind the facade for perhaps the first time in years. He left Jasmine alone in the lounge so that she and Cleante could have their reunion in private.

Cleante had insisted that T'Shael accompany her; T'Shael had as adamantly refused. It might have become a full-fledged quarrel if Cleante hadn't remembered McCoy's saying about winning an argument with a Vulcan.

"But you'll join me in a little while," she said, not asking. "I especially want her to meet you."

"Perhaps," T'Shael said softly.

How to explain that the levels of meaning of mother and daughter, dimensioned by human emotion and contrasted with her own Vulcan rootlessness, might be more than she could comfortably encompass? Yet she did arrive after a time, after the embraces and the tears and the catching-up-on-what-they'd-missed—not only for the six months of Cleante's captivity but for a lifetime of strained relations—were over, and mother and daughter sat contemplating the blue tranquility of the planetoid looming large below them. The quiet shush of the door to the VIP lounge seemed a fearful racket in contrast to the silence of the Vulcan who crossed its threshold.

Cleante came and took T'Shael's hand, bringing her into the room. Jasmine stood and almost locked into her diplomatic mode from sheer habit—Vulcans had always made her feel artificial, she supposed rightfully so. She had also, always, disliked Cleante's friends on principle. But Cleante's talk had been filled with this one, and the changes Jasmine could see in her butterfly of a daughter, now grown deep and thoughtful and mature, could only have had one catalyst. The High Commissioner put her arm around her daughter's waist and held out her other hand to the introverted one, drawing her into the circle as if she had suddenly acquired a second daughter.

"I won't be running for a second term," Jasmine told Cleante sometime later. "You'd be surprised at how fatiguing forty-odd years of smiling can be. I've a chance at ambassador-at-large next year, and if I don't get that—well. I'll sit home with my feet up and do a memoir, or lecture. This life has really become a bore lately."

"You're sure it has nothing to do with my going back to T'lingShar as a Warrantor?" Cleante asked suspiciously.

"Of course not!" her mother protested, fooling no one. "Besides, Mikhail has asked me to cut down on my planet-hopping just a little. He feels it detracts from our time together, and since he's been such a dear through all of this . . ."

" 'Mikhail,' " Cleante repeated mischievously. "Let me see: he's two meters tall and blond and rippling with muscles and he has those wonderful Slavic cheekbones, and he's a lot younger than you but of course he has the *most* mature mind, and he's an attaché with the Martian contingent. Or is he the Pan Slavia ambassador's bodyguard? Am I close?"

Jasmine tried for a contrite look; it didn't work. Cleante burst into giggles.

"Mother, you're impossible!" she said. "And I love you for it."

She studied her mother's face closely for the first time and saw the months of strain and worry, the gray streaks in the jet black hair that had never been there before. Jasmine took her hand and squeezed it.

"It's going to be different for us from now on, Cle," she said with a catch in her voice. "Promise!"

"I know, Mother," Cleante said, then tried to lighten the mood. "Besides, if I could teach a Vulcan to love, you should be easy!"

"What did you do to her?" Jim Kirk wanted to know as he and Spock watched T'Shael and Cleante together, an attractive portrait of two young females born under different stars, joined by a bond that owned no alienness, no differences. "You must have presented her with quite a case for survival."

"I, Admiral?" Spock wore that characteristic deadpan which could disguise a great many things. "It was not the Vulcan influence but the human which drew T'Shael across the chasm to the side of life. My role was insignificant."

Kirk gave him a that's-not-good-enough-Spock look, and Spock tried a different approach.

"The Vulcan who relishes debate is still on the side of life," he suggested.

"Meaning you picked a fight with her. Dared her to keep on living."

"Crudely expressed, but essentially correct."

"A new Variant on a *cha'* match," Kirk suggested. "I would have loved to listen in on that one."

Spock gave him a bemused look.

"What kind of odds do you give them now, Spock? Now that the crises is over. Will they be able to make this—friendship bond—hold up under the day-to-day?"

"I am prepared to speculate that the divergence in their personalities might result in a certain degree of friction. Unavoidable where humans are concerned."

"Where humans are concerned with Vulcans, you mean. But on the whole you'd give them a fighting chance?"

"Jim, since the odds against you and me sustaining a friendship over this many years, and uncounted crises real and imagined, are approximately forty-seven-point-three-five to one—"

"I see your point," Kirk cut him off, preoccupied with watching the two across the room, sharing their harmony vicariously. He was reminded of a very young, very grim Starfleet cadet and a very silent, very serious Vulcan junior officer who had met over a chessboard at the Academy several lifetimes before. "Have I ever told you you talk too much?"

Spock said nothing. He too had his memories.

"Mother and I are returning to Earth, at least for now," Cleante said. "We'll stop over at the starbase for a few days. There's a starliner taking the slow route back to the in-planets. Come with us?"

"Does this starliner also stop at Vulcan?" T'Shael wanted to know. Of all the decisions she had had to make in the past six months, why did this small, impermanent one cause her such difficulty?

"It does," Cleante said. "Is that what you want, to return to T'lingShar?"

T'Shael did not answer. She did not know what she wanted.

"I wouldn't stand in your way if you did. It might be good for you to touch base again, to return to the crafters' shop, to T'Sehn and Sethan. And of course your students at the settlement. Do you think that's what you'll do?"

"I do not know," T'Shael said softly.

What place was there for her on Vulcan now? The crafters' shop was her place to mourn the Gifted One, the place of the Masters for mourning Master Stimm. A return to her ancestral lands meant mourning the proud and unfortunate Stalek. The settlement was for mourning Resh and Krn and Jali, the Old City for mourning the savage past of her race. All of Vulcan was her mourning ground. No, not this, not now. Perhaps another, later time. Spock had said the universe was vast. What could Cleante offer as an alternative?

"Come with me to Earth," Cleante was saying. "Let me show you the blueness of our skies, the depths of our oceans, this thing we call snow. We'll eat falafel and climb the pyramids and sail the Nile in a reed boat. I'll introduce you to a dolphin and take you to the opera and—Oh, come with me, T'Shael, please?"

"If you wish it," T'Shael said.

"But do you wish it?" Cleante asked, not for the first time.

"Yes" was T'Shael's answer.

THE STAR TREK PHENOMENON

THE

⟍⟍TAR TREK⟍

PHENOMENON

_____ **STAR TREK– THE MOTION PICTURE**
67795/$3.95

_____ **STAR TREK II– THE WRATH OF KHAN**
67426/$3.95

_____ **STAR TREK III–THE SEARCH FOR SPOCK**
67198/$3.95

_____ **STAR TREK IV– THE VOYAGE HOME**
63266/$3.95

_____ **STAR TREK: THE NEXT GENERATION:
ENCOUNTER AT FARPOIINT**
65241/$3.95

_____ **STAR TREK: THE KLINGON DICTIONARY**
66648/$4.95

_____ **STAR TREK COMPENDIUM REVISED**
62726/$9.95

_____ **MR. SCOTT'S GUIDE TO
THE ENTERPRISE**
63576/$10.95

_____ **THE STAR TREK INTERVIEW BOOK**
61794/$7.95

_____ **STAR TREK:
THE NEXT GENERATION:
GHOST SHIP** 66579/$3.95

_____ **STAR TREK: THE NEXT GENERATION:
THE PEACEKEEPERS**
66929/$3.95

_____ **STAR TREK: THE NEXT GENERATION:
THE CHILDREN OF HAMLIN**
67319/$3.95

**POCKET
BOOKS**